RED SKY RADIO

Other Novels by Matt Howarth:

The Eden Retrieval*

Progression
Enriched Visions
Itself
Toofer
Separation Anxiety
Tuners
Beyond Meat Time
Hungry Thunder
Stalk Exchange
Dreamtime Awry
The Blue Light
Imaginary Numbers
Haunted

For more information on books and comics by Matt Howarth, visit www.matthowarth.com

*Coming soon from The Merry Blacksmith Press

RED SKY RADIO

by MATT HOWARTH

The Merry Blacksmith Press

2011

Red Sky Radio

© 2011 Matt Howarth

Previous edition published in 2004 by Trantor Publications

"Diver" first published in 2002 in *Oceans of the Mind*

For information, address:

The Merry Blacksmith Press
70 Lenox Ave.
West Warwick, RI 02893

merryblacksmith.com

Published in the USA by The Merry Blacksmith Press

ISBN— 978-0615520698
0615520693

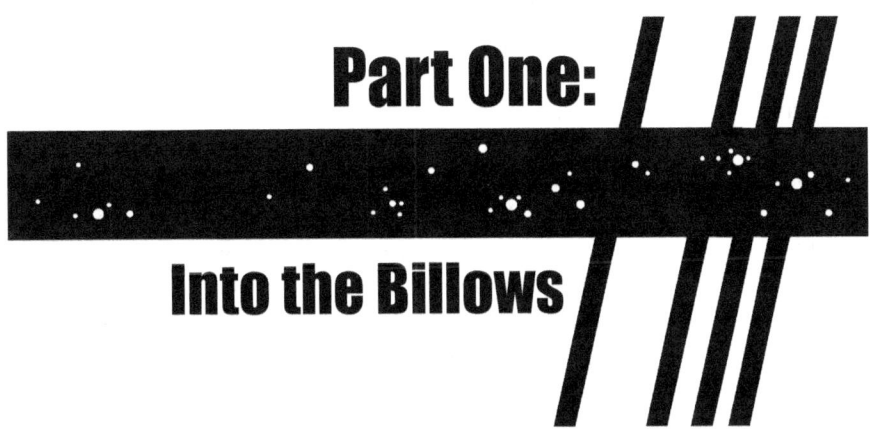

Part One:

Into the Billows

This was the part she liked the best: descending toward the scarlet clouds, all billowy and inviting like a forever wall of baby's-bottoms.

Once inside the gas giant's dense atmosphere, Peri's view would be artificial, a conglomeration of sensory impressions assembled by the circuitry that resided in her utility belt and transmitted to receptors just under her skin. Her brain was augmented to handle this flood of foreign perceptions, sorting infrared scans and climatic pressure readings with the same ease as her brain digested visual, auditory and tactile sensations. The spectacle found in these clouds was breathtaking, but what Peri saw was an environmental assessment, not a representational image. It did not exist as a four dimensional realization, for her complete view involved a multitude of perceptual overlays ordinarily unfound in routine human senses. She tasted a particle's quantum spin as vibrantly as she thrilled to the caress of its chemical composition. Electromagnetic pulses gave her a stomach ache, while X-rays stimulated her libido.

But before she plunged into that gaseous majesty, expanding her perceptions into a fractalized analysis, she liked to restrict the view of her fall to her visual cortex. That image was her favorite.

The forever wall rushed toward Peri as she plummeted into Baltuss' massive gravity well. The cloudbanks seethed and roiled with turbulence, vast plateaus of cloying vapor bigger than moons surging and melting back into the intangible uniformity. There were so many shades of red—more than her heart could count, and each one tickled her retinal cones a different way.

This was the equivalent of Peri Fairchild's commute-to-work.

She lived in a capsule-community that drifted in the void safely beyond the gas giant's influence. The complex consisted of a double-platform arrangement of domicile capsules (most no bigger than 2x2x4 meters). These kilometer-wide wedges of interlocking dom caps hung in space parallel to each other, anchored at their corners by larger pods devoted to administrative and recreational pursuits. Thousands of gas divers such as herself dwelled in these cramped capsules, but everyone spent most of their hours—their days, their weeks, their years, their lives—diving in the alien atmosphere. Many of them sought the golden score, the capture of a cloud of rare ingredient. Some of them dove deeper, searching for the compressed remains of ancient asteroids that had fallen into the bowels of the planetary behemoth. There were even a few odders who hunted for alien artifacts as foretold in primitive cinema. While Peri never discounted the chance that she might find a golden score, her diving was motivated by other passions. She sought a more intangible reward than financial profit.

Peri was addicted to the clouds. The long hours of lazy swimming through gaseous strata of remarkable presence. The tranquillity of the depths. Their visual serenity, their auditory ambience. The dynamics of turbulence among the mists, the topographies of chemical density. Peri was never happier than when she was lost in the gas giant's terrible atmosphere.

Theoretically, divers went down into the clouds to collect precious gases for commercial resale through the platform's Gas Exchange. Although this was the reason behind most dives, bagging gas was not Peri's personal goal. Finding a profitable cloud would inevitably end her fun. Freeform diving was difficult to manage with any degree of grace once the diver was encumbered with a full sack of snared gas. The bags tended to act as flotation devices, dragging divers to loftier and less dynamic altitudes. How could she enjoy her vaporous joyrides with such an annoying buoyancy tethered to her belt?

Not unexpectedly, Peri's secret vice kept her from capturing marketable clouds with any dependable regularity. She took the time every once in a while to bag enough gas to cover her necessary expenditures, but she rarely possessed the discipline to earn creds when there was no burning need. Her poverty never bothered her, for riches could never enhance her private joys. But it bothered Taz Bailey, often infuriating him at the most inopportune moments.

Like this morning…

After a glorious night of epic coupling, they had drifted in their recreational capsule for an extra hour, half-awake and torpid with the afterglow of their ecstasy. Peri had gone ballistic when she had finally realized the time. "We agreed," she had challenged him, untangling her pale, lithe limbs from their erotic knot. "Up and out by five. I can't afford my share of an extra hour, Taz. You know that. Why didn't you wake me?"

"Don't fry," he had remarked in his calm manner. "I can cover it."

That hadn't been the point, and she had told him so. "I wanted to catch the accelerator before the morning rush."

"You spend altogether too much time Down, Peri. You never have anything to show for it either. Why do you keep at it?"

"You think I'm a terrible diver..." she had pouted, hoping to divert him from this discussion about her endeavors—or lack of them.

In vain.

"But you're not," Taz had declared. The luminous tattoos that embellished his brown skin had attributed a dramatic flavor to his bewildered frown. "That's what makes it so murky. I've seen you dive—you're a natural. Why do you always come back empty-bagged?"

She had chirped something about already being late, then had jetted from the rec cap. The stass field at the capsule's end had blended with her own field as she had entered the raw vacuum, allowing her to slip from the compartment without disrupting its environmental contents.

Far too often Taz stumbled dangerously close to uncovering Peri's secret pastime. Sometimes, she feared that he already knew, and that was why he wanted to partner with her—out of financial pity. Taz was a successful diver, with several big scores on his record. By spacer or grounder standards, he could definitely be considered "rich". He could have afforded to leave and buy himself a tasty private asteroid long ago, but he stayed. Sometimes, in the tender moments after lovemaking, Taz revealed that he stayed to be with her, but Peri suspected those claims were simply post-coitus platitudes. She had her own suspicions: that Taz stayed because he was an odder searching for some elusive treasure among Baltuss' deep clouds.

Whatever the man's motives, Peri was not willing to share her secret with anyone. Not even Taz, who actually inspired a fair degree of earnest affection in the girl. Some things were too personal to admit to anyone. Not that she was embarrassed by her clandestine behavior. No, she hoarded her secret thrill because it was a *private* matter.

Taz often teased her for being secretive about the stupidest things.

He was right, though.

There was an awful lot she had never told her lover about herself. In truth, her secrets outweighed the mask she wore.

Taz knew that Peri was physically augmented (out here, everyone was), but he had no idea the incredible extent to which she had been *augmented*. The average diver carried implants needed to generate their personal stass field, with basic neural enhancements to accommodate additional sensory input. Peri's artificial neural nets were a thousand times more sophisticated than the sharpest human intellect. Her brain was no smarter as a result of all these implants, only capable of processing a higher load of input. The intricate tattoos that covered her flesh were actually extensions of organically embedded circuitry. The average diver was outfitted with an oxygen converter that relied mostly on biological foodstuffs for its raw material. Peri had replaced her left lung with a pressurized tank capable of storing enough raw material to fuel her air-recycler for over a week. Her entire skeletal structure had been replaced with lightweight but indestructible plastic. Beneath the skin of her silky thighs, conversion jets waited to unfold and blaze into action, propelling her through the clouds. Her scalp was hairless, but a crest had been grafted to her temples connecting around the back of her skull into a headdress of cartilage spikes that secretly doubled as a supplementary sensory array of antennae. The average diver's sensory pickups were confined to facial implants and long-range detection equipment located, quite literally, at their fingertips. Peri's fingers could telescope out to a length of over three meters. She never mentioned these unconventional augmentations. She was, you will recall, prone to secretive behavior.

The survival of everyone out here depended on the battery that drove each person's stass field. Keeping one's battery fully charged was a necessary obsession. The stass-skin protected its wearer against all external conditions, or lack thereof, as in the case of the vacuum of space. It wasn't really a physical suit; in actuality it was only a mirrored force field produced by implanted generators. A regulator field conformed the stass field to the body of the wearer, becoming a silvered second skin. Peri's bio-battery was unique in that it was capable of recharging from ambient environmental energies. If she had so desired, she could have stayed Down for weeks at a time without experiencing power shortages, or atmospheric or dietary deficiencies.

Peri was careful to never reveal these capabilities to anyone, for it might draw unwanted attention to her. People would puzzle all the more to understand why she regularly returned from her dives empty-bagged. All of her physical secrets were designed to facilitate her confidential vice.

At times, her emotional secrets were more difficult to conceal. Peri was a private person, not used to sharing her inner thoughts with even her lover. She rarely discussed her previous life on Earth, and when she did, it was always in the vaguest of detail. Blinded by her own determined denial of her past, she remained unaware how this implied that she was obviously running from something. Meanwhile, this mysterious demeanor made her alluring in Taz's regard. She hardly ever thought of the life she had escaped, for her present lifestyle was so enjoyable. Her secret past did not live up to any vicarious rumor, though.

She had not come unprepared to the Petrie platform. Her choice to retreat from civilization had been well-thought-out. She had exhausted her inheritance funding the operations that had transformed her into a lifeform that could brave the vacuum or the savage pressures of diving into a gas giant's atmosphere. Her new self exceeded her expectations, allowing her the freedom to indulge herself among the glorious clouds.

As she kicked off from the recreational capsule, Peri decided that she might as well grab a quick breakfast. The linear accelerator would be crowded at this hour with commuters desperate to get Down. She could afford to wait until the traffic jam had passed. It wasn't as if she had any need to hurry her day, no financial motivation spurred her to race into the clouds this morning. She snared a tow line and rode it in the direction of the nearby corner pod. Her ride was brief, for the rec caps were located nearby the community pods for obvious reasons.

Normally, Peri inhabited her own personal dom cap, which she rented on a monthly basis so that she had a place to crash and store her few belongings. More and more, lately, she had been sharing rec caps with Taz. The rec caps were designed for occupation by two people, again for obvious reasons. Although pleasurable, her cohabitation with the amorously agile boy was beginning to tax Peri's meager funds. It had been days since she had even visited her artificial "home."

She realized what this meant, and sighed mentally (conditioned to derive her oxygen from an internal source, inhalations or exhalations were superfluous). Her next dive was going to have to be wasted on responsible pursuits. She needed to bag a profitable cloud in order to replenish her depleted capital. Now, she felt, there was even more reason to postpone that departure.

As she neared the massive structure of the pod, Peri paused to momentarily survey the void. She crawled along a plane of dom caps that hung like a wall in space. There was no gravity here to establish any up or down, leaving her mind to unconsciously label the platform as "beneath" her, making everything else "up." The crimson face of Baltuss hovered in this dark vacuous sky, huge despite its distance. Seen from this vantage, the planet looked hostile and menacing, but Peri knew what glories lurked behind that blood-red facade. Brownish bands crowded the world's equatorial regions, cradling a series of minor hurricanes big enough to swallow a moon. The gas giant possessed several lunar bodies, a few were visible as tiny dark orbs traveling across the scarlet sphere. The Petrie platform drifted hundreds of kilometers from the great planet, hiding in the empty void. The rest of the sky was black, sparkling with a loose density of stars. Cacio Trumpis was a vivid blue star located on the rim of an arm of the galactic spiral. She was peering "up" into those lustrous depths now, while the sky hidden by the platform was generally barren of stellar twinkle. Cacio Trumpis itself was a distant cinder, noticeable among the starfield only by its azure brilliance this far out in the elliptic plane. Possessing an equatorial diameter of 148,532 kilometers, Baltuss was the sixth planet in the system, located over nine hundred million kilometers from the star.

And all of this, she reminded herself, *is a solar system in a different galactic arm than the one that contains the planet of my birth.* She smiled; there were people in her hometown who had never traveled beyond the city limits. But Peri had journeyed so far that she could not really comprehend the actual distance separating her from mankind's planet of origin. The psychological sense of displacement might have been overwhelming had it not been for her realization that space in the Cacio Trumpis system was fundamentally no different than the void back in the Sol system. The warm comfort of familiarity that other people derived from a proximity to their birthplace had been transferred in Peri to the clouds of Baltuss. This void was her home now, for it bordered on the magnificent clouds offered by the gas giant.

She returned her attention to the tow line in her grasp, for she was approaching the pod's bulbous bulkhead.

Entering the corner pod through the access hatch, her stass-skin blended its mirrored surface with that of the stass-door. The two fields became conjunctive, allowing her to effortlessly pass through the barrier which otherwise kept the air inside the facility and the vacuum out. Initially, this technology had dazzled and amazed her for months after she had received the field generator implant. But this transition had become commonplace to her in the three years since she had come to the freelancer platform. She hardly noticed it anymore.

Inside, a corridor led into the facility's labyrinth of chambers and concourses. She swam along the metallic hallway, humming to cheer herself up. The people she passed were already stassed-up for imminent departure, so she recognized no one until she reached deeper, more populated regions of the inner chambers. She headed for the cafeteria, where she deactivated her own stass-skin and splurged on a lavish triple serving of nutrient paste.

This hunger was hardly motivated by any actual appetite. Her physiology had been redesigned to be capable of drawing sustenance from her internal storage tank of raw nutrients. Peri was using breakfast as an excuse to delay her descent into Baltuss' clouds, for now that she had determined that her next dive should be spent bagging gas, she was innately reluctant to embark on this stale task. She resented life's financial needs for they intruded on her private time, denying her the enjoyment of diving for the sake of diving. This resentment was far from subconscious too. Despite her current meager funds, she spent her last few precious creds on a superfluous meal whose real purpose was postponing any replenishment of those dwindling funds. Of course, she did not consciously identify this illogical dichotomy, perceiving her actions only as a simple procrastination in order to avoid doing something she did not want to do. Her obsessive need for isolation ran far too deep to actually show up in her surface thoughts.

Settling into a small dining stall, Peri plugged her bio-battery into the recharge line and started sucking on her first food packet. Most people preferred to secure themselves in place by using the foot braces provided at the base of the booths. But Peri preferred to drift free. Freedom of motion had been one of the things she had sought coming out here, she saw no point in reminding herself of gravity. She quickly emptied the second food packet, and so held off on the third one to give her reason to stay where she was. The quicker she finished her meal, the sooner she would have to descend to the drudgery of common labor.

She fiddled with the wire connecting her to the stall's recharger, absently estimating how low her battery had been. She had been diving for two days before returning to spend last night with Taz. At normal activity levels, she figured the thing couldn't have been lower than half-charged. Most of her real exertions had been with her lover, for diving was a relatively passive recreation. Floating aimlessly among alien vapors required very little strenuous physical effort.

Their lovemaking had certainly left her famished, though. She bit into the third food packet, her hunger overcoming her discipline.

Taz could be remarkable. His prowess in the pursuit of zero-G sex was incredible, if not expected—for he had been raised in orbital stations. Peri, however, had spent the first twenty-three years of her life as a grounder, living at the bottom of a gravity well. The novelty of space life was still fresh to the girl, but Taz Bailey had never known ground beneath his feet. Indeed, he no longer had feet, for they had been surgically replaced with supplementary hands while he was a child. A lot of spacers went that route, altering their outward physiology to accommodate their offworld needs. Taz's legs had undergone alteration too, so that they bent forward and could function as a lower pair of arms. This difference afforded the man a wondrous variety of additional sexual intimacies, of which Peri was personally quite fond.

The rest of him was conventional enough. He had a wide torso like a bear. If he had originally possessed any body hair—which she suspected he had, for he looked the type—genetic tinkering had removed that nuisance. (Again, most spacers wanted no part of such a temperamental body part—in space, a stray hair could prove fatally hazardous should it foul any equipment necessary to maintain a habitable environment.) His skin was smooth and brown, almost silky in her carnal memory. His body tattoos were done in a luminous pale ink to stand out against his dark flesh. He had his share of handsome musculature, and all four of his hands were large and agile. His stass-skin and breathing recycler were of particularly average manufacture, which puzzled Peri when she remembered how wealthy Taz was. He could certainly afford better implants.

Personally, Peri found his face adorable. The blunt angles of his skull were adorned by a charismatic brow and noble nose and wide earnest lips. His eyes were dark blue, giving his dreamy gaze a steely air. Peri believed their color was attributable to some tech enhancement. When he smiled, his features fell into place to grab at Peri's heart. She was very comfortable with Taz…but she doubted that she loved him.

That would have been too clichÈ: to have traveled across interstellar distances to finally meet her soul mate in orbit around a gas giant in an alien star system. No, she had left Earth chasing another prize, and she found that every time she dove into Baltuss' endless atmosphere. Taz was important for many reasons, physical, emotional, and social, but he was no challenge to Peri's real weakness. No man could compete with an entire planet, even if most of it was just super-pressurized mist. Her hidden heart belonged to Baltuss.

As she was leaving the cafeteria, Peri ran into Dezi. The man was distraught over something, so Peri decided to dally and try to cheer him up. Yet another opportune distraction to delay her inescapable departure.

Although she knew him only casually, Peri felt sorry for Dezi Annucci. He was definitely an odder, and one who had been here for many years, according to rumor. But Peri found his wiry nervousness endearing. If she didn't take him too seriously, they got along famously. The man was, though, far too weird to endure on a regular basis.

There were few elderly spacers—a direct testament to the dangerous nature of life in space. Dezi had to be at least seventy years old. For someone who had spent the majority of his life in the void, his skin was pale and paper-thin. His flesh hung loose on his gangly gaunt frame. His head was overlarge and all flaps with a prominent nose and ears that stuck out like radar dishes. Eyes that had once bulged were now buried in mountains of wrinkled skin that rarely opened more than a squint. His lips were thin and creased. When he wasn't stassed-up, the plate in his chest announced the ancient nature of his augmentation. He wore teller screens implanted into his forearms, and Peri was fascinated by the antediluvian hardware.

The downside of interaction with Dezi involved his vehement delusions. He was not prone to violence, or even annoying preaching, but he was willing to freely share his opinions. He carried quite an impressive array of odd notions in his old head. He believed in several interstellar conspiracy theories, and even hinted that Baltuss was inhabited by intelligent snails. He was openly abusive when he talked about Harvest Corp, but then part of the man's legend included a stretch diving for the mining corporation that ruled Baltuss' airspace. Try as she might, Peri could never get Dezi to admit to that claim; either it was false or so traumatic that he refused to relive those days.

Peri found the man's outrageous opinions tremendously amusing. In his own way, Dezi was the platform's storyteller, spinning wild tales to entertain the population-at-large. He was harmless.

Accompanying him through the process of purchasing a meal, Peri joined the old man in a dining booth. Like her, the spacer rejected the stall's seat-struts, preferring to drift in the air. This was a subtle testament to how long the man had lived in space. He hung loose, but tension was still visible in how he held his arms and legs.

"What's the biz?" she asked congenially. She sucked a juice bulb the man had bought for her.

Dezi shuddered his shoulders, announcing with his body language how distressing the news was that he was about to eagerly relate. With the old-ster's predilection for fantastic conspiracy theories, his latest beef could be expected to be wildly entertaining. He grunted in his gruff voice, "It's those HeeVee Execs."

"What're they up to now?" she inquired with honest interest. News about HeeVee—as the locals derisively called the Harvest mining corporation— could possess actual impact on her immediate livelihood. The Corp Execs were constantly devising new ways to torment the freelance divers. HeeVee claimed absolute ownership of the cloud-mining rights here, and they were determined to defend the exclusive nature of their proprietary rights regarding the gas giant's atmosphere. To evade detection by agents of the nasty Corp, the Petrie platform hid itself in uncharted space beyond the orbits of the planet's moons. In this manner, if the Corp discovered their location, the freelancers could quickly move the station to another position. Threat of a HeeVee raid was never far from the freelancers' minds, though.

With growing distemper, Dezi told her about a rumor that the HeeVee Execs were planning to dispatch robotic units programmed to search-and-destroy anyone not carrying a Corp code. There were darker rumors that these robot drones had exhibited over-violent responses, repeatedly failing to correctly recognize a HeeVee diver's Corp code. These attacks had failed to deter HeeVee's urgent desire to release these killer guard bots into Baltuss' airspace and clouds.

"And *clouds*?!" Peri moaned.

Dezi advised her that it would be prudent to avoid going Down for a while. Sooner or later, the Corp's own Workers Union would force HeeVee to recall their killer drones; the company divers would not tolerate working under such potentially dangerous conditions. Rather than risk legal intervention from Greye's Authorities, HeeVee would back down and busy themselves with finding another way to torment the freelancers. "Until that happens, though," the old man declared, "you should keep your pretty little ass away from Baltuss. You wouldn't want to get caught by one of those killer bots."

There was *no way* Peri was going to abstain from diving for a couple of days! Her need for the clouds was too great to deny. Anyway, she had to bag some gas soon in order to pay for her immediate survival on the platform. There was no such thing as welfare relief here. Those who failed to pay their way perished.

Dezi's latest rumor couldn't have come at a worse time.

But then, she reminded herself, it *was* after all only another of Dezi's extravagant *rumors*. How much credence could she place in his story? He was a kindly old man, but he *was* an odder. It was hazardous to trust in the opinions of odders. Peri had no intention of upsetting her life over some outlandish tale professed by a crank.

She was reticent to insult Dezi by denouncing his latest rumor, however. The old man was entitled to whatever beliefs rattled around in that wrinkled head. She liked him, and hoped to avoid hurting his feelings. She had, she recalled, accompanied him with the intention of bolstering his spirits. Debunking his story would hardly cheer him up, so she chose to play into his version of reality.

"I'll betcha Fast Eddie can set anybody up with a fake Corp code," she commented slyly. "Then everybody can safely dive again."

"Too risky," Dezi countered with earnest anxiety. "Those killer bots've been malfunctioning, remember? And attacking Corp divers who have the right codes."

She nodded, exhibiting a thoughtful frown for the man's paternal concern. *Just agree to stay on the station and be done with it,* she chided herself. She could do as she pleased once she had left the old man's company.

"I guess I'll be sticking to the platform then," she voiced her decision to take Dezi's advice. "You're right. My pretty little ass would be too much of an attraction for those killer bots." She smiled, thinking herself an expert liar.

Dezi frowned, visibly dubious of her quick acquiescence to his counsel. His eyes disappeared in the creases of a suspicious squint.

"You'll keep an ear out, right?" she prompted. "And let me know when the coast is clear?"

The old man's doubts melted away, and he nodded solemnly. It was charming how he treated her like a co-conspirator now.

As it was, she was unable to head directly Down once she left Dezi in the cafeteria. If she was going cloud-hunting, Peri needed her bagger rod, which was back in her personal domicile capsule. Upon leaving the community pod, she moved her way along the tow lines that ran the width of the platform. Her pod was a cheap one, located far out in the middle, away from any convenient facilities. It took her a few minutes to drag herself across the landscape formed by the interlocked plastic shells of the dom caps. The surface was uniformly bulbous, stretching out into the darkness in every direction. It glowed orange in the scarlet light given off by the gas giant.

She glanced at the distant planet. It hung massive and high in the heavens, but she knew its stratosphere was actually many kilometers away. The planet was so incredible enormous. Unos was quite prominent as the moon swung around on its outermost orbit. It stood out as a dark gray blotch against the gas giant's vivid crimson facade. The upper regions of gas surged in an array of turgid streams, swarming in patterns around the storms that wandered across the atmosphere's global face. To her augmented eyes, the surface was a swirling ocean of luminous twinkles. These sparkling textures swam like oily mists, describing magnificently intricate designs. The rhythm of the atmospheric dance mesmerized her. It took some concentration to pull herself away from gawking at the spectacle. She continued along the tow line until she came to a juncture necessary to reach her residence.

The confines of her dom cap were claustrophobic and depressing after the sensory grandeur of moments ago. Despite the merry decorations painted on the close walls, her room seemed positively tomblike. Her entire material life fit into a single carry satchel that was clipped to the back of the capsule. Inside, she hunted through her clothing and pix disks and toiletries and a back-up bio-battery and finally found her bagger rod. She pulled the device out, and gave it a cursory examination. It resembled a staff a third-of-a-meter long and as thick as her wrist. The actual machinery was metallic, encased in a protective shell of durable plastic. With the flick of a few switches, the nozzle could extend like a snake, sucking in the target cloud and storing it in an inflatable sack that expanded from the rear of the staff. She clipped the device to her utility belt and was about to leave when she noticed her cred chip in the satchel. With a fatalistic sigh, she picked it up. The touch of her fingers activated the chip, it flashed her Ident number and the sum total of her wealth. The low total distressed her, corroborating her worst fears concerning the status of her finances. With renewed resignation, she replaced the cred chip in her satchel and zipped it closed. There was no denying it: she desperately needed to score some high-priced cloud. Turning away, she exited the cap. Her stass-skin automatically activated itself, protecting her lissome flesh from the hostile vacuum. She dragged herself along the tow lines heading toward the launcher.

The launcher's structure was mounted at an exterior end of the platform. Towering far out into the void, it consisted of a linear accelerator that could pivot to point at Baltuss' remote face. Commuters were fired off at the planet.

There was no crowd now, the early morning throng of hungry miners having departed on their daily collection dives long ago. Only a few late-comers drifted in line at the ticket booth's mechanical facade. Her wait was minimal, and soon she was transferring the price of a launch ticket into the station's accounts. Once she received the go-ahead light, Peri crawled into the cramped elevator and was conveyed to the apex of the tower. There, she positioned herself at the rear of the tunnel of magnetic accelerator rings and awaited the launch signal. Thirty seconds later, the large metal rings glowed with an eerie light. Momentum was transferred to her mass, and Peri was summarily fired out into space. Safe within her stass-skin, she was untouched by the savage forces employed to produce her trajectory. Incredible though the process was, the experience was too familiar to awe her any more.

The ride was just the tantalizing overture for the splendor of the dive ahead.

She tongued a switch at the back of her mouth, one of a series of teeth that had been replaced with controls for her hordes of implanted hardware, and the radio filled her head with noise. Waves of interplanetary static collided with the hiss of heavy radiation expelled by Baltuss' active bulk. Muttering behind this wall of cosmic interference, a hundred voices discussed descent vectors and cloud-strata conditions. Mixed with these personal transmissions were the more demonstrative HeeVee broadcasts, announcing pompous corporate policies, border warnings that went unheeded by the freelancers, weather predictions and burn ratios arranged by hemispherical vector. Toggling the tooth with her nimble tongue, Peri dialed through the miasma of frequencies until she had filtered out the majority of the conventional channels, leaving her receiver primed to detect the elusive signal of Red Sky. Gradually, for fine-tuning the roving pirate broadcasts was not for the impatient, she locked on to the illegal transmission and her dive gained a soundtrack.

The music surged with electronic keyboards, multi-layered to enhance their drama. Sinuous threads of synthetic percussion sparkled in the undulating net of riffs. As the melody looped, its structure grew more insistent, as if foreshadowing a momentous imminence. The dynamic soundscape became part of her planetary-bound flight.

This was the part she liked the best: descending toward the scarlet clouds, all billowy and inviting like a forever wall of baby's-bottoms.

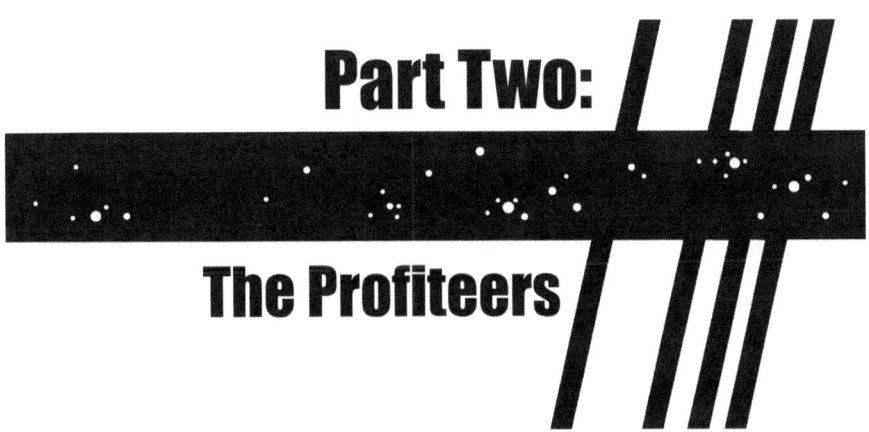

Part Two:

The Profiteers

Trust was not an accredited commodity to the corporate mentality.

Once a month, the three Executives who managed Harvest Corp's Baltuss operation conducted a Review Board. The Execs never conducted their meetings in the flesh, always appearing via vidcasts to prevent any risk of assassination. Their mutual hostility was rooted in a long tradition of vicious coups and commercial backstabbing prevalent in an extreme capitalist society. Although no registered threats had passed among the trio, they knew to guard their lives with constant vigilance. This was the corporate way.

Harvest Corp maintained its Baltuss facilities on Natt, the gas giant's twelfth moon. This base consisted of an enormous and sturdy cube that crowded the edge of a vast plateau of crystallized methane, overlooking a plummeting crevasse that reached deep into the frozen lunar mantle. Contained within this block was an entire city inhabited by the corporation's employees, roughly fourteen thousand personnel. The Executive class occupied the top level of the cube, leaving the lesser officers and the workers to reside in the urbanized middle floors. The foundation layers were devoted to the industrial complex required to process the chemicals collected from Baltuss by the Corp's mining divers.

The Executive Review Board convened, and one by one, each of the base's Departmental Domos stepped up the podium and delivered their reports to a trio of vid-screens. When it came his turn, Security Domo Theo Sloane announced himself and commenced his summation. From their vidscreens, the three Execs stared at him.

There was Pa'dash Uwu, the Raga nationalist who had fled war crimes on Earth to hide among the stars. Using his stolen wealth as a lever, he had usurped his way up the corporate ladder, scoring a third-share of Harvest Corp's Baltuss cloud-mining operations. From everything Sloane had heard, Uwu's climb to ultimate power had barely begun. His arrogant superiority commanded every feature of his swarthy face, from his wizard's nose to his intolerant forehead to his derogatory lips. His lithe fingers curled naturally into a possessive rictus when they reposed before him on the marbled surface of the distant conference table seen at the bottom of his video image.

There was Evelyn Hannigan, the ex-seductress of a thousand porno clips who had invested unscrupulously and found the corporate lifestyle more to her liking. Although Sloane never tired of staring at her stunning face, he was not blind to the manipulative desire that sparkled in her cold blue eyes. Her physical beauty had not faded since her cinematic retirement, the Security Domo could personally attest to that. However, no matter how many times the woman changed her hair or skin color or her height or build—she always retained an indefinable aura that could curdle milk at a distance.

There was Nigel Bester, the aristocrat who sprang from a long line of presumptuous monarchs. Behind the man's angular forehead and colorless gaze lurked an inscrutable mind, betraying no trace of emotion or intent with his compressed lips. He was supposed to be quite diminutive in height, but having never met the man in person, Sloane could not corroborate this fact. Although his ancestry was responsible for hideous atrocities, this Bester had yet to perpetrate any overt horrors on the universe-at-large, as if he was saving his worst for a future day. Or maybe his crimes had been so perfectly crafted that no one could recognize his complacency in them. Either way, he was rumored to be the more dangerous of the three Execs, a man no one wanted to call their enemy *or* ally.

The Security Domo kept his summary minimal and vague, for—in all truth—he had achieved minor success in keeping the gas giant free of pirate activity. A group of the thieves had even broken into the Natt base only a week ago. Sloane longed to find some way to overlook this incident, but as he suspected: the Execs already knew every detail of that raid from their own spies. In defense of his capabilities, Sloane had prepared a compelling oration lamenting the understaffed and underfunded nature of his Department. The Execs were unsympathetic to (as Uwu worded it) "the failings of an inadequately managed security force."

Hidden behind his thin lips, Sloane's teeth were grinding with irritated exasperation. He kept his wide jaw firmly clamped shut, knowing that anything he might say would only inspire more vituperative reprisals. He held his military-buff body motionless, betraying no trace of his internal rage.

"These pirates are malicious industrial terrorists, profiteering off territory legally under our exclusive domain," growled the Exec. "Your inability to route them from this planet is deplorable, but allowing them to violate the sanctity of our own reputedly-secure base is inexcusable."

Wrinkling his leathery face with resentment, Sloane wisely ground his teeth and endured the insults.

Hannigan, though, was interested in seeing him twitch under pressure. She politely requested that the Security Domo describe this recent break-in.

Hiding an exasperated sigh in a preparatory inhalation, Sloane recounted the incident for the edification (and entertainment) of the Board. "Last Tuesday, at 0324, a group of individuals managed to invade the base through an open waste flush pipe."

"These intruders," Bester interrupted softly. "They made off with several cases of circuitry, did they not?"

"That's correct," Sloane grudgingly admitted. "Fortunately, the circuitry had not been formatted or biased, so the thieves got none of Harvest's programming."

"*Unfortunately,*" hissed Uwu, "they broke in and stole something in the first place!"

"I have, you'll recall," Sloane officiously pointed out, "filed previous recommendations concerning the security breaches inherent in the waste disposal depot's purge hatches."

"Are you attempting to hide your failure with hindsight, Security Domo Sloane?" Hannigan's accusation was silky.

"I'm bringing it up in order to get your authorization to correct this weakness in the base's defenses," Sloane countered smoothly. "I'd like to install a series of compartmentalized air locks to conduct waste products as they are ejected from the complex. In my opinion, it is vital to avoid a repeat of this incident. If the pirates could sneak in that way once, they will try again."

"How much is this going to cost?" Uwu inquired. His harsh features were immobile.

"If you want the pirates to come back and steal some more equipment, that's your business—because this *is* your business you're talking about. You're the bosses." Only by a Herculean effort did Sloane keep his caustic remarks free of any trace of sarcasm. "It is *your* prerogative to ignore my professional recommendation."

"Funds do not come from nowhere," Bester observed.

"The market is currently unstable," grumbled Uwu. "Profit ratio curves are not meeting fiscal expectations."

The Security Domo glared at the trio of vid-screens without comment.

"The matter will be taken under advisement," Hannigan finally broke the stalemate.

As the Executive screens abruptly went dead, Sloane realized that his report was done.

The pirates were definitely the most irascible dilemma on Sloane's professional agenda.

Further troubling him was the fact that his Department was a feeble deterrent to the problematically persistent trespassers. Security was severely ill-equipped to cope with policing an entire planet. Sloane had repeatedly petitioned for additional manpower, but the ranks of his patrol officers remained without the necessary reinforcements. Meanwhile, the Security Domo was forced to rely on the efficiency of his crew of sixty-three patrol officers. They were decent people and capable, but ultimately their efforts were inadequate when it came to patrolling the gas giant's entire atmosphere. According to intel, the pirates outnumbered his patrol force by an astounding percentage. How was anyone expected to combat an opposition of that magnitude?

Months ago, he had requisitioned a set of robot drones with the intention of using them to patrol the regions beyond the reach of his Department's meager personnel. After an initial assurance of delivery, these drones had never arrived—at least, they had never been delivered to *his* Department.

The Harvest base on Natt had its share of secret projects, any one of which could have nefariously gobbled up his requisitioned drones for their own guarded purposes. Just because he was Security Domo did not mean that he was privy to every secret found on the base; in fact, all *those* details were known to only three very elite individuals.

Trust was not an accredited commodity to the corporate mentality.

Part One Resumed:

Returning to the Billows

I t took time to reach her goal.

The scarlet face of Baltuss rose to meet her, a vast landscape of seething gas that grew bigger and bigger, filling the sky. The drop—from linear accelerator to impact with the gas giant's stratosphere—often took hours. There was ample opportunity for minds to wander among the freelance divers.

Peri's train of thought flowed from baby-bottoms to warm-and-comfy to a flash of childhood memory involving her favorite blanket to the sting of growing up and being jilted to the oppressive burden of living at the bottom of a gravity well.

Her life as a grounder had been drab and stifling. Born into a well-to-do family, Peri Fairchild had spent her teen years rebelling vehemently against the arrogance of the wealthy class, which had brought her to odds with her snooty parents. They had never understood that when they disassociated themselves from her, their "punishment" was the exact goal she was striving for with her rejection of the tawdry entitlement that accompanied the family wealth. As clueless as her own parents, Peri had wandered the four corners of Earth's globe in search of purpose. Finding no guidance in aimless travel, she had settled down in Amsterdam, finding employment as a waitress in an Italian restaurant. There she had remained, unfocused and unsatisfied, until her parents had revealed their true malicious nature in death, bequeathing the entire family fortune to their estranged daughter. Her sudden financial windfall had left her torpid and even more unsatisfied. Sickened by society in general, she had decided to get away from it all—everything. She would go out to a frontier world where civilization was simpler and existence was more challenging.

Choosing the world of Baltuss, Peri had burned through her abundant afflu-
ence financing the biological adjustments necessary for her to survive in that
region of deep space. She had conducted extensive research into the lifestyle
and requirements of freelance gas divers before she had chosen her implants.
She had been careful to go for the upper-end hardware, knowing that no expenditure was really extravagant when it came to protecting her from the
harshness of life in a vacuum. Once she was out in orbit around the alien gas
giant planet, her survival would depend entirely on the capacities of her new
lungs or her sensory array or her bio-battery or her stass field generator... She
had been unwilling to accept all these enhancements until she comprehended
their scope versus the actual conditions in which she would be living. The notion of escaping Earth's overcrowded urban sprawl for the wide-open void and
endless clouds of the crimson gas giant had been impossible to resist. She had
grown fixated on the freedom implied by large open areas, and had visited the
Nevada salt flats repeatedly during her final land-bound months.

Coming to Baltuss had been the right decision. It had definitely been
her pivotal choice in life, moving her into closer proximity with her ultimate destiny. With her debut dive she had known: this was where she was
supposed to be. Swimming through the gas giant's dynamic atmosphere was
more rewarding than sex! She was finally *happy*.

She smiled with warm gratitude at the vivid clouds that billowed beneath her—ahead of her—above her—perspective did not seem to matter.
She was the center of the universe, a sentient singularity with a limitless wall
of inviting vapor coming toward her. There was no up or down, only the
integral relationship between herself and the approaching horizon of scarlet
clouds. That proximity alone was all that existed, it was all that mattered. And
it filled her with a tremendous joy. By diving into the gas giant's atmosphere,
she was joining the planet's spirit, becoming part of the grand emptiness she
so admired. Her dive achieved a unity with the universe-at-large that no experience had ever achieved in her distant grounder life. She was fulfilled and
emotionally invigorated by the experience.

And she adored the view. The rush too. The impetuous spectacle was a
high whose addictive qualities she gladly welcomed. She knew her fascination with this experience would never pale from repetition. The thrill was
intoxication incarnate. She was *very* happy.

Wisps of vapor began to dance by, passing like nebulous specters in the
cold vacuum immediately bordering the atmosphere. Her enhanced senses
caressed each streamer and foggy cloud as it moved past her, examining each
with quantum curiosity. These puffs of gas had traveled far through the gas
giant's aerial mass to reach this region of the stratosphere, leaping from the
planet with wanderlust dedication, striving to detach themselves from their
home and explore space as separate entities of rarefied substance. Their out-

bound voyage was courageous, and deserved to be immortalized.

An annoying hiss had crept into her soundtrack, she corrected it with a few agile pokes of her tongue against the tuning tooth. Once the music was clear again, she boosted the volume of the radio receiver embedded in her neck, and the tenuous murmur rose to a dynamic crescendo in her ears. The melody's agitated coda suited the drama of her view, excellently matching the tension generated by her headlong plummet toward the crimson wall of clouds. She began to unconsciously bob her head with the electronic tempo that lurked in the music's elegant symphonic presence. Growling synthesizer passages surged and receded, almost in tandem with the arms of stratospheric vapor that rushed by around her.

The planet's outermost regions were getting nearer. Soon, she would enter the actual gas envelope and commence the real part of her dive. The colored clouds would surround Peri, swallowing her with their welcome yet intangible embrace. She had to remind herself that this dive was for purposes other than her regular frolic. With a brush of her tapered fingers, she touched the bagger rod that hung clipped to her utility belt, reassuring herself that the device was still with her.

But then…filling her gas bag would take only a few moments once she had located a suitably profitable cloud. And finding such a score would hardly be difficult for her. Although she wasted little time actively collecting gas, her private sport took her to a wide range of depths where the composition of the cloud-strata was truly exotic and exceptional. In effect, she knew these clouds better than most divers, for her wanderings were rarely interrupted by bagging any of the clouds she saw. She spent her hours observing the glorious panorama, giving her a rudimentary familiarity with the seemingly random distribution of particular gases throughout this vaporous environment. (These same tactics were regularly employed by Harvest Corp to determine the location of the richest gas deposits. Crews of divers were dispatched whose sole purpose was to wander through the clouds, scouting the positions of profitable gases. Markers were left to guide later divers to these riches, thusly precluding the need for the Corp's cloud miners to waste diving time searching for lucrative clouds to bag. Peri was unaware of the similarities between her secret joyrides and corporate mining techniques.) She knew where the layers of raw oxygen lurked, which billows of methane actually concealed lithium cores, how to track the more mobile radium deposits by following the tighter whirlpools left in their spurious wakes. When the infrequent times came that she needed to do some gas collecting, she knew exactly where to go to score a high-priced cloud.

So, she thought, *there's actually no reason I can't indulge in a few loops and drops for my own enjoyment first. There's time enough later to bag some gas.*

In fact, she knew of a tasty deposit of irradiated fermium that would do nicely to replenish her dwindling cred account. It was deep and far to spinward, but the journey there should be thoroughly delightful. With a satisfied smile, she swooped lower, plunging headlong into a cloudbank of deep purple tin. The gaseous metal swirled like an angry liquid as her stass-skinned body slipped through the aerial river. She exited the seething mist, sliding effortlessly into the next cloud-strata.

Her stass field protected her from the deadly ecology, maintaining her body temperature and tolerable physiological pressure in the midst of the super-dense clouds of vaporized elements. Wild radiation storms raged among these clouds, but Peri was untouched by their vicious sting. When she encountered regions undergoing electrical discharges, she swam calmly through these labyrinths of contorting lightning bolts, unworried and secure in her inevitable safety. None of the indigenous lifeforms could penetrate her glistening silver skin. Nothing could get through a stass field; even her perceptions were routed to her brain through intricate apparatus intended to codify sensory data into more manageable bitstreams. The EM fields that generated her stass field savagely warped the fabric of space-time to produce an energy zone that detached her from the physical universe, protecting everything within that field. Theoretically, her stass-skin would allow her to survive a dive to the core of a blazing star. She had only a basic understanding of the complex science behind the principle, but she used the process every day now to live in space and make her dives into Baltuss' atmosphere. This inviolate armor had become a second skin, a new body part like the airtank that resided inside her chest; it was an extension of her new self, as noticeable as her spleen or any particular tendon in her left foot. Like her nose or nipples, she took the stass-skin for granted.

Immersed in cloud and music and rapture, Peri failed to detect whatever it was that struck her. Protected by her stass-skin, she was uninjured by the impact, but it startled her as she rebounded into a spinning tumble through the clouds. Using her thigh-jets to steady herself, she cast about with her artificial senses, hunting for whatever she had hit. It had been solid. There were not supposed to be solid masses among Baltuss' clouds, certainly not at these heights.

Her scan spotted a dark silhouette against the vaporous background. The readings she got told her that it was not only solid—it was metal! And refined metallics at that.

She had heard the tales of how there "had to be" a lot of cosmic debris hiding in the gas giant's extreme depths: asteroids, lost equipment, alien artifacts, fabulous islands of mystery—mostly flights of fancy in Peri's opinion. Granted, some asteroids and comets had probably been swallowed up by the gas giant over millennia, but what rubble might remain of them was guaranteed to be deep in the planetary mass of gas. In such regions of hellish storms and monstrous pressure, it was doubtful that much remained of these solid objects, their bulk inevitably rendered into fine debris by the savage environment. Only odders—and even then, only the most extreme odders—would dare such dives as would be necessary to hunt for such legendary treasures. There were stories of "things" that dwelled in the lower regions, nasty things that ate unwary divers. She tended to disregard those myths too, for never in all her extensive diving had she ever encountered a dangerous lifeform in these clouds.

There was life aplenty in the dense and alien atmosphere, but a lot of it was microscopic, and the larger specimens were relatively diaphanous. A poked finger could inflict fatal punctures to the drifters' gas-bags, leaving the creatures to sink to their death. She had a hard time imagining that any drifter was capable of successfully worrying a stass-protected diver.

Monsters aside—for those type of thoughts were foolish and unproductive—whatever she had hit in her dive was solid and metallic. It must be an asteroid that had recently fallen into the gas giant's attraction. Such a mass might not have sunk to the sargasso depths yet. This was far more profitable than any fermium deposit. What a score! Probably rich with iron and magnesium and all kinds of solid stuff that would bring premium prices at Petrie's Gas Exchange. And she had found it by accident!

She moved toward the object on subtle bursts of her thigh-jets. As she approached it, the mists parted and her asteroid came into view—but it was no lump of coarse rock. It was a machine! A piece of lost equipment…?

"Or one of HeeVee's new search-and-destroy robot drones?" she heard Dezi's garrulous voice in her memory. Great Void—was the old man's latest conspiracy rumor actually true this time? Had she blundered right into one of these deadly killer bots?

She froze, expelling a reverse jet burst to halt her advance through the drifting mists. She hung at the vague terminator boundary between a dark brown cloud and a strata of translucent vapor. The not-an-asteroid-thing hovered in this pearly mist, its two-meter-diameter shape bristling with intimidating spines. It certainly looked hostile to her. Its chromium shell was pitted with decay, giving the thing an arcane appearance. Slowly, she increased her reverse thrust, moving in careful retreat. For all the fear that was rising like a scalding gorge in her, Peri refused to panic. She cautiously backed away from the dreadful machine, praying that she had somehow escaped notice of the robot's sensory apparatus.

As she slowly retreated through the brown cloud, a swarm of confetti fish exploded around her. They came from her left, abruptly immersing her in their flittering passage. They swam in a thick flock measuring several meters in diameter. She almost freaked out when they appeared, startled by their untimely arrival. Only her fear of the killer bot kept her from spazzing out and betraying her presence to the murderous machine. With every muscle in her body clenched in dread, she watched the confetti fish rush by. Individually, they were tiny things: no bigger than her thumbnail and flat as a scrap of paper. Alone, they were incapable of animate movement; only in swarms could they move about. Supposedly, these swarms traveled at a rising velocity, zooming through Baltruss' clouds until they fragmented into smaller streams. In this manner, the confetti fish propagated. To most divers, this was purely speculative legend. Peri, though, had frequently witnessed such bifurcations during her secret dives, marveling at the biological elegance of these minuscule creatures. Now, however, their presence was unwelcome and potentially life-threatening. She was visibly grateful once their swarm swiftly passed to neighboring regions.

Finding herself twenty meters or so from the killer bot, she considered herself fairly secure in the suspicion that the robot was not coming in pursuit of her. She twisted around and jetted herself high into the roiling billows. Forgotten now were thoughts of joyriding or precious asteroids or golden scores or depleted funds; her only concern now was flight. Her playground had suddenly become a dangerous place. For the first time, Peri desperately longed to be out of the clouds.

Her jets carried the girl back into the vacuum and across the gulf that separated the freelancers' platform from the gas giant's mining skies. Frantic fear that refused to subside was her only company during this escape.

Somehow, the impact of bumping into the deadly robot had fouled her ability to tune in Red Sky Radio. She made her escape in oppressive silence.

She remembered very little of that journey beside an undercurrent of regret for having been driven from her playground by a sense of overwhelming terror.

By the time she reached the platform, she had regained a measure of her composure.

When she passed a grumbling Dezi Annucci in a corridor, she gripped his shirt and drew him close to hiss at him, "They're already there!"

"Who?" the old man inquired.

"The clouds are full of HeeVee's killer bots!" she moaned.

"What are you talking about?" Dezi shook loose her frantic grip and peered at the girl as if she were insane.

"I saw them!" Peri wailed. She was frustrated that she could not make the old man understand. Her anxiety was returning, and with it a rising nausea.

Before Dezi could respond, her stomach lurched, and Peri was forced to flee. She found a public toilet where she lost her breakfast in a private stall. A disturbing cold sweat sheathed her like an uncomfortable second skin as she crept back into the communal passage.

Dezi was long gone, so she lethargically made her way to her personal dom cap. Once inside, she curled into a fetal ball and begged her fear to wane.

It took time to reach her goal.

Part Two Resumed:

Malevolence in the Proximity of Profiteers

He was buzzing with anticipation.

An hour from now, Security Domo Sloane had a clandestine appointment with a man who was reputedly involved with one of the numerous secret projects being conducted on Harvest Corp's Natt base. Mr. No-Names-Please had promised to deliver information that would reveal the nature of this research to Sloane. Finally—after months of digging and prying, he had found a weak link in the chains that bound Harvest Corp's innermost secrets. Soon, one of those secrets would be betrayed to him by Mr. No-Names-Please.

Sloane privately scoffed. As if the Domo of the base's Security Department was unaware of the man's name and entire history. Sloane had chosen Algol Caffino because of what he had found in the man's logged profile jacket. Weak and easily swayed by figures of authority, Caffino was the optimum prey for Sloane's style of forceful intimidation. The research technician had turned out to be perfectly spineless. Sloane could only be amused by Caffino's obsession that his identity was somehow a secret. It showed how truly naive the tech was.

Storing his patrol officers' summaries in his database, Sloane examined his desk for signs of anything that required handling before his secret rendezvous. No disks had spat into his Danger bin, implying that it had been a slow day without any significant pirate raids. There was no point in opening any current investigation files for review—if they hadn't been solved by now, the chances of an arrest were highly unlikely. Tracking the rogue culprits was an impossible chore. The void beyond Harvest's territory was too vast, the pirates could be hiding anywhere.

Soon after he had won the job of Security Domo at Harvest Corp's Baltuss cloud-mining facilities, Theo Sloane had realized the true futility of the corporation's struggle with the pirates. No matter how many trespassers his patrol officers caught, there were always hundreds more waiting to swoop down to steal Baltuss' clouds. His troops could never hope to apprehend each member of such an elusive horde. By virtue of this realization, Sloane saw that the only way to do away with the pirates was to eliminate their base. Without a hideout retreat, they would perish in the empty void. The trouble was: the pirates guarded the location of their base better than a devout eunuch defended its virtue. Only once, long before Sloane had arrived at the Natt base, had Harvest's forces managed to uncover the actual location of the Viper Nest (as he unofficially called it). The data regarding this incident had been deep-filed in an attempt to erase the embarrassing failure from public record. It had taken Sloane three days to hack the coded report into a readable format. Harvest's assault squad had fallen on bad luck, and by the time back-up had arrived, the pirate base had been long gone. *Something* had happened, leaving only a few surviving officers to be rescued by reinforcements. No amount of decoding would explain what that *something* had been, though.

Nowadays, the pirates chose to regularly move their base. Sometimes Sloane wondered if they kept their Nest in perpetual motion. There had to be some explanation for the inability of his best efforts to find their insidious hideout. Sloane knew that his Department was not to blame for this failure, for his determination and the efforts of his officers had remained unflagging in pursuit of uncovering the criminals' lair.

Ruefully, he resigned himself to dealing with some backlogged paperwork, trivial but bureaucratically necessary.

Time flew, and soon Sloane was marching along a public avenue dressed in clothes that were more innocuous than his security uniform. Even dressed in common streetwear, Sloane's muscled physique could not be easily disguised. The mighty pillars of his legs strained the material of his pants, his biceps stretched the sleeves of his dark blue jacket. Both his coat and shirt remained unbuttoned at the top to accommodate his burly neck. The jacket was several sizes too large for him, so that at least its broad drape concealed the girth and power of his torso. He hid his potent hands in its deep pockets. All this camouflage was pointless, for his robust anatomy was distinctly noticeable among the wiry and flabby figures of the others who strolled the base's avenues. He wasted no concealment on his square head, for few average employees knew his wide jawline or the misshapen gristle of his repeatedly broken nose or his beady, ever-alert eyes. Those few who had met the Security Domo had done so as felons, and were soon-after incarcerated or exiled from the Corp's lunar base. Sloane rarely made public appearances, insuring that his face was not readily recognizable by the average Harvest employee.

The street bustled with pedestrians, the second of the three lunchbreak periods spread over the twenty-four-hour-day had just begun. Hundreds of hungry workers rose from the industrial depths to converge on the base's restaurant district. Maneuvering easily in the moon's .73 gravity, Sloane threaded his way through these crowds. He headed for a game center which, as he had expected, was vacant during this shift. There, Caffino nervously awaited him, clutching a personal play-unit in his lap as he sat at one of the shop's CGI game stations.

Impatient to examine his spy's report, Sloane contemptuously dismissed the man without discussion. Caffino stumbled to his feet and made a clumsy show of "absent-mindedly" leaving his play-unit behind when he finally scurried out of the game center. Sloane sighed with dismay at the fool's ineptitude. Boldly striding over to the "forgotten" play-unit, he popped its disk and pocketed it. A moment later, he was back on the street again.

Within minutes, Sloane accidentally (for real) ran into the foreman of the base's waste disposal system. Concealing his frustration at this impromptu diversion, Sloane was courteous to the man. The Security Domo admitted that official authorization was still forthcoming on the installation of airlock baffles in the flush pipes. "Funding," he grumbled, casually blaming bureaucracy for the delay.

The foreman shared a rumor with him regarding the potential application of the base's waste byproducts. It was no secret that Greye, the next planet in this star system, was a prime customer when it came to basic fuel. Harvest Corp had intentions of offering the colony world a discount in exchange for a long-term contract for hydrogen at a locked-down basic purchase rate. The Corp was already sucking the colony dry over the price of oxygen, which was needed to finish terraforming Greye. In an attempt to sweeten these negotiations, Harvest was planning to browbeat a few colonial industrial concerns into buying the base's waste products as fertilizer for Greye's struggling agriculture.

Sloane saw his point. If the base's waste disposal Department could generate new profits, it would help convince the Board to approve the airlock modifications. He promised to advise the Execs of this development, but when he finally returned to his office, he found his Department in frantic disarray as his officers strove to handle a full alert.

For a while, the notion of paying for the new airlocks by selling off shit was gone from Sloane's mind. He even forgot about the disk in his jacket pocket.

There were pirates to chase.

He barked command codes at his officers, rousing them from their confusion and stinging them into action. Scrambling into his own battlegear, Sloane checked each suit and pulse rifle before he passed them over to his troops. When he came to Officer O'Donnell (whom everyone called "PeeWee" behind his back), Sloane directed him to stay, for the Security Domo wanted only his burliest and spriest men accompanying him on this strike. Anyway, someone had to man the comm; if subsequent information was forthcoming, Sloane needed that data immediately forwarded to him on-site.

Before hurriedly ushering his troops into the dispatch pod that would convey them to a pursuit skimmer, Sloane downloaded the alert specs into his wrist unit. Then he dashed after his men, yanking the pod's hatch closed behind him. As the pod zoomed through passages, heading for the skimmer hangar, its sudden velocity forced them all deeper in their crash couches.

Moments like these brought back memories of Sloane's military days. Unexpected alarms motivating entire squads into speedy and carefully practiced maneuvers. Cramming himself into combat suits, then checking his deployment buddy's gear as the other swiftly examined his own suit and weapons. Crowding into assault cruisers that smelled of sweat and lubricant. Reviewing attack formations as the soldiers traded smokes and tense humor. Although Sloane enjoyed the benefits of the private sector, he often waxed nostalgic for the military's strict discipline.

These officers who accompanied him into battle now were competent, but they lacked the rigid training and bloodthirsty dispositions generated by a military regimen. They were motivated by salary, not dedication, and that distinction would impair their proficiency if this impending encounter became mortally desperate. Sloane knew that he was the only one of them who possessed the right stuff. The only person he could truly rely on to watch his back was himself. The trouble was: as Domo, he was also responsible for protecting the backs of every man under his command.

At the hangars, he double-timed his troops into a skimmer and requested immediate launch priority from the dispatch center. Haste was vital, but so was avoiding a crash with any freighters about to dock at or deploy from the Natt base. The skimmer was advised to wait for thirty-six seconds while a massive ship jockeyed its way out of a neighboring hangar. Gritting his teeth to appease his furious frustration, Sloane watched the spacecraft's storage capsules sway as its turgid thrusters strained to elevate the bloated freighter. When the traffic controller's go-ahead came over his comm, Sloane was already firing up his skimmer's jets.

The sleek vessel leapt from the hangar. Designed for speed in atmosphere, slender wings and tiny turbine coils swept along the pursuit craft's tapered fuselage. A white fusion exhaust blazed from the effulgent tail of the ship. Gaining altitude, it soared over Natt's landscape of frozen methane. The heavens were occluded by the swirled crimson face of the moon's gas giant primary.

Handing off the skimmer's navigation to an officer who could cope with the simple task, Sloane found a seat in the back of the cabin and punched up the alert signal stored in his wrist.

A Corp diver had reported sighting a group of nine unscheduled stassed individuals in the vicinity of a gatherer depot stationed near the stratosphere in sector 449. When these strangers had failed to respond to a hail on Corp wavebands, the diver had immediately called in the pertinent facts. Outside of grid coordinates, the diver's report was basically useless; the experience had stressed him out, and the man had babbled like a hysterical child.

But then, coordinates were enough for Sloane to initiate his defensive assault against the intruders. Once his strike force was within range, the skimmer's scanners would pinpoint the pirates for him. Then the chase would begin.

The skimmer's trajectory followed the curve of Baltuss' gaseous face, heading into the spin of the planet's rotation. The target sector was still beyond the horizon, even at its best speed the pursuit ship would take nearly an hour to reach the threatened gatherer depot.

Such delays endlessly exasperated Sloane. Even in his military days, he had never adjusted to the travel-time involved in space travel. His impatience had inevitably been the cause of his departure from the Space Navy. Seeking employment in the private sector, he had hoped to find work that would spare him the tedium of space voyages. And yet, here he was…flying a troop of patrol officers across thousands of astral kilometers to foil a pirate raid. The chances were very remote that any of the trespassers would still be on-site by the time his security force arrived. There was every possibility that the depot itself might even be missing, for Sloane knew better than to underestimate the avarice of the pirates.

How was he supposed to combat these nefarious trespassers while travel-time hampered his efforts?

It was infuriating to be so helpless against the enemies of his employers, but it was even more maddening to know that the best he could expect was to apprehend these lawbreakers and turn them over to Greye's Courts for trial. Personally, Sloane ached to see each pirate die horribly and slowly under his own brutal touch.

By the time they approached the hovering mass of the gatherer depot, Sloane was inwardly seething with repressed impatience. He ordered his officers into the airlock, releasing them one by one as the ship swooped through Baltuss' outer clouds. The depot swam like a bulbous island in the stratosphere, the blue dome of its inflated carriage towering above the mists like a swollen pustule.

There were no signs of any struggle among the loose throng of silver man-shapes hanging like gnats around the enormous depot. *We're too late,* he mentally moaned. *The pirates are long gone.* But when Sloane switched to Harvest's recognition code scan, then overlaid this with the physical view on the skimmer's display screen, the intruders stood out like turds in ice cream.

"Gotcha, you bastards," he growled.

"We caught them red-handed, sir," remarked the sole officer remaining with him in the skimmer's cabin.

He grunted agreement, but internally Sloane fumed with regret. They weren't red-handed at all. As long as the pirates maintained positions above the stratosphere, they were not technically trespassing in Harvest territory. The bastards had found another manner in which to flaunt their existence. But the Security Domo knew there was more to this almost-a-violation than simply embarrassing the legal limits of the Corp's ability to respond to their presence. They were after something. The gatherer depot was too big for them to steal, but any amount of its hardware might be the thieves' actual target. They might even be looking to release the chemicals the divers had already deposited at the depot.

Via comm-links, Sloane ordered his officers to spread out and surround the flank of the depot where the intruders were carelessly gathered. Against his personal opinions, he sharply instructed his troops to restrain from firing on the pirates, "Unless they enter the clouds—then they've actually violated Harvest airspace, and we can use force to evict them." Sloane would lead the attack with the skimmer. His plan was to startle the pirates with the appearance of the Harvest pursuit ship, scaring them into flight. By approaching from above the plane of the gas envelope, he hoped his advance would drive them deeper into Baltuss. Then he and his troops could respond with legal sanction.

The pirates fled in the wrong direction, however, scattering to merge with the other Corp divers who loitered about doing their jobs. Sloane cursed vehemently. Gripping the controls, he chose a single pirate and set his sights on the criminal. Relentlessly, the skimmer dogged this individual across the perimeter of Baltuss' clouds. The pirate refused to be driven into breaching the atmosphere, dodging pursuit with remarkable expertise. The skimmer trembled under Sloane's reckless guidance as he forced it through maneuvers far too extreme for its construction. Strapped in beside him, his co-pilot officer gasped at every sharp turn and unrecommended pull-about.

The chase was a chaotic blur zigging and zagging throughout the sky. Coming into frequent contact with aerial pedestrians as it jetted about, the skimmer knocked silvered divers tumbling head-over-heels out of its path. Their stass-suits protected them from any injuries from the impacts, Corp divers and, unfortunately, trespassers alike. As the ship dove through their midst, the divers and officers mixed with the fleeing pirates until no one could recognize their neighbor. Avoiding the hyperactive and unpredictable trajectory of the skimmer was hardly the only worry for these loose people. Someone was firing weaponry and being rather indiscriminate with their choice of targets. The energy blasts were no threat to the divers, for their stass-skins protected them from all harm. But the gunfire was creating a panic.

"Dammit," Sloane ground his teeth. "I warned those guys not to discharge their weapons."

"Maybe it isn't one of ours," offered the co-pilot.

That would be nice, but Sloane knew that fortune was not on his side in this encounter. The pirates had baited him into attacking them then they had scattered to lose themselves in the throng of legal divers. Their maneuver was a blatant insult to Sloane's tactics, as if the pirates were giving him a collective finger. They were playing with his security troops, relishing the frustration produced by this stalemate. Sloane ached to strafe the bastards, catching as many trespassers with the skimmer's weaponry as he could before common sense stifled his impulsive anger. The ship's armament would be just as ineffective against the stassed pirates as the rogue energy rifle blasts had been. Shooting the criminals was not a viable option, he needed to *capture* them. He abandoned his pursuit of the solitary nimble pirate, bringing the skimmer into a position high above the people dispersed around the gatherer depot. From this vantage, he broadcast a recall to his officers, at the same time instructing all company divers to report to the Natt base for debriefing. He had hoped that this might divide the crowd, identifying any stationary figures as the guilty pirates. But that notion was too whimsical. None of the figures on his screen hesitated, each one moved in one of two general directions. The greater numbers headed in the direction of Harvest's lunar base, while disturbingly only a few came to reboard the waiting skimmer. Clearly, the corporate wavebands were known to these interlopers. The pirates had outwitted him again, blending in with the legal divers by complying with the Security Domo's recall broadcast.

Sloane was furious to discover that five officers had vanished during the confrontation. No one recalled seeing anyone get shot, but neither would any of the nervous officers attest to witnessing the defection of the missing individuals. They shrugged and faced the Security Domo with vacant expressions.

There was no chance that foul play had taken the missing officers. Such defections were becoming more and more frequent, depleting his already sparse manpower against the vile pirates. Sloane considered these escapees cowards and traitors, never once questioning what might have inspired such disloyalty in the first place.

Nor would any officer admit to firing their weapons during the fiasco. Examination of their gear corroborated this claim. Whoever the mystery gunman had been, it was not one of his men.

Before leaving, though, Sloane directed the gatherer depot to return to Natt. There was no point in risking the equipment to a possible return visit by the pirates. It was possible that his assault had thwarted whatever the trespassers' scheme had been, and Sloane felt it was prudent to maintain that meager success.

Five men lighter and with nothing to show for it, Sloane's skimmer escorted the depot satellite back to the lunar base.

The data in his pocket remained forgotten until late that evening when Sloane stomped into his quarters and wearily cast off his jacket. Pulling it from the pocket, he fingered the black disk like a long-lost treasure.

After his failure to apprehend a single pirate, Sloane was elated to discover something that might turn the day victorious.

He pulled on a relaxation robe and settled down at his private console... only to find a communiquÈ awaiting him from the Executive Review Board.

They had decided to approve his waste disposal system modifications. To cover this unexpected expenditure, the Security Domo was instructed to release five officers from the employment of his Department, for their salaries would finance the construction he had recommended.

His furrowed brow expressed his displeasure. "Those bastards," he grumbled anew. It seemed that everyone was a bastard today. "How am I supposed to maintain security if the Board downsizes my Department? They're sabotaging my ability to perform my duties."

Well, he knew which five officers he could fire without causing any disturbance in the ranks of his troops. At least their cowardly disappearances could be put to constructive use.

In the end, the airlock baffles would get installed, and there would be one less route for the pirates to sneak into the base. To expedite the construction, he promptly forwarded the Board's approval to the waste disposal foreman.

While sipping a vodka-spiked java, Sloane remembered the black data disk, and his spirits regained some altitude. Popping it into his console, he ran the spy's report disk.

What he read made him happy.

The secret research was devoted to the development of a weapon of mass destruction. The process was some sort of disintegrator, the details of which befuddled his mediocre knowledge of quantum physics. He skipped through a large section that consisted of dense theorems, finally reaching a summary text.

Project Godbreath had succeeded in generating something that induced a complete disintegration of matter. The basic difficulties at this stage involved the overt instability of the process itself. It was feared that, once initiated, there might be no way of turning off the deadly weapon. Therefore, all experimentation had been limited to theoretical computer models...until recently.

In the last weeks, the researchers had made a breakthrough in the ability to control the malevolent process.

Requests were going through channels for increased funding so that this new control could be investigated.

Immediately, Sloane saw an application for this secret weapon, one that would definitely solve his own problems with a single strike. All he needed was to discover the location of the pirates' lair.

If he could learn their location, Sloane proposed to take them out from a distance. He would not launch any assault craft, he would simply subject the Viper Nest to the Godbreath disintegration process. It would dissolve the pirates' base right out from around them, leaving them naked to the unsympathetic vacuum. Their stass-suits would probably protect the pirates from the dissolution of their hideout; indeed, those stass fields would preserve their bodies long after they all died of starvation. Oh, how Sloane wanted to see a thousand pirate corpses drifting helpless through the void. Their carcasses would orbit Baltuss as a grim testament to the futility of crossing Theo Sloane.

And now, according to this stolen report, the disintegrator was nearing perfection. Soon, he could add it to his arsenal against the pirate menace. But—the deadly weapon was useless unless he knew where to use it. He needed to track down the pirates' elusive base. He needed to discover the best-kept secret in the entire solar system.

How hard could that be?

He was buzzing with anticipation.

Part One Resumed:

Shunning the Clouds

She was so sad and helpless. All he wanted was for her to be happy again.

Not even Taz's loving caresses could dispel Peri's gloom.

Her mood had not improved since her terrifying encounter, and Taz Bailey was beginning to grow concerned.

Privately, he had zero belief in the cause of her fears. He suspected that she had simply bumped into some HeeVee research drone. With Annucci's ridiculous tales of killer bots still fresh in her highly-suggestible mind, it was no wonder Peri had misidentified the "thing" and fled in a panic. Whatever the case, though, she was safe now, back on the colony platform and far from the threat of any actual or illusionary objects. There was nothing to fear here. Why couldn't she relax?

The threat could not be real, for there were no other reports of any strange mechanical drones wandering the clouds. He pointed out how many others were still diving safely among the gas giant's clouds, but she refused to be cheered up.

He had to admit, though, that there were beneficial sides to her weakness. Unable to bring herself to return to Baltuss' clouds, Peri found her funds bleeding away with alarming speed. She had finally agreed to share a full-time rec cap with him, reluctantly announcing her decision two hours after the lease lapsed on her own personal domicile. Taz didn't care; by effort or default, he was happy to have finally won a commitment from her. The extra housing cost barely scraped his wealth, but the expenditure was worth it if it helped tighten his relationship with the girl.

The 24/7 availability of her company was a thrill he continued to appreciate, but the darkness of her withdrawn personality was wearing away at his compassionate patience. Her mood began to separate them, as if her despair was determined to isolate her soul from him. Taz missed the Peri with which he had fallen in love. Whatever had happened to her down in the clouds had robbed him of that carefree spirit. His best efforts to revitalize that joy were proving to be useless. He watched her descend slowly into a terrible depression. Her days were empty and uneventful, her nights were haunted by robot monsters.

Taz had no idea what to do. The colony had no psychotherapist, and the platform's acting quack of a medical doctor was liable to poison her with some speedy misdiagnosis. There was no one to turn to for professional help…his own resources were all he could use to battle her emotional decay.

He looked at her now, saddened by how her lithe figure seemed withered. Her long limbs were coiled about her, as if struggling to contain her despair. Even her head crest was retracted and folded across her skull. Her tattoos stood out starkly against her pale skin. He could not see her face, but he suspected it was pinched with internal distress, wrinkling her small nose and tainting her sensual lips with a pathetic grimace. Her dreamy brown eyes were undoubtedly scrunched closed, shutting out the universe-at-large.

He scowled, wishing he could master a bit of her oblivion right now.

Loud thumps and a guttural bellowing were resounding from the rec cap next-door. Alligned in compact rows, the capsules readily transmitted vibrations.

Over the years, the divers of Petrie platform had evolved a fundamentally easy-going society. While the camaraderie of life in the void made them all unspoken brothers in this cosmic frontier, most spacers embraced a strong sense of privacy born of the stress of living in such close proximity. People tended to be more considerate in these conditions. The smartest "rule" was: don't be a pest. There were no police aboard the platform, but nuisances invariably found themselves excluded from social contact. Troublemakers got themselves spaced.

Right now, Taz thoroughly wanted to space his noisy neighbor. This was not the first annoying outburst; the ruckus had been going on since the man had appeared a week ago. Had he no sense of decorum? Did he never tire or pause in his noisy habits?

The rude intrusion bothered him all the more for how he imagined it must distress Peri. In her depressed state, the ruckus was undoubtedly oppressively monstrous. With an angry scowl, Taz decided to put an end to this disturbance.

Making certain that Peri was safely asleep, he left the rec cap and approached the stass-hatch of his neighbor's capsule. As he had expected, the portal was locked barring his entry. He rang the buzzer, announcing his vehemence by pressing the worn switch viciously again and again. Despite his relentless buzzing, it was several minutes before the admittance light blinking on, signaling that the stass-hatch had been retuned to accept his own stass-field.

Taz was not given the chance to enter, though. Brusquely blocking the entrance, the noisy neighbor emerged, stassed-up but visibly infuriated by the interruption. The man communicated his verbal abuse over the public comm frequency.

"You got some gall bothering me, you silverface!"

"Look, Barker," Taz responded with momentous restraint, "these caps carry sound like an amplifier network. You've got to cut back on the—"

"Where do you get off telling *me* what to do?" boomed Barker's shrill voice.

"I was only—"

"You got the stones, you bighead. Y'think I don't know who you are? Big high-and-mighty rich-boy. Yer Bailey, aincha? Spoiled brat rich-punk, thinks he's entitled to boss everybody else." Barker leaned forward and stabbed at Taz's startled chest with a sternly prodded finger. "You go ahead and order me around and see what it gets you, cloud-headed farty-boy."

"Do everybody a favor and learn how to be a human being, huh?" snapped Taz. He brushed aside the brute's rigid appendage.

For a second, it looked as if Barker might explode into lunatic violence. His stout head wavered back and forth on his bull-neck. His silvered fists were spastic blurs at the ends of his taut arms. The airwaves communicated his wordless breathing, it rasped with hateful ambition.

By the time Taz realized he was defiantly standing his ground, the moment had passed, Barker's hair-trigger psychotic episode failed to erupt. The man regained his sardonic composure and resumed his verbal abuse.

"You got my Paw's stones, Bailey," barked the noisy diver. "Don't ever touch me again."

With that, he whirled and retreated to his rec cap. The instant Barker had disappeared through the stass-hatch, the locked light blinked on, its yellow glitter snidely denying Taz any last words.

Dirt-eater, he muttered to himself. Sometimes it took newcomers a while to adjust to the platform. But if this breach-hole didn't wise up and start acting civil, he was looking at a remarkably short tenure here.

Unfortunately, the man's uncouth audacity doomed Taz to return to a noise-bombarded rec cap.

At least Peri was managing to sleep through the din.

When Taz announced that he was going out for a while, Peri's desperate expression forced him to assure her that he was not planning on leaving the platform. He wanted to fetch some food from the cafeteria, and he was thinking of renting a movie for their enjoyment. Did she have any preferences? In diet or entertainment?

Her reply was openly unspecific.

Leaving their living quarters did little to alleviate Taz's distress. He could not shake his concern for Peri's mental health.

Outside, Baltuss' crimson mass dominated the heavens above the Petrie platform. A crescent of its horizon glowed brightly as tiny but brilliantly blue dot that was Cacio Trumpis edged from behind the alien world's massive girth. Polished by interplanetary dust, the wall of dom capsules glittered with the combined illumination of the far planet and the even more distant sun. Taz squinted in this reflected incandescence, then stepped down his visible range to avoid burning out his mechanical eyes. This left him hanging next to the colony in a murky gloom which only enhanced the mood he was looking to cast off.

Gripping the tow lines with his bottom hands, the man pulled himself along while maintaining an upright position. He hurried through the vacuum, eager to be out from under Baltuss' ruddy regard. The greater muscles of his legs propelled him more swiftly than the arms with which he had been born.

Once inside the platform's commercial facility, he returned his visual senses to their normal aperture. He had imagined that proximity with other people might soothe his emotional tempest, but the freelancers he passed in the corridors only reminded him of his own anguish. Their casual smiles taunted his tortured soul, proclaiming how unproblematic were their lives in comparison to his. They were happy and their loved ones were not tormented by psychological demons. All of his wealth could not cure Peri's depression. He was powerless to save her, and he feared he was doomed to share her deterioration. All these apprehensive worries maintained his tension level, not allowing him the clarity he so desperately needed right now.

To his dismay, he found the cafeteria closed for repairs. He was forced to turn back, reentering the void to make the long climb to an opposite pod to visit another food dispensary. This exasperating detour only served to further frustrate him.

While hovering in line at the far cafeteria, Taz encountered someone he had not seen in months. Besides moving in different social circles, the acquaintance had never really endeared himself to Taz. While most freelancers distrusted the HeeVee presence in local space, this man was zealously outspoken regarding his hate for the vile Corp. He was almost fanatical when it came to decrying every aspect of Harvest's existence. The excessive volume of his relentless denunciations had gained him the nickname "Din."

"Haven't seen you in weeks," the acquaintance remarked in his loud voice. "What's up? You find a better party circuit that I should know about, Taz?"

He admitted that he had lost touch with the party scene. "I've sort of settled down."

"With that grounder?" Din smirked. "Taught her any useful positions yet?" He chortled at his crude wit, collecting his food from the dispensary slot and moving aside to allow Taz to place his order.

"Her name is Peri." At the last second, Taz chose a pair of vodka bulbs instead of a meal. His maudlin spirits were no longer interested in sustenance. Perhaps some alcohol might deaden his defeatism.

Together, they moved to a stall where Din could ingest his dinner and Taz could imbibe his intoxicants.

Between mouthfuls of nutrient paste, Din explained: he had been Down off and on for nearly a week, searching in vain for a score that might enable him to cancel his gambling debt. The clouds were frustratingly bare, he revealed. He was not the only diver to return empty-bagged lately.

Careful to not imbue his inquiry with any degree of reason-to-worry, Taz probed after any strange sightings in Baltuss' clouds. When Din laughingly accused him of doing research in preparation of going odder, Taz rolled with the jape. The vodka was already blurring his judgment, and he unwisely mentioned a rumor he had heard about dangerous robotic drones prowling the gas giant's atmosphere.

His whispered tale drew the attention of someone at a neighboring dining stall. The eavesdropping man turned out to be Petroff, the colony's questionably talented medical doctor. Petroff was curious where Taz had heard that rumor.

"Dezi Annucci mentioned it," he reluctantly revealed.

"That old man and his mouth," the doctor sneered. "I'm going to miss his crazy rumors when he's gone."

"Is he going somewhere?" mumbled Din.

"Sick," announced Petroff with a furrowed brow. "Bone cancer. He's got it bad."

This news spoiled Taz's mounting torpor. Although he had no fondness for the old odder, he wished the cruel reality of mortality on no man. Word of Annucci's condition sobered him, and he found his mood reverting to its prior state of agitated despair. He sucked down the second booze bulb in a single gulp, hoping it might restore his inebriated detachment. Unfortunately, the drink delivered no fresh numbness to his fretful consciousness. Leaning to press his back into the cushion set into the booth, Taz listened as Din and the incompetent doctor traded platitudes devoted to old man Annucci.

"My favorite," Petroff confided, "has always been Dezi's claim that Baltuss is inhabited by sentient beings."

"The ones that no one have ever seen," nodded Din. "Including Dezi himself."

"That's a mainstay in every one of the odder's rumors, y'know," agreed Petroff with a derisive snicker. "Never once has *he* witnessed or seen evidence that might corroborate any of the tales he tells."

"It's an awfully big planet," Taz remarked. "How can anyone be so sure it doesn't harbor intelligent life?"

"Oh, c'mon, boy," the doctor chided insultingly. "Don't tell me that you *believe* that stupid myth…"

"I see no harm in keeping an open mind," Taz replied. But he was already regretting his statement, for now he saw the "harm". He could detect amusement rising in the pair like sharks zeroing in on bloodstained waters. His "open-mind" policy was marking him as a diver sliding into odderhood. Their friendly tones were turning dismissive. How fast would word of his budding madness circulate? How soon would Taz find himself the target of the same insults he had once thrown at Annucci and the other delusionary wretches who lived among the freelancer colony?

"I'm just playing devil's advocate," he explained unconvincingly. "News of Dezi's sickness has scrambled my mind. My girlfriend, Peri, you heard we moved into a rec cap, right? She always liked the old odder. Hearing about his cancer is really going to upset her. She hasn't been herself lately…"

"You should send her to see me," grinned Petroff. "I'll fix whatever's ailing her."

This was the other reason that Taz didn't like the man. Besides his ineptitude with medical matters, Petroff openly lusted after Peri. Taz had never challenged him on the matter, and perhaps because the doctor seemed to enjoy flaunting his improper desire in Taz's face.

He wanted to say: "You're so incompetent, you couldn't cure a healthy patient. Why, I'll bet Dezi Annucci doesn't really have cancer at all—you just misdiagnosed his condition." But instead Taz smiled and commented what a pity it was that the doctor could not fix what was ailing Dezi.

With a frosty look, Petroff returned to his own booth.

Remaining unaware of the undercurrent of rivalry between the men, Din offered his condolences for Peri's ill-health, predicting that she would perk up soon enough. He made some more idle conversation, attacking the overripe taste of the paste he had just consumed and finding an absurd reason to blame the flavor on HeeVee interference. Then he politely took his leave. "Have to head Down, Taz. I need to bag some gas if I'm going to eat better. I don't know how long I can tolerate this general-issue slop…"

He's got a point, Taz told himself. The food here was dreadful. Taz could not bring such a bland offering back to Peri, not if he expected to boost her deflated spirits. It seemed that every minute of his brief escape from their rec cap was only whittling away what little resolution Taz had left. There was no way he could return to her in this state of distress.

He decided to splurge. That might cure the dejected disposition they both shared.

Of all the businesses that maintained offices or outlets in the freelancer colony, RFC was the most expensive, the most elite, the most exclusive. Getting a table at RFC without a reservation was an absolute impossibility for most…but not for Taz.

He had learned long ago that wealth was useless as long as one hoarded it in one's account. "Spending" was hardly the only, nor the most effective, means of divesting oneself of personal funds. "Investing" provided growth potential, gradually increasing his overall fortune. "Investing" in local businesses made him an entrepreneur, proving that he had faith in the Petrie community. There were hundreds of businesses eager for some extracurricular funding, and Taz Bailey spread his investments around. He owned shares in three of the independent clothing suppliers, an all-purpose Everything Market, and several less legal professions. His financial dealings had repeatedly attracted offers from the colony's Administrators to join their ranks and become an equal-share owner of the rogue station, proposals Taz had graciously declined, for he harbored no political aspirations. Besides, he harbored acute anti-Admin attitudes which he preferred to not advertise. He was satisfied to see his money improving the quality of life among the freelance divers, for that elevated standard was something that benefited everyone—including himself.

Very few of the businesses found in the colony's commercial pods were branches of interstellar chains, for the Petrie platform existed in a gray legal area and most corporations wanted no part of Harvest Corp's ire. Most of the platform's businesses consisted of one-man operations that provided highly specialized services. RFC had started out that way: small and informal, with Roget Thibuit cooking private meals for discriminating individuals of considerable opulence. Soon, his reputation saw him serving private parties. As word circulated through the platform, Roget found himself in need of facilities bigger than the meager rec cap he rented. With Taz's financial assistance, the chef had rented office space in a commercial pod, and Real Food Central became an actual restaurant, competing with the insipid pastes offered by the public cafeterias and their lowlife competitors. RFC's prices were outrageous, but business boomed. The value of home-cooked delicacies went far beyond simple currency, especially in a station orbiting an alien world. Roget's pasta was worth a king's ransom to someone who normally dined on unpalatable gruel. As RFC's popularity soared, so did the price of a table in their serving rooms. For years now, reservations were necessary and usually hard to get. Some diners had to schedule their incredible meals more than a month in advance. These facts did not deter Taz from showing up unannounced. As a partner in the restaurant, he was entitled to preferential treatment, although he rarely afforded himself of such honors.

The staff greeted him with sincere congeniality. They escorted him to a private dining room, where Roget promptly appeared full of contented enthusiasm. The men discussed pleasantries for a few minutes, during the course of which Taz mentioned Annucci's cancer.

Roget was horrified by the news. Outside of the station's Administrators, the old man was rumored to be the colony's longest-standing inhabitant. He and his outrageous tales had become fixtures on the platform, he would be missed by many who knew him only casually.

Taz agreed that it was a tragedy—if the man was really sick.

Roget made an inquiring noise.

"The news comes from Doc Petroff," he revealed.

"Who is not the greatest authority when it comes to medical matters," the chef remarked sagely.

"Right."

Roget announced that—true or false—the rumor had inspired him to contact Dezi Annucci and offer him a free meal. "If he really is sick, that's the decent thing to do," commented the gourmet chef. "If he is not sick, he is still worthy of respect for his decades of diving."

Taz concurred. To avoid embarrassing the old odder, he suggested that RFC conduct a contest. Annucci could *win* his free meal.

"That's a marvelous idea," Roget declared. "We can offer two grand prizes, and do a real contest."

"You're the boss," Taz reminded him with a wry smile.

"And tonight, *you* are the customer. What culinary pleasure can I get for you this evening, Mr. Bailey?"

"Something simple will do," replied Taz. "Give me two servings of whatever you have in surplus. And they're to-go."

"You are not staying?" The chef looked hurt.

"I'm planning a romantic dinner with my honey back in our rec cap," Taz revealed with a faint smile. "Besides, then you can put this private room to more profitable use, eh?"

Roget nodded, flashing a somewhat bawdy grin before vanishing to his kitchen.

Ten minutes later, the chef was back, bearing a hermetic backpack filled with plastic containers and a thermos. "Beef and noodles in a cheese sauce," he informed his business partner, "with a sparkling fruit wine as the beverage." Drawing attention to a squarish box, he whispered with drama, "And for dessert: a pair of chocolate eclairs that are barely an hour old."

Taz thanked the man, then offered him his cred chit. When Roget refused payment, his partner deferred out of respect.

Making his exit of the restaurant, he felt good, energized by Roget's generosity. The chef was a remarkably amiable individual, his cheer had been effectively infectious. Coming here had been a fortuitous choice. Taz was leaving with superior food and a restored optimism, both of which would hopefully be positive influences on Peri's depression.

Before he departed the commercial district, he stopped into an entertainment depot and arranged for a movie (a comedy with light romantic overtones) to be made available to his quarters in a few hours. Now he was armed to take down her funk.

Look out, Peri's blues, he chuckled.

When he returned to their rec cap, Taz found Peri coiled in the same spot and the same position as he had left her. Her lassitude drained his revitalized confidence.

Her skin was sallow, and Taz was worried that she was running a fever. Generally unresponsive, she stared up at him with vacant eyes. Her mind seemed buried under layers of desensitizing dread.

What was the matter with her? Why had her fear mutated into this near-catatonic withdrawal? What terrible monster had driven her away from him?

She was so sad and helpless. All he wanted was for her to be happy again.

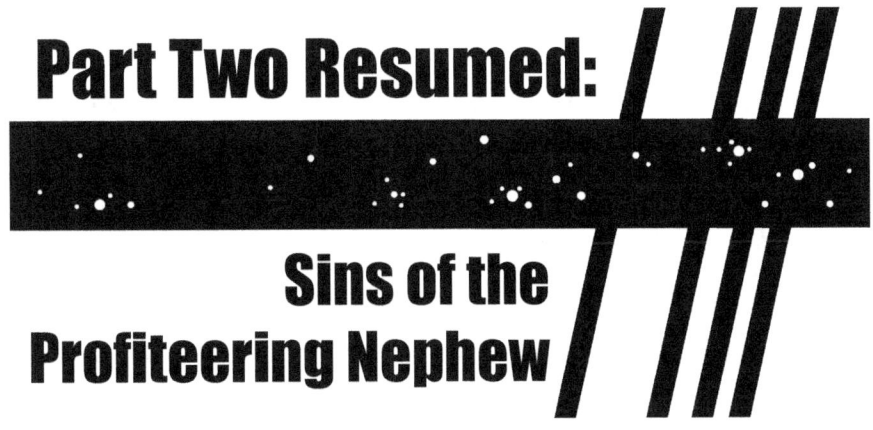

Part Two Resumed:

Sins of the Profiteering Nephew

How impressive…

And certainly achieved at no small expensive, mused Ted Hein with an insolent pucker of his harsh lips. *It's a shameless display of self-importance.* Hein was careful to keep his criticisms unvoiced, though, for he suspected that Executive Bester maintained fastidious audio-visual surveillance of all who approached this lair.

The design and construction of Nigel Bester's private sanctorum had challenged the architects the Executive had ferried in from Greye, but those elite engineers had proved equal to the task. What had once been a two-floor block of the penthouse level of the Harvest base had been hollowed-out and converted into a single vast chamber modeled to resemble the interior of some archaic British castle. Pillars featuring tierceron vaulting walled the circumference of the enclosure, striving to give it the feel of a coliseum. The ceiling was incredibly high, lost from sight in the hall's murky ambience. At one end of the chamber a ramp of stairs led to a dais that might traditionally sport an impressive throne. (The lack of such an extravangance did little to dissuade Hein from his opinion of Bester's overwhelming arrogance. *If it were* my *lair,* Hein sneered inwardly, *I'd have put a throne there.*) Instead, the lofty dais supported a modern control console. A hoverchair of excessive comfort drifted before the rank of machinery. Adding a primitive flair, the area was lit by the flickering taper of holographic flames. The primary illumination for anyone seated at the console came from the flickering monitors. Except for this console (and the luxury mattress located in a curtained alcove behind the chamber's stout pillars), the entire sanctorum was done in facsimilated stone.

The vast floor of the hall took Hein's footfalls and threw them into resounding echoes around the steep dome. He suspected these acoustics were intentional, the purpose being to bombard visitors with the amplified sound of their own arrival.

Not that Executive Bester entertained many people here. Rarely was Teid Hein allowed to enter his uncle's sanctuary. In Hein's opinion, he *deserved* access to the sanctorum for both familial and professional reasons. He fully expected that one day he would inherit Bester's Executive Privilege. Until then, Hein made himself useful by handling matters of social delicacy for his uncle.

Like the girl he had just decommissioned for the Exec. There were always dirty little chores to do in the shadow of corporate depravity, and there would always be nasty little men who would enjoy handling such unpleasant tasks. Hein was, at heart, such an individual.

Related to the Exec through his deceased mother, Teid Hein was a handsome man in his early twenties, full of vigor and stamina and ambition. He stood just over two meters in height, possessing wide shoulders and a bodybuilder's torso. His limbs were similarly corded with impressive sinews. A shock of bleached-white hair cascaded from his cranium, hanging down his neck in elaborately braided dreads. His face was a masterpiece of artistic reconstruction, reputedly styled after some ancient American cinema star. His money had been well-spent, for Hein now wore the body and profile of an Adonis. He made full use of these faculties, bedding as many women as he could, and being the biggest bully in any given group. Without his blood-linkage to the Exec, Hein would have been a surly thug. By virtue of his genealogy, though, he became a dangerous agent behind the scenes of corporate life.

He ascended the steps, and his uncle came into view hunched over an array of display screens at his console. Bester wore a long, flowing robe that transformed him into a draped shroud with a human head and arms. The robe was made of that new miacle material that conducted light pulses through its weave to produce an animated picture on the cloth. Hein jealously admired the fabric, wishing he had enough corporate clout to requisition a suit of his own. A stormy coastline raged on Bester's cloak, complete with windswept crags of threatening rock and an ill-fated schooner that traveled around the man's haunches to crash itself on the cliffs on his thigh. In the sputtering holographic light, Hein could not make out his uncle's mood. Bester's aristocratic features were turned away as he studied his screens.

When the Exec gave no sign of noticing his presence, Hein coughed, unable to keep impatience from his utterance. He stood on the last step, unwilling to go further until he was acknowledged. Minutes passed while the Exec puttered with his work and the bulky contender poised petulantly beyond the dais' plateau. Hein could not be certain, but it seemed that the Exec's ears were muffled by a pair of headphones.

Old fool, Hein grumbled privately. *You waste my time with this waiting game, and my time goes for a much higher premium than yours. Despite your Executive Privilege, only a very little of the real power is yours. You might give the orders, but it's other people who turn those directions into reality. When you pass a corporate edict, it's processed and implemented by workers. When you need some covert action taken, it's me who sees it's taken care of. And I have things to do.*

Bester finally turned to notice his nephew. Switching off the headphones, the Exec removed them from his bald head and placed the silent speaker-cups on the console at his elbow. When he spoke, his words were few, cutting right to the point.

"She's decommissioned and in the freezer," Hein assured him. "You have nothing to worry about, Uncle Nigel."

Bester flinched at the name's familiarity. He lowered his gaze, shaking his head at some unfortunate recollection. "The state of things is in constant decay," he mumbled.

"Physically or morally?" Hein asked snidely.

His uncle ignored the slur. He spoke of unexpected difficulties in the negotiations with Greye officials over exchange rates for a proposed oxygen deal. The colonists were being obstinate, refusing to accept Harvest's unflattering offer.

Uninterested in the Board's souring business deals, Hein asked if there was any way he could further be of assistance. When Bester shook his pale head abstractly, the youth took it as an answer. Hein turned and left, never having ascended to the final step.

In the finite confines of the base/city maintained on Natt by Harvest Corp, the ebb and flow of people and their interactions could be considered a network of lines. In Hein's mind, each line represented a separate person. These lines crossed the paths of others when social interactions occurred. They ran in tandem groups that represented the people they came in contact with on a daily basis: family, co-workers, friends. Certain lines were not intended to intersect. For instance: Exec Bester was not liable to run into lowly scrape tech Norman Normal. That was an extreme example, though, and not a viable model to judge circumstances. Take instead the life-line of Algol Caffino, a research tech attached to one of the base's secret research projects. (Make no mistake, Hein was aware of such activities as result of his association with the Board. Although he possessed no detailed knowledge about these clandestine affairs, he knew they existed. To his frustration, he had found that these secrets were too secure to reveal themselves to even Hein's nefarious curiosity. In the end, this did not overly bother him, for Hein doubted that he would have understood the technical jargon necessary in order to comprehend the research being conducted behind those closed doors. Knowing that such classified projects existed was enough for him. If the need ever arose, the simple existence of such secret labs was adequate to provide him with harmful leverage against the Execs should—*when*—he needed it.) Back to this Caffino guy—he was an average Al who rarely got drunk and stayed out of trouble, his life-line had no reason to intersect with the base's Security Domo's line.

So what were Theo Sloane and Algol Caffino doing together in a game arcade in the middle of a public lunchbreak? What deviltry was the Security Domo up to now?

Hein kept track of these kinds of things. It was not his weirdest hobby.

Of all the people Hein had ever met, he had more than a passing aversion for the Security Domo of Natt base. In fact, Hein coveted the man's job, for he had convinced himself long ago that the most comfortable application for his particular skills was the field of law enforcement. The echelons of that occupation were a plausible access route to his ultimate goal of membership on the Executive Board. Also: the Security Domo had interfered with Hein's unofficial practices more than once, thwarting several schemes that would have been financially rewarding. Since these endeavors had been unsanctioned, Hein had been unable to hang the Security Domo for his meddling. Beyond these political objectives, though, Hein hated Sloane for very basic and intensely visceral reasons. Everything about the wretch infuriated Hein, from Sloane's sexual prowess to the way the man breathed in long, even inhalations. Hein wished him an eternity of misfortune. Any inconvenience he could add to Sloane's life was well worth the effort.

Much to Hein's professional embarrassment, Sloane spotted him spying on the man. Brazenly adding salt to this psychological wound, the Security Domo's greeting was publically sarcastic. Hein had no choice but to rise to the slanderous insult.

"While *you* waste Harvest's time lunching with subversives in an amusement bar," Hein sneered. "You're certainly putting what little talent you have to adequate use, Domo."

"I'm conducting an investigation," Sloane announced. "And I do not appreciate being stalked by someone with your unsavory reputation."

"Coming from you, that's a compliment." Hein instantly regretted his retort. It was crude and banal—far too unsophisticated for someone of Hein's stature. Resorting to verbal scorn was demeaning. Words were too eloquent to waste on this low-life. He must avoid sinking to Sloane's vulgar level. The Domo simply brought out the worst in him.

Sloane was a disgraceful example of ordinary breeding, his strengths lay in his bluster. There was no wit to the man's cunning—not like Hein's razor-sharp artifice. He had no doubt that Sloane's miserable bravado would crumple and shrivel when faced with the handiwork of a master strategist. The Domo deserved a truly momentous penalty for his sins.

"Run along," advised Sloane. "You're interfering with official business."

Official business, Hein vowed, *will be your downfall, you audacious cretin.*

Word had reached Hein's ears of the Security Domo's latest encounter with the pirates that regularly preyed on Harvest's clouds. *Here,* he thought, *was the perfect opportunity to plague his sworn nemesis.* While combating the pirate menace, Sloane had ordered the threatened gatherer depot satellite to return to the Natt base—with its storage tanks less than half full! Enhanced with the right phraseology, this action could be transformed into an impropriety that damaged the Corp's fiscal identity. Official charges could be filed against the man responsible for this loss of profit.

It mattered very little to Hein whether this accusation bore any resemblance to reality. It was too perfect a downfall to pass up. Facts and evidence could be created to support this accusation. There was even the chance that the evidence really did exist.

Let the pompous Domo think he's secure in his position. All the better if his dark fate creeps up on him when he least expects it. Sloane is finally going down.

Hein was convinced he had finally found the necessary means to eliminate the man, which would leave the position of Security Domo open. And who better to fill the position than the enterprising person who had uncovered the previous Domo's corruption? Hein's vengeance would be all the sweeter if it gained him the job he secretly wanted. Meanwhile, disgraced and possibly imprisoned, Sloane's life would be ruined.

All it would take was a whisper in the right ear.

How impressive.

Part One Resumed:

Separating Rumors from Face

She had to do it herself.

For all the valiant efforts applied by Taz to remove Peri Fairchild from her deep depression, the girl found her own salvation in a dream.

Darkness surrounded her, hiding the dreamscape from her. She reached out to investigate her hidden environment with inquisitive fingers. Things were uncomfortably familiar to her groping touch: the satin seatcovers and the finely-carved ancient oak table and the porcelain curves of dishware. There was food on the plates, its warmth reached her touch before its odors reached her nostrils. There were other scents in the dark air, expensive perfume mixing with a salty breeze. The familiarity of it all was maddening, for she could not identify why. Her toes clenched deep in the plush carpet under her feet, and she realized that gravity held her in place.

This had to be back on Earth, before she had left the planet of her birth…

Lights sprang into brilliance, painful after the soothing embrace of the darkness. She squeezed her eyes shut, but the sudden glare pierced her translucent lids with a fuzzy pink glow.

Sounds followed, rising to torment her with clarity and attach her surroundings to a childhood memory.

"Happy birthday, little Patrice," announced a chorus of voices. "Today, you are twelve!"

"I'm older than that," she insisted. "I'm an adult now." She kept her eyes closed, though, refusing to look upon the resplendent repast that accompanied the recollection.

"Don't be foolish, little child," a voice cooed. Peri recognized it as the delicate diction of her mother. "You'll always be my baby girl."

"Our perfect little princess," declared her father's voice.

"Always in such a hurry to grow up," an unfamiliar voice chuckled. "What's the rush? Adulthood will bring you no new responsibilities, not as long as your family is here to watch over you."

"I'm a big girl now," she whimpered.

"You'll never have to want for anything. All you need do is ask, little child, and everything is yours."

"I want my independence!"

"That is something you'll never have to worry about, dear," her father's voice admonished her.

"I need to be self-reliant," Peri moaned. "I need that!"

"Why would you want that? Self-reliance is a myth created as a refuge for those who cannot interact with other people."

"You'll always need someone," her mother's voice sighed with diminishing patience. "You are not whole by yourself. You will never be the master of your own destiny as long as you're afraid of accepting help from other people."

"I don't need anyone!" Peri cried. Her sobs were laced with anger. "I don't need you, or your money!"

"Do not so readily dismiss wealth, little child," spoke her father with authoritative command.

"I want to return to my clouds," Peri moaned. "I want to be left alone..."

"Only money can solve your problems."

Her screams of anxiety dissolved the dream from her slumbering mind.

Although she woke with no coherent recollection of her dream, Peri found her despair melting away to be replaced with a desperate need to revisit the clouds of her ultimate rapture.

As she dimly recalled the ennui that had imprisoned her soul, she was shocked that her reaction had been so extreme. To have abandoned her only reason for existence was a drastic response to the threat she had encountered. There were hundreds of things that made diving into the atmosphere of an alien gas giant a hazardous pursuit. Lethal pressure, radiation storms, capture by HeeVee patrols, asphyxiation, systems failure...did a few killer robots make the clouds any more dangerous?

But then, her nervous breakdown had not come about as a result of any personal vulnerability. Her psychological collapse had resulted from her inability to return to Baltuss, not from the trauma of going face-to-face with the mechanical drone. The severity of her withdrawal troubled her, for it revealed a weakness of character Peri thought she had left behind when she had fled

Earth. It took courage—or madness—to make the transition from grounder to diver. To learn that she still carried some flaw that could incapacitate her so thoroughly—this realization contradicted her own self image. She needed to prove to herself that she was the only master of her body and mind. She needed to brazenly defy these irrational fears that filled her mind.

She needed to return to the clouds.

There was no sign of Taz when she crawled from the sleep netting. She was the rec cap's sole inhabitant. At first, Peri was disappointed by his absence, for she remembered the lengths he had gone to in his attempts to cheer her up. He deserved a special brand of gratitude for his concern. But then, she realized that he would be unconvinced by the abruptness of her restoration. Taz's concern would impel him to force additional convalescence on her. And she was not about to endure another hour deprived of her clouds.

Knowing that her absence would panic him, Peri left her lover a brief note on the cap's vid-pad. Her wording was intentionally upbeat, and just as deliberately vague. She might be anywhere on the platform, eating, relaxing, wandering through stores…the last place he would think to look was Down.

Once she had recharged her bio-battery, she stole from the rec cap and hauled herself along the tow lines necessary to convey her to the linear accelerator. Fortunately—against her own protests—Taz had transferred creds into her depleted account; otherwise she might not have been able to afford the simplest amenities.

Her present need was driving her into immediate action. She had no wish to grant herself any opportunity to revert to her insidious weakness. As soon as she was launched Baltussward, there would be no chance for her to question the wisdom of her impulsive determination.

Within minutes of being fired out of the platform's linear accelerator, Peri tuned in Red Sky Radio so that she had music for her voyage. The trip was going to be long, and she still dreaded a relapse of her unreasoning fear. Music, she hoped, would help steer her mind into more decisive directions.

The radio station was playing a set of power pop tunes, perfectly designed to keep her smiling. The frenzied rhythms succeeded in firing her up, while the familiar melodies enabled her to sing along as she plummeted through space at a velocity of a hundred kilometers a minute. Fortunately, no one had to suffer her caterwauling, since she was not broadcasting her utterances. Sadly, for all her love of music, Peri was quite tone deaf when it came to "singing along." Unbothered by her dreadful voice, she wailed and bebopped with the music, humming fill-in words in place of the lyrics she could not remember. Her spirits ballooned with each happy chorus.

She *so* appreciated the existence of the pirate radio station.

HeeVee's version of musical entertainment was dreary by comparison, consisting of marching operas and vile stretches of corporate commercials. She could not believe that even the career workers on Natt enjoyed the music prescribed for them by corporate decree. Life under HeeVee house-rules must be insufferable.

The corporation was fanatically possessive when it came to defending their claims on Baltuss. Their license agreements with local authorities granted them exclusive cloud-mining rights to the planet. By association, HeeVee perceived that every aspect was covered by that ancillary domain. They aggressively fought to keep out intruders, jealously guarding the world's entire atmosphere. (For all the good those efforts did. Freelance divers had been sneaking onto Baltuss for over a century.) In HeeVee's opinion, the Corp owned the planet's atmosphere and surrounding space. Peri knew that the Petrie platform was a burning thorn in the corporate butt, and she suspected that Red Sky infuriated them just as much with its continuous transmissions. Not only was the pirate station broadcasting in flagrant violation of HeeVee's local frequency regulations, Red Sky displayed a better understanding of its audience's needs, delivering varied selections of quality music—without advert interruption.

No one knew who was behind Red Sky, no one knew the location of their transmitter. Although Peri had heard rumors of corporate attempts to silence the pirate station, there was no evidence to support any trace of success in those schemes. Red Sky was always there: free and easily accessible and bursting with delightful music. Whoever programmed the illegal airplay was a genius. Their choices indicated that they were intimately familiar with the emotional needs of the freelance divers as they kept the selections in tune with the platform's overall temperament. There had to be a whole network of people behind Red Sky, for it was too efficient an operation for a small group. Big or small, this group managed to conceal their identities from everyone with eerily airtight conspiracy. Peri could not recall ever hearing Dezi recount a rumor involving the secret staff of Red Sky Radio. Whoever they were, they were *that* good at hiding their complicity.

Which Peri thought was stupid. HeeVee were the ones threatening Red Sky; the pirate station had nothing to fear from the freelancer divers. In fact, to everyone she knew, Red Sky's staff were heroes. If they ever chose to unmask themselves, they would be treated like royalty for the invaluable service they brought to every freelancer's life. Peri could not imagine living without music, not back on noisy Earth, and even less so here in the forever quietude of space. Without music, humanity could never survive out here.

There were even tales that Red Sky's signals reached as far as Greye, the next planet sunward in the Cacio Trumpis system, where the population openly appreciated the pirate station's entertainment in their dark cities. These tales came from people other than Dezi the rumormonger too; she had heard them from the lips of traders who smuggled freight from Greye to the freelancer platform.

Everybody loved Red Sky Radio (with the exception of the HeeVee tightasses), but no one loved Red Sky more than Peri. Their music had been her constant companion during all her previous joyriding dives into the gas giant's atmosphere, it was only fitting that she reenter the clouds today accompanied by the merry soundtrack they provided.

The frivolous nature of the songs playing now helped diffuse her anxiety about returning to Baltuss. The mindless cheer conveyed by the music made her fears seem trivial and over-exaggerated. It was a huge planet; the chances of running into one of whatever-she-had-run-into again were statistically diminutive. There was no reason to be uneasy in the imminent presence of the clouds she so vividly loved—and needed. Everything was okay, and soon she would be reunited with her precious freedom among Baltuss' vapors.

We're talking about a dangerously powerful addiction here, Peri's conscience warned her. *You went into catatonic withdrawal because you thought you'd never be able to dive again. It's unhealthy to allow anything to have that much control over our psyche.* She hated that tiny inner voice, for all it ever did was preach the abolition of fun.

I'm my own master, she reminded herself. *Nobody forces me to do anything I don't want to do. I'm going diving because I want to.*

Need to.

Want to, she insisted. *What I* need *to do is prove to myself that I can still do it. I know it won't kill me, but I have to go through the motions to prove that to myself. Actually,* she realized, *you're the one I need to prove it to. I already accept it as a truism*—you're *the disbelieving voice of uncertainty inside my head.*

Her conscience made no reply, withdrawing from the flow of her consciousness.

Everything was okay once more. She swept toward the wall of crimson mists, with uptempo tuneage bouncing in her head and the anticipation of a horny virgin tickling her gut. It was as if this dive was her first venture Down…she was leaping headlong into a wildly new world. Environmentally, she knew what to expect, but *emotionally* the clouds represented the unknown, simultaneously possessing the ability to please or scar. The only way to learn what would happen inside those mists was to go there. There was no turning back now. Well, actually she could use her thigh-jets to abort her planetfall, but taking that route was not an option as far as Peri was concerned. She was going Down, and nothing was going to stop her. The proof that everything was okay lay hidden in that alien atmosphere. Once she swam in familiar clouds, she would be whole again, healthy and satisfied.

Fate smiled on Peri as she pierced the gas giant's turgid stratosphere. The music sequewayed into her all-time favorite song, empowering her joy with supernatural intensity. Familiar rhythms defined a simple-but-engaging beat, while fuzz-box guitar wailed through a catchy riff. The bassline was fluid and scalding. The vocals were masculine and harsh, following a harmony that was separate from the melody pursued by the other instruments. Bellowing the all-too meaningful lyrics in her own brutally off-key tones, she reentered her wondrous playground after a forced exile. The chemical signatures of the clouds called out to her, their tenuous density caressed her silvered limbs, their infrared content sparkling across her augmented vision. Her passage into the clouds was an ecstatic one.

She sank through a region of scarlet fog that was so dilute that her passage failed to make visible eddies in the mist. That spilled her out into a vast cavern of orange immensity. Roiling cloudbanks formed this chamber's walls. She fell through the rarefied gas that filled this air pocket. The next strata of cloud that she encountered was a murky brown haze that oozed like gelatin. She swam in this aerial river, reveling in the thrill of returning to these favorite places.

Meanwhile, Red Sky Radio seemed to playing specially for her. The cluster of gleeful pop tunes gave way to a moody electronic composition. Dense layers of sequencers erupted like newborn lavaflows amid a soundscape of gurgling tonalities. The ghostly call of synthetic flutes drifted through the mix, evoking moist everglades and summer mornings. In the distance, tribal percussives echoed across eons to establish a racial link with the shadowy melody. The obscurity of the music was a perfect compliment to the vapors of Baltuss' infinite atmosphere. Peri was awestruck by the majesty bestowed on the compressed effluvium by this momentous soundtrack. This return to her clouds of joy was exceeding all of her wildest hopes. Her heart was replete with confidence. The clouds became her rightful and proper milieu, and for a moment she and this congruous environment were all that existed. She drifted at the epicenter of a universe of heavenly infinite scope. The alien clouds welcomed her with mollifying undulations, tendrils of mist uncoiling like searching fingers until they sensuously merged with the neighboring gaseous embankments. Everything was exactly as it should be, each molecule of gas poised in tandem with her rapt physiology.

A stray perception spoiled this epitome of peace: at the periphery of her scans Peri caught a concentrated heat signature. This meteoric distraction ruined her nirvana. An instinctive recognition of the brief profile presented by her scan dragged Peri back to mundane reality.

It was another diver. Swooping down on radically efficient thruster jets, this figure slid through the effervescent muddy soup. In a second, the intruder was gone, descending to the next lower cloud strata. What startled

Peri was how the figure seemed masked from detection; if not for the blazing heat of their jets, they would have escaped her notice completely. Beyond the basic reflective nature of a stass field, she was unfamiliar with any cloaking technology capable of veiling a stass field itself. *This* unprecedented factor drew her in pursuit of the new diver.

Later, she would realize the folly of her curiosity. Any person in possession of such concealment could only be in HeeVee employ, out testing some new stealth hardware which would inevitably be used to stalk unwanted freelance divers through Baltuss' dense clouds. Her mind was still too pumped from the bliss of her descent to identify the stupidity of following such a stranger.

She maintained a respectable distance from the mystery diver. He might be masked against detection, but Peri's own stass-skin was equipped with no miraculous camouflage. There was every reason to expect her prey to discover her chasing form, but the diver continued without pause into a purple cloudbank that was vaguely familiar. She chose to avoid directly following the man into this mist, instead maneuvering around a few meters to approach from her target's side. At the nebulous perimeter of this fog, she held back and observed the man's actions.

Close enough to pick him up in the visible frequencies now, Peri could tell the diver was masculine from the squat lines of his silvered body. Beyond the man's gender, though, she could discern little more. The opaque and mirrored veneer of his stass-skin concealed any features that might aid her in identifying the man. (This perfect masquerade had always annoyed Peri. It was effectively impossible to recognize even one's most intimate lover with their stass-skin activated. The absolutely impervious surface presented by the field's exterior rebounded light and all other frequencies, producing a fluid reflection that tended to further obfuscate the topography beneath the mirrored field. It wasn't until she was far offworld that she stared into the silvered face of another shielded person and finally understood why stass-skins were outlawed on terran soil—a criminal wearing one would not only be uncapturable, but unidentifiable.) As a result of this inevitable impossibility of recognizing one's stassed-up friends, the freelance divers regularly broadcast a mild Ident signal, announcing their identity to passers-by. This diver was transmitting no such Ident code. He hung warily in the purple mist, as if suspicious of his solitude.

His next action drew a verbal gasp from Peri.

Reaching into a cumulous wall, the man pulled into view the spiny mechanical monster that had driven Peri from Baltuss. Her chest constricted with a rush of panic as she recognized the thing. With its corroded, egg-like central mass bristling with extremely long dark needles and barbed thorns, the thing certainly looked every bit like a killer robot. It really did exist, and she had run into it *again*! This time, however, it appeared she had found drone and master.

The mystery man's movements implied an intimacy with the hideous object. He bent to open a panel in its metal side, exposing the drone's machinery to the vaporous environment. He was too far away for her to make out the type of fiddling he conducted, although she could tell he had produced a set of long tools to accomplish his tinkering. From her vantage, as the man hunched over the frightful-looking machine, she could see a cubish metal carton hanging from his utility belt. After a few minutes, he paused his technical modification to withdraw a cartridge of data discs from inside the machine. Taking another cartridge from the box at his hip, he inserted it into the drone's guts.

He's reloading the thing with new orders, she realized. *Or maybe he's retrieving the bot's surveillance tapes.*

Peri was suddenly overcome with the conviction that important secrets were stored on the disks which the man had taken from the bot. If she could get those disks, the freelancers stood to gain an invaluable advantage over HeeVee's murderous scheme to exterminate the competitor divers. There was, she knew, only one way for her to obtain those disks, and now—while the HeeVee diver was distracted resealing the bot's carapace—was the optimum chance to steal them. Probably her *only* chance too. To make use of it, she had to act *now*, for the man's distraction would not last forever.

So pumped up was she that Peri never considered the foolhardiness of her actions. The sudden threat of finding herself face-to-face again with the killer bot—not to mention its mysterious master—had scrambled her normally methodical mental process, allowing her to entertain these reckless prospects of acting the hero. Had she paused to consider the possible outcome of her courageous bravada, she would never have been so impulsive.

Firing her thigh-jets at maximum thrust, Peri shot from her place of concealment, diving on the HeeVee agent from behind. She held her breath as she approached him and reached for the carton at his waist. Her hands missed the box, and she collided with the man. For a brief instant, their stass fields joined at that point of impact, reverting to their individual integrity as the divers rebounded apart. Floundering back from the man, Peri scrambled to clutch his carry carton. Her frantic bungling only managed to detach it from his utility belt. She grabbed after the box, but it tumbled away from her desperate fingers, sinking out of view into the never-ending depths. She moaned.

Meanwhile, the man had recovered from his surprise and was struggling with her. His blows were feeble, but delivered with a raw anger. His retaliation succeeded in disorienting her sufficiently for the man to grab her leg. Now he held her firmly. She was helplessly trapped by his iron-grip.

"What the hell do you think you're doing?" the man demanded over a comm frequency.

With a start, she recognized his graveled voice. "Dezi?"

"How do you know me?" he growled. "Who are you—?"

"It's me—Peri Fairchild. You're hurting my leg," she whimpered.

"Peri?" Dezi released her and drifted back. "Why did you jump me, girl?"

"I didn't know it was you." She massaged her numb leg. "I thought you were…a…"

"A what?" His question was calculated, badly hiding the speaker's tension.

"A HeeVee diver," she told him. "What're you doing with one of their killer bots?"

His unexpected guffaw rang in her ears.

"There's nothing funny about that thing," she declared. She stabbed an accusing finger in the object's direction and spat, "It's one of those HeeVee search-and-destroy robots you told me about. It chased me off Baltuss last week."

"You've…encountered this *thing* before…?" Again, his query was laced with obvious hidden agendas.

"Last week." Peri informed him how she had bumped into the thing in the clouds, instantly recognizing it for what it was. "I barely escaped it."

"So," Dezi muttered. "That was *you*…"

"What were you doing with it?" she asked. "Sabotage?"

"Umm, the less you know, Peri, the better it'll be for you."

"Is it still dangerous?"

"What, uhh, makes you think its 'dangerous'?"

She snorted. "Just look at the thing. All those stabbing needles…"

He nodded solemnly, appraising the robot as if for the first time. "You have a point, yes."

"I'm sorry I lost your carry carton, Dezi," she sighed, hanging her arms by her side and waggling her hands with fretful worry. "I hope it didn't contain anything important."

"That's okay. Nothing I can't replace," he replied, turning his mirrored face back to regard her. "Are you all right, though? You hit me pretty hard."

"I'm sorry. I thought you were a…"

"A HeeVee spy, I remember. I suppose that would have seemed the likeliest explanation, yes."

"Shouldn't we get away from here?" she suggested. "What if that thing's real owners show up?"

"Umm, yes. We wouldn't want to meet *them*," he agreed.

Together, they soared into an adjacent cloudbank, leaving the thing hovering in their wake. It made no move to follow them. In fact, once they were gone, the unit purred slightly and glided back into its hiding place inside the stream of gaseous tin.

Before they parted company in the clouds, Dezi Annucci made Peri promise to tell no on about what she had seen—neither the "killer robot" nor his "tampering" with the device. He assured her that his involvement in no way implied any collusion between himself and HeeVee, nor would his actions bring any harm to the freelance colony. "Quite the contrary," Dezi hinted, but he refused to elaborate.

She accepted this secrecy based on her fondness for the old man. Dezi had never exhibited any antisocial behavior; he might have been an odder, but he was one of the less weird ones. It was not in Dezi's nature to do anything that might produce unpleasant repercussions. Whatever he was up to, it was not something she could help him with—for she knew she never wanted to see one of those dreadful killer bots again.

She only hoped that his scheme helped to rid Baltuss' clouds of HeeVee's killer bots. When she told him this, he chuckled mysteriously.

He flew away, ascending through the vapors, vacuumbound. She hung for a while in a yellow stream of what she assumed was some type of chloride, fitting recent discoveries into her worldview.

Triumphantly, Peri had reclaimed her beloved playground, mastering the fear that had driven her into catatonic withdrawal—only to learn that killer robots did indeed prowl her precious clouds. Somehow, Dezi Annucci was working to eliminate these killer bots, making Baltuss safe for Peri's secret joyrides…and everyone else too.

That part troubled her. It was unfair—if not outright criminal—to withhold information about the killer bots from the rest of the freelancers. Each time someone dove into Baltuss' atmosphere, they unknowingly risked their lives. The colony deserved—*needed!*—to know about the threat. But…Peri had promised Dezi to tell no one.

Nearby, a six-of-veils exited a cloudbank with placid grace. She watched as its fragile fins rippled, launching the diaphanous beast on a torpid crossing of the environmental gap. The thing was twice as big as a human, the span of these multicolored flukes extending in an elegant array. The body that sprouted these sailing pinions was spindly and brown, consisting mostly of the knotted muscles necessary to manipulate its airfoil plumage. As she gazed idly at the exquisite creature, another lifeform appeared: a cotton feeder, sliding into view like a dazzling yellow needle. The diminutive predator dove on the six-of-veils, tearing through its willowy sails like a fierce arrow. Driving its sharp nose into the drifter's flimsy torso, the cotton feeder extended gaunt mandibles, pinning the unwary victim in its invasive clutches. Oblivious to the presence of the parasite, the six-of-veils continued on its stately path.

Even here in these alien mists, there existed a cycle of eat-and-be-eaten. There were always predators looking to prey on weaker individuals…just the way HeeVee sought to oppress the freelance divers.

How could the actions of a single person undermine one of HeeVee's murderous plots? Dezi was an old man, he could not vanquish the robotic horde alone. Was senility the basis for his belief that he could single-handedly defeat HeeVee's army of killer bots? She was unwilling to suspect that Dezi was a HeeVee spy. That left madness as the only explanation for the odder's overconfident expectations.

I should never have promised him not to tell, she reprimanded herself. *I hadn't thought it all out, hadn't put all the facts together yet.* The platform needed to know about the robot menace. If anyone died now, their blood would stain Peri's conscience.

Someone had to warn the freelance divers of Petrie platform.

She had to do it herself.

Part Two Resumed:

Why Some People Hate Pirates

He dreamt of killing pirates—literally.

Although Theo Sloane was unaware of the origins of this sentiment, the roots of his pathological hate were deeply rooted in the man's childhood.

Raised on the heavy-gravity world of Crunch, little Theo was the only progeny of a zealous district judge whose rulings were harsher than necessary. Magistrate Sloane was a firm believer in extremism. (Possibly, the father's mania was some attempt to conform judicial law to the planet's hostile environment, creating a philosophical unity between civil disobedience and the lethal ecology. But this was supposed to be a glimpse of insight into little Theo, not his domineering father.) As a result of his parent's strict and judgmental demeanor, the boy was quiet, almost meekly deferential. This in turn placed him in the role of most popular victim among his peers. Little Theo lacked any evidence of the body-mass he would attain as an adult; he was quite scrawny. He was the target of every bully that crossed his adolescent path.

The most traumatic of these beatings occurred when he was five years old. He was playing in a sewer crawlway when a gang of youths appeared and commenced to beat the crap out of him. The thugs were dressed as pirates, for that's what they were playing. The incident was no more brutal than any other beating little Theo had received during his childhood, nor had the beating instigated some momentous emotional transformation. It was simply the random straw that permanently scarred the boy's young psyche. From that day on, everyone who picked on little Theo became a *pirate* in his vague perceptions of blame.

It was many years before little Theo stopped being a public victim. The boy became a man when he was drafted into Crunch's Space Navy. The military life strengthened the weakling, giving him backbone and muscles. Now, Theo Sloane was able to fight back—more than that, now he could beat the crap out of most everybody else. He might have become a bully himself if not for an interplanetary threat that suddenly struck the heavy-gravity planet. The Space Navy was dispatched in full force to combat a swarm of—surprise—pirates.

(Who says it's a random universe?)

Major Theo Sloane distinguished himself in the struggle to route the invading pirates from Crunch's solar system. He was involved in several skirmishes, and was always among the soldiers who boarded the enemy vessels and slaughtered hundreds of the vile space criminals. He received official commendations for his service record during the "Crunch the Pirates War." There was a particular irony in Theo's eyes for being decorated for venting his aggressions on someone who was synonymous in his mind with anyone who had ever victimized him. He never consciously acknowledged this duality of satisfaction, and gradually forgot all about it.

After the War, his daily routine was too tame to satisfy War Hero Sloane's newly sated bloodlust. He retired from the military with honors, and pursued more adventurous careers in the private sector. Harvest Corp snatched him up right away.

Unknown to him, Harvest's headhunters had been keeping an eye on him for a few years, ever since his battle experiences had made him a brief war celebrity. The cagey Corp agents had drawn a connection between Major Sloane's hate for pirates and a certain difficulty another branch of the corporation was experiencing in the Cacio Trumpis system. When Sloane became a free agent, these headhunters filed strong recommendations with the Home Office that the man be hired and sent to handle the Corp's pirate problem on Baltuss. As a soldier, Sloane had proven the manner in which he dealt with pirates.

(There it is again: the universe behaving in a blatantly unrandom fashion.)

Theo was honored to accept the position of Security Domo for Harvest's Natt base which managed the Corp's Baltuss cloud-mining operation. When he learned about the pirates who plundered the gas giant's atmosphere, Theo was enthusiastic to tackle the problem.

Since arriving at the Natt base, Sloane had discovered the true depths of that problem. Baltuss' clouds were too vast and uncharted to track the trespassers. Apprehending stassed individuals was so awkward as to be considered ridiculous. And the bastards always escaped to their secret hideout adrift out in space beyond the lunar base's sensor range. Adding insult to injury, the Security Domo found himself severely muzzled when it came to executing these pirates—should he ever capture one of them. The Authorities on Greye were quite specific when it came to limiting the amount of "killing" done by any member of the private sector. Regardless of his authority within the territories licensed from Greye by Harvest, Sloane was powerless to actually enforce the Corp's own regulations within those territories. Defanged by these local laws, Sloane ached all the more to find a way to slaughter every last pirate in the system with his own bare hands. But the bastards persisted in eluding apprehension, robbing him of even the opportunity of venting his anti-pirate wrath.

Security Domo Theo Sloane was a very tormented individual.

He dreamt of killing pirates—literally.

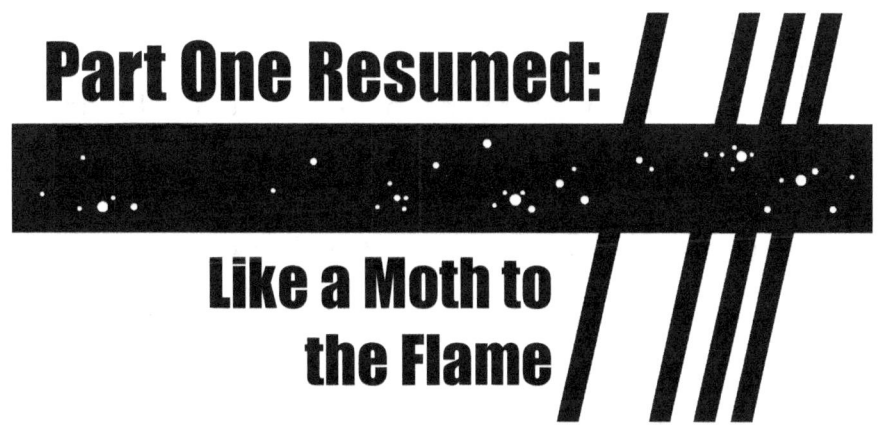

Part One Resumed:

Like a Moth to the Flame

Some yelling was to be expected.

Taz was furious with Peri for having run off to go diving without telling him. Unconvinced that she was fully recovered, he citing her newfound obsessive delusion as proof of the continuance of her unbalanced state of mind. He credited no belief in her stories of killer robots down in Baltuss' clouds.

Nor did anyone else when she tried to spread the dire news.

So committed was Peri to warning everyone, she forswore her own secret vice to inform the platform's populace. She spoke with people in the cafeterias, in the corridors, in the stores. She harangued commuters as they waited to use the linear accelerator. She demanded the Administrators issue official warnings. Everyone ignored her. No one took her seriously.

As far as they were all concerned, a new odder had surfaced among the freelance divers. This one believed in killer bots breeding down in the clouds (her story got tweaked somewhat in the retelling). This one even argued publicly with other odders.

One afternoon Dezi Annucci caught her preaching to passers-by outside a commercial gym. The oldster exploded on Peri, accusing her of violating a trust. Much of their confrontation consisted of the old man yelling "You promised!" with her declarations that "The public deserves to know!" arranged in a looping cycle. When some pedestrians attempted to calm the arguing pair, Dezi grew phobic and stormed off. The peace-bringers took hasty leaves when Peri launched into her tales of robotic doom with almost evangelistic fervor. She could not comprehend why people refused to heed her warnings.

Unsuccessfully, Taz tried to explain things to her several times. She wanted no part of his doubting excuses.

"Why has no one else spotted any of these killer robots?"

She imagined that those who did discover the bots swiftly became victims. Dead divers told no tales.

"But there're no missing divers."

Records were being tampered with. The conspiracy to hide the existence of the killer bots must involve very high circles.

"Now you're saying the colony's Administrators are in bed with Hee-Vee?"

Stranger alliances had happened…although no, she couldn't give him an example right now. She had never claimed to be a historian.

"You're not being rational, Peri. You've gotten hooked on an urban myth, one of crazy old Annucci's conspiracy theories."

And she would remind him that she had seen these killer bots—*twice*! She was *not* the only diver who knew about them either. Dezi had seen them too. In fact, he had special knowledge about them.

"Sigh…you realize how credible that old man is, right?"

Was he calling her an "odder"?

"That's what other people are saying, honey. I'm trying to understand why you're acting odd."

He thought she was *odd*! Peri was mortified, and more than slightly angry at Taz. She stormed out of their rec cap, full of embarrassed fury. How dare he challenge her beliefs. She had seen the bots, he hadn't. Why couldn't he accept that they existed?

The public deserved to know about the killer robots. They were risking their lives every time they dove into Baltuss' clouds. Measures needed to be instigated to protect the freelancers from HeeVee's murderous machines. Besides the threat of slaughter, there existed the political ramifications too. The Corp would never survive if word about the killer bots got out. Once the things had been scattered throughout the clouds, HeeVee's corporate dick was on the chopping block. They would allow no survivors to point an accusing finger. The robots were there to wipe out all of the freelance divers. This was a real threat. Why was no one listening to her?

For that matter, why was Dezi hiding the existence of the bots from the platform? Could the old man really be a HeeVee spy? He had expected her to remain silent about the deadly bots, and now he was mad at *her* for doing the right thing.

People needed to know!

She could only go so long before her addiction compelled her to return to Baltuss' glorious clouds.

Enduring the jeering catcalls of the techs manning the linear accelerator (for they recognized her as the one who begged people not to go Down—and here she was, breaking her own rule), she bought a launch ticket and fled the platform.

Back in the void again, she took solace in Red Sky Radio and the familiar-but-always-engaging panoramic approach of Baltuss' scarlet clouds. She felt more relaxed out here; there were no people to criticize her opinions. The matterless state of the astral vacuum extended to an absence of tension or worry for Peri. Her fears melted away to be replaced by a soothing darkness that was dark because it was unequivocally empty. There were no divers ignoring her warnings, there were no killer bots stalking her this far outside the gas giant's atmosphere, there was no bloodthirsty Corp behind it all. There were no problems with Taz, her disagreement with Dezi melted away, her rejection of her Earthly origins even ceased haunting her for a while as she drifted (at a hundred kilometers a minute) through the vacuum.

The soundtrack provided by Red Sky for this journey consisted of experimental jazz compositions: mellow basslines, nimble piano, soft percussives, fiery trumpet passages. A funk influence lurked in the pale blues, transforming the melody into a passionate expression of triumph. It seemed a bad omen to her that the music reached its inspirational crescendo long before she entered the embrace of the planet's stratosphere. Things were out of sync this time. Her detached demeanor placed her dive in a different personal context. It was not a perspective she enjoyed.

Big empty darkness.

Disassociation from society.

Withdrawal from reality.

Fixation on the killer robot threat.

Sublimation her own emotional fears.

Fear that her romance with Taz was failing…or succeeding?

Fear for the stability of her own mind?

What if she really *had* gone odder? And there were no killer bots…there was no deadly conspiracy…no reason for the freelancers to worry…no reason for Peri to avoid the clouds…

These conditions implied that Peri was losing the capacity to fit in with the other divers. Her terrible realization that she "didn't belong" had driven her from Earth…only to find that she didn't "belong" out here either. Was her life to be an endless series of flights to escape emptiness?

Yet, the emptiness of the vacuum pacified her anxiety. How could one void cure while another void tortured her so?

This mental dance did her no good. The questions she pondered only raised deeper enigmas, imponderable mysteries that were all based on the validity of her own perceptions. Of her own experiences. The prospect that there was reason to doubt her own memories troubled Peri. If her mind was flawed, then how could she even trust her present sense of doubt?

Her fear might be illusionary.

The nightmarish killer robots could be a product of her own overactive imagination.

Her very search for answers could be unreal.

But wait, she reminded herself, Dezi Annucci's displeasure with her was very sincere, wholly tangible. If there were no killer bots, then why was the old man furious at her for breaking her vow of silence?

She decided that she did not enjoy philosophical debates.

There was one reality she refused to question: the grandeur and majesty of the clouds that loomed to fill her horizon. This undeniable truth rushed to surround her, to remove her from the doubts and unease of her life. Only now, these clouds that offered her emotional escape had (theoretically) become the realm of dangerous robotic monsters that sought to exile her from her therapeutic joyriding. Barred from diving through the mists, Peri suspected that her mental disturbances would grow all the more worse. To alleviate her stress, she needed to return to her threatened playground, to confront her fears and validate or debunk their authenticity.

How many times, her conscience chided her, *do we need to encounter these killer bots before we* really *believe in them?*

It had never been her intention when she had come to this alien world to search for conspiracies hiding in the gas giant's mists. She had never looked for lost spacecraft or sunken asteroids or mythical alien artifacts. Her discovery of HeeVee's killer bots had been accidental. These traumatic encounters had only disrupted her happy calm. All she had ever wanted in life had been found in Baltuss' limitless clouds. Peri had already achieved her emotional fulfillment, she needed no intrigue or anxiety to spice up her existence.

Spreading her limbs, Peri arched her neck until she fell face-first into the glutinous atmosphere. Sensory input flooded her mind: chemical constituencies (hydrogen and argon at these heights), atomic weights (electron counts varying per element in the soupy mixture), infrared signatures (basically low Celsius readings, attributably mostly to stellar irradiation since the planet's gaseous mass didn't seriously heat up until one reached significant depths), electromagnetic fluxes (generally minimal at this altitude), particle velocities (a storm of turgid motion, disturbed by interplanetary detritus striking Baltuss' stratosphere), and a score of technical codifications, all designed to mingle into a coherent planetary portrait in her artificially augmented perceptions. Her consciousness brushed aside these quantum specifications so that she could appreciate the artistic beauty of her view. In her ears, a fresh jazz tune buzzed, accumulating modern sensibilities that carried its traditional groove far beyond fusion or prog, sliding into contemporary slap overtones.

This was what she lived for, breathed for, and dreamt of. Her relationship with Taz could never compete with this rapture. No lover had ever brought her physical or emotional bliss that could compare with the ecstasy she found in cloud diving.

There was no menace so intimidating that it could coerce her to abandon this secret vice. Not killer robots, not carnivorous monsters, not planetary disaster, not even a stellar nova could convince her to restrain from indulging. The addiction's payoff was too great, too satisfying.

It was such a vast planet too. Each time she plunged into its atmospheric mass, Peri encountered different gas strata and exotic currents and convolutions of fluidic motion. She never ceased to be amazed by the versatility of the vapors lurking below Baltuss' crimson outer pale. This variety was hardly surprising, considering the variegated selection of gaseous chemicals that made up the planet's volume. The vast atmosphere was subjected to wild pressure storms and electromagnetic bursts that kept everything in constant chaos. Gaseous streams kilometers thick could be invaded by a hundred different eddies, scattering the prior zone into a multitude of stratified layers. Radiation tempests could fuse separate flows, transmuting elements into unlikely compounds. This embroiled nature was undoubtedly what made Baltuss' clouds so commercially profitable.

While Jupiter, back in her homeland solar system, sported a single Red Spot, a colossal hurricane bigger than most planets, Baltuss' atmosphere was spotted with numerous storms of lesser scale. And not all of them were evident from the surface. In many ways, Peri's playground-of-choice was a perilous dominion.

She passed through rivers of yellow methane. She soared across regions of rarefied neon. She dove through the fringes of a submerged hurricane's vehement bluster.

Peri's plummet brought her into a vast separation between air fronts, a chasm that stretched for many kilometers among the clouds. It was as if some cosmic force had cut and lifted a sliver from the sky, leaving behind an empty void as a negative barricade between the mountainous cloudbanks. Falling into this expansive gap, she found she was not alone. Something was following her.

It was not the mechanical dreadnought of her nightmares that swooped upon Peri like a malevolent hawk, it was a man…a diver encased in stassskin, but armed with instruments of violence. It was a HeeVee patrol officer!

She almost laughed with fright. Of all the dangers she had dreaded finding among Baltuss' clouds, a HeeVee cop had never crossed her mind. She had been so lost in contemplating implausible hazards that she had overlooked the very normal and very real threat of being apprehended by the Corp's police force of thugs. *Idiot!* she chastised herself.

There was little chance that she could outrun the cop. Her thigh-jets were good, but hardly equal to the officer's expensive corporate thrusters. In other circumstances, she might have been able to elude him by hiding in a dense cloud that would mask her presence from his scanners—but this region was too big, too open. There was nowhere to hide.

He flew down beside her, oddly making no hostile gestures. His weapon—a pulse rifle—remained clipped to his utility belt along with an assortment of nasty-looking police equipment. Otherwise, in his silvered second skin, the man looked no different than any other diver. It was impossible to discern any facial expression through the shimmering mirror of his stass field.

"Uh, hi," she ventured on an open channel.

"You're a pirate, right?" came the man's gruff reply.

How the hell do I answer that? There are no tourists on Baltuss; what else can I be but a trespasser in HeeVee's eyes? What good will denying it do? On the other hand, she was leery of admitting to being a "pirate."

"I'm a freelance diver," she told him.

"Yeah, right," the cop snickered.

She didn't know what to do. They had paused in their flight and were hovering now in the great open chasm of mist, facing each other while they conversed over a public comm frequency. The situation seemed at a standoff. Then the cop reached out his hand to grip her arm. And Peri responded with innocent panic.

With thigh-jets blazing, she fled from the officer. Her trajectory took her from his side quick enough to dislodge his loose grasp on her wrist. She soared into the chasm's gaseous ceiling, zooming through the upper cloud strata in desperate escape. Flight was her only hope, but it was pretty flimsy as far as expectations of success were concerned.

"Hey—" the voice of the pursuing HeeVee cop called in her ear. She found the volume of his call disquieting, as if the man were physically close enough to shout at her.

All of a sudden she ran into someone! *What—how did the cop got ahead of me?* Although their impact was abrupt, they did not rebound and tumble. The stranger grabbed Peri around the waist and held on. She flailed in her captor's grip, yelling wordless objections.

"Peri—stop it—it's me!"

That was Taz's voice, she realized. *What is he doing here—?*

"You followed me!" she accused him. "You crummy—"

"I'm sorry," he admitted, "but I was worried about you. I tried to catch up to you, and I just missed you at the accelerator, so I had them fire me off after you, but I lost you a few cloud layers up. I was starting to fear that I wasn't going to find you, but—"

"There's a HeeVee cop after me," she gasped. "We have to—"

"Oh, Peri. Not more delusions.... Maybe coming Down wasn't such a good idea for you."

"Be quiet, Taz, listen to me. I'm not crazy—there really is a—"

"Is he a pirate too?" came the officer's voice. If Peri could hear it, odds were that so could Taz.

"Who's that?" Taz grunted. He released her to gape around, finally picking out the officer's body rising among the bilious vapors.

"I told you—it' a HeeVee cop," she pleaded with him to understand the hard reality that pursued her. "He's looking for 'pirates.'"

"That's correct," the cop remarked.

Peri slapped her thigh and complained, "My stupid jets. They fired on their own." She shrugged to the cop who hung nearby now. "I'm sorry, officer. Luckily, my friend was here to rescue me."

"We don't want any trouble," Taz muttered.

"That's nice," the officer commented. "Then you'll take me back to your pirate base."

"We can't do that," Peri whispered.

"Of course you can."

"She's right," announced Taz. "You know we can't betray the rest of the colony."

"Who's asking you to?" the officer harumphed. "I'm looking to join up."

"Huh?"

"I've had it with the Corp's rigid rules and lousy pay," the man confessed. "My own damned Domo almost ran me down with his pursuit skimmer. So I decided to defect. I want to be a pirate now."

"You're joking," groaned Peri.

"Never been more serious in my life, girl," the man declared. "I've had it with Harvest getting rich while I never get a pay raise. I'm going to join you pirates and start ripping off the Corp's clouds for my own profit."

"First of all, we're not *pirates*," Taz stressed. "We're *freelance divers*. We're here because we dispute the validity of HeeVee's exclusive claim on the clouds of Baltuss. There is no criminal intent behind our actions, we're fighting for the concept of a free market."

"I'm not much for politics," the defector reported to them. "I'm looking to do some ripe plundering and make a fast fortune, y'know?"

The encounter had grown far too surreal for Peri. To move so quickly from a dramatic chase into the black comedy twist that the pursuing officer was looking to defect because he wanted to be a "pirate"…it was all too weird and ridiculous. *It's not fair to torment me with craziness like this,* she complained to herself, *when minutes ago I was wondering whether or not I was psychologically disturbed.* What had happened to transform her into a magnet for such recurrent strangeness?

Taz was arguing with the ex-officer about the moral necessity to break "laws" established to protect a financial monopoly. Most of the carping was being done by Taz, though, for the other man showed little interest in philosophical or sociological quandaries. He—whose name was Juul Ragle—was only interested in money. Somewhere, Ragle had gotten the impression that freelance divers were wealthy from their "plundering." Lost in defending his own ethical position, Taz remained ignorant of this misconception.

When Peri tried to correct the man's error, Ragle rejected her claims of constant hardships with a boisterous laugh.

"Yeah, right. Everybody knows how rich you pirates are. Well, I want to be rich too."

Turning to Taz, Peri shrugged. "Why hassle him? He'll discover the truth soon enough."

"I'm worried that he might be a HeeVee spy," Taz confided to her.

"There've been other HeeVee defectors," she pointed out. "Dezi used to dive for the Corp, and he's not a spy." *At least, I hope he isn't.*

"Forget spying," the ex-officer snorted derisively. "There's no money in espionage."

"I'm still not convinced," proclaimed Taz. "There's too much at risk here…"

"Tell *me* bout it, huh?" Ragle snarled. "Do you know what the Corp'll do if they ever get their hands on me? By now, my absence has definitely been noted. Depending on the Security Domo's pissy quotient when he fills out his report, I'm either AWOL or MIA. Neither condition will carry much sympathy if the Corp police find me. I'm kind of putting my life in the hands of you two…"

"Gee, thanks," Taz grumbled.

Their argument had grown too tit-for-tat for Peri, her attention was momentarily distracted by a glassy shard that had drifted near the group. Approaching from behind Taz, the man never noticed this tiny intruder as it advanced on him, ultimately withering as it plunged itself into the muted exhaust of his stabilizer thrusters. Peri watched the creature's suicidal course with a mild regret. Glancing around, she saw that a flock of soft glass chips had emerged from a nearby cloudbank. Up close, these organisms were flexible disks, the diameter of their flattened membrane rarely bigger than a few centimeters; seen from a distance, a flock of the creatures resembled a hovering light show as their gyrating bodies caught and reflected random light with their polished skins. The fragile lifeforms were advancing on the group, attracted by the heat of their jets. With sad determination, the tiny creatures threw themselves into the blaze that lured them, vanishing in unheard puffs of dissolved protoplasm. Even stepped-down to drift mode, the humans' jets were powerful enough to vaporize the gossamer physiologies of these cloud-dwellers. Peri smiled without humor, perceiving a loose parallel between the self-imposed fate of these soft glass chips and the life-path chosen by this defecting HeeVee wretch.

"I say we believe him," Peri declared. Her words surprised even herself.

"Huh?"

"He just wants to be a pirate. Let him come along so he can find out what it's really like."

"You've got to go back sometime," Ragle warned them. "I could just follow you then."

"Oh, that's nice—threatening us," sneered Taz.

"Cut me a break, huh? I've got nowhere else to go, okay? Believe me, Harvest doesn't forgive people who run out on their employment contracts. I simply couldn't take it anymore—all the strict rules and the slave wages." Ragle was growing agitated. "When the Domo took us to prevent pirates from raiding one of the Corp's gatherer depots, I saw my chance to get away—and I took it. While the rest of the patrol officers were trying to round up the pirate saboteurs, I deactivated my Corp transmitter and hid myself in the loose crowd of company divers who were on the scene. When the workers were ordered back to the Natt base, I went along with the group, but I slipped away en route. I've been wandering the clouds ever since, looking for somebody to help me find my way to the pirate base. You've got to help me out, pal. I haven't got much oxy left…"

"Wait a minute," Peri muttered. "What're you talking about? Pirates—I mean, freelance divers don't raid HeeVee satellites. We're not terrorists, we're just people who refuse to submit to a corporate contract."

"Actually," Taz remarked, "there is a group who've been going Down on thieving runs. Admin is apparently overlooking their actions. You know the slogan: anything that hurts HeeVee, helps the colony."

"That sucks vacuum," Peri declared. "That's giving HeeVee the idea that we're *all* thieves. No wonder they're seeding the clouds with killer bots to get rid of us."

"Huh?" This time, it was the ex-officer's turn to express puzzlement.

Taz had no desire to share Peri's delusions with this stranger. He avoiding the point by asking the man, "What were you planning to do if you failed to run into any 'pirates' in the clouds?"

Ragle glumly admitted that he did not know.

"That's not too smart," Taz observed.

"I was in a hurry, okay? It wasn't something I planned to do. All of a sudden, there was shooting going on, and I decided I had to get out—so I ran."

"I believe him," Peri repeated her conviction.

"Well, if he is a spy, he's not a very bright one," Taz resolved. "It'd be inhumane to let him run out of air just because he's stupid."

"Hey—"

"You're either a cunning spy—or a dumb pirate wannabe. Which one do you think gets saved? The spy or the doofus?"

"Okay," Ragle sighed. "If I have to pick, I'd rather be a living idiot."

"Cut it out, you guys," Peri chided them. "Time enough to play dominance games once we've gotten Juul more oxy."

"Girls just don't understand this kind of stuff," mumbled Taz.

"It's a guy thing," Ragle agreed.

Peri tuned them out. Somehow, Taz's uncharacteristic display of harassment had created a bond with the defecting officer. By trading insults, they had cemented a kinship. Sometimes, there was no comprehending the masculine mentality.

"Let's get moving," Taz announced.

The three of them ascended into the clouds, heading for the void and the remote Petrie platform—the "pirate's secret base."

While jetting through the vacuum beyond Baltuss, Ragle had some questions.

"Is there an initiation to become a pirate?"

He was reminded that they were not "pirates," but preferred to call themselves "freelance divers". He must get used to this distinction if he expected to survive in the colony. They were not criminals, they were independent workers. But no—there was no initiation ritual. The Petrie platform was generally devoid of community spirit or ceremonial procedures.

"How do I set myself up as a pi—I mean, a freelance diver?"

The process was explained to him, revealing how freelancers conducted their business. Solo dives, bagging the choicest clouds, bringing the gas back to the Petrie Exchange Office, trading gas bags for creds—most of which went to cover food and board on the platform. There was no official registration, no licenses were needed in order to dive for gas. A person became a freelance diver by virtue of being there on the rogue station with the other unlicensed divers. Just as there were no tourists on Baltuss, there were no slackers among the freelancers.

"What're the hours like?"

He would be his own boss, setting his own schedule and habits. As long as he avoided antisocial behavior, his destiny would be his own to decide.

"How's the retail situation? I mean—are there quality stores and clubs and bars and all at this platform?"

He learned about the commercial pods and the profusion of stores and trade shops and game centers. Taz even mentioned a gourmet restaurant that was well worth the expense.

"Oh yeah—and what's *this*?" Ragle's transmission crackled, then a second signal was spliced into his broadcast.

Peri instantly recognized it. "That's Red Sky Radio."

"*This* is Red Sky…?" Ragle seemed confused.

The music was a selection of calypso tuneage now. Energetic rhythms crowded the airwaves, with sultry bass and chugalug acoustic guitars fleshing out the melody.

He was told about the pirate radio station. In defiance of HeeVee's (he was gradually getting accustomed to thinking of the Corp by this derisive pair of syllables) proprietary claims of ownership over all airwaves in the region of Baltuss, unknown individuals had established an illegal station to broadcast better music than the pathetic marching band music that dominated all the HeeVee radio channels. The pirate station had existed for years, providing the freelancers with free entertainment.

Ragle expressed a smug amusement that the freelancer colony had its own form of "pirates."

Later, after Juul Ragle had been settled into a domicile capsule (grudgingly paid for by Taz at Peri's insistence), the lovers returned to their quarters to discuss their own problems. Unfortunately, they had different ideas of what those problems were.

Peri was still concerned about killer bots, although her fear seemed somewhat abated by her recent voyage into the clouds.

Taz felt it was significant that she had *not* encountered any more killer robots on this dive.

"Yeah," she remarked. "This time I found a defecting HeeVee cop!"

He expressed concerns for her mental health. Her continued fixation on imaginary homicidal machines was self-destructive.

"It's not a fixation, because they really do exist!"

"It doesn't matter whether or not they exist, Peri. Don't you get that? The problem is your preoccupation with the subject. It's an unhealthy obsession—most obsessions are."

"It's important that people know about these killer bots," she professed. "Everyone's risking their lives each time they—"

"C'mon, honey. Don't preach. We're discussing your fanaticism, not the object of your fanaticism."

"But somebody's got to warn people. I'm the only one who knows these killer bots exists...the only one besides Dezi. I don't understand why he's keeping silent about them."

Taz thought he knew. During Peri's unbalanced emotional state, Taz had found it judicial not to mention the old man's cancer. He told her now, suspecting that it might explain the man's stranger-than-normal behavior.

Peri was distraught to learn about Dezi's affliction. The old man was clearly important to her, for her anguish was lavish and passionate. Reacting with immaturity, Peri vented her frustration as anger. Taz became the focus of her condemnations.

Some yelling was to be expected.

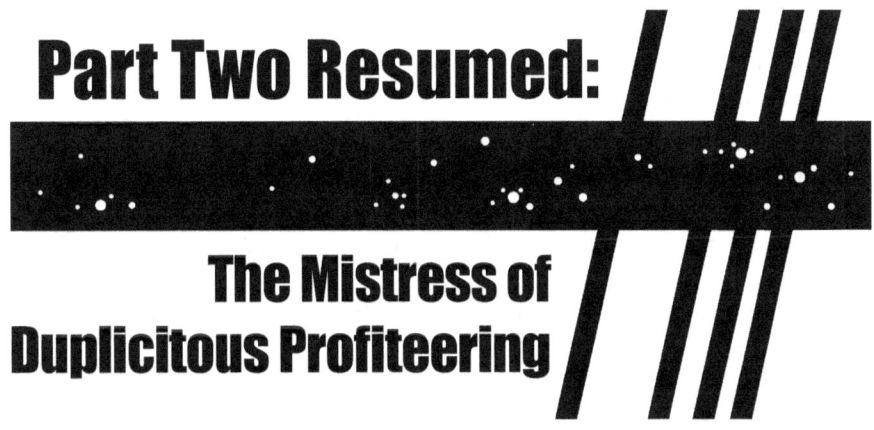

Part Two Resumed:

The Mistress of Duplicitous Profiteering

Each new day seemed devoted to perpetuating yesterday's tedium.

Today, Evelyn Hannigan wore unorthodox flesh, hued a benign orange and textured like velvet down. Her supple fingers traveled along her new skin, appreciating the tactile quality of the delicate nap. Her muscles rippled and twitched under these caresses, eagerly responding to her touch like a lover who has been celibate for far too long. Each stroke fed fresh endorphins into her thin bloodstream, filling her body with a carnal tension.

Years ago, she had foregone ignoble couplings with commoners, deciding that only she was worthy of her own delights. Only her own fingers deserved access to her moist niches, for those digits understood each of her special desires and how to stimulate them. These novelties had grown stale, though, leaving her bored with and irritated by her opulent self and surroundings. Like every resolution she dedicated herself to, such decisions were fleetingly transient.

The covers moved next to her, falling aside to partially reveal a man's sweaty shoulder. The orange woman curled her lip, recalling the abject ecstasy she had derived from that well-muscled body. She resented the man for his lusty acumen. The unmitigated gall of his proficiency infuriated her. Suddenly, the masculine warmth in bed beside her revolted the hedonistic Exec. Her carnal afterglow sputtered, quickly extinguished by the memory of the ribald pleasures she had experienced in the brute's arms. A cold tension swept through her veins, and she had to restrain herself from violently kicking the man from her boudoir.

No, she struggled to calm her breathing. A scandal was inappropriate at this time. Anyway, for all her loathing, Hannigan had no real desire to alienate this individual from her embrace. Despite his socially inferior status, he was by far the best lover she had had in decades, professionally or for the purposes of personal entertainment. With age came wisdom, and she knew how rare it was to have access to such a talented performer. She refused to deny herself future trysts just to satiate an impulsive revulsion.

She nudged the man with her foot. His grumble was muffled by the plush blanket. He roused slowly, stretching his mighty limbs. His hip grazed her thigh, sending spasms of aversion racing to her brain. Before she could sidle away from him, the man cast off the covers and sat with his naked back to her. The sound of his grinding teeth came to her over his wide shoulder. Sight of his rippling muscles stirred her shallow values, but that tinge of lust was quickly smothered by her desire to murder the man for tempting her so effortlessly.

Rising from the soft mattress, he pulled on his dark and menacing uniform. Without a word, the man departed, leaving his employer alone in her private quarters.

For nearly half-an-hour, Evelyn Hannigan remained unmoving, sitting up in her massive bed on a mountain of mollifying cushions. The ragged wheeze of her stressed-out breathing was the only noise in the perfumed air. All around her, the walls were draped with vivid red curtains. A single holo-light glimmered in the center of the ceiling, directly above the bed.

Reaching out suddenly she snatched the still-pungent roses from her bedside table. As she pulverized their expensive petals across her orange breasts, she cursed the man's virility. The crushed flowers mingled with the blood drawn from her heaving bosom by the thorns' cruel passage across her flesh. The pain conquered her rising libido, stifling her physical needs.

Leaving her with the desire to share her emotional agony with everyone.

Having adjusted her mood to her preferred temperament, she busied herself with work. Never once did the woman ever smile in the presence of witnesses.

Each new day seemed devoted to perpetuating yesterday's tedium.

Part One Resumed:

Sidereal Factors

She was still new to the nuances of life in space.

At least she had stopped throwing up a week ago. Medication and her own innate obstinacy had gotten her through the nausea and spatial disorientation. Those first few weeks had been difficult though. Denise preferred to forget them.

In retrospect, she imagined that her space sickness had been a type of death preceding her rebirth out in the Cacio Trumpis system. Her new life was beginning now, there were no reasons to dwell on the past. When Denise Coleman had departed Paulen, she had left nothing behind, no family, no friends, no acquaintances, no outstanding debts, no fortune, all her possessions had been converted into the funds necessary to travel offworld. She had taken a commercial spaceliner to Greye, squandering valuable creds on a private cabin in order to hide her physical discomfort. Her savage nausea had kept her from socializing with the other passengers, which was a pity, for her evangelistic fervor might have been sobered by exposure to her fellow travelers.

Denise's reasons for leaving the Paulen colony were noble and altruistic. She had been "called." It never occurred to her that the other people who traveled to alien worlds did not think of themselves as valiant pioneers. She remained ignorant that commercial trade comprised the bulk of space travel; interstellar tourism was a luxury available only to the very wealthy. By remaining reclusive in her cabin throughout the voyage, she had missed the opportunity to interact with an assortment of fabulously rich and spoiled individuals. It was probably for the best.

By the time the spaceliner docked with a station orbiting Greye, Denise's space sickness had abated, allowing her to appreciate a few hours of her journey. Loitering by a portal, she watched as the spaceliner returned to realspace and approached the station that handled offworld traffic. The complex satellite swam out of the darkness, taking visual form only when the murky face of Greye swung into place as a cosmic backdrop. The spaceport looked so flimsy, barely more than a chaotic pincushion of unconventional design, all spokes and slender wedges. The geometry of the station bewildered her, for it compared to no architectural logic she knew. A novice to space life, she had yet to grasp the restrictions imposed on design by gravity. As the spaceliner neared the terminal, she saw that its wedges were actually other spaceliners docked at the orbital port. The station itself was even more ephemeral than she had thought. A tangle of tubes connected randomly positioned structures—which, she realized, must each be nearly a kilometer tall. As the station proper swooped into view through the portal window, she felt intimidated by the construction's immense scale. What she had mistaken for "tubes" were actually tunnels wide enough to accommodate a battleship. From a distance, the orbiting spaceport had appeared to be a delicate thicket of wires; up close, it became sturdy and imposing…and huge.

After debarking (??) the spaceliner and subjecting herself to the indignities of customs bureaucracy, Denise purchased a little 3D holomap of Victoria Terminal to enable her to navigate the station's intricate structure. The facility maintained artificial gravity in some sectors, and she was grateful for that. She knew she would have to accustom herself to a zero-G environment soon, but right now her stomach deserved a brief respite after her all-too-recent bout with space sickness aboard the interstellar liner. Frequently consulting the holomap, she made her way through the station's winding branch-work and eventually found herself standing in the doorway of a particularly squalid bar.

Smeggy's Zonk Tavern was a dive, devoid of character and couth. Its walls and floor stickily proclaimed the passage of years since it had last been washed. She avoided the stools, wary of the same tacky patina, and chose to stand at the bar to order an innocuous drink. Wrinkling her nose at what she was served, she took the concoction and retreated to a corner booth. From there, she had a good view of the entire tavern and its motley clientele.

Seated at the bar were a group of spaceliner officers, wearing crisp uniforms and flashing toothy, overeager grins at every woman that passed. Their leering regard had tracked Denise as she had entered and bought herself a beverage, finally losing interest in her voluptuous curves when she chose a booth removed from their informal camp at the counter. The officers seemed a jovial group, slapping each other across the backs and stomping their heavy-booted feet to punctuate their lewd declarations.

There was an incredible hunk seated in a booth on the opposite side of the oval tavern. Dark of skin and ample with sinews, the man devoured an unruly sandwich with immense gusto. From his pale olive jumpsuit, Denise assumed he was one of the Terminal's ranks of grunt laborers.

An old man huddled in a corner booth, unmoving. With his elbows splayed on the table and his head hung low between them, he seemed to have drunk himself unconscious.

One booth was crammed with teenage girls. That they were tourists was quite obvious, from their giggly amazement to their telltale Texan accents. With extravagant flips of their puffy hair and bats of their longing eyes, they were attempting—unsuccessfully—to attract the randy attention of the spaceliner officers.

Another booth was occupied by a man and woman. From the way their hands cupped each other's, presumably they were lovers. They gazed into each other's eyes with rapt interest, oblivious to their surroundings. Denise wondered whether their romance was native to the orbital station, or perhaps they were reuniting here after a long and painful interstellar separation.

At the far end of the bar, she saw an example of the other end of the love spectrum. Well in his cups, a swarthy man was grumbling loudly about infidelity and unpleasant surprises. The bartender spoke with him, attempting to quiet his disgruntled tirade with a mug of hot java.

A few other people cradled their drinks at the bar. Sitting alone and in silence, they would have been innocuous and unmemorable if not for their unconventional physiologies. Denise had known to expect to find altered individuals out in space, for the practice was intended to aid the human form to function in zero-G environments. She knew she would be encountering such people in her future job, but she had not consciously made an effort to acclimate herself to this strangeness. So she inspected these examples from across the tavern with covert curiosity.

One man no longer possessed legs, having replaced them with what appeared to be boneless tentacles. It seemed to her that walking in the Terminal's artificial gravity must be awfully painful now for the man. She was startled to see his unconventional eyes, and it took her a few moments to identify that the man had replaced his retractable eyelids with a pair of permanent hard domes, giving him a very fish-like profile.

Another was a woman who sported an extra set of arms. Additional shoulders decorated her side where the auxiliary arms joined her torso, providing the limbs' muscles with sturdy joints to anchor their mobility. When the woman turned her head to call for the bartender's attention, Denise noticed that she had no nose.

One man had a tail. Long and sinuous, it was curled around the base of his stool. Its end was split into a nest of wormlike tendrils that writhed with relentless agitation. Otherwise, this man was physically normal. No, wait—when he shifted in his seat, Denise could see that his legs possessed secondary knees halfway down the femur, allowing him to crouch in a most peculiar posture.

Another person had undergone such drastic surgical redesign that he no longer resembled a human being. His torpedo-like body squatted on a bar stool, held in place by a myriad of wiry stalks. She was amazed that such tenuous limbs were able to support the man's inhuman weight. The only attire worn by this spacer were a series of leather belts adorned with sturdy pouches, revealing the ex-man's flesh to be a richly mottled green. Staring with morbid shock at the extremely altered person, Denise realized that the patterns covering the individual's skin was far from a random coloration. When viewed carefully, what she had mistaken for a mottled pattern was actually a representational rendering of an aeroplane in flight across a green sky littered with majestic blue clouds. She wondered whether the picture was an elaborate tattoo or literally a product of redesigned skin pigmentation.

Space travel offered such a variety of surprises.

It surprised Denise when the one who approached her turned out to be the rumpled oldster. Somehow, she had hoped that the ebony hunk would be the one to reveal himself as her contact. But no—Denise did *not* leave Paulen to take a job offer among the stars, only to find sexual fulfillment at the hands of an interplanetary adventurer. Instead, Denise came to Greye and didn't even get to go down to the surface of the colony world. She had to rendezvous with a grubby old man who looked as if he was the poster model for "feeble."

"Coleman, right?" coughed the old man. His voice sprang from a pair of thick, wide lips hidden in a grizzled and unkempt gray beard. His sad eyes blinked constantly, as if conducting some secret code. He glanced at a palm-pad he wore, then peered at her, announcing, "You match Coleman's pic." He flashed his palm screen at her, and for a brief second Denise stared at a tiny facsimile of her own face.

Denise was, as she knew, considered a "looker" by most men. The curves of her short body had been compared to vivacious starlets by the many men who had yearned to take her as a lover back on Paulen. Her oval face was a delicate arrangement of pert features and satiny dark skin. Her over-large eyes were a vibrant pastel blue, giving her stare an ethereal quality. A magnificent mane of blonde hair framed her appealing face.

"You're Dirk Masterfield?" she asked. Although she had entertained no expectations regarding the appearance of her future employer's contact, the man's name had implied a certain flair…calling to mind a spacer of heroic stature, not this decrepit codger.

The old man nodded. He crumpled into the booth across from her, almost deflating, with his elbows splayed wide on the table. He released a raspy breath and mopped his hairy brow. When he finally looked up to discover her worried expression, he smiled and weakly waved a reassuring hand. "I'm okay. Not used to gravity, that's all. It wears me out quicker than a woman these days." He chuckled to himself, suddenly lost in some ancient recollection that he gratefully refrained from sharing.

"Oh," grunted Denise. She fidgeted, unsure how to react. If Masterfield was suffering, then this meeting should be brief to allow him to return to the comfort of one the station's zero-G sectors.

"I'm not sure what we do next, Captain Masterfield."

"Eh?"

"What happens now? Do we leave right away? Or do you have to refuel your ship or something?"

"We can leave any time we want, Coleman."

"Now?"

"Eager to get to your new job, huh?" he chuckled again, his gaunt throat transforming the sound into a spectral rattle.

She blushed.

"Well, come along then." He pushed his aching bones erect and gave her a shrug. "Where's your luggage?"

"In a locker at the docking station," she informed him. She slid from the booth, leaving her drink untouched. As she sidled by him Masterfield snatched up the glass and drained its contents behind her back.

She followed the old man out of the grubby bar.

Denise Coleman never saw the outside of Masterfield's spacecraft. If she had, she might have refused to entrust her mortal coil to its confines.

The ship was a squat bullet-shape, bearing the obvious signs of patchwork construction and even sloppier-looking repairs. Mismatched panels were welded into place without concern for neatness, no attempts had been made to match similar metals or paint the hull to conceal its chaotic appearance. It almost looked like an entire junkyard had suddenly been squeezed into a blunt cylinder by some industrial compactor. Belying that impression, a series of elaborate antennae sprouted from the craft's nose, while a pair of crude ramscoop burners had been grafted to the ship's rear. Further enhancing the vessel's patchwork nature, both of these ramscoops were of dissimilar design, clearly originating from different cultural backgrounds. Despite the unorthodox and derelict demeanor of the craft's assembled parts, these pieces shared a single characteristic: nothing gleamed with newness, everything had been tarnished by time and previous owners. The sight of Masterfield's spacecraft was not a construction that inspired any confidence.

From inside, though, Denise remained unaware of the vessel's unreliable appearance. As far as she was concerned, it was four rooms (two living quarters, a dining area, and the control chamber) connected by a pair of corridors. She knew there was more—like engines and fuel tanks—but she presumed those regions of the ship were offlimits to passengers. Masterfield had warned her away from the control room, and she had no intention of investigating the man's bedroom, so the living space available to Denise during this final leg of her interstellar journey was confined to her own quarters and the spartan dining room. She spent most of her time in her bathroom, vomiting and moaning into the toilet.

For Masterfield's ship operated without artificial gravity, plunging her unprepared digestive tract back into zero-G discomfort. Apologetically, the old man confessed that his ship was not designed to provide gravity.

"I've got to get used to it sooner or later, Captain," she sighed. "The colony's zero-G too, isn't it?"

He nodded.

"That'll take some getting used to," she told him. "I've lived my whole life in Granola City."

"That's on Paulen, right?"

"Yes, on the East Coast of the Telurian continent."

"I saw a map of Paulen once. There sure were a lot of land masses—all separate and far apart. Most planets settled by man out in space have just single continents." He slapped his thigh playfully. "Ha—Baltuss don't got none. It's a gas giant. No solid core at all. All atmosphere."

"The Baltuss colony mines the gas clouds, doesn't it?" she inquired. "I mean, that's supposed to be the chief employment there."

"Just about everybody out by Baltuss dives for a living. Not much point of being there if you're not bagging gas."

"It must be a big colony. Is it on one of the moons?"

Masterfield grunted, "It's big enough, missy. And full of surprises." His eyes, what little Denise could see past his crinkled cheeks, sparkled as if they held a secret too good to reveal just yet.

Reaching for her drink bulb, she overshot the target. In an attempt to halt her tumble, she caught the table with her other hand. The combination of moves sent her into an aerial somersault that soared over Masterfield's idling figure. The old man shot out an arm and steadied the girl before she injured herself against the bulkhead.

"How much practice have you had in zero-G, missy?"

"None," she admitted.

With a glottal sigh, the seasoned spacer set to teaching her the basics of handling herself in the absence of gravity. The girl had a lifetime of grounder habits to forget.

Not all grounders were able to comfortably adjust to living offworld. Some of the lifestyle changes proved too insurmountable, forcing a percentage of emigrants to seek their fortunes on the surface of nearby planets.

Masterfield revealed that almost a third of the people he ferried out to the Petrie station ended up taking refuge on Greye, for few of the failed pioneers possessed the funds necessary to afford the expensive interstellar trip back to their distant homeworlds.

"That's an awfully high rate of physiological rejection, Captain," she observed.

He intimated that not all the hardships that drove people to ground were physical in origin. Some were psychological, many were simply financial. Not everyone had the fortitude to face the strict regimens of living in space.

Denise pondered this while the old man showed her the graceful way to maneuver down a gravityless corridor.

She was beginning to realize that her life on Paulen may not have been all that unendurable. The loneliness that had ruled her prior existence might be preferable to the stress she was discovering at the old man's instruction. Not everything he showed her was confined to physical balance. There were aspects of living offworld that Denise had overlooked in her stubborn desire to flee her solitude.

There were, the old man told her, two deadly threats out here: the vacuum, and loneliness. A stass-skin would protect her from the first, but she must be alert to avoid the pitfalls of isolation. Diving into the gas giant's atmosphere was an extreme adventure; many people could not cope with the vastness of the clouds.

Neither the vacuum or the alien atmosphere would be a bother, since she had no intention of "diving" or going outside. She kept this to herself, though, for she was embarrassed by her own inability to properly prepare herself for her new offworld life. She would simply have to make allowances for those inadequacies.

She learned how to move about in zero-G, *that* was an immense improvement. Once she was no longer stumbling around, Denise found that she quite enjoyed this mode of travel. Floating free, she slept better than she ever had before. The zero-G toilet took some getting used to, but it was hardly as horrific now as it had been her first day aboard the old man's interplanetary ferry ship. Even though she took the necessary chemical supplements to compensate for calcium loss and muscle atrophy, she exercised regularly. After a few days, her calisthenics lost their clumsiness, adopting an elegance that was unique to her new environment.

She learned how annoying it was to have long hair in space. Her long tresses were a constant inconvenience, refusing to remain orderly. They thrashed about like animate appendages in the gravityless air. Early on, she had bound her mane into a ponytail, but Masterfield had clucked his tongue and advised her that the wisest solution was to trim her hair to a much shorter length. He recommended applying a special salve that would permanently remove all hair from her scalp, but she rejected the extremism of his suggestion. Instead, she transformed her voluptuous locks into a sporty bob.

She learned that Masterfield did not like being called "Captain," for he thought of his "ship" as a "home." Beyond its signature code, his spacecraft was nameless. "Homes have numbers, not names," he announced with exaggerated insight.

She learned a smattering of the old man's history. Masterfield had been a spacer for many, many years. A native of one of Greye's orbital settlements, he had jobbed for an assortment of spacecraft before owning his present ship. He was, the old man revealed, far from unique. There was a fleet of privately owned tugs hauling commercial freight between Greye and Baltuss.

"Don't you get lonely?" she asked. "Out here all by yourself? With the closest human being sometimes thousands of kilometers away?"

"I have friends," Masterfield told her. "I may not 'see' them very often, but we stay in touch through comm."

Denise nodded grimly, absorbing the wisdom hidden in the man's casual admission. Physical solitude did not have to include loneliness. Comm-links were the obvious answer. The important part of that solution, though, was to know people with whom one could trade friendly calls. Masterfield had lived his entire life in space, he undoubtedly would have numerous acquaintances scattered through the Cacio Trumpis system. Newly arrived, Denise Coleman knew no one yet. No one except Masterfield. She was embarrassed to ask if she could be one of his comm-buddies. She had never made friends easily; even though she had traveled far from the planet of her birth, there was little reason to expect her social ineptitude to improve.

She hung on every word uttered by the old spacer, soaking up clues on how to conduct herself in her new life.

The prospects of this impending new life filled Denise with a vibrant thrill. On Paulen, her skills had been average, but in the Petrie colony, she would become a valuable addition to society. Her presence there might even mean the difference between life and death for some unfortunate colonist.

Nurses did that sometimes.

Nineteen days later, Masterfield's space tug docked with the Petrie colony. In order to escort his sole passenger to her new employers, the old man accompanied Denise through the airlock. An agent of the Administration was waiting to meet her, for Masterfield had called ahead.

Denise gawked despite the absence of any impressive panoramas. Her surroundings were windowless corridors, far more cramped than the expansive hallways back in Victoria Terminal, and starkly uncluttered. There were only a few pedestrians swimming past the alcove in which she hung with Masterfield and her official guide, who introduced herself as Erin Lansky.

Denise gawked, and everything she saw was rich with incredible implications. This was a *human space colony* in another *solar system*, an astounding achievement for a bunch of evolved monkeys. And she was here, actually a part of this effort to tame the interstellar frontier. Her name might never become famous, but she was an inviolate part of mankind's brave cosmic expansion. A sense of purpose swelled her ample chest.

Speaking privately with Lansky, Masterfield was conferring some informality to the one-woman welcoming committee. Denise only caught the phrase "she thinks it's a colony," which failed to alert her at the time. She was still drenched in the heroic actuality of being here.

Masterfield gallantly bid her goodbye, claiming he had other business to attend to aboard the station. Denise watched the old man leave: he nimbly launched himself from the alcove into the curving tunnel beyond, expertly joining the darting colonists without disrupting their graceful flow.

"Well, here I am," Denise declared, presenting herself to Lansky.

"I expect you'd like to see your quarters." The woman took Denise's single piece of luggage under her arm, then turned to leap into the corridor. "Then I can show you the medical facilities."

Denise accepted the woman's guidance. As they made their way through the station's zero-G hallways, she looked Lansky over. The female spacer was short and stocky. She wore an orange jumpsuit that gave the impression of being a uniform with its glittery trim and cinched cuffs. A thick mechanical belt surrounded her waist, a profusion of gadgetry dangled from it. Her Caucasian features were fused with an Oriental flair, showing up mostly in her huge, expressive eyes. The rest of her oval face was angular and tight with muscles. At first, it seemed that the woman's hair was a closely cropped metallic red, but then Denise realized that Lansky's scalp was merely tattooed with the illusion of a crimson buzz-cut. She maneuvered the corridors with a sinewy command that impressed Denise. When she studied the woman's movements to copy her skill, Denise realized with a start that Lansky's knees swung both ways. There was no chance that Denise could duplicate much of her guide's unnatural calisthenics.

As they moved along, Lansky was silent.

When they came to a silver hatch at the end of a particular passage, the spacer slid through the mirrored surface as if it was without substance. That hatch, however, stopped Denise like a stolid barrier. She rebounded, her forehead smarting from the impact. Whatever that hatch was made of, it felt like cold metal.

A minute later, Lansky's torso poked back through the surface of the silvered hatch to peer at Denise. "What's the matter?" the spacer asked.

"What the weed is that thing?" She pointed at the hatchway.

"It's a stass field. The only thing that can pass through it is another stass field. We use them instead of physical exit hatches. Is yours malfunctioning?"

"I…I don't have one," Denise revealed hesitantly. She had hoped to conceal this deficiency, assuming that only divers left the security of the station.

"That is going to be a problem," Lansky admitted. She drifted back until her entire body reappeared in the corridor, passing through the unbroken smooth stass field like a ghostly mirage. "Umm," she mumbled, rubbing her pointed jaw with a finger. "Are you hungry? Let's retire to a cafeteria. I need to think this out…" She guided Denise through a few more corridors.

The cafeteria consisted of rows of communal tables established in a three-dimensional grid to accommodate zero-G access. The walls—and floor and ceiling—were lined with private stalls containing more intimate booths. The large room was not crowded, so they were able to pick a secluded booth in which to settle. Lansky left her there, jumping off toward a dispensary wall. Denise used the opportunity to familiarize herself with the strange seating arrangement. The table was small and conventionally rectangular, protruding from the wall. Each side was flanked by "seats" that were set against the walls of the booth, resembling braces designed to fit a person's back more than their buttocks. These braces, she soon realized, were secondary. The real means of support was hidden under the table in the form of rows of plastic tubing. These rods were lined with loose loops that functioned to stabilize the diners while they ate. One slipped an ankle through a loop, securing oneself by effectively hanging in place. The back cushions made sense to her now.

When Lansky returned, the woman carried an assortment of squeeze tubes which she identified as nutrient paste. Each tube was labeled as conventional flavors, but once Denise started sucking on the "chicken" one, she discovered that the label was more psychological than descriptive.

"I thought Masterfield was joking," Lansky remarked as she perched across the booth. "You think this place is on a moon, don't you?"

"Petrie is a space colony, isn't it? I assumed the station must be orbiting the main facility on the moon."

Lansky shook her head. "This 'station' is it, girl."

"Huh?"

"This is a free-floating platform. We're not affiliated with any lunar body or other station. This isn't a 'colony', either; it's a space station used by the freelance divers as a base. Do you even know about the quasi-legal nature of this facility?"

"I was told that Petrie was in competition with some corporation over cloud-mining rights."

"Outright hostilities is a better description of the relationship between HeeVee and the freelance divers. We can discuss that part later." The woman wrinkled her brow with worry-lines. "Whatever possessed you to come out here without getting a stass field generator implant? Were you *advised* to dispense with that necessity?"

No," Denise admitted reluctantly. "The employment agency made it very clear that I should get the field generator. I...the decision to skip the surgery was mine."

"Are you prone to making the wrong decision a lot?" Lansky asked.

"What? I—"

"Because out here, wrong decisions can get you killed—really fast. And if you're unlucky enough to make a really *big* wrong decision, you could end up killing other people too."

"I'll be careful...I won't make any wrong decisions..." She realized how lame that sounded. "I guess that's kind of stupid... How am I supposed to know *right* from *wrong* in an unfamiliar environment?"

"At least you can see that much," Lansky grunted.

"I was afraid of the surgery," Denise sobbed suddenly.

"A squeamish nurse?"

"No. I just don't like the idea of *me* being the one who gets cut open."

"Your hangups are your own business. I'm more concerned with your immediate survival. Admin didn't spend all the creds to ship you way out here to lose you to the first vacuum you encounter. You're an expensive acquisition, Miss Coleman. If you fail to live up to expectations, heads are going to roll."

"I don't understand..."

"Later. First, we have to figure out how to handle your stass-less state."

"Why? I don't need to go outside..."

"Girl, that's not the way this station is designed. No matter how much this place might sometimes seem like a city—it isn't. Think of Petrie as a big hotel in space, because that's how Admin runs the station. There are public facilities like this cafeteria, gyms and game centers and stores and all the trapping of a city, but it's all here to serve a clientele who rent quarters and pay for everything they need—from food to air. The parts of the station you've seen so far are all contained in one of the commercial pods. There are four of them, positioned at the corners of the twin dom cap platforms. The divers live in those domicile capsules."

"Can't I get a room here in this part of the station?"

"There aren't any. Everybody lives in the dom caps, or the rec caps for couples."

"Even families?"

Lansky frowned. "Families just rent more than one rec cap."

"Then I'll have to live in one of these domicile capsules."

"And how are you going to get there without killing yourself?"

"Surely there must be access corridors."

"The only access is through the vacuum."

"That's absurd. What about people who—"

"*Everybody* out here has stass field generators implanted in them to protect them when they go outside."

"Oh..."

"You begin to see the extent of your problem, Miss Coleman."

In truth, Denise's plight was not as desperate as Lansky implied.

It turned out that quarters were indeed available on the commercial pods. She was not the only one on the platform unwilling to venture outside. Several merchants preferred to reside in conjunction with their businesses, and one of them was found who was willing to rent her a room. Grudgingly, Lansky admitted that this solution apparently took care of the majority of Denise's "problems." The short woman seemed frustrated that the dilemma had been so easily solved.

Denise was thoroughly grateful for the simplicity of the solution. She could commute to work, for those medical facilities were located in this very pod. If she ever needed to leave the pod to visit another part of the platform, she learned that she could rent a hardware pressure suit to protect her. This option was ill-advised though, for the suits were expensive, and very few hatches were rigged to pass anything not contained in a stass field. In the long run, she found it easier to reconcile herself to the fact that she would not be going outside—which thrilled her, for she had no desire to visit what lay on the other side of the station's bulkheads. Her entire life would fit within the confines of this commercial pod: work, sleep, eating, playing. She would make friends and see them in these corridors. She would never miss not having a stass field generator implanted inside her body.

For that matter, no one needed to learn that she lacked this implant, or any other biological augmentation. "Right?" she pleaded. Reluctantly, Lansky agreed to keep her secret. Denise feared that people might somehow think less of her if they discovered her deficiencies, so she told no one. Not even Doc Petroff.

Her introduction to the doctor and his offices revealed more things which Petrie's Administrators had neglected to tell the employment agency that had recruited Denise back on Paulen. This time, the surprise involved the political infrastructure of the colony. (No, it was a "base". She had to stop thinking of Petrie as a "colony" and readjust to the reality of it being a station out in the void.)

Apparently, Admin maintained a public medical facility for its clientele. The personnel of this office consisted of a single man: Doctor Ivar Petroff. Admin had failed to share with the doctor their decision to supplement his staff, resulting in the man taking an instant dislike to Denise Coleman when they were introduced.

Petroff flew into a wild rage, demanding explanations that Denise was unable to supply. The man was unsatisfied with the answers given him by Lansky. He stormed off to "confront the Administrators about this insult."

"What was that all about?" Denise gasped once the handsome man had left.

"The truth?" Lansky shrugged. "Doc Petroff is a lousy doctor. This station needs better medical staff, that's why Admin hired you. In his arrogance—you noticed his incredible ego, right?—Petroff remains ignorant of how bad a doctor he is."

"Great," sighed Denise. "My boss hates me."

"Technically, Admin is your boss."

Denise threw the woman a scowl, and Lansky agreed with a wry smile.

"This sucks."

It took a few weeks, but Doc Petroff finally warmed to Denise. By that time, she had witnessed enough evidence to support Lansky's off-the-record evaluation of the buffoon. As Petroff took an interest in her, Denise found the man less and less attractive. His callous nature and egocentric personality effectively ruined the obvious appeal of his handsome physique and features. She discouraged his advances, which returned their relationship to its original distant temperament.

Her work environment offered her no opportunity to make friends, for Denise felt awkward attempting to befriend the sick and injured. So she took to frequenting game centers, but her unfamiliarity with the limited range of zero-G sports earned her no acquaintances. For a while she retreated to her own company, wandering the pod and familiarizing herself with the extent of her neighborhood, for her world effectively ended at the outer bulkheads of the station.

This commercial pod measured a third-of-a-kilometer in diameter, and was used on an average by half the three thousand freelance divers who resided at the base. It featured a cafeteria, extensive merchant districts including a variety of privately owned novelty shops, an inadequate public gym, an adequate commercial exercise facility, an adequate—and getting more competent by the day—medical office, and several public courtyards that doubled as meeting halls for the rare official function. The entertainment shops were well-stocked with movies and documentaries. She even found one that detailed the birth of "The Petrie Colony".

From its very title, Denise knew it to be blatant Admin propaganda. By now she understood than no diver thought of the Petrie platform as a colony. Lansky's private description of the station had been painfully exact. The platform was a business, it existed to feed off the divers who fed off Baltuss' clouds. As someone who worked directly for Admin, Denise was spared the financial scramble that permeated every diver's daily routine, but she still existed here only by the grace of her employers.

She rented "The Petrie Colony" and viewed it back in the privacy of her rented room above a clothing shop.

Ninety-seven years ago, in 2207, Danyel Peesmont organized a commercial collaboration among several Greye businesses to fund the construction of space hotel which would orbit the planet in conjunction with Victoria Terminal. The scheme was to deflect a percentage of tourists arriving at Greye's main spaceport into occupying the newly fabricated Orion Arms. The endeavor proved considerably profitable, generating excessive fortunes for Peesmont and the other investors.

Among the ranks of these investors, there was a man named Danner who was known to think outside the box. Danner proposed a scaled-down, utilitarian version of the Orion Arms to handle the overnight turnover of travelers arriving at or departing from Victoria Terminal. A no-frills operation of this type was expected to be an instant success, but it was not. The Orion Overnight went ignored in lieu of the more convenient lodgings found on Victoria Terminal. After barely a year in operation, the OO closed down in financial disgrace. Undefeatable, Danner found a solution outside the box—way outside the box.

The next planet out from the Cacio Trumpis sun was Baltuss, where Harvest Corp conducted their cloud-mining operations. Channeling the Corp's freight was a multibillion cred business in the skies above Greye.

One day, Danner heard a rumor that not all the cloud divers bagging gas on Baltuss were under the Corp's employment. Some were—gasp!—renegades, uncontracted individuals poaching Baltuss' atmosphere. Right under the nose of the mighty Corp! These pirates were operating from their own spacecraft parked in hidden orbits around the gas giant. The entire thing sounded like an urban legend, but it inspired Danner to conceive of a scheme that might possibly save the Orion Overnight from being sold off as parts.

The dormant OO was moved from its orbit above Greye and relocated out near Baltuss. There, the hotel made itself available to any divers who wished to mine the clouds without relinquishing a share of their profit with a soulless corporation. What had previously been overnight sleep capsules became long-term domicile units. A selection of shops and basic services were installed in the station's larger pods.

And slowly, the dom caps began to fill up with adventurous individuals looking to score big in Baltuss' prosperous clouds. Danner and his staff ran a slick operation, offering minimal comforts and reaping high rents. After a few years, they even installed a catapult to help the divers reach Baltuss' atmosphere. They also established the Gas Exchange which purchased divers' collected clouds at wholesale rates, then shipped the booty off to buyers at Greye. As an overnight hotel, the OO had failed; as a secret hideout for space pirates, it flourished.

Somewhere around its thirtieth anniversary, the OO began to call itself the Petrie colony. Efforts were made to create a community spirit among the freelance divers. Public medical facilities were made available to the divers—for a price. Several prosperous divers invested funds in local businesses, and the exchange rate went up three creds per liter.

While the Administrators of the Petrie colony were struggling to create a social entity, Harvest Corp's disapproval was a constant hazard for the freelance divers. In orbit in free space, the platform imagined that it was safe from corporate harassment. Danner and his Administrators imagined wrong, though.

In 2282, an attack had been made on the Petrie base, while Danner was still alive. The colony's founder had led the settlement in a courageous defense against Harvest's murderous assault troops. Denise was thankful that the documentary included no footage of this battle, its description was terrible enough for her. She gasped to hear how Danner had fought insurmountable odds and managed to escape destruction by unexpectedly moving the crippled base while the attackers awaited reinforcements after an arduous stretch of space combat. The Petrie platform retreated to the open void, where Harvest's evil reach could not find them.

Reconstruction was conducted, and the Petrie colony survived. The commuter catapult had been destroyed in the battle, it was replaced with a more modern linear accelerator. Old man Danner died before the station was fully restored. Taking charge as the colony's Administrators, his heirs saw the base rebuilt and revitalized.

It startled Denise to learn that the colony/hotel/base had undergone an attack by hostile forces. Fortunately, the chances of this happening again were apparently low. For nearly four decades, the colony had managed to avoid further reprisals from the wicked corporation. She hoped this standoff would continue while she was here.

The part that troubled her the most was the section toward the end of the documentary that dealt with the "lies and slander" conducted by Harvest Corp when it came to sullying the public reputation of the Petrie colony. According to the film's spokesman (who Denise later learned was the son of one of the Petrie Administrators who had since left the platform to seek an acting career on distant Greye), Harvest had attributed the colonists with the actions and bloodthirsty nature of space pirates. Freelance divers were accused of outright gas thievery, acts of terrorism and sabotage against the Corp base on Baltuss' Natt moon. Every atrocity the corporation had subjected the colony to was turned around and blamed on the vicious pirates. Supposedly, these scoundrels relentlessly tormented the honest, hardworking corporation. The Petrie colony gained the reputation of criminals in the public eye as a result of Harvest's media spin teams.

Denise was no fool, though. She could see what was really going on. Despite its mercantile origins, the freelancers of Petrie platform were engaged in defending the rights of the individual in the oppressive shadow of the soulless interstellar corporation. It was a classic case of everyman versus the company. There was no question who was in the *right* and who was in the *wrong*.

She was still new to the nuances of life in space.

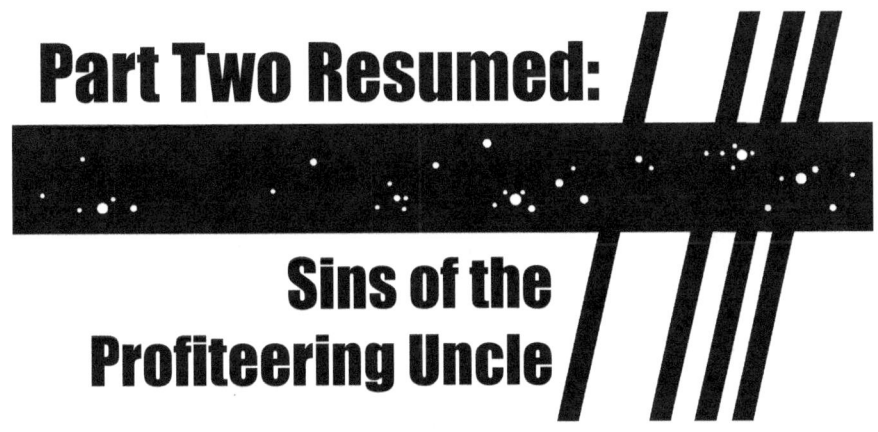

Part Two Resumed:

Sins of the Profiteering Uncle

There were parts of Executive Privilege he regretted.

The afterhours hallways of the Executive Sector were always thick with intrigue. Lesser ranking officials conducted their backstabbing in the shadowed corners of these corridors, while those same passages were used by the higher powers to exchange messengers and saboteurs between the districts of the three reigning Board Execs.

Years ago, there had been a fourth and a fifth Exec on the Board presiding over Harvest Corp's Baltuss cloud-mining facility. The fifth Exec, a man named Jersey, had gotten too sloppy with his greed; he had perished in a purge openly engineered by Exec Uwu. The fourth Exec had lost his franchise for being not greedy enough; Rennf had been crushed by a buyout scheme maliciously masterminded by Exec Hannigan. Since then, an uneasy armistice had existed between the three surviving Board members.

Sometimes, Nigel Bester missed old Rennf. The man should never have risen as high as he did within Harvest's cut-throat corporate structure; sadly, his compassion for strangers had undermined his power base. Despite the man's fatal character flaw, Bester had always liked Rennf. Perhaps as a result of his misplaced trust, Rennf had had an easygoing quality about him, his smiles had been earnest and his interest in "your health" had been untarnished by any hidden agendas. Bester had enjoyed many fine dinners with Rennf before the man's altruism had attracted the fiscal sharks. Rennf's unnecessary demise had taught Bester a very important lesson, one it would take him years to appreciate.

The Exec lay down his utensils and took a final sip from his wine goblet. He sat back and smiled across the dining table at his wife. She smiled back, her still-attractive face wavering with a minor technical glitch.

Not again, he fretted. Her holocube was getting more and more temperamental. He knew the day was coming when her recording would fail. He feared that terminal malfunction, its prospect was forever waiting to happen. Any minute, he could find himself in the middle of what would become his last conversation with his dead wife. Her magnificent, titan-tressed image would flicker, her last words would garble, and finally she would wink out like a spent cinder. Then she would *really* be gone forever. He wondered if he could survive losing her a second time.

After her unfortunate death, Bester's survival had been achieved with the aid of a holocube recording of her. The illusion of her presence had kept him sane. What would he do when that illusion was finally silenced?

He sighed, and for the thousandth time put aside that thought to concentrate on something else. His plate and goblet had been covertly removed while he had been lost in contemplation. A mug of java steamed before him now. Warming his palms by cupping the drink, he surveyed his dead wife's remarkable beauty through the elaborate deco grid of the table's hanging candelabra.

The woman's hair dominated her entire persona, lending presence and elegance to what was basically a particularly slutty face. Her features were astounding to Bester's sensibilities, but to others the woman had the used lips and defeated eyes of a public prostitute. In her husband's eyes, those traits made her a mixture of waif and brat. His ears were deaf to the coarseness of her laugh, and the pathetic way her left eye constantly leaked tears went unnoticed by his lovesick adoration. In the thirty-three years since her death, his wife's holocube had been slowly degrading, blurring her true image and voice worse than Bester's idealized memory. What remained now bore only a rudimentary similarity to the man's recollection of how his wife looked and sounded.

Soaking up her reassuring appearance in order to motivate himself to live through the night, Bester switched off the holocaster. She disappeared, depriving his solitude of any illusionary company. It was prudent to conserve use of the master recording before that holocube degraded to the point of losing its functional integrity.

He rose from the table and walked away, taking no notice of the robots that scurried to strip and sterilize the table in his absence.

In the privacy of his sanctorum, there were no robotic drones to get underfoot. He sealed the doorway, wanting no interruptions by chance visitors.

With mild trepidation, he remembered the recent visitation by his creepy nephew. Teid was always showing up unannounced, as if that lent him some eerie upperhand. The boy worried Bester, for the Exec could recognize the signs of a psycho-about-to-blow. For years Teid had wallowed in the most unpleasant pastimes he could find, and that exposure had warped the lad, transforming him into an arrogant sadist. The nasty boy was getting restless, things had been calm for too long. Teid Hein needed to regularly vent his cruelty, lest it turn on him. He was on the prowl, looking for something to destroy. Bester pitied the fly this monster selected to de-wing.

He had not come here to think about wicked little Teid, he reminded himself. He had retreated to his sanctorum to escape such petty and intrusive elements. Bester was looking to relax. There would be time enough later to cope with Teid's ill-tempered tantrums and the Board's omnipresent duplicity and the stubborn resistance of the Greye negotiators and the rest of the endless problems that clamored for Executive solutions.

Turning from the locked door, Nigel Bester left his corporate persona behind. It was a younger soul who suddenly moved his body in a complexity of dance-moves across the cobbled floor. With no one to witness, he cavorted like an over-enthusiastic opera character, bending to stroke the ground with his fingertips, sliding around the ribbed pillars that walled the chamber, pirouetting and twirling with romantic abandon.

When he reached the ramp of steps, Bester had to sit down and catch his breath. He was getting too old for this nonsense. Soon, he'd have to find alternate means to express his inner self. Puffing mildly, he glanced around at his surroundings.

To most, the chamber's antediluvian decor appeared gloomy and foreboding. The coarse stone that produced this appearance seemed cold and damp although they were actually dry and smooth. In the dim light, the mighty columns that supported the lofty ceiling dome were shrouded in secretive shadows. In that same minimal illumination, the floor seemed to ripple as the flickering light danced across each cobble's curvature. At his back, the source of that light—his holographic lantern—made his shoulders twinkle in his peripheral vision. His shadow fell upon the floor before him like an angular stain.

To him, though, the mood evoked by this castle facsimile was one of hidden inspiration. The coarse stone and rustic flooring captured a courage and glory that Bester had read about in his youth. According to tradition, the Bester lineage had originated in Earth's British Isles, where some ancient ancestor had reputedly established an early stage of the family fortune by stealing possession of a castle of stark grandeur. As a strapping lad, Bester had imagined the bloody battle for supremacy of a magnificent structure of regal proportions. As an adult, he had conducted deeper research, discovering that the attack had been quite cowardly, the castle little more than a rudimentary dirt fort built into the side of a hill, and the "fortune" had consisted of the privilege of lording over three local farmers who grew mud better than crops. Despite these hard and dismal realities, Bester was certain that an amount of courage must have gone into the capture of the castle. He drew strength from this theoretical bravery, and the castle imagery became synonymous with such fearless heroism.

When the time came for him to choose the decor for his private sanctorum, Bester had readily demanded a castle motif. The construction had been expensive and exasperating, as he obsessed over each detail and the cost escalated with each knitpicking refinement. The final product, however, had validated all the stress. His sanctorum was perfect. While filling him with a private sense of ancestral power, the dismal chamber psychologically battered visitors with its archaic solemnity, making Bester the alpha male of every encounter. It amused him that the facade that invigorated his spirit was found so repellent by others.

His wife had not been intimidated by his gloomy castle. For reasons of her own, never known to Bester, she had shared his passion for granite architecture.

But now there was only him.

Wearily he rose to his feet and climbed the stairs to reach his desk. He dropped his gangly frame into the contours of the floating chair. With tired eyes, he surveyed his machinery. A few screens were still running data corrolations from his last session; he ignored these, turning his attention to a pair of headphones that rested on the console. He fit these on his angular head, then pressed a few switches on the control board at his elbow. Music filled his head.

Electronic percussion rolled so fast and tight that the rhythms became a liquid wave oozing across a landscape of rolling hills. The beats were soft and delicate, purring like angry bees. The tempos they described were sinuous and languid. Growling in the background: a sheet of vibrating metal cast off haunting noises. These spurting sounds were captured by a melody, compressed into a riff of energetic quality. Blooping with electronic rapture, the beats merged with the loops to produce a sonic tapestry of hypnotic dynamics.

Nigel Bester, Executive member of the Board managing Harvest Corp's Baltuss cloud-mining operation, was a fan of eclectic music. Which meant that Bester was a secret listener of Red Sky Radio, for nothing like this music would ever grace an official Harvest broadcast.

For a while, he simply relaxed in his hoverchair and enjoyed the abstract impressions conjured by the lively electronic music. His mind emptied of tension and details, giving in to the compulsive beat. He let the music carry him along, confident that whatever it revealed to him would prove entertaining.

Vistas of rustic countrysides opened inside his head, shrouded in a morning mist that oozed off the forlorn moors like a gaseous creature. The landscape before this seeping mist was green and verdant. Silhouetted against the huge yellow orb of the rising sun was a grand castle of lofty towers and pointed caps flying immense banners. Although possessing noble majesty, this fortress exuded a foul foreboding that Bester knew was attributable to the terrible miscreants who ruled this castle. He smiled as the mists parted to swirl in celebration around the flanks of the righteous knights come to vanquish the evil lords and punish them for the atrocities they had visited upon the peasants who dwelled in this magical land.

As a group of E-perc rhythms clustered to rattle into a synchronous vibration, he imagined a flock of war hawks launching into the morning sky. Their stark forms filled the heavens, driving back the depressing mists and hurrying the heroes on their assault of the distant castle.

Finally revitalized, Bester opened his eyes and stared placidly into the shadowy heights of his sanctorum. The flickering of the illusionary candle gave the view a smoldering undercurrent. These earthy concepts helped ground his consciousness as he sequewayed back into the real world.

A light was blinking on his console. He reached for it, activating the transmission. A tiny voice reported that the base's Security Domo had ordered a gatherer depot to return to the lunar base ahead of schedule, leaving its position in the gas giant's clouds before filling its tanks to the estimated quota. Official charges were being brought against the man for his unauthorized interference in Harvest's cloud-mining operation.

Bester sighed.

This incident had crossed his desk days ago. He had ignored the report once he had determined that the Domo's actions had been involved in protecting the depot from a pirate raid. The man's breach of protocol was justified in Bester's opinion, he had been doing his job.

Others, apparently, did not share Bester's view of Security Domo Sloane's ability to improvise in the field.

The tiny voice from his console went on to enumerate the failings, professional and personal, of the Security Domo, going so far as to repudiate the man's hygiene. As the accusations grew progressively outlandish, Bester's attention to detail flagged. He could recognize a smear when he heard one, and this one was particularly crude. He thought he detected Teid's hand in this, for the Exec was well-aware of his wicked nephew's rivalry with Theo Sloane. Normally, Bester enjoyed watching the evil brat be bested again and again by the Security Domo, but he feared that this time the scowl was going to be on Sloane's face. An official Board accusation was not as easy to dodge as covert slander.

There was an economic foundation supporting the charges against Sloane. The Domo had ordered the gatherer depot back to base before its tanks were full. This premature recall of the huge satellite had hurt this week's quota. Dispatching the gatherer depots were costly endeavors. According to the litany of the official charges, Sloane's interference would cost Harvest greatly. The Executive Board could not afford to allow this transgression to pass without reprimand.

Bester would be sorry to see Sloane punished, for the Security Domo made such a perfect foil for the rambunctious intrigues of the Executive's unpleasant nephew, Teid Hein. As a Board Exec, though, Bester would be one of the three who decided Sloane's predestined guilt.

There were parts of Executive Privilege he regretted.

Part One Resumed:

Escape to the Clouds

She was unaware of being watched.

When Peri sought out Dezi Annucci, he refused to speak with her.

The old man was just leaving an electronics supply shop, and seemed to resent the attention she was drawing to him. Hoisting the satchel of his purchases over his stooped shoulder, Dezi tried to evade the girl's approach by dodging down a side passage, but Peri followed him with unwavering determination.

As they passed an open-fronted 24/7 tavern, several inebriated voices chanted at them.

"Dizzy Dezi! Dizzy Dezi!"

"And Little Peri Worrybutt!"

"Look out for killer bots!"

"Peri's got a *neeew* boyfriend…"

Dezi ignored them, continuing to swim his way along the zero-G corridor, but Peri paused to scowl and fling a derogatory challenge into the bar. The drunks cackled with ragtag glee, the slurred syllables of their amused insults echoing after the pair. When Peri and Dezi had moved beyond view, the boozers puffed with intoxicated pride over their unkind humor. They laughed among themselves until a new figure came to hang in the tavern's open facade. Taz Bailey's disapproving frown silenced their joviality, for they recognized the entrepreneur and had no desire to annoy him.

Taz had been following his emotionally disturbed girlfriend from a distance, careful to keep just beyond Peri's range of detection. While his concern had driven him to shadow her, Taz understood the argument this would incite if Peri realized that she had a guardian watching over her. The last thing he wanted to do was aggravate her.

By the time he caught up to her, Peri had cornered Dezi and was forcing her grief on the old man. Taz observed from a safe distance as Dezi rebuffed the girl's distress with a flood of vitreous verbiage.

They were arguing about some "secret." Taz pursed his lips with resignation, for he knew that his girlfriend had no deficiency of those. Even the old man had his secrets.

Steadying his aged form with an outstretched hand against the bulwark of the passage, Dezi faced Peri and loudly denounced her unreliability.

She replied with a brief burst of indignation, but an edge of dubious uncertainty crept into her sultry voice.

The oldster was unmoved and unconvinced by her solicitous apologies. From his hiding place, Taz could see how darkly the man's normally pale face flushed with his unhappy allegations. It was clear that Dezi was furious with the girl over some indiscretion she had committed. From the stubborn nature of Peri's response, Taz imagined that the alluded-to blunder involved her delusional killer robots.

She can't talk to anybody these days without bringing her obsession into the conversation, Taz ruminated sadly. Her fanaticism was truly out of control. Peri, of course, remained obstinately blind to the extent that her obsession was alienating everyone around her. In Taz's opinion, this was all the old man's fault—if Dezi had kept his absurd conspiracies to himself, then Peri would never have gotten caught up in this delusion. The decrepit rumormonger was responsible for Peri's mental distress, he deserved to be plagued by her preaching rants.

Taz failed to comprehend, though, why Dezi was so angry with the girl. Even now, the old man was indicting her with vicious scorn. Whatever transgression Dezi imagined Peri had committed, he was adamantly opposed to forgiving her. In return, the old man's resolute attitude was irritating the girl, spurring her to shriller recriminations.

"I think it's time that people know you're involved with these killer bots," Peri announced at a volume that carried to Taz in his hiding place. "For all we know, *you're* a HeeVee spy!"

The old man's reply was hardly as loud, so Taz was deprived of hearing its specific content. The method in which Dezi waggled a stern finger at the girl was easily readable, however. Although Peri seemed oblivious to it, the warning was not lost on Taz. Expecting the oldster to resort to violence, Taz tensed, ready to throw himself to the defense of his beloved.

Dezi confined his vehemence to his mouth, though. When his words failed to quiet Peri's ongoing outburst, the old man kicked off. With a spry grace, he slithered around the girl and rebounded away down the corridor, leaving Peri arguing with empty air.

Considering her present mood, Taz thought it unwise to "accidentally" run into Peri. He had gotten enough of her cruel censure back in their rec cap before she had stormed off. Withdrawing, Taz maneuvered his way from the region.

As he threaded between other off-duty freelancers, Taz mulled over the best place to avoid his girlfriend. Now that she was all worked up from her confrontation with Dezi Annucci, there was no telling where she would seek solace, or whether she would even take the time to unwind. Considering her current disposition, Peri might start bothering passers-by with her chicken-little warnings. This practice could take her anywhere on the platform as she harangued divers, urging them to refrain from pursuing their livelihood. Taz needed some Peri-less time to sort out how to deal with things.

Down, he decided. With the exception of this morning's dive, which had been done entirely with the intention of retrieving Peri, it had been a few weeks since Taz had ventured into Baltuss' atmosphere. Possessing a surplus of funds from his lucrative economic investments, the man had little reason these days to regularly go in search of profitable clouds. There was no lack of alternate duties to occupy his daily routine, monitoring the status of his financial interests was often a full-time pursuit. A high percentage of his hours had been spent lately watching over Peri as she recuperated from her dilapidating depression. He felt a sudden urge to escape the colony and prowl the clouds of Baltuss in search of distraction. Perhaps stalking a fresh cloud would ease his stress.

He took the next left corridor, for that route would take him to the nearest exit hatch. On his way to the linear accelerator, Taz detoured briefly to grab his bagger rod from his possessions in the recreational capsule he shared with Peri.

He was startled (and somewhat suspiciously annoyed) to discover Doc Petroff loitering outside the rec cap. Although unhappy to have the man in his living space, Taz waved the man to join him inside the capsule. Once they entered, their stass-skins flickered off, revealing their faces to each other.

Foregoing the courtesy of any greeting, the medical quack expressed dismay that Peri was absent.

"She's out about today," Taz remarked, hoping his ambiguity was obvious enough for the man.

"I was hoping to catch her in," Petroff mumbled. "I remembered your mentioning how she wasn't feeling very well, so I was going to see if I could help."

Right, Taz privately fumed. *A little physical examination would be just the thing—to give* you *a thrill, you pompous fraud.*

"She's feeling better," he told the intruder.

"I think *I* should be the judge of that, Taz. After all, who's the one with the medical training here?"

That'd be neither *of us, you fake.*

"I'll tell her you were looking for her," Taz spoke through grated teeth. Finding his gas-bag, he clipped the rod to his utility belt.

"Don't forget now, okay? Peri is far too gorgeous to deserve to be sick," Petroff insisted in his snide voice. "Going diving, huh?"

Taz shrugged. He drifted near the cap's stassed hatch, indicating that he desired to leave.

Ignoring the social cue, the doctor hooked an ankle in a foot-strap and made himself comfortable. "I'd've thought you had no time to go scrambling around bagging clouds for petty creds, Taz. Or is your fortune in peril? Bad investments taking their toll?"

"There's nothing wrong with any of my investments," Taz responded with visible rancor. This subject was another of the endless reasons that Taz disliked the doctor. Years ago, when Taz had begun to spread his money around to support various businesses in the freelancer colony, Petroff had approached him with the notion of opening a jolt parlor aboard the platform. Taz had little tolerance for the practice of using electrical surges to desensitize the human brain for the purpose of entertainment, much less here where a jolt addict could endanger everyone with their sloppy behavior. Taz viewed with horror the prospect of such a service opening on the Petrie platform. His refusal to fund Petroff's quasi-legal enterprise had been brutal and deprecating. The doctor had responded by circulating the story that he had approached Taz with a proposal of opening a socialized medical center, but the "rich-boy" had derisively refused to fund such a thing. It had taken Taz months to undo the subsequent damage to his reputation. He still craved revenge on the undesirable physician for that slander.

"That's not what I heard," Petroff commented. The doctor exaggerated his casual tone to imply how intimately vital was the information he thought he knew.

Taz possessed no interest in the man's inferred confidentiality. Whatever it was, the news could only be bad—that was, of course, if Taz placed any faith in secrets known by the unlicensed physician, which he didn't. Any secrets that Petroff knew were so old and impotent, they had to be no longer worth knowing.

"I'm late," he told the annoying visitor.

"Don't let me keep you from your trivial rendezvous," Petroff chuckled. "I'll wait here until Peri returns."

Not in this lifetime, Taz vowed. His patience finally overtaxed, he grabbed the doctor's ankle and flung him from the rec cap like a javelin of flailing meat. As Petroff plunged through the hatch's stass barrier, his own stass field activated itself, sparing him from organic decompression as his body reached the vacuum outside the domicile.

By the time Taz left the capsule, the doctor had vanished. The fraud had probably scuttled off in shame, for Taz knew he wasn't lucky enough to have thrown him farther than the man's thrusters could handle. Since he had no desire to clutter his attention with misgivings over the doctor's health, Taz forgot about the wretched lech and made his way along the tow lines running the length of the row of capsules.

A few hours diving in Baltuss' clouds would hopefully clear all unpleasantness from his mind.

Taz had never been very athletic. His buff physique was more the product of his metabolism than any skillful exertion on his part. He wore his muscles without complaint, for strength could not be considered a disadvantage while surviving in space.

He prided himself on being pragmatic about life. He accepted things, in himself and in his environment, for there was no profit in bemoaning the inevitable or the immutable. (A child of dirt might have found Taz's physiological augmentation to be a contradiction undermining his acceptance of his body, but grounders would fail to take into consideration that, as a child of void, Taz had received his implants while he was a young child. All spacers were augmented early, for children are notoriously experimental, and such immature antics could prove fatal aboard an spacecraft or orbiting station. As a result, Taz had grown up thinking of his implants as natural parts of his body.) Because of this stoic outlook, Taz possessed little tolerance for frivolous entertainment. If something failed to contribute to his survival or peace of mind, it was not ignored, just given unimportant status. Nonessential factors existed for him, they were simply relegated to his sensory background.

Diving through the multicolored mist, Taz was unmoved by the panorama. As far as he was concerned, the clouds were inert and impersonal. They were gas, to be collected or rejected, not appreciated. This philosophy was not something that existed in his conscious thoughts. So basic was his lack of artistic appreciation that he never considered the subject, certainly not while viewing the roiling clouds of Baltuss. The idea of atmospheric conditions possessing artistic merit never crossed his mind.

He was not entirely soulless, though, for he had a fondness for orchestral music.

Tuning in to Red Sky Radio's pirate broadcast as he descended through the vaporous stratosphere, Taz was pleased to find them playing one of Holtz's compositions. Even tone-deaf spacers were familiar with Holtz's "The Planets", the symphonies had extraordinary significance to anyone born and bred in the void. The grandeur of the music stimulated Taz's sense of wonder. It made him think of love.

It made him think of Peri.

For some time, the girl had been an important part of his life, a source of great pleasure and fulfillment. Taz had thought he had finally found his soul mate, but now…he didn't know what to think. The girl had changed so much in the last week, transforming from a carefree slacker into a fanatical cultist. Her charming mirth had been replaced with an expression of fervent obsession. Her demure shyness had vanished, and now she aggressively forced her wild opinions on strangers. And now she was lying to him, sneaking off to dive when she should have been resting. What would be next?

He was loathe to admit it, but his heart ached with the fear of losing her. He loved Peri so much, but he wondered how drastic her transformation would have to become before her changes taxed his deep affection. How much would he endure to perpetuate the illusion of having someone to love?

She was no longer the person he knew; further change would only greaten those differences. Her present personality bore little resemblance to the girl he had fallen in love with. Yet he emotionally clung to her as if she were the only girl left alive in the universe. He knew he would tolerate her reckless new moods, for he could not bring himself to abandon the minuscule hope that she might undergo some astounding regression and revert to her old, happy-go-lucky self. That tiny and implausible chance would hold him in this relationship long past its prime. He would suffer for this inability to cut himself loose, but he recognized that as a psychological pattern he could never resist. He was trapped with Peri. No matter how ugly things got, he refused to forsake her.

The music had changed. Now it was loud in his head: caterwauling hillbilly blues, full of lament and emotional loss. Taz found it annoying, especially in tandem with his present train of thought. He switched off his reception of Red Sky's broadcast. The descending silence became oppressive, somehow accentuating his distraught mood.

It's time, he decided, *to pick a cloud to bag.* That might distract him from the maudlin bias of his temperament.

Curtailing his downward flight, Taz surveyed the surrounding clouds through the strictly analyzing regard of his augmented senses. The mists faded to near-invisibility as the sensors located in his utility belt probed the mists for profitable chemical signatures in his vicinity. Spectrographic critiques flowed across his vision, cataloging the molecular ingredients of his immediate environment.

For a second, a stray statistic flickered before his eyes, then it vanished. He frowned, for the reading had featured a number of refined metallics and even a coherent isotope. But—that was not possible. Such a concentration of heavier elements could not be present in gaseous form, and there were no traces of any denser mass lurking among the nearby vapors. He rescanned the direction in which his sensors had briefly detected this implausible reading. No, nothing. *It must have been a momentary glitch,* Taz told himself. He made a mental note to have his utility belt checked out once he returned to the Petrie colony.

Selecting a precious cloud, he unclipped his bagger rod and aimed it. Holding the device forward and slightly to his right, he pressed the go button and the rod's nozzle plunged into the target mist. The rear end of the staff began to extrude an opaque balloon. As the rod sucked in the gas, the sac swelled.

Trusting the rod to do its thing, Taz's eyes wandered across his surroundings. The spectacular cloudbanks were just walls of vapor to his regard, possessing no traits to pause his surveying glance. Sudden movement past his left shoulder made him twitch, but the unexpected motion was only the emergence of a confetti swarm. With an urgent eloquence the swarm swept between the roiling clouds, the high velocity of their passage generating colorful eddies in the mist. As he watched, the speeding swarm branched into two, then three groups. These new crowds dove off in different directions, quickly vanishing from sight in the gaseous strata.

Curious behavior, he thought. Had something frightened the confetti swarm, prompting the creatures to flee in separate groups? A casual scan of the region revealed no predator or anything that might have panicked the alien lifeforms. They certainly hadn't been intimidated by his presence, for their strange division had occurred some distance away from Taz's position. The trajectory of the passing swarm had never come near him. *Curious creatures,* he mused, dismissing their puzzling antics as some trivial quirk practiced by confetti fish. After all, they were an alien species. Shouldn't they be expected to conduct themselves in a manner thoroughly bewildering to a human observer? Especially one like Taz, who was no authority on Baltuss' exotic biota.

He returned his attention to the bagger rod. It was merrily humming in his hand, filling the growing bag with precious contents.

Despite the rarity of the lithium he was collecting, Taz decided to avoid overstressing his equipment. With the infrequency over the years of his need to dive to earn creds, the rod he was using was almost two decades old. It was worn and temperamental, more a sentimental keepsake now than a useful tool. He had no desire to burn it out, especially not on a cloud he was bagging out of boredom.

But…maybe this gas didn't have to be bagged without a purpose. Maybe he could put it to good use.

What would happen, he wondered, if he took this cloud and sold it to the Gas Exchange in Peri's name? How would solvency affect her obsessive mania?

He tried to remember Peri the way she had been before falling prey to fanaticism, soft and friendly and diving all the time but never managing to bag much vapor... How would that Peri react to a sudden fortune? Her worries should dissolve away. Freed from the restrictions of her poverty, she should relax, becoming more centered and rational. She should reject her delusion, and forget all about her imaginary killer robots. She should be herself again.

Yes, that was the thing to do.

All he had to do was figure a plausible way to introduce the creds to her account without raising her suspicions.

Oh, this was such a clever plan!

He joyfully continued to fill his bag, willing now to tax the device's tolerances in order to benefit his beloved.

For all their expanded range, his artificial senses remained ignorant of the metal beast that hovered barely five meters to his left. It's spiny bulk hung immersed in an embankment of liquid tin, its presence effectively concealed by its cloaking circuitry.

Sealing his bloated gas-bag, Taz clipped it back on his belt and launched himself in departure.

He was unaware of being watched.

Part Two Resumed:

Surrounded by Pirates

His enemies were everywhere.

Unfortunately for his professional dignity, the Security Domo was not alone when he learned of the official charges that had been filed against him regarding his handling of the pirate raid on the gatherer depot. Sloane was in the process of chewing out his officers for their laziness when the summons was delivered. The clerk had felt compelled to read the charges aloud.

At first, Sloane had fumed over the interruption that halted him from redressing his troops. Then he had raged over the absurdity of the accusations implied by the charges. He bellowed at the clerk, informing the man that, with the exception of the Board itself, there was no one more loyal to the corporation on this base than the Security Domo. "My decisions insure the safety of everyone on Natt," he yelled. "From the divers to the lowest, most insignificant clerk—you'd all be living in socialist anarchy if it weren't for me!"

Although the clerk paled to almost deathly color, he refused to take the blame for an Executive Summons. He reminded the Domo that he was "only the messenger."

Sloane still sent him off with a broken nose.

His officers knew to restrain their amusement until such time as their violent leader was not present.

With the summons disk clutched in his meaty hand, Theo Sloane stalked off to brood in private.

The entire thing was just ridiculous, he fumed. His actions had prevented the depot from falling prey to pirates who might have sneaked back for another shot at their target. How could the Corp punish him for saving the depot?

These charges were exaggerated, blowing fragments of the truth out of proportion while twisting those fragmentary facts until they pictured him as utterly irresponsible.

How could the Board overlook the danger to the depot?

Shots had been fired against his officers!

Men had been lost during the mission, bravely giving their lives while defending Harvest's valuable equipment! (A stretch of the truth, perhaps, but no more outrageous than the half-truths contained in the charges levied against Sloane.)

Several divers were even claiming mental stress from the incident!

He could see the Board challenging his competence for failing to capture any of the trespassing thieves. But to reprimand the Security Domo for rescuing the depot from potential sabotage or theft—this was simply ludicrous.

Sloane sensed a more vindictive hand behind this travesty than just bad luck. Even Exec Uwu wasn't this irrational with his imposing edicts. This madness had to be the handiwork of Bester's sleazy nephew, Teid Hein.

For several years, Sloane had been aware of the hate Hein felt for him. The Security Domo had foiled more than a few of the brat's illegal schemes, but he had never been able to produce enough evidence to officially implicate Hein with these nefarious endeavors. He knew Hein was guilty, though. Just as certainly as he knew that Hein knew he knew.

Without solid evidence—of the ultimately damning kind—Sloane knew he could never hope to arrest the vile nephew of an Exec. Hein was protected by his bloodline. Absolutely irrefutable proof would be required to bring him down.

Sloane hated the brat.

Pirates…his idiot troops…and now an Inquiry Review…

His enemies were everywhere.

Part One Resumed:
Premonitions of Circular Clouds

She was going about this all wrong.

Given the fact that no one would heed her warnings, Peri realized that she needed to find a way to capture one of the killer bots and bring it back to the Petrie platform. Then everyone would *have* to believe her!

She had no idea how to go about this, though.

She was going to need help.

Her first choice of co-hunter was Taz, but her lover was unsupportive of her plan. He reprimanded her for "taking this craziness too far", warning that she was going to get herself hurt if she continued to escalate her worry over these killer robots. At least he was polite enough to avoid condemning her obsession outright, for Peri was well aware of Taz's disbelief in her phantom machines. Although his opinion hurt her feelings, she accepted it, just as he accepted her unwillingness to rely on his money for her own livelihood.

When she confided her scheme to a few acquaintances, she learned how deep those friendships ran. No one was willing to credit her proposal with more than a wry smile and a condescending shake of their head. Peri remained unaware how widespread her odder reputation had become among the denizens of the platform.

Finally, she decided to approach Juul Ragle to assist her in capturing one of the deadly HeeVee robots. Her logic was based on the assumption that Ragle: one—should possess some familiarity with HeeVee technology; two—might still have his security officer pulse rifle (which could be very handy in overpowering a killer bot); and three—definitely owed her for getting the ex-cop to the Petrie platform. Besides, he was new to the freelancer community and might not have the same narrow-minded resistance to her story. Having just escaped from HeeVee's "slavery" (his words!), the man already knew what kind of worst to expect of the corporation.

No one answered at the dom cap Ragle had rented, so Peri started cruising the platform's bars in search of the man. She found him on her fifth try, hunkered down in the back of Millie's Tavern (a really nasty joint) with a grizzled old man who was introduced as Dirk Masterfield.

"I've heard of you," she remarked pleasantly. "You're one of the smugglers who keep the platform supplied with stuff."

"I've never thought of my cargo as 'stuff', Miz," the old man replied congenially.

"Smugglers and pirates," chuckled Ragle. "This is the life."

"I'm sorry," Peri blushed, "You, uh, you don't mind me calling you a 'smuggler', do you?"

"Girlie," Masterfield leaned forward with a twinkle in his eye (which *had* to be artificially induced), "I've been a *smuggler* longer than you been a girl."

She smiled, relieved that she had not embarrassed herself. Not only was she looking to impress Ragle with her veracity, she had nothing but respect for anyone who was willing to brave both Greye's export Authorities and HeeVee's proprietary blockade protecting the space around Baltuss. Without daring pilots like Masterfield, the Petrie platform would want for many basic luxuries.

"Juul here is quite the rascal too," Masterfield chuckled. "He's been asking me about acquiring a ship of his own so he can compete with me."

"Aw, hey, no," the ex-cop objected. "I'd never compete with *you*. I was just examining the exciting range of options open to me. There's not much excitement in bagging gas."

"You looking for some excitement?" she asked Ragle.

"What kind of excitement you got in mind, honey?" the ex-cop responded with a smirk.

She elbowed him in the side, "Keep it in your pants, soldier. I'm talking heroic kind of excitement."

"I can be pretty heroic in the sack—" he guffawed into a grunt as she elbowed him harder. "Okay, point taken. Ouch. I'll behave."

Hooking her feet unconsciously into the brace at the bar counter, she settled beside Ragle and began telling the man about her encounter with the mysterious-but-menacing robot down in Baltuss' clouds.

The ex-cop was dubious, but had to admit that HeeVee could be up to anything. "There's rumored to be a lot of classified projects running out of the Natt base."

She explained that these bots could only be a threat to the freelance divers, describing the monstrosity to support her fears. "They're nasty brutes, all armored and spiny like a pincushion. Yuck."

Masterfield listened without offering any comment.

"These things could mean trouble, huh?" Ragle commented.

"Every freelance diver is in danger of becoming a potential victim," she assured him.

"These robots you're talking about could be something innocent, you know," Masterfield offered. "Survey drones, or even stray pieces of equipment."

"If you had seen it, you'd know, Mr. Masterfield," she professed. "It looked like an angry insect, all pointy and malevolent."

"Somebody should do something about these things," Ragle declared. He pounded a fist into the palm of his other hand, a gesture that marked him as a child of dirt.

"My thoughts exactly!" agreed Peri. "And I have a plan! But it needs some help."

"Let's hear it, honey."

Invigorated by the moment, Peri revealed her idea of capturing one of the killer bots. "We can bring it back and show everyone. They'll have to believe they exist then."

"Sounds ambitious," observed Ragle.

"Sounds dangerous," Masterfield observed.

"Think of the glory," Peri intoned. "There might even be a reward."

"Ah!" cooed Ragle.

Gotcha, she cheered mentally.

Ragle turned out to be a bit of a control freak.

In retrospect, Peri should have expected no less from the HeeVee security-officer-gone-renegade.

She was too elated to argue with him. Anyway, his assault expertise was one of the valuable skills he brought to the partnership; taking charge was part of the role he played.

And what's my *role?* she wondered.

If Ragle was the muscle and the point man and the strategist and the insider intel, then what was Peri's function in this plan?

Well…I'm the one who came up with the basic idea and convinced him to get involved. Oh my God, she realized, *I'm the Machavellian manipulator—I'm the corporate Exec!*

Peri was eager to be about their mission, so they wasted no time. After stopping by his dom cap so Ragle could grab his old patroller equipment ("Never thought I'd need this stuff again!"), they launched from the platform's linear accelerator.

"Show me how to find the good music," Ragle begged her as their silvered bodies soared toward the gas giant.

"Red Sky Radio?"

"Yeah. Gimme that good old rock'n'roll, baby."

She guided him to the proper frequency, then advised him how to best tune into the pirate signal. She was amused by the fact that freedom was not the only benefit Ragle was enjoying now that he was liberated from HeeVee's employment.

Nimble-fingered fusion guitar seared over the airwaves, full of crisp reverb and slithering through catchy riffs with effortless glee. Dynamic drumming pounded along, while rumbling bass resounded like a vitreous oil-slick disturbed by the recoils of a pulse cannon. It was power rock, and its ripping pulsations filled the void with a positive energy. Personally, Peri thought the soundtrack validated their mission with its overt drama.

Ragle was thoroughly enjoying the music. "Back at the HeeVee lunar base, they don't have anything this good," he gloated. "Back there, they're always piping ugly marching tunes over the public address speakers. It's enough to drive a man loopy."

She agreed that life was a better place with Red Sky Radio along for the ride.

He probed for more intimate information about the radio station itself. "Who runs it? Where's their transmitter?"

"Nobody knows." She giggled, "But I think it's a safe guess that Red Sky isn't coming out of HeeVee."

"*That's* for sure!"

She told him that even people on Greye enjoyed Red Sky's broadcasts.

"No shit? That's an impressive signal." He was silent for a moment, then announced, "Naw, that's not possible. It's over six-hundred-million kilometers from here to Greye. They've got to be using multiple transmitters to send their broadcasts that far. They must have satellites in orbit around Greye."

She had never noticed that dilemma, but his deductions were probably true. Certainly the part about the distance between Baltuss and Greye. By the time the signal reached Greye, it would be fuzzy and garbled by the outwardly bound solar wind. No normal signal could maintain coherency over such a distance, not enough to enthrall an entire populace. Ragle must be right: Red Sky had to be simulcasting its music across the Cacio Trumpis system. Such an accomplishment implied a bigger operation than Peri had imagined for the radio pirates. Somehow, she had always pictured them as a small group of rebel divers who were really into music, messing around and goofing on HeeVee's strict no-fun radio policy. Like most counterculture activism, it was highly entertaining and, by its own choice, made no profit.

Peri was eternally grateful for the pirate station's existence. Their music gave her days depth.

Another song was playing now. From the meatier quality of the dense percussion, she could tell it was a modern slap tune. The melody's pace grew more frantic, as if each beat rushed to smother the next rhythm. The vocals were literally (and probably intentionally) unintelligible.

"They've got access to current releases," he observed. "This song here is from a recent album. I recognize it..." His voice flustered momentarily. "An ex-girlfriend sends me ripped copies of music. I guess I won't be getting any more shipments from her. She wouldn't know where to send them."

"You can get mail," she told him. "What do think we are at Petrie platform—savages? Smugglers like Masterfield make runs between Petrie and Greye all the time."

Baltuss was drawing near. The pair of stassed humans were still at least five hundred meters from the planet's atmosphere, though. Even so, the gas giant had become huge, eclipsing half the sky with its crimson vapors. It was as if they were falling toward an enormous wall in space. To their right, a swirl of ebony mists marred the planet's scarlet face. Luckily, their descent would bring them down far from the ferocity of this gigantic hurricane.

"Weird how I never heard about any smugglers while working for Harvest," the man remarked pensively.

"What reason would a smuggler have to work for HeeVee?" Peri laughed. "They're running cargo through Heevee's blockade, Ragle, not to the corporate base."

"Hey, the Corp is endlessly haranguing about the evil pirates and all the trouble they cause. Y'think they'd complain about the ones who keep those pirates supplied with fresh food and clothes and stuff. It's not like Harvest to overlook an opportunity to condemn its enemies." After a moment of silence, he muttered, "It's a miracle that Harvest hasn't bribed some ruthless smuggler to expose the location of the platform."

"The smugglers are on *our* side," she protested. "Out here, everyone is HeeVee's enemies."

"Y'think there're a lot of these smugglers?"

"I really don't know how many there are," she admitted. "You'd have to check with someone like Mr. Masterfield about that."

"Always room for one more, huh? Ripe market, growth potential."

"You're serious about becoming a smuggler, aren't you?"

"Like I told you, there's just not enough excitement around here. Don't get me wrong, I'm not unhappy—just bored." Ragle strained his voice to emphasize his boredom. "Bagging gas is such a monotonous way to make a living. I crave a more challenging career."

"Dashing pilot, running blockades and flaunting the law..."

"That too, yeah."

They both chuckled as they plummeted toward Baltuss' huge atmosphere.

"So," she whispered, "what's the plan?"

"Well, first you have to find us one of the things," Ragle advised her.

"Why me?"

They dove through dense mists now, several gas strata down in the planet's atmosphere. About them, the effluvium billowed like semi-liquid explosions, running from horizon to horizon like sinuous aerial rivers. The divers plunged through these vaporous swirls, leaving a wake of swirling eddies. If there had been visible light at this depth, their trails might have glowed with a chaos of fluid colors; as it was, the visible frequencies were decidedly murky, but their environment registered to their acute artificial senses in a variety of vivid frequencies. Amid this vaporous milieu, their stassed forms slid, mirroring their surroundings. Ragle was stark and sleek to Peri's augmented perceptions. She undoubtedly looked the same to him: silvered curves and supple limbs, her figure arched in descending flight through majestic clouds of alien origin.

"Cuz you're the one who found them twice before," he told her.

Ragle made sense, and that annoyed her.

"But—it's not as if I know where to look," she whined. "I stumbled on them by accident."

"So, let's have another accident."

"Don't be ridiculous, Ragle. I can't just call up an accident by sheer willpower."

"Okay—what do *you* suggest we do?"

The pair of hunters had paused and were hanging now in a nebulous concoction of oily orange peppered with streaming veins of luminous green.

"We wander around and hope to…"

"…run into one of the brutes by accident," he interrupted. "Then let's get to it."

They wandered, passing vertically and horizontally through the vast atmosphere in an aimless search pattern. At one point, she found herself in the spot she had first encountered the killer bot. She recognized the flow of gaseous tin. Ragle was skeptical about her assurances that this was the spot. Rather than press her claim and risk revealing too much of her hidden talents, Peri left her statement undefended. After all, there was no sign of any killer bot here now.

They moved on, cruising the clouds. As their weariness increased, their tenacity flagged. The fury of their outrage was not surviving, the search was dampening their fire. Ragle was beginning to grumble, and although she refrained from letting him know it, she was starting to share his irritated impatience. Back and forth they swam through Baltuss' luxurious mists, but each pass they made proved unrewarding.

Of HeeVee's murderous drones, there was no sign. But the clouds were far from empty, harboring a profusion of indigenous occupants. New to such things, Ragle expressed fascination in these novel lifeforms. He urged Peri to identify each species they encountered.

"Those are confetti fish," she told him. "They travel in swarms."

"Are they dangerous?"

She laughed. "How can anything be 'dangerous' to a person who's stassed-up?"

"Yeah…I guess that's true…"

"Anyway, none of Baltuss' lifeforms are what you'd call strong. Most of them are pretty fragile. A sneeze would tear them to bits…if you could sneeze on one of them, that is." She was feeling foolish, explaining fundamental drifter biology to someone who should know such things. How had Ragle spent his time diving for HeeVee and not encountered any of the creatures that populated the gas giant's vast environment? "I thought you were a HeeVee diver," she muttered. "How come you're so unfamiliar with the clouds?"

"I was a cop, not a diver," he pointed out. "The time I spent in this soup was devoted to hunting for pirates, not admiring the local lifeforms."

This struck Peri as a sloppy survival habit. It was advantageous to know one's environment, especially when that environment was so basically hostile to human survival.

"What're they?" called Ragle, pointing a silvered arm in the direction of another inhabitant of the dense clouds.

"That's a baby's paw blowtorch," she told him.

"Who the hell came up with these silly names?" he grunted, unable to stifle an adolescent giggle.

She surprised him with a serious answer, for this was a subject with which Peri had meticulous familiarity. Her long hours diving in Baltuss' clouds had sparked a personal curiosity about the diverse and weird species that shared her alien playground. After much research, she was actually somewhat of an expert on the gas giant's biota.

"When humanity first came to Baltuss," she explained, "all these creatures were discovered and given ridiculously complicated names by the scientists who comprised those exploration surveys. Aero-this and ichthyo-that, stringing together tongue-twisting syllables that would even befuddle intellectuals. So incredible were some of the creatures they found that new phylums had to be created to accommodate the unusual lifeforms. Making matters worse, each member of a discovery team wanted to inject their own name into the creature's technical label, hoping for immortality in some ob-

scure galactic textbook. Some of the names they attached to the poor drifters are so long that you need to pause for a breath halfway through saying
them."

The classical music which Red Sky was currently broadcasting was a
suitable accompaniment for her casual lecture. The melody even conveyed a
subtle bestial undercurrent, matching the biological nature of her discourse.
Horns blared like the trumpeting of wild elephants. Swarms of violins filled
the mix with a cerebral buzzing. Fancilful piccolos echoed down canyons
walled with library bookshelves.

"The 'silly' names, as you so whimsically put it, came later. They were a
product of the early divers who mined Baltuss' clouds. The divers were looking for simpler names to call the lifeforms that drifted through the gas giant's
vast atmosphere."

"Sounds like a smart idea," Ragle remarked. "Why'd they do such a silly
job of it?"

"Actually, the names they devised aren't so much 'silly' as 'straightfor-
ward'. They may not have been artfully clever, but the words they picked were
inherently quite accurate."

"Aw, c'mon. 'Baby's paw blow-ranch'?"

"It's baby's paw blowtorch. And it's on-the-nose, once you watch the
creature move along." She directed Ragle's attention to the beast as it chugged
its way through the mists.

The creature's body seemed to be a tangle of undulating tentacles until
one studied it for a moment. Only then did it become apparent that the nest
was actually a pair of appendage groups located at opposite ends of a squat
tubular torso. These nests convulsed with a rhythmic pattern, seeming to
squeeze the creature's bulbous cylinder with each constriction.

"So?" Ragle shrugged. "What am I missing?"

"See how the stumpy limbs wrap around its torso? Don't they resemble
the hands of an infant closing on a parent's extended finger?"

"I suppose..." he reluctantly conceded.

"Now look at how the creature's actually moving," she instructed.

With each constriction of the baby paws, the creature's torso was releasing a burst of gas which acted as a propellant.

"It's a windbag," Ragle grunted.

"The spurts are quite hot in reality," she told him. "Hence 'blowtorch'."

"It's still a silly name."

They encountered several more drifters, each one requiring identifica-
tion by Peri, but the hunters saw no killer robots in the clouds they traversed.

"Maybe they don't want to be found," Ragle muttered.

It had not occurred to Peri that the killing machines would have cause
to conceal themselves. Skulking, yes; but hiding? Wasn't their purpose to

seek out the freelance divers and—watch, hunt, slay—do whatever they were programmed to do? The behavior of both killer bots had been, now that she thought about it, highly uncharacteristic of a machine that was supposedly designed to search-and-destroy. Neither of the robots she had encountered had made any aggressive moves against her. Both bots had allowed her to escape alive. The second bot had even allowed Dezi to tinker with its hardware. *Gee,* she ruminated, *these bots are really pretty incompetent...*

"Maybe they've camouflaged themselves," she suggested.

"What—you think they're really there, but we can't see them?" There was a sudden, wary tension in the ex-cop's normally swaggering voice.

She had to agree—that was an excessively disturbing notion. They could be surrounded at this precise instant, swimming unaware in the middle of a swarm of invisible stalkers. If this were true, they were as good as dead.

But...nothing had attacked them. So, the bots weren't invisible and tracking their every move. Or...the killer bots weren't programmed to be hostile.

She giggled. Nonviolent killer robots—now, there was an oxymoron.

"Don't you go hysterical on me, girl," growled Ragle. "We could be in a mess of trouble here."

"I'm okay," she assured him.

"How do we determine whether they're all around us or not?"

"You can't prove an absence of something you can't see."

"Maybe...we should get out of here," he proposed. "Retreat and regroup and rethink this whole attack plan. We need to figure out a way to detect the things."

"But we haven't found one yet..."

"That's the point, Peri. We're not going to, either, not until we get ourselves a better plan."

"There *is* no better plan," she asserted. "All we can do is look until we find one of the bots. They're here." She paused, narrowing her eyes behind her silver stass-skin. "You're not starting to doubt they exist, are you?" That was it, she realized. His disappointment had become disillusionment, turning him into a disbeliever.

"If they're here, they're not going away. We can find them tomorrow." He had slyly avoided answering her accusation.

"They exist," she breathed.

But there was a modicum of wisdom in his suggestion. Their efforts had been fruitless so far. HeeVee's robots were hiding from them. Until a way was found to draw the brutes out, Peri and Ragle were just wasting their time.

The tension of their search and the frustration of finding nothing was occluding even her basic ability to enjoy the dive. How could she relax and appreciate the multicolored clouds when any bank of mist could be hiding one of the killer bots? Masked by its hypothetical stealth hardware, the things could jump out of nowhere and gut her and her companion without warning. Such suspicions did not generate any calm in her. Peri was wired and defeated by her inability to uncover any of the evil machines.

Reluctantly, she joined Ragle in an ascending spiral through the clouds. She was loathe to leave the atmosphere empty-handed, but there was no alternate recourse at this point. They had been exploring for hours without a hint of success.

Making casual conversation, Ragle was relating the details of his visit to Petrie platform's resident doctor. The ex-cop had felt that it was important to have his HeeVee Ident code removed as soon as possible, so as not to compromise the location of the pirate's secret base to the oppressive Corp.

Only half paying attention, she commended him on the sapience of that decision.

"I was worried that getting it out was going to be a hassle," he told her. "That the HeeVee implant might be too integrated into my physiology. But there were no probs with its removal."

Peri found this surprising, for Doc Petroff's ineptitude was no secret aboard the platform. His coarse libido had hardly endeared the man to any of the divers, male or female. Peri herself disliked the way Petroff's eyes were eternally hungry, always roving across her bosom and rump as if sizing her up for some imaginary intimacy. The doctor's gaze was the most uncomfortable she had ever encountered in her life. His look conveyed a foul uncleanliness that made her feel dirty without provocation.

"I never got to see the doctor," Ragle remarked. "A nurse handled the whole procedure."

"A nurse?" Peri was unaware that the doctor had hired any staff.

"I got the impression she was new. A real looker too."

Anything that might distract Ragle's amorous advances from Peri was worthwhile in her opinion. She liked the ex-cop, was willing to overlook his enemy-camp background, but his charms and physique did not strike a chord with her personal tastes.

He was a stumpy man, his bones wrapped in pudgy flesh that he wore with an aggressive disposition, as if daring anyone to accuse him of being chubby so that he could explode on them to display his hidden strength. When not obscured by the silvered veneer of an active stass-skin, Ragle's face exhibited a slight cruelty that Peri found unnerving. A pair of wickedly deep vertical furrows habitually wrinkled his brow between his heavy eyebrows whenever something perplexed him. She had finally convinced herself that these lines of suspicious disapproval that creased his forehead and flanked his mouth were leftovers from the man's servitude to the corporation; given time, she expected his face would relax and he would lose this haughty expression. From his verbal idioms and his physical mannerisms, Peri knew he was originally from Earth, but she could detect no trace of any accent in his voice to pinpoint his birthplace more specifically. His burly features and thick black hair made her suspect he carried a degree of Italian blood in his veins, but then "Ragle" was hardly a Mediterranean name—she had no idea what nationality had spawned the name, in fact. If anything, his given name implied African roots. Ultimately, a person's ancestry meant very little among spacer communities. Living in the void generated a kinship that ignored geographic or cultural heritage, celebrating a new brotherhood defined by braving the harsh ecology of the vacuum. Ragle had used to be a grounder, and he had used to work for HeeVee, but now…whether he chose to become a pirate diver or smuggler pilot, the man was a spacer.

He was still talking about Petroff's new nurse. Her name was Denise, and she had only recently left the dirt behind. Apparently, according to Ragle's estimation, she had the cutest face with such huge blue eyes. He revealed that he found her sturdy build more appealing than the willowy physiques of the women he had found at the Natt base or the Petrie platform. Denise's wide hips reminded him of home, or at least of the girls he had bedded in his youth.

So enraptured was Ragle with his amorous recollections, that the ex-cop flew right past the robot without noticing it. He saw Peri hit it, though.

It was not the first time she had ricocheted off one of the killer bots, so—after the initial surprise of the impact—she was not unfamiliar with the tumbling rebound.

As if somehow attuned to what was going on down in the clouds, the music playing in her ears took a dramatic turn. Each instrument plunged up the scales to wail with startled exclamations. The orchestral crash mutated into an electronic squeal, piercing and emphatic in its sonic anguish.

As she overcame her gyroscopic disorientation in the mist, Peri heard Ragle exclaim, "Where the hell did *that* come from?

"Quick!" she cried. "Shoot it!"

"Damn," he grunted. "That's one of them, isn't it?!" With spastically uncooperative fingers, he fumbled his pulse rifle from its place on his utility belt.

The confrontation lasted only half-a-minute at most, but the moment stretched into a slow-mo dissection in Peri's augmented perception.

The man's weapon swung into play with agonizing lethargy. The rifle was sleek and designed to be held by a single hand. Since it was an energy discharge weapon, there was no recoil to disrupt the shooter's grasp. Everyone called them "rifles", but they were more comparable to bulky revolvers. The gun's nasty pulse charge was contained in a small battery that clipped into the top of the chassis. The majority of the weapon's mass was devoted to containing and ejecting the charge once a shot was fired. This action was achieved via a traditional handgrip and pull-trigger arrangement. The gun's nozzle was a tapering funnel of squat construction.

Ragle's silvered form glistened with an optical life of its own. Arcs of free electricity were dancing about him, the entire region was alive with the lively discharges. Jagged bolts of current leapt between the surrounding clouds. This flickering luminescence sent vibrant trails swarming along the mirrored surface of the man's body as he tensed in response to the sudden discovery of the enemy.

In slow-motion, the twisting lightning bolts became an electrical forest of glowing fracture-lines. They bisected space, delineated the region in a puzzlework of chaotic chunks of existence. As their slow undulations progressed, these spatial chunks contorted, their shapes as liquid as the incandescent bolts that defined their oozing quadrants. The pale orange clouds of this strata gave the scene the impression of being inside the heart of a star.

Even the soundtrack provided by Red Sky Radio seemed touched by the stasis of the moment. The music flowed into a tapestry of minimal tonalities, generating a seamless continuity that defied progression or change. The synthesized drones pulsed with such lassitude that the harmonies drifted frozen in an immobile structure.

The menacing killer bot hung unmoving in the mists, its protruding spines seeming to waver as denser gas drifted by, briefly eclipsing the dark needles. The bot did not deviate from its sedate hover. The robot gave no indication that it was cognizant of the presence of the two humans or the threat they hoped to pose to its mechanical future. In fact, the thing gave no sign that it was aware of any part of its surroundings. Of all the aspects of the confrontation that were caught by Peri's artificial senses and elongated into a dramatic moment, the killer bot was the only component that displayed no motion. The spastic electrical discharges, the seething clouds, Ragle's quick-draw action—all these things moved, albeit at a decelerated velocity. The robot, though, was stationary, as if it existed outside of space and time.

This illusion was shattered as the pulse blast from Ragle's gun tore a hole in the bot. The shot ripped through the robot's corroded carapace and pulverized a section of the thing's internal apparatus. Debris drifted from the hole, then spewed like sharp vomit from the exit wound created by the force of the pulse blast. The robot shuddered under the violating impact, bobbing in the orange haze.

Peri grew aware that she was yelling, incoherently and with great volume. Ragle was shouting too. Their cries rang in each other's ears.

It was not until after Ragle had killed the thing that Peri noticed how the clouds' electrical discharges strangely avoided the bot's metallic shell.

"I got it!" cheered Ragle.

"Grab it before it falls or drifts away!" she urged.

"It's not going anywhere," he muttered. Nevertheless, he did reach out to grab the bot by one of its long needles, steadying the wobbling metallic shape. "I've never seen anything like this before." He turned to glance in Peri's direction. "Are you sure it was hostile?"

"Just look at it," she insisted. "It's got all those nasty pointy spines…"

"I don't see any actual armament on this thing," Ragle commented. "These 'spines' are only transmission antennas."

"It's a killer bot," she asserted with vehemence. "We dispatched it before it could attack us."

"The only way this thing could've hurt us is if we impaled ourselves by accident."

"It's dangerous. At least, it *was* dangerous…"

"Stop!" a new voice resounded over Peri's comm-link.

"Huh?" she heard Ragle grunt. "Who's that?"

"I'm too late, aren't I?"

A blur appeared at the periphery of the farthest range of Peri's scanners, taking human form as it approached. She did not need subsequent readings to tell that the newcomer was stassed, there was no other way a person could survive the savage depths of Baltuss' dense atmosphere. The raspy voice was familiar too. A second before he spoke again, she realized the man was Dezi Annucci.

"Dammit, you didn't have to shoot it up." He swooped in to examine the mechanical corpse. "Once I heard what you were planning, I came to head you off, but I didn't know which unit you'd find."

"Dezi!" Peri cried.

"You know this guy?" asked Ragle. His tone communicated his mounting suspicion.

"Do you have any idea how expensive one of these things are?" Dezi spat. He had ceased probing at the drone's severe wound, and was now facing the girl and her ex-cop companion.

"That's the Corp's worry, not ours," Ragle replied triumphantly. "If nowhere else, we hurt them financially."

"Correction, idiot—*I'm* the one who's going to have to afford repairing this unit." Dezi shook with barely restrained fury. "Who is this dirt-head?" he demanded of Peri.

"Who you calling a 'dirt-head'?" the ex-cop bristled. His hand tightened on the grip of the pulse rifle he held.

"This is Ragle," Peri introduced the man to the oldster. "He's helping me capture one of the killer bots."

"Dammit, girl," Dezi growled. "They're *not* killer bots!"

"Hold on," Ragle interrupted. "You claim this thing belongs to *you*? What—are you in league with HeeVee or something?"

The old man laughed hoarsely. "Not likely, dirt-head."

"And we're supposed to believe you because you say so?"

"You're starting to really piss me off, punk," Dezi snarled. "You have no idea how much trouble you've caused."

A part of Peri suddenly realized that the musical voice of Red Sky Radio had stopped. Somehow, the fragments fell together in her confused mind, and she understood the horrible scope of what they had just done.

"It's not a killer bot, is it?" she muttered. "It's a transmitter."

She had gone about this all wrong.

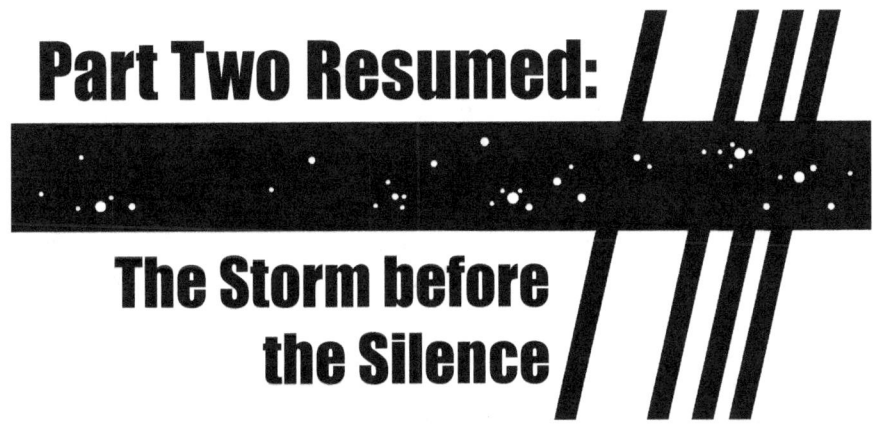

Part Two Resumed:

The Storm before the Silence

Some schemes were paying off.

Once he had disabled all the covert spy-eyes and assured himself that the corridors were clear of any pedestrians, Theo Sloane slipped from his concealment and strolled up to the door of Mr. No-Names-Please's quarters. He did not press the call button, instead he slid his all-pass chit through the door's lock apparatus. The Security Domo was instantly admitted without any fuss or warning.

Inside, Sloane paused a second. As his eyes adjusted to the dim lighting, he frowned at the gloom. Not half-an-hour ago, Sloane had witnessed Caffino retire to his rooms. Why were the lights off? Was the tech already asleep? In the middle of the day?

He edged carefully across the room, his ocular radar steering him around the tech's modest furnishings. The apartment was cluttered with crates of textbooks and ragged circuitboards. It was obvious that Caffino entertained few visitors. A faint heat trail guided the Security Domo toward the sealed doorway that led to the tech's bedroom. At that plastiform barrier, he paused again to listen for signs of activity within the sleeping chamber. Perhaps Caffino was with a lady friend who had arrived before the tech or his shadow. But the only sound Sloane's augmented hearing detected beyond the door was the wheeze of a single occupant's breathing. He noted, though, that the breathing was not even or slow, in fact it seemed deep and ragged.

Even better, Sloane smirked. *Not only do I catch him unaware, I catch him in an embarrassing moment.*

The Security Domo had decided the time had come for his pathetic little spy to produce something more tangible than detailed progress reports concerning Project Godbreath. Knowledge about the classified research project had stimulated Sloane's imagination. He wanted more than information this time. Toward this goal, he had decided that his best course of action was to accost the paranoid tech/spy in his quarters. By threatening the man in what was normally the safe privacy of his lodgings, the Security Domo expected to intimidate Caffino into doing the unthinkable.

Let's do this while his pants are still down, Sloane urged himself from his reverie.

Sliding open the door with a sharp snap, Sloane strode into the bedroom. "You have a surprise guest," he announced. He slapped the light switch beside the doorframe, banishing the darkness to reveal Caffino's form reclining on the foam slab.

The sudden illumination brought Algol Caffino alert. He sat up on the bed, dragging a pair of headphones from his ears as he gaped at the intruder.

What's this? Sloane grunted, ignoring the man's stumbling surprise. The tech was fully dressed. He was not involved in any intimate impropriety… or was he? A degree of shame tinged Caffino's startled expression. He had been doing *something* improper. Sloane took quick stock of the room and the man's personal possessions. Everything seemed innocuous enough, the type of junk a physics technician would keep around: uneven stacks of textbooks and ragtag log reports, 600dpi color printouts of metallurgical scans pasted on the wall, a collection of newage abstract blocks scattered on the bedstand, clothing surprisingly distributed in neatly folded piles, grooming apparatus poking sloppily from the drawer of a bedside console.

The damning clue to Caffino's vice was auditory, though, not visual. Music squealed from the headphones that hung around the man's gulping neck. Melodies that were far too uptempo and raucous to be from Harvest's approved selection.

He's listening to unsanctioned music, Sloane realized.

He interrupted Caffino's feeble objections to the Security Domo's intrusion. "That's Red Sky, isn't it?"

"What I do with my off-duty time is my own business," the tech responded with clumsy bluster.

"Not as long as you're under contract to the Corp, Caffino. Everything you do is my business." He stooped to flick the man's chin with a stern finger. "You could be a *security risk.*"

Mr. No-Names-Please edged back uneasily on the bed. Suddenly, he became aware of the music coming from around his neck. He reached over and switched off the bedside console, silencing the rock'n'roll. His face was drenched with guilty sweat by this point.

"What do you want with me?" Caffino wheezed.

"A research technician like you, don't you have any imagination? Surely a creative intellect such as yourself can guess why I'm here."

"I've given you all the data there is," the tech whined. "What more can you want?"

"I want a sample," Sloane told him coldly.

"You're insane! I can't get a—" His response became a high-pitched scream as the Domo advanced on him. Sloane pulled the tech from the bed by his hair and dragged his head halfway up the wall. His lunatic mask growled centimeters from Caffino's cringing face. "When I tell you to do something, you thank me for the honor. And then you *do as I tell you!*"

Mr. No-Names-Please moaned and sputtered wordlessly.

"You have two days," Sloane warned the wretch. "And if you think any of this is negotiable, you need to have your hearing adjusted. All that illegal music has scrambled your brain."

He left the technician with one ear intact.

Pleased with the way the encounter had gone, Sloane took the long way back to the offices of his Security Department. His detour took him through a crowded concourse filled with needy shoppers bustling from store to store. Pausing at the rail of an elevated balcony, his relaxed thoughts were suddenly troubled by a strain of music filtering up from the crowd that filled the busy concourse. It wasn't the same rock'n'roll he had heard in Caffino's bedroom, but the symphonic swells were just as unsanctioned.

Red Sky Radio again. This time, the transgression was public. Someone in the crowd was playing the illegal music for other people, involving them in the criminal offense. Sloane shook his head, appalled at the brazen violation.

Pirates were an exhausting adversary for Sloane's depleted security forces. The trespassers frustrated the efforts of his troops, constantly eluding capture. But at least with the sneak thieves there was a physical presence to pursue. When it came to Red Sky Radio, though, it was simply hopeless to combat a signal in the air. There was no effective way to block or jam the pirate transmission, not without severely disrupting Harvest's own communications network. The radio pirates invariably eluded the interference by switching their broadcasts to another waveband, and within a day, word had spread, notifying their audience of the change. The signal came from too many sources, its actual point of origin was impossible to determine. As to the masterminds behind the illegal radio station, his intel told Sloane that not even the pirates knew who operated Red Sky. It was like a disease: its infection rate was incredible, and it swiftly adapted to hostile environments.

Getting rid of the pirates was difficult enough. Silencing the voice of Red Sky was an impossible endeavor. The damned pirate signal seeped in everywhere, tempting the workers with its seditious music. It annoyed Sloane that he was exerting maximum effort to chase trespassing ghosts, while this sonic invasion crept deeper into the base, captivating new listeners every day. And there was nothing he could do to stem the increasing tide of converts who were discovering the pirate station's illicit music.

Several schemes had been proposed over the years to silence Red Sky Radio, but none had ever succeeded. If things went according to his plan, though, Sloane might be able to eliminate the pirates and their unlawful music.

Personally, Sloane couldn't have cared less about music. Rock'n'roll, jazz, classical, electronic, even Harvest's authorized marching band tunes—they all meant nothing to him. He had no interest in music, so he had no taste to be offended or appeased. The rules dictated loyalty to the Corp's authorized music; as Security Domo, Sloane was sworn to uphold those rules without question or leniency. If tomorrow, the rules changed to demand that everyone listen to Red Sky Radio, Sloane would enforce that edict with equal determination. To him, it was a job, no more and definitely no less.

Although he was not consciously aware of it, Sloane's feelings for the people behind Red Sky were hardly that mercenary. These people were more than criminals—they were *pirates*. Should he ever find himself forced to accept Red Sky Radio, his heart would still long for the painful deaths of every individual who contributed to the station's broadcasts, just as he dreamt of personally eviscerating each freelance diver who violated Harvest's exclusive cloudspace.

He sighed, resigned to the futility of tracking down the offender in the crowd below. The only way to make sure of reprimanding the actual culprit would be to apprehend and punish every member of the crowd, for he could guess that no one would finger the insurgent without severe coercion.

As he sighed, the music abruptly stopped—and was replaced by a coarse growl of static. Sloane nodded smugly, pleased that the offender had come to their senses. Or possibly it had been another worker who had silenced the illegal music, convincing the offender of the error of his ways. Either way, it was reassuring to see respect for the rules prevail.

Walking away from the balcony, he failed to notice the groan of disappointment that spread behind him through the crowd in the concourse.

A disturbance seemed to be going on inside the Security Office. As Sloane pushed open the doors, the uproar spilled in his face, forcing him to wince.

The reception area was alive with shouting officers. They grew aware of Sloane's presence, and turned to bellow at him. Their fervor, he could see, was not one of anxiety. They were cheering.

"Have you heard?"

"Red Sky's off the air."

"We've won!"

Some schemes were paying off.

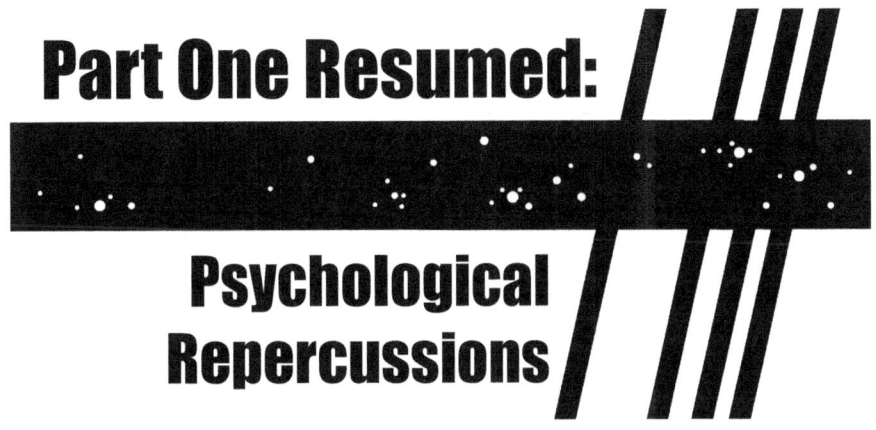

Part One Resumed:

Psychological Repercussions

There were so many things for Denise Coleman to learn about life aboard the Petrie platform.

Her time was painfully divided between adjusting to these new routines and sorting through the chaos of the station's mismanaged medical records.

Erin Lansky's whispered allegations had barely touched upon the actual depths of Ivar Petroff's incompetence. The man's medical acumen was shamefully lacking. And, as she had discovered from his relentless, crude advances, the Doctor was so full of himself that there was no chance of him recognizing his inadequacies—professional or personal.

While attempting to organize the medical office's files, Denise had encountered numerous glaringly inaccurate diagnoses. Glandular disorders dismissed as common rashes. A blatant tendency to over-medicate the simpler ailments. Why, one man had been told that he had bone cancer, when the truth was that Petroff had misread the test results, making a mistake that even a novice intern would have caught. Everywhere Denise looked, the Doctor's errors were legion.

Her attempts to contact the misdiagnosed cancer patient had been fruitless so far. The man must be down in Baltuss' clouds, beyond the range of the platform's communications web.

Adding to her distractions, the medical office had been packed all morning with people complaining of hearing loss. When she asked Doc Petroff about this strange epidemic, the man had smirked and explained that they were all crazy. "There's nothing wrong with their hearing," he remarked. "They just can't access that stupid pirate radio station. It must finally be off the air...and good riddance." The arrogance of his statement did little to assuage Denise's concerns.

Maybe, she thought, *the time has come for me to file a report with Admin regarding the Doctor's incompetence. It's literally life-threatening to have such a buffoon supervising everyone's health.* If something was not done about Petroff, someone was liable to die as result of the man's ineptitude.

There were so many things to learn about life aboard the Petrie platform.

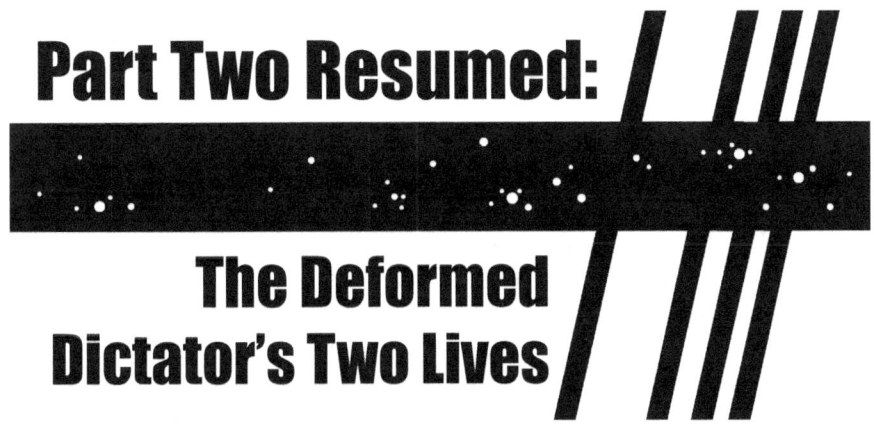

Part Two Resumed:

The Deformed Dictator's Two Lives

Beset by the severest misfortune, Uwu survived…with a vengeance.

To understand the devious psyche of Pa'dash Uwu, one must look to the man's state of health, not his traditionalist Raga upbringing. His affliction was the root of the man's madness. And that madness had crushed all trace of his pacifist philosophies.

The Uwu that everyone saw via the Exec's vid-casts had not existed for nearly a decade. That Uwu had aged slightly through the subtle alteration of the CGI program that constituted the man's public face. Practicing corporate paranoia, Uwu never interacted with any other individuals, conducting all his business and activities through electronic proxy. No one ever knew that this video persona bore no resemblance to the abomination the Exec had become.

Fifteen years ago, Pa'dash Uwu had been diagnosed with a rare case of leprosy. The Corp's medical officers were at a complete loss to explain how the Exec had contracted this incredibly rare disease—much less in the closed environment of the Corp's base on Natt. For some strange, unspecified reason, inquiries into the origin of Uwu's affliction were ceased, and the files were sealed. (Officially, they were "sealed." In reality, they had been "deleted" long ago.) Using his corporate wealth, Uwu summoned medical specialists from all over the galaxy. For six years, these experts scrutinized the afflicted man, probing and scanning and biopsying and irradiating and taking more tissue samples from his already dwindling body. Inevitably, the specialists could offer no means to halt the disease's cellular rot. In the end, Pa'dash Uwu simply rotted away. He refused to die, though.

Through video trickery, he kept himself alive to the public. He found other ways to perpetuate his real flesh. More tissue samples were taken, and once these pieces of his flesh had been genetically wiped of the leprosy, they were subjected to growth hormones and an attempt was made to clone Pa'dash Uwu.

When Uwu awoke in his new body, there was good news and there was bad news.

The good news was that he had woken up at all. The transference of his mind and personality from his near-corpse to his new body had been successful! His life would go on past the failure of his withered original body. Why, using this method, he could live forever.

The bad news was that the genetic wash had been flawed. His tissues had not been purged of the horrible disease. Worse—the genetic wash had screwed with his DNA, leaving his cells with unclear directions of what they were supposed to grow into. His cloned body was a hideous malformation of boneless meat with an exposed brain growing like a tumor from its mottled flank. It measured a meter in diameter, weighing no more than a healthy canine. It had no limbs, but it did have a mouth that attached to a rudimentary digestive tract. Uwu's sight needed to be artificially restored with neural jacks. He was a monster! And—using this method, he could be a monster forever!

(Wait, it gets worse.)

Uwu may have been a monster, but he was still thinking, breathing, aware and able to communicate. He was still alive! His new body might be a monstrosity, but at least he still had a corporeal vessel to house his vital intellect.

But that body was still tainted with leprosy, which was slowly eating away his lumpish new flesh. His only salvation lay in the constant growth of fresh tissue by artificial means, forcibly replacing his bodyparts as they decayed. To achieve this process, his grotesque new body was installed in a grow booth. Through electronic networks, Uwu was kept alive and in contact with the universe-at-large.

Beset by these severest misfortunes, Uwu survived. He was determined and courageous and rich and powerful enough to achieve this wretchedly aberrant continuance. The struggle changed him, but it did not make him evil. He was already an unethical deviant. The traumas he suffered only increased the degree of his fundamental depravity.

Every medical specialist who had labored to save him was assassinated. Each technician who had worked to give him new body was slain. All traces of the fabrication of his salvation grow booth were destroyed, along with everyone connected with that construction. Eradication of all evidence of the true nature of Uwu's flesh was relentless and absolute and prevailing.

From the confines of his grow booth, Pa'dash Uwu fought his way to the position of dominant Executive on the Board that managed the Corp's Baltuss operation. While he conducted scathing business negotiations via vid-casts, a myriad of robotic tools amputated newgrown portions of his body and transplanted that healthy flesh to replace areas that his disease had eaten away. His eyeless body was subjected to a ceaseless bath of radiation that would fry a normal human being. Had this new body's network of nerve fibers not been surgically disconnected from his brain stem, the agonizing pain of simple existence would have shattered his already-diseased sanity. He schemed and plotted, and he remained unconcerned that his physical mass changed appearance on a daily basis from the never-ending rearrangement of body tissue.

His attention was habitually required to attend to more profitable matters than his hideous profile.

There were hundreds of illegal and highly volatile research projects being conducted throughout the Natt base. Most of these projects belonged to Uwu. His most maniacal fantasy could spark the creation of a wild new research project…like finding a cost-effective way of killing matter. The Exec was quite insane by this point, and emphatically homicidal. He was always looking for new ways to inflict suffering or simply destroying things for the sake of destroying them.

He also practiced this egocentric pathology in his business judgments. His deals were brutal, and often insulting to the buyer…but the victims always signed the contract when the deadline came. His ruthless nature was infamous; only a suicidal fool would dare to cross him.

To earn this aura of absolute intimidation, Uwu regularly indulged in wanton assassinations among the Boards of rival interstellar corporations. He took to punishing the flimsiest slur with a grisly demise. His vengeance was excessive and indiscriminate.

Acting through a vast network of artificial and organic agents, Uwu's wrath could manifest anywhere across the galaxy, without warning and often without justification. His eyes were everywhere.

He knew that Security Domo Theo Sloane had met with a technician assigned to Project Godbreath. The passage of classified files between the men had been noted.

Uwu also knew that Teid Hein, the unsavory nephew of that spineless Exec Bester, was spying on the Security Domo. Hein's rivalry with Sloane was no secret to the mutating lump of ugly flesh. It would not take Hein long to uncover whatever Sloane was doing.

This did not fit in with Uwu's overall plan. Hein was a useful tool, albeit a bit ambitious. But Uwu saw more promise in Sloane. He was depending on the ex-war hero's vicious anti-pirate animosity to blossom into a bloodbath that would someday exterminate all troublesome trespassers from Baltuss. Eliminating the brazen freelance gas-thieves was more important than any personal vendetta bratty Hein was carrying around.

Considering how Uwu treated unintentional slander among the general public, his ire was quite intense when it came to those who publicly flaunted the regulations he had set down to govern the territories immediately under the Exec's control. These freelancers were fools to reject employment with Harvest, and they were insane if they imagined that the Corp would tolerate their persistent thievery. No amount of judicial leniency on the part of Greye's interfering government was going to save the pirates from Uwu's malevolent punishment. Whether by Sloane's zealous hand, or the handiwork of the spies Uwu had aboard the freelancers' pathetic hideout, the Petrie platform was guaranteed a terrible doom.

The more people that died, the happier the deformed Exec was.

Beset by the severest misfortune, Uwu survived...with a vengeance..

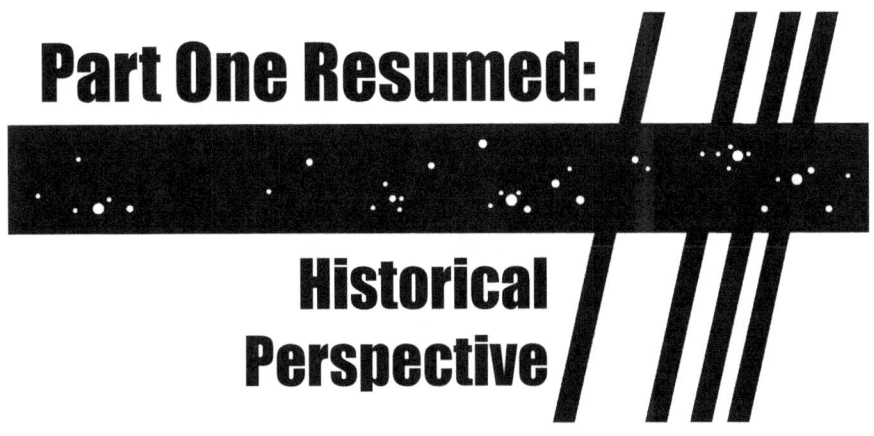

Part One Resumed:

Historical Perspective

This much was obvious.

For over two decades (specifically twenty-two years and four months, as reckoned by Earth Standard Days, the unit of time measurement mankind irrationally persisted in impressing on each alien district visited by humanity), Red Sky Radio had always been there. Entertaining the freelance masses and everyone else within hearing. HeeVee had struggled long and hard to silence the pirate station—scouring the vacuum in the vicinity of the gas giant for the station's secret transmitter, jamming the airwaves with everything from Sousa marches played at the wrong speed to an endless stream of self-promotional adverts. None of the corporation's vile schemes had managed to interrupt the pirate broadcasts.

It had taken a witless girl hunting delusions of killer HeeVee robots to silence Red Sky.

Dezi wanted to condemn Peri Fairchild, but the old man knew that he was partially to blame. He had planted the seed of his undoing when he had told the girl the rumor about the "killer bots." She had grown increasingly obsessed with that bit of modern folklore, until it had dominated her waking desires.

Spreading unsubstantiated rumors had become Dezi's hobby over a decade ago, a casual amusement intended to spice up what he had perceived as a doldrum stretch on the platform. This verbal vice had entertained Dezi so much that he had never abandoned the pastime. In ten years, he had passed along thousands of wild tales, often jazzing them up with seditious embellishment if he didn't just concoct them from scratch himself. The more outlandish the rumor, the wider and quicker it would spread. He had swelled with pride when some of his better fictions had come back to him years later from sources off the platform.

Over time, Dezi had refined his rumormongering to an art-form. He knew the wisdom of keeping the stories simple, allowing others to flesh them out in the retelling. He kept tabs on the temperament of the divers, their moods, faves and dislikes, in order to customize his tales to appeal to popular trends. If a chance storm on Greye spoiled crops, depriving the Petrie platform of fresh fruit, it helped to deflect the divers' ire from the unfortunate farmers, redirecting animosity toward Harvest Corp and their endless parade of wicked schemes designed to undermine the survival of freelance competition. These kinds of conspiracy theories not only entertained the masses, they were socially therapeutic.

Never before, though, had one of his rumors come back to haunt him.

It's my own fault, he recriminated himself. *I should have given Peri an innocuous cover story when she stumbled across me updating that transmitter's packet of play disks. I should have seen that going along with her own explanation would cause problems.*

Already fixated on the killer bot rumor, Peri had instantly assumed that the transmitter was one of the fictitious deadly HeeVee machines. By failing to correct the girl's assumption, Dezi could see now that he had started the chain of events that had led to this disaster. If he had offered her a safer lie, everyone would have been spared this current silence.

Although this unit was only one of a series of devices hidden throughout Baltuss' dense clouds, it's abrupt destruction had brought about a system failure among the entire network, silencing the pirate signal in the vicinity of the crimson gas giant.

At least this crisis would be confined to the local network of transmitters. Red Sky's broadcasts would continue uninterrupted for the audience on Greye, for the transmitters orbiting the other colony operated as an autonomous system, separate from the original machinery concealed in the gas giant's atmosphere.

Some of that equipment had been in use for over twenty years, secretly lurking in the clouds and filling the airwaves with quality music. As required, Dezi had ministered to the needs of the machinery, repairing minor malfunctions and even replacing parts like the antennas, for they were forever exposed to the turgid mists' ethereal corrosion. Harvest Corp was hardly Red Sky's only enemy; erosion and circuitry fatigue were every bit as deadly to the radio station's operations. Frankly, Dezi was amazed that the network had lasted this long. In his opinion, upgrading the entire system had been necessary for quite a while. The only thing keeping him from doing this was poverty.

He was an old man now, no longer agile enough to bag the volume of precious clouds required to finance the purchase of new equipment. He also suspected that he lacked the stamina anymore to ferry the machinery piecemeal down into the clouds and reassemble the new transmitters among the clouds. It would be so much easier if he could conduct this reconstruction openly, lowering new equipment into the planet's atmosphere, but that would be suicidal as long as HeeVee remained vigilant and hostile. Assistants would be invaluable too, but Dezi was quite obsessive about protecting his secrets.

He had more than his share of those.

Under another name, Dezi Annucci had been born on Levin, one of humanity's farflung colony worlds. The circumstances of his escape from that planet were the oldest of his closely guarded secrets.

Levin was a ball of pulverized soil, a global desert without signs of surface moisture. Once, the planet had possessed vast oceans, as evidenced by the deep basins that girdled the equator. Scientific authorities postulated that a massive solar flare had vaporized Levin's waters centuries before mankind discovered the world. That cosmic wave had sterilized its soil of any trace of organic residue, burning off most of the atmosphere, leaving the desert world shrouded in a thin shell of inflammable and unbreathable ammonia. The planet harbored no valuable mineral deposits. It was too far off the gradually evolving interstellar shipping routes to have any value to commercial concerns. It even lacked any strategic potential for military use, for sadly (and endlessly to the frustration of Earth's Space Navy) no extraterrestrial species had ever been found to fulfill mankind's instinctive need for an enemy.

To anyone but a cunning bureaucrat, Levin was an utter waste of the outrageously expensive exploration ship that had discovered it. In a desperate attempt to keep colonization funding from losing public support, some nameless desk jockey suggested that the desert planet might serve as a offworld prison facility for criminals and madmen who were beyond possible rehabilitation. ("Giving *Levin* some *worth*" became a catch-phrase that made no sense to anyone who didn't know the history of the Old American penal system.) Somehow, this proposal grew into a popular cause in a United Nations election year.

And so: Levin became a prison colony.

Thousands, then millions of incorrigibles were shipped off to the dead world and dumped unceremoniously into Levin's global wasteland. There was no need of on-site guards to keep the prisoners alive, no need to even leave wardens in orbit to monitor the population. Their fates were unimportant to the rest of humanity. The prisoners were going nowhere—there were no ways off the desert planet. As far as most "law-abiding" people were concerned, exile to Levin was the equivalent of a death sentence without the unpleasantness of having to pull the kill-switch.

Individually, people can be quite intelligent; collectively, they can be quite naive.

The prisoners exiled to Levin did not die off. Well, a percentage of them failed to live very long—the crazies and the sex offenders—but the strong-willed ones rallied the survivors together. By diplomacy and by force, the remaining inmates transformed a rabble into a society. Water was found in underground pockets. Food was unearthed while digging for that water—in the form of subterranean fungus that flourished below the sand. Villages were built from the cannibalized remains of the drop capsules that had brought the prisoners to Levin. As more and more criminals were dropped into Levin's gravity well, the newly formed society grew. Villages expanded into towns, then into cities. Sympathetic outsiders smuggled technology to the prison colonists. Industrialization came to Levin, and several generations later, the Levinians developed their own space program, launching explorers back into the universe that had rejected their ancestors.

After nearly a century, Earth and the other colony planets were still dumping their undesirable lawbreakers on Levin. The rest of the galaxy seemed unaware of or unworried by the society that was growing on the desert world. The proper authorities took notice, though, when the prison colony started sending its own undesirables offworld.

Earth was forced to take action. Guard stations were placed in orbit around Levin, designed to shoot down anything that tried to achieve escape velocity from the prison world. Now, no criminals could sneak away from Levin and cheat their exile.

The terrible irony was not lost on some who realized that Earth and the other colonies were spending trillions of creds per annum to ship their criminals halfway across the galaxy. Then, while trying to escape this prison, a percentage of these exiles were fired on and killed by the orbital guard stations—constructed and maintained at astronomical expense. It would have been far cheaper to simply euthanize the convicts on their homeworlds.

The sad irony was that the individuals slain by the guard stations were not attempting to escape at all. They consisted of the truly undesirable offenders, the sickos and deviants that not even the Levinians would tolerate. Instead of dealing with these murderers and rapists themselves, the prison colonists gave them back and washed their hands of the consequences.

The hidden irony was that there were very few actual "criminals" to be found among Levin's surface population anymore. The descendants of the early exiles far outnumbered the influx of "new" prisoners. The smarter newcomers abandoned their antisocial behavior, motivated by the fact that those who didn't were ejected into space to become targets for the guard stations that ringed the planet. The average "citizen" of Levin was well-behaved and law-abiding.

The Levinians were very unhappy about the fact that they were denied access to the universe-at-large. Their objections went unaddressed by the galactic authorities.

Getting off Levin was a mythic achievement that remained undocumented for the obvious reason that anyone who succeeded in escaping the inescapable prison colony was not about to advertise their accomplishments and risk recapture and return to the desert planet. There *were* those who had achieved the impossible, though. Dezi knew this, for he was such a person.

Under *no* circumstances did Dezi ever discuss his origins.

When he reached civilization (specifically a settlement on one of the moons of Aert in the Bootes system), he took the name Donald Flint and earned himself a technical degree in the field of astrophysics. By his mid-twenties (he had escaped Levin in his mid-teens), Professor Flint was entertaining job offers from a variety of corporate fronts. Tasty projects and lucrative funding were dangled before the young scientist. He chose Harvest Corp, for they were offering him a position in cloud-mining research, a subject that had attracted his personal interest for years. Harvest Corp assigned him to their industrial complex on Natt in order that he have close access to Baltuss' atmosphere to pursue corporate research.

The fourteen years he spent working for Harvest Corp comprised another of Dezi's secrets. This was a double-edged secret, for he feared exposure by both the Petrie platform and HeeVee. The freelancers would condemn him if they ever learned about the procedures he had perfected for Harvest, while the Corp would come after him for running off with classified data when he had violated his contract and disappeared

The nature of the research he conducted for Harvest Corp was ethically questionable, but it had been the job's illicit property that had attracted him to take it. To have the opportunity to dabble with the transmutation of matter had lured his inquisitive soul with a passion that had sated his immature self. Now he reviled the fact that he had so cheaply abandoned his sense of decency. At the time, though, Donny Flint was quite full of himself and keen to show off his intellectual acumen. He attacked the research with his full vigor, an enthusiasm which he maintained for twelve of his fourteen years under contract to Harvest. His blind eagerness was killed by the discovery that the Godbreath contagion was being developed not for military or scientific purposes, but in accordance with an infra-corporate agenda. (What reason would a corporation that traded in raw material have to conduct research into methods of destroying matter? Such a process could only be profitable as warfare technology. All this intimated a vicious side that Harvest Corp kept hidden from the universe-at-large.) That discovery transmuted Flint into an enemy of Harvest, finally bringing about a reclamation of his long-lost ethics. He carefully plotted against the Corp from within. His position as a project co-director enabled him to secretly subvert all tests from that point on. The project began to fall out of favor in the fiscal eye of the Corp's Review Boards. Flint imagined that he had outwitted the corporation, defusing a destructive avenue of their research. He was quite surprised when the Board informed him that he was being removed from Project Godbreath and placed in a subordinate position working for the base's waste disposal department. All of the project's top staff were being replaced—with ambitious new technicians who would attack the problem with fresh approaches. The Corp's own rigid efficiency had sidestepped Flint's covert efforts, defusing his own sabotage. Flint responded by sneaking into the lab one final time. Before erasing every trace of data from the system concerning Project Godbreath, he made a copy for himself. Then, slipping out through the pipes of the base's waste disposal facility, he fled the Harvest outpost on the Natt moon and took refuge with the colony of freelance divers.

Professor Donald Flint ceased to exist, and Dezi Annucci came into being.

Unfortunately, Dezi lacked the funds to put interstellar distance between himself and his angry previous employer. He knew that the Corp would find him if he went to ground on Greye. No, if he wanted to elude HeeVee's malicious reprisal, he needed to find a more secure hiding place. The Petrie platform was the perfect solution for his dilemma. For several decades, Harvest had unsuccessfully labored to drive the freelance divers away from Baltuss' clouds. These trespassers had managed to elude the Corp's best and most aggressive efforts. Among these pirates, Donny/Dezi found escape and security.

Over time, he grew to appreciate that the Petrie platform was more than a pirate base for unlicensed divers. It was a community of independent adventurers who challenged the arrogant corporation's claims over every gas molecule contained in Baltuss' atmosphere. Their "piracy" was a declaration of freelance commercialism. Their bravery impressed Dezi, for by then he understood the harsh and spartan lifestyle endured by most of the divers who struggled to live aboard the rogue platform. In their own way, Petrie's Administrators were as greedy as HeeVee's Board. Under the guidance of Karel Danner's unscrupulous greed, Admin gouged the freelancers with outrageous dom cap rental fees and exorbitant prices for substandard nourishment. The platform's facilities were minimal in those days.

Dezi empathized with the divers' oppressed state, for he was being victimized by the same outrageous fees and exorbitant prices. The Admin-run Gas Exchange offered insultingly low remuneration for bagged clouds, then leached back those creds from the struggling freelancers.

When the HeeVee assault force struck in 2247, the Petrie platform was defenseless to repel the corporate troops. The freelancers were no match for trained soldiers. The Administrators were unprepared to handle such a crisis, for Danner had never anticipated an armed attack on the Orion Overnight Hotel. HeeVee's attack would have ended the colony's lifespan if it hadn't been for the brief return of Professor Flint.

Without a doubt, what Professor Flint unleashed was the most guarded of Dezi's secrets. Flint's terrible solution rid the Petrie platform of HeeVee invaders in a particularly unpleasant manner. Horrified by the consequences of his brazen action, he never consciously allowed the memory to cross his mind outside of feverish nightmares.

In a blatant showing of his true colors, Danner claimed credit for the coup. (Dezi never forgave Old Danner for that lie, but he kept his dissatisfaction unvoiced, lest anyone learn about his real identity and exactly how he had saved the platform.) In truth, however, the only part of the platform's salvation that was really Danner's idea was to run away as fast as possible. While the stunned HeeVee survivors of the assault squad watched from their crippled ships, the Petrie platform used its tiny stability retros to slip off into the void.

Undoing the damage and returning the platform to a comfortably habitable state took years. The process broke Danner's fortune and spirit, fragmenting his iron control of the platform into the hands of his greedy protÈgÈs. Meanwhile, the worst of times settled in for the freelance divers. With the platform's catapult disabled by the attack, there was no easy way for the divers to reach Baltuss' distant clouds. And even if they did, the Gas Exchange was in no condition to brokerage the bagged gas. At no time did Admin cut any of their customers a break; the new owners showed zero tolerance for anyone unable to pay their bills aboard the platform. These hardships forged the freelancers into a community.

It was during this worst of times that the idea of a pirate radio station occurred to Dezi.

While drunk on fungi-sterno one night, Dezi became involved in an epic gripe session with some buddies. They were all dissing HeeVee's obnoxious radio broadcasts and lamenting the pathetic musical content of those transmissions. Dezi was quite familiar with these oppressive broadcasts, for reasons he would never admit. At some point before he drank himself into unconsciousness, he wondered why no one tried to compete with the HeeVee radio station.

In the sobriety of the following morning, the question was still valid and unanswered. Over the next few days, he observed that the platform needed something to bolster its waning spirits. Reconstruction was troublesome and tedious, and everyone's mood was turning ugly. Even Admin's lame renaming of the platform failed to rally any community pride or bolster any freelancer's personal hardship. Dezi decided to secretly save the day.

Stealing the necessary equipment from an Admin supply depot, Dezi made the long dive to hide his first transmitter in Baltuss' clouds. Using a meager selection of tunes downloaded from public databanks, Red Sky Radio began broadcasting an alternative to HeeVee's dreary signal. The problem was: how to get people to discover the new transmissions. But while he struggled to concoct the right rumor that would announce Red Sky's existence to everyone—keeping himself anonymous and unconnected to the broadcasts—fate took care of his problem.

HeeVee's broadcasts were suddenly denouncing the presence of an illegal signal originating somewhere within range of Baltuss. This pirate broadcast was in flagrant violation of territory rights, and the Corp demanded that it desist immediately. Within twelve hours, every freelancer had explored the airwaves and found Red Sky's frequency. Their curiosity turned into delight. The pirate station was an overnight success...with the divers. HeeVee, however, fumed and ranted and vowed eternal harassment until the illegal signal stopped broadcasting.

Dezi was quite pleased with himself. He had succeeded in lifting the spirits of the freelancers. And at the same time, he had managed to drive an annoying thorn into the Corp's arrogant hide.

He revealed to no one that he was behind Red Sky Radio. By this point, secrecy had become a dominant part of Dezi's lifestyle. He saw no reason to deviate from that pattern. Besides, he was on the lam from HeeVee. Celebrity would only undermine his ability to avoid the Corp's vengeance—for his previous data-burn and flight, and now for masterminding the pirate station that was so infuriating the Executive Board. To guard his own life, Dezi denied himself the accolades of his peers. Unknown to everyone, the man they cheered skulked among the divers, carefully gauging their likes and dislikes, quietly basking in their profuse acclaim.

He learned the profile of his audience and applied that information to increase their enjoyment of Red Sky's broadcasts.

The music lifted the spirits of all the freelancers, even stirring the cold hearts of the Administrators. Positivism swept the platform, and stability returned to the community. Prosperity started to poke through the battlescars. The ruined catapult was replaced with a secondhand linear accelerator, and the freelancers were able to resume their dives on a more regular basis. And Dezi put every cred he could spare into increasing Red Sky's selection of music and purchasing the parts necessary to construct more transmitters.

After two decades on the air, Red Sky consisted of a network of fifteen transmitter satellites scattered throughout Baltuss' dense clouds. With the aid of smugglers who knew not what they ferried for the old odder, a similar series of transmitters soon orbited Greye too, offering those colonists access to the broadcasts. The radio station was entertaining every human in the Cacio Trumpis system, with the exception of the hardnoses at HeeVee's Natt base. Red Sky's earnest enemies were actually very few, for the majority of Harvest's divers and base personnel were closet fans of the pirate broadcasts. Appreciation for Red Sky Radio was widespread.

And the whole affair had been taken out by a girl obsessed with nonexistent killer robots. There was simply no way to plan for a thing like that.

Peering across the holed carapace of the wounded transmitter, Dezi scowled at Peri.

I have only myself to blame for this, he reminded himself. The recrimination did not ease his stress, though.

"I'm *sooo* sorry, Dezi," moaned Peri.

No amount of sincere apology was going to repair the damaged unit and bring the network back online. He refrained from pointing that out to the girl. Clearly, she had realized her mistake and felt bad enough about it. The time had come to put blame aside and focus on fixing the damage.

"Help me move the unit," the old man instructed the girl's companion. "I want to get it out of the atmosphere before the clouds corrode any exposed circuits."

Dezi recognized the man' equipment as HeeVee issue; he must have recently fled the Corp to join the freelance divers. Despite Peri's assurances, the old man was suspicious of this Juul Ragle. But—there was no one else to ask for help right now.

Together, the two men grabbed hold of the transmitter. Igniting their jets, they bore the unit into the murky orange heights. Peri followed them, still mumbling amends.

"Do you think you can, uh, repair the thing?" inquired Ragle.

"I have more immediate problems," Dezi sighed. "I need to get Red Sky broadcasting again."

"So…you're really the guy who's behind the pirate radio station, huh?"

There was no point in denying the obvious now. Later, Dezi would worry about finding a way to buy the silence of the girl and the ex-cop. The old man hoped that Ragle's defection to the platform was sincere, for if the man was still on Harvest's payroll, then Red Sky's secrets were destined to fall into HeeVee hands.

What could Dezi do if Ragle was a HeeVee spy? He was certainly not strong enough to overpower the ex-cop. Plus: Ragle had a gun, while Dezi was unarmed. No, if the man was a spy, then Dezi's safe haven was forfeit, and there was nothing he could do to prevent it. His only recourse was to trust that the man's loyalties no longer lay with the Corp.

"I guess that's a stupid question," Ragle grunted. "At this point, huh?"

"I'm…involved with the station, yes," Dezi admitted. If he kept it vague, maybe he could evade the man's probing curiosity. Implying that there were more personnel behind the conspiracy against Harvest—that was the wisest approach. "I'm just a grunt, though. Policy, playlists, integral knowledge of the operation—I'm not in-the-loop on that kind of stuff." *Make him think that Red Sky will live on if he chooses to capture me for the Corp.*

"Pretty cool job," the man remarked. "I'm new to the platform. I never got to hear Red Sky back at the HeeVee base. I wish I had. It's a pretty cool thing—the radio station and the music you, uh, they play."

"Hopefully there'll be more, once the network gets back up."

They had left the gaseous stratosphere and were guiding the damaged unit through rarefied vacuum now.

"I'd like to help if I can," Ragle told him as they paused in the void. "I feel kind of responsible, y'know?"

As he bent to examine the extent of the damage, Dezi replied that he could probably use all the help he could get.

That much was obvious.

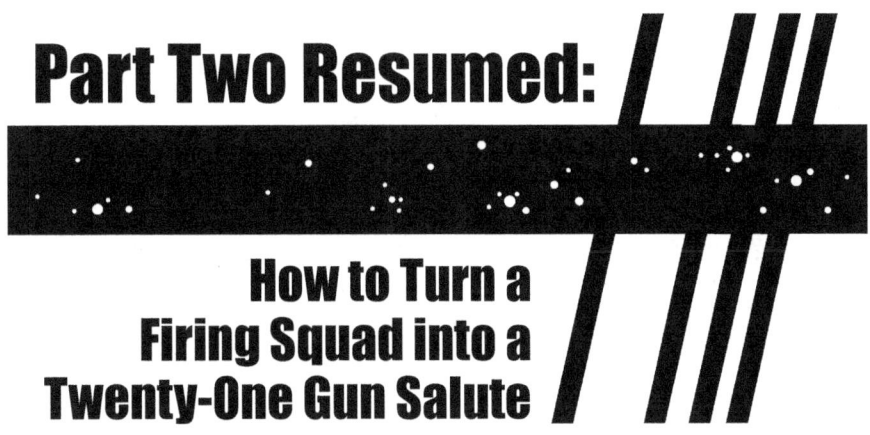

Part Two Resumed:

How to Turn a Firing Squad into a Twenty-One Gun Salute

Some farces must play out in order to defuse themselves.

An Inquiry Review had been initiated against Theo Sloane in connection with his decision to order a gatherer depot to return to base before the satellite's tanks had been filled to capacity. Although Exec Nigel Bester believed that his wretched nephew, Teid Hein, was behind the accusation, the complaint against the Security Domo had been filed on the Executive level, by Evelyn Hannigan.

Bester viewed this hidden link with some trepidation. Relations between the three Execs on Natt were hostile in every manner. If Hein was defecting to an enemy camp, then Bester could expect to find himself gutted by his nephew's treachery. The boy was privy to countless behind-the-curtain actions, for he had been the merciless instrument carrying out most of those unofficial disposals. Of all the skeletons in Bester's closet, Teid Hein was the biggest and the ugliest.

In typical Executive fashion, Hannigan and Uwu arrived late, later even than Bester who activated his desk fifteen minutes after the appointed time. They had probably been monitoring the Review chamber, waiting to see which of their rivals would lose political face by logging in first. Security Domo Sloane had arrived early and was fidgeting in the accusation seat. According to protocol, Sloane was the only flesh-and-blood participant present in the chamber for this Review; if he had any witnesses to support his actions, their testimonies would be on-disk and offered into record once the Domo had verbally submitted his own case.

Naturally, there was no sign of the Machiavellian Hein. Bester knew his nephew was observing the proceedings, though, using any one of a variety of spy devices "borrowed" from Bester's covert collection. At any time, the Exec could have neutralized this selection of secret devices, but doing so would have alerted Hein. Bester had no intention of warning the schemer that anyone was aware of his nefarious pursuits.

Bester knew that Hein considered him to be a doddering relic, perhaps even the weakest link on the Executive Board. Hein had never made any pretense of showing proper respect for his elder, his uncle, his employer, his superior. There was no doubt in Bester's wary mind that his evil nephew coveted an Executive seat on the Board.

A light on Bester's console revealed that Hannigan had come online. Ten seconds later, another light winked on, announcing that Exec Pa'dash Uwu was finally in artificial attendance.

Without preamble, Uwu called the Inquiry Review to order.

Safe in his private chambers in the upper levels of the base, Bester frowned at this breach of corporate etiquette. Since Hannigan had been the one to levy charges against the Security Domo, it should have been her who initiated the proceedings. This impropriety made Bester uneasy. Were both enemy Execs in league with Hein? Keeping his concerns to himself, Bester silently listened as Uwu recited the official accusation into record.

"What do you have to offer in defense of these unauthorized actions, Security Domo Sloane?" intoned Hannigan.

Another breach of protocol, Bester noted. While he had originally intended to voice his support of the Security Domo's actions, the cagey Exec was beginning to suspect that he needn't bother. If Hannigan and Uwu were rallied in alliance against Sloane, the Security Domo didn't stand a chance of surviving this Inquiry. On the other hand, if the two Execs continued to violate corporate covenant, the Domo might actually stand a chance of beating this rap without outside assistance, if only in appeal. Bester could not understand why they were conducting this Review in such a slipshod manner. There had to be more involved this time than Bester had discovered or deduced. In his private estimation, *that* suspicion was more worrisome than their unprecedented cooperation.

Two Execs in collusion, backed by the unscrupulous coercion of Hein— *there* was an enemy alliance capable of destroying Bester. Threats like this made him realize how trivial the pirate menace really was. The biggest danger to Harvest Corp lurked at the pinnacle of its own power structure.

Sloane was giving his report of the incident in question. Being familiar with the details of the Domo's official log, Bester paid little attention to the man's strong-voiced verbal account. The Exec's mind wandered through mental hallways filled with hypothetical threats.

Teid Hein: skulking in the shadows behind every curtain, armed with an insidious array of spy-eyes and deadly assassination devices. Alone or in a pact with the other Execs, Hein's growing lust for power had transformed

Bester's nephew into a professional liability that the Exec could no longer tolerate…or ignore.(Make this 'ignore… Or tolerate.)

Evelyn Hannigan: pursing her lips with mock interest and leaning forward to reveal her deadly cleavage on-screen. The woman held a special grudge against Nigel Bester, for the Exec ranked among the few men-of-importance who had spurned Hannigan's carnal temptations. Besides coveting Bester's corporate stock and powerbase, the woman lusted to see Bester degraded and destroyed for refusing her advances. Sooner or later, one of her schemes were going to take him out…unless he acted first.

Pa'dash Uwu: lording over the mining operation like a dictatorial spider, surrounded by impervious defenses accrued through years of seniority. The ex-Raga nationalist was probably the biggest threat aboard the Natt base. Although he did not abuse his power with public display, Bester knew that Uwu controlled most of the Departmental Domos. An attack from this enemy could come from any direction and never be traceable back to the cunning villain. As far as Bester knew, Uwu had no personal loathing for him; the ranking Exec's jealousy was purely professional…which was scarcely a consolation.

The Home Office: sitting in remote judgment of every decision, relentlessly increasing the quotas expected from the cloud-mining operation. For all the malevolent power wielded by the three Execs in residence at the Baltuss operation, they were insects compared to the corporate might and wrath of those who sat on the Home Board back on Mars. Fortunately, the Baltuss operation was proceeding smoothly, keeping its problems secret from outside scrutiny. There was no reason to expect intervention from that direction…unless something attracted their attention.

The Petrie pirates: trespassing among Harvest-owned clouds, stealing gas from the Corp. This threat was obviously the most insignificant, warranting little concern on Bester's part. The pirates were thieves, not assassins. They coveted Baltuss' clouds, not Bester's Executive Privilege. They were only parasites feeding on Harvest's mammoth as-yet-uncollected wealth. Even the bold raids they conducted, like the one Sloane was now recounting, were pathetically feeble actions, gaining the thieves scarcely an armload of stolen hardware. Harvest's losses were so trifling that no doctoring was required to hide them in any fiscal report.

"My squad encountered several pirates in the vicinity of the gatherer depot," the Security Domo was explaining. "Officers were dispatched to apprehend the trespassers. Although no captures were made, we did succeed in routing their assault team, preventing them from stealing any equipment from the gatherer." Sloane paused to regard each Executive's image on the screens that towered before him in the Review chamber, then he resumed, "Because we were unable to apprehend any of the pirates, there existed a strong chance that these thieves might return to plague the depot once my officers had left the area. Rather than leave the depot to be plundered by them, I ordered its immediate return to the Natt base."

"Without consulting with base," Hannigan remarked tersely. "You were unconcerned that the depot's collection tanks were nowhere near full."

"My priority," Sloane revealed, "was to prevent the depot from being cannibalized by the pirates. If they had returned, they might have even stolen the collected gases. Then—Harvest would have been left with a damaged depot with completely empty tanks."

"That would have been unfortunate," Hannigan conceded. "But it was not *your* decision to make."

"If I had consulted with base, Ma'am…would you or the other Execs have instructed me to risk everything and leave the depot down in Baltuss' atmosphere?"

Bester chuckled silently as the woman grudgingly admitted that the Executive Decision would probably have been to remove the gatherer depot from any potential vandalism.

Sloane utilized considerable restraint by not capitalizing on her admission. Instead he took a long breath, and spoke of something that did not immediately seem to be associated with the matter at hand. "As you are no doubt aware, my Department is rigorously searching to uncover the secret location of the pirate's rogue base. In the course of these investigations, some information has come to light."

"What does this have to do with our Inquiry?" Uwu snarled.

"Indulge me for a second, sir," Sloane smiled. "The data's pertinence will become apparent. It involves the intentions of the particular raiding party of pirates which my officers and I routed from the gatherer depot.

"We learned," he continued, "that the thieves were after the depot's comm circuits. Apparently, Red Sky Radio needed the parts to conduct repairs on their pirate transmitters. Deprived of these parts, the pirate radio station has gone off the air."

A hush dominated the Inquiry Review for a moment.

"Hindsight is no excuse, Domo Sloane," announced Pa'dash Uwu.

"Hindsight has nothing to do with it, sir," Sloane countered. "I was aware of this information prior to my encounter with the pirates. In order to insure that Red Sky's scheme be thwarted, I ordered the gatherer depot back to base. My actions not only saved the depot from being plundered, but it brought about something that the Board has been after for thirty years. *I silenced Red Sky Radio.*"

Nicely played, Bester noted. Sloane had cleverly saved himself by linking two unrelated incidents. The Board could hardly reprimand him now for saving the gatherer depot from being gutted by pirate thieves, especially if the stolen parts might have kept Red Sky Radio on the air.

Word about the abrupt cessation of the pirate radio station's signal had swept the base that morning. But Bester had known the instant it happened, for he had been listening to the illicit music in his private sanctorum. The silence had troubled him—not just because it implied that something was going on among the hiding pirates, but because it robbed the Exec of the music itself.

For several years, Nigel Bester had secretly become addicted to the pirate station's sonic offerings. Spurning the Corp's sanctioned marching band songs (abhorrent things, imposed on all employees by a demented official in the Corp's dim ancestry), Bester took solace in the versatile and evocative offerings found in the pirate broadcasts. His preference was rock'n'roll, especially the archaic classics that Red Sky played in the late mornings; the hyperactive hard rock music helped revitalize him for work.

As a closet fan, Bester had rarely initiated aggression against the pirate station. When one of the other Execs would voice their outrage at the continued existence of the station's sonic blight, Bester would casually draw attention to the latest trespasser and raid statistics. The Board would agree that the pirates doing the cloud-stealing were the ones that really needed to be stopped…and the threat of Red Sky would be forgotten for a while, downgraded to a simple nuisance.

But now—it was gone. And no one knew how or why.

Bester entertained no belief that there was any substantial connection between the potentially targeted depot and the mysterious silencing of the pirate station. Sloane was profiting off the coincidental proximity of these events. The man's spin doctoring skills were quite masterful.

You've found yourself a capable nemesis, Teid, Bester privately commended his nefarious nephew. *Sloane's ruthlessness might rival your own.*

In fact, the Security Domo might just deserve to be added to the threats stalking the Exec's overcautious mind.

Pa'dash Uwu was tight-lipped, Evelyn Hannigan was fuming, and Nigel Bester was feigning similar surprise. It was clear that Sloane had beat the rap with his nimble connect-the-dots logic. The evidence—real and illusionary—was stacked in the Security Domo's favor. The Board would have to go through the motions of "discussing these developments in camera", but there was no question of a complete exoneration for the accused.

Some farces must play themselves out in order to defuse.

Part One Resumed:

The Fruitless War Council

Peri knew it was a stupid question, but she had to ask it. "What are we going to do?"

Dezi Annucci hissed at her, reminding Peri that he would discuss nothing while they were in public corridors. Falling silent, she sulked and kicked along behind the old man. Chuckling without rancor, Juul Ragle followed at her heels.

There was something amiss aboard the Petrie platform, even Peri could tell that through her self-absorbed worry. Some people were spread out normally, traveling the passages in pursuit of their daily routines, but there was a profusion of groups clustered in corners. Some of these crowds almost blocked the zero-G hallways. It was evident that these people were agitated about something, sharing their distress with friends and strangers alike.

Frowning at the inconvenient traffic jams, Peri dodged around these human knots as she soared through the corridors. As she passed by, she caught vocal fragments.

"...and then it was gone!"

"What're we going to do?"

"...think that HeeVee might..."

"...gone too far this time..."

"...in the middle of their best program too..."

"...not going to tolerate this..."

"...we need our music..."

They were talking about Red Sky, she realized. The pirate station's music was a constant companion to most of the freelancers. They had noticed its absence. Several hundred individuals had probably been listening when the damaged transmitter had silenced the station's popular broadcast. And naturally, no one knew what to make of it. The silence was more than a sensory deprivation for the divers, it harkened ill solar winds. It was inconceivable to them that Red Sky would have abandoned their audience by choice; that inferred that foul play must have been involved. Everyone instantly believed that HeeVee was responsible.

"...think a Corp attack squad is going to hit the platform?..." Peri heard as she came to a juncture of passageways.

Dezi swam into the left branch, unconcerned whether Peri or Ragle followed. Diving after the man, Peri grew anxious that the notion she had just overheard might sweep the platform. Aided by people's comm-links, word-of-mouth could circulate among the divers with astounding speed and ease. In ten minutes, there wouldn't be a person aboard the Petrie platform who didn't know that Red Sky was off the air. In twenty minutes, radicals would be demanding violent retaliation.

It didn't feel right knowing the truth as she did, and not being able to share it with anyone. She was certain that the populace would appreciate knowing that this was not the first strike in some HeeVee attack on the platform. The truth might avert panic, perhaps even forestall reckless retribution. But her lips were sealed.

Long before they had left Baltuss orbit, Peri and Ragle had sworn to keep Dezi's secret. Although she had no idea how trustworthy Ragle was, it was a promise that Peri took seriously. She was all too aware of the unfortunate repercussions of her prior broken vow.

Dezi had informed them that he did not need help to handle this crisis. But Peri had argued vehemently that they—Ragle and herself—were ethically bound to offer any assistance they could muster. It was immaterial whether her offer was motivated by guilt or civic responsibility, her intentions would not be dissuaded. Her refusal to separate from the old man had been adamant; accompanied by Ragle, she had followed Dezi back to the Petrie platform, relentlessly pestering him until he had accepted their company. He refused to discuss the problem, though, until they were safely alone.

She had faith in the old man. Dezi would fix Red Sky, and the pirate transmission would resume. Everyone would rejoice, and life could return to normal for all the pirate station's loyal fans.

And for herself too. With no killer bots to fear among Baltuss' clouds, Peri could comfortably indulge once more in her secret vice.

"Where're we going?" asked Ragle.

"Somewhere we can talk privately," was all the elderly spacer would supply.

His choice, she discovered, was the platform's hydroponics gardens.

With a key code Peri suspected he shouldn't have, Dezi gained them access to one of the gardens. She was dazzled by the overt, almost oppressive humidity. A flurry of odors assailed her nostrils, earthy smells Peri thought she had forsaken when she left Earth. Mulch and dampness and germinating greenery. The vegetative perfume was not unpleasant, just unexpected. Despite the station's refiltration air system, the rest of the platform was permanently tainted by decades of human occupation; it taken her a few weeks to get used to the ripe odors of the closed environment. The verdant smell of loam and shrubbery was a welcome escape from the locker-room stench.

The garden was an enclosed hangar whose walls were covered with cultivated fungus. The low ceiling featured an immense array of incandescent grow lamps. The chamber itself was divided into a pair of horizontal levels by a plastiform membrane that separated the water from the air in the zero-G environment. Dotting this plastic sheet were plants: their roots submerged in the nutrient liquid, their leaves and produce reaching through the rich air for the artificial light. Locked in plastic embrace, this vegetation could easily be harvested, then new seedlings would replace them in the grow pouches set into the plastic divider. New roots would dangle in the nourishing fluid, new leaves would sprout and bear fruit, producing new crops awaiting harvest.

With Dezi in the lead, they swam in the air through the leafy stalks, pulling their way along by snagging the spongy vines.

"It stinks in here," Ragle complained. His olfactory displeasure did not keep him from plucking a few ripe tomatoes, though. He munched them as he trailed behind Peri.

"This will do," Dezi finally announced. He paused to hover beside a thicket of vines that were crowded with budding onions.

Peri took position next to a diminutive maple tree. "Can you fix it?" she inquired.

Dezi Annucci expelled a long breath that effectively answered her. "It's going to take parts," he elaborated. "The problem is: there's no way to pay for them."

"I wish I could help," Ragle muttered around his mouthful of juicy red pulp. "But I'm new to the freelancer platform, and I'm tapped cred-wise."

"I told you," Dezi grumbled, "I don't need any help. Especially not from *you*." He glared at the swarthy man.

"Hey" objected Ragle. "I told you I was sorry."

"I don't know how you even found the transmitter in the first place," muttered the old man. "It's stealth hardware is supposed to keep it camouflaged from even the most acute sensors."

"I flew into it," Peri confessed, embarrassment briefly coloring her pale cheeks.

"That's the second time you did that," Dezi remarked with visible impatience. "You are either blessed with clumsiness—or cursed with bad luck."

"How is it 'clumsy' to run into something that's 'supposed' to be invisible?" Ragle smirked.

"That won't be a problem now," growled Dezi. "The one you damaged was the master unit. It coordinated all the other transmitters. Now, the entire network is not only down, every unit is exposed for discovery by casual scans."

"Look, I was only following Peri's instructions," Ragle retorted. His hostility was rising in proportion to Dezi's thinly veiled recriminations. "It... looked as if it was going to attack us."

"Cut it out!" Peri spoke up, interrupting the tirade that was on the tip of the old man's tongue. "We can't undo what we did, Dezi, but we want to help you fix it."

"Only money's going to fix this," Dezi reminded them. "And I've only got fifteen creds in my account."

"What about the other Red Sky personnel?" Ragle inquired. "Why can't they supply the necessary funds?"

"Because...they don't exist," the elderly spacer hissed. "There's only me."

"Thought so," the ex-cop nodded with evident satisfaction. "No reason to be embarrassed, old man. It's a pretty impressive achievement for a single person. My compliments. Pity you don't have secret partners, though, cuz their money would be mighty handy right about now, huh?"

When Dezi offered no reply, Ragle cocked his flabby head in Peri's direction. "What about you, sweet-cheeks?"

Flushing with embarrassment, Peri confessed that Dezi was fifteen creds richer than her. "I've been living off Taz."

"That's right. Your boyfriend's loaded," commented Ragle. "He's an okay guy. He fronted me the creds to set myself up here. Why not ask him for a loan?"

"I..." Peri's reply fizzled in her mouth. Despite their intimate relationship, she disliked being indebted to Taz. Normally, Peri strove to be self-sufficient, but her recent distress over the HecVec killer bots had plunged her into a destitution that had only been survived by cohabiting with Taz.

All that stress and worry that she'd never again safely dive in Baltuss' clouds—and the killer robots were not real. Peri resented Dezi for seeding her mind with that rumor, but then she realized that her panic had been of her own devising. She had mixed up fact and fiction, convincing herself that the threat existed, allowing herself to become a victim of her own mistaken imagination. Dezi had tried to warn her not to worry, but in the throes of her fanatical overreaction, she had ignored the old man's advice.

"No!" Dezi was declaring. "It's bad enough that you two know about Red Sky Radio now. I will not allow the secret to spread any farther."

"Taz doesn't have to know what the money's for," Ragle suggested. "Peri could just borrow it for herself, on some pretext…"

"I…can't…" she whispered.

"Aw, c'mon," the ex-cop grunted. "He's a decent guy. He loves you. He'd give you the creds."

How could she explain it to him? She didn't even know how to tell Taz.

The truth of the matter is, Peri's conscience reprimanded her, *we don't even know how to explain it to* ourself.

Realistically, Taz was a dutiful and loving potential mating partner. He was wealthy, and he was well-respected on the platform. He made no secret of the love he had for her, and he seemed willing to accept her reluctance to commit herself emotionally to anyone or anything other than her diving. In return, Peri loved Taz, but she knew she was not "in love" with him. Sometimes she felt as if she was living a lie: sharing a full-time rec cap with him. She knew Taz did not mind supporting them both, but Peri could not shake the opinion that she was taking advantage of the man's affection for her. In light of this emotional imbalance, she was loathe to beg more creds from Taz.

Peri mumbled something about not being able to explain. Baring her soul was not the topic of discussion. There was no way that her confession was going to help Red Sky Radio get back on the air. Money was needed, money she could not bring herself to take from her lover. The money would have to be found elsewhere.

Her pathetic avoidance went unchallenged. A lethargic silence descended on the hydroponics garden, as each one of them retreated to their own thoughts.

Picking a small onion, Peri took a bite. The acrid juices filled her mouth. As she chewed the succulent pearly orb, she surveyed her companions.

Dezi was sullenly feeding baby tomatoes into his wrinkled mouth. His distress was vividly apparent. The old man hung in the air with a beaten slope to his upper spine. He held his elbows close at his sides while he ate. His head was bent to avoid meeting anyone's eyes, and he shook it every once in a while in disagreement with some private rumination. The clothes he wore looked ancient, giving him a very shabby demeanor. She had known Dezi for years, indeed she was one of the few who treated the odder with any modicum of respect. Even so, it was difficult for Peri to accept this elderly rumormonger as the mastermind behind Red Sky Radio.

Ragle was investigating an exotic growth he had pulled from a nearby bush. It resembled a lettuce, but was the size and consistency of a coconut. He seemed unperturbed by the dilemma that faced them. His olive features were unwrinkled with concern. He held his chubby body confidently, betraying his officer training. How committed was the ex-cop to restoring Red Sky Radio? Peri had no real understanding of the man's ethics or personality. His dark face seemed to exude a relaxed charm, but she had no idea how earnest this amiability actually was. She felt partially responsible for knocking out Red Sky's network, but it had been Ragle's actions that had done the literal damage. It remained to be seen whether he was going to atone for this mistake.

"What happens if you find some money?" Ragle asked the old man. "Where would you get the parts you need?"

"From hardware suppliers here on the platform," Dezi told him.

"Would these suppliers front you the stuff? Then you could raise the money later."

Dezi laughed. "You really *are* new to the colony aren't you?"

"What about heisting what you need?"

"Absolutely out of the question. I am a radio pirate, not a thief," Dezi declared indignantly. "The radio station exists to benefit the Petrie community. I cannot sanction criminal activity to support Red Sky."

"But—if you're a radio pirate, you're already breaking the law."

The old man spat, "HeeVee laws! Bah! The Corp is the enemy."

"Then what about stealing the hardware you need from them?"

That suggestion gave the gangly codger(?) pause. His jaw ceased masticating the tomatoes in his mouth. His tiny eyes vanished as he squinted to consider this possibility.

In Peri's opinion, it was "stealing" no matter who the victim was—friend or foe. But then, it was not her decision to make. Red Sky was Dezi's responsibility, the ultimate judgment rested with him. Stealing from HeeVee would potentially solve the problem of "affording" the necessary repairs to the damaged transmitter satellite. She was pleased, though, when the old man denounced the option of stealing anything from Harvest.

"No," Dezi declared. "Not even from them."

"Okay," Ragle shrugged. "Hey, I chose a career in commercial security enforcement because I wanted to help make a difference against crime. I applaud your values, even if they are screwing you over this time."

"We'll have to find a legal way to raise the money," Dezi announced without much verve. "That means diving for clouds."

"So? What's the problem?"

"The problem is *us*. *I'm* too old to bag enough gas. You," he jerked his head at the ex-cop, "*you're* too inexperienced. And, no offense, Peri," he nodded meekly to her, "but *you've* got a heavy rep for always coming back empty-bagged."

"I can do it," Peri told them, but they overlooked her tiny declaration.

"It doesn't sound as if we've got any other choice, Dezi. Unless we raise the creds by bagging gas, your transmitter stays broken."

"I know where there's a golden score," she asserted, finally getting their attention.

"Girl," Dezi remarked skeptically, "If you knew where to find a prize cloud, you'd have bagged it long ago for yourself."

Not necessarily, she privately disagreed. How could she get them to believe that in the course of her extensive and unprofitable diving she had become intimate with the location of hundreds of golden scores? The answer to that question was obvious: she could convince them only be confessing her secret joyriding vice. Was she willing to make that desperate sacrifice?

Even as she asked it of herself, Peri knew that was the stupidest question of all.

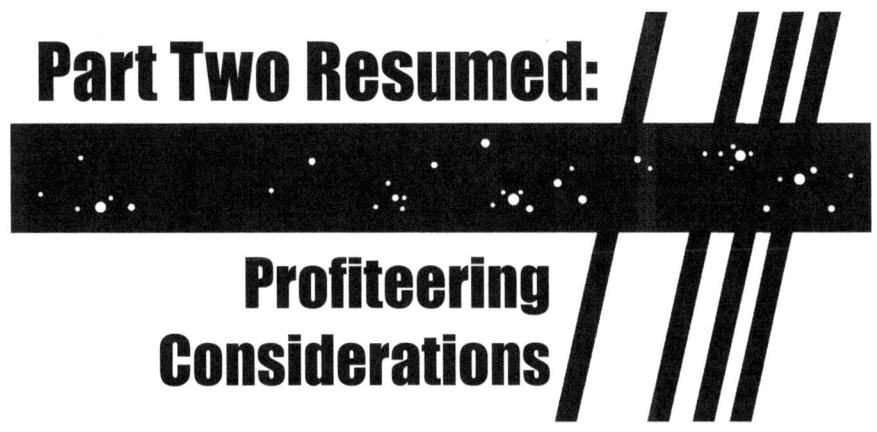

Part Two Resumed:

Profiteering Considerations

To anger Pa'dash Uwu was a lethally dangerous pursuit.

The distance between the inhuman Exec's approval and vehement condemnation was often measurable by the casual blink of an eye. The reasons for such changes of Uwu's mood were difficult to predict.

Many years ago, while Exec Uwu had still possessed his original, debilitated body, he had been engaged in an unholy alliance with another Executive assigned to the Board on Natt. The pair had schemed to usurp complete dominance of the cloud-mining operation, ridding themselves of the other Execs through covert assassination. Abruptly, on the very eve of their master coup, Uwu had turned on his coconspirator, murdering Jersey and assuming control of the Exec's wealth and position. Only Pa'dash Uwu knew the reasons that had caused him to violate his pact, for only Uwu had heard Douglas Jersey's offhand comment. Over a shared dinner, Jersey had remarked how healthy Uwu appeared that evening. Uwu had heard the words correctly, but his distrustful brain had sensed a different interpretation lurking in the statement. Infuriated by the insult he imagined to have been hidden in his partner's polite compliment, Uwu had ordered his guards to shoot Jersey and his retinue. The conspiracy against the other Execs had been forgotten in Uwu's triumph over Jersey's insolence.

Exec Uwu was especially alert for aspects that remained invisible to other, less suspicious individuals.

When Exec Hannigan had filed official charges against the base's Security Domo, Uwu had assumed that the foolish man had done something to irritate the Executive. At first he had thought it was only a lover's spat, dragged out into public view by the vindictive fury of a woman spurned. A cursory examination, however, revealed that the interfering hand of Teid Hein was actually behind the professional attack on the Domo. The disturbing implications of this datum flickered through the cerebral cluster that dangled on the exterior of Uwu's grotesque body.

Hein was allying himself with Hannigan, and the two of them were conspiring to destroy the anti-pirate Security Domo.

In Uwu's opinion, Security Domo Sloane represented the best chances of ridding Baltuss' clouds of the thieving pirates. Any attack on Sloane was an indirect assault on Uwu's personal agenda, and thereby an affront on him personally.

As a result of this, Pa'dash Uwu had intended to vote to exonerate the Security Domo, expunging these ridiculous charges from the man's record in a show of defiance against Bester's nefarious nephew and that Hannigan whore. And although he voted to acquit Sloane, Uwu's opinions had changed during the course of the actual Inquiry Review.

On one hand, he admired the audacity of Sloane's self-defense. The Security Domo had cleverly evaded the charges, trumping his enemies' accusations with ghostly accomplishments.

On the other hand...Theo Sloane had dared to cheat Pa'dash Uwu of being the one to save the Security Domo. The man had stolen the Exec's opportunity to thwart the smear campaign being conducted by Hannigan and Hein.

I will make Sloane pay for this indignity, Uwu vowed.

And who would champion Harvest now? Who would vanquish the thieving pirates now that war hero Theo Sloane had failed to live up to Uwu's discriminating expectations? These failures were more reasons to revile the audacious Security Domo. The man had disappointed Uwu on so many diverse and vital levels.

The mound of malformed meat that was the Exec's hideous body trembled with increased rancor for the Security Domo.

To anger Pa'dash Uwu was a lethally dangerous pursuit.

Part One Resumed:

Ragle to the Rescue

Heroics were often beset with unexpected twists.

The girl was crazy. Her intentions were righteous, but somewhere along the way her synapses had gotten all scrambled with eagerness and a strong desire to contribute something, leaving her overbooked and incapable of meeting her own basic needs.

Juul Ragle had seen it before.

His first wife had been like that: too nice a person to say no, with too few hours in a day to attend to the things she had promised to do for others. In the end, her health had suffered. Unwilling to disappoint the people who "needed" her, she had continued her relentless pace, unmindful of the consequences. When she had died of a heart attack, she had left a long list of chores undone, favors ungranted, promises unfulfilled. Most of all Juul had resented the leaches who had claimed to be her friends, those callous bastards in whose service she had perished, for they had failed to comprehend how savagely they had abused her kindly nature.

Peri Fairchild was like that. The girl longed to help people. When she had believed that the gas giant was overrun by killer robots, she had been desperate to save everyone from these imaginary brutes. Now, she was stubbornly determined to solve Dezi Annucci's problems. (After their secret conference in the hydroponics garden, Peri had confided to Ragle that the old man was already ill, battling a recently diagnosed case of cancer. "He really needs our help. He isn't up to handling any of this.") Eager to help Dezi get Red Sky Radio back on the air, she vowed to produce the creds necessary to purchase the parts Annucci needed to repair his damaged transmitter and get his network broadcasting again.

From what Juul had heard, though, the poor girl was a wretched gas bagger. She barely covered her bills—in fact recently, she had failed to do even that. By her own vague admission, she survived now as the mistress of Taz Bailey, the Petrie colony's most successful diver. Juul thought there was a certain irony in that pairing, the best and worst divers sharing a bed. Although he had known her only a few days, he could tell she was no gold-digger. She was just confused. Unaware how much certain people cared for her, Peri was desperate to win the affection of strangers. Juul even suspected that her reluctance to borrow the necessary creds from her lover was based on her ignorance of much Taz loved her. Even Juul could see the sincerity of the man's devotion.

But Peri was determined to prove that she could save the day by diving into Baltuss' clouds and bagging a golden score. The fact that she was a terrible cloud-miner did not daunt her in the least. Somehow she was going to draw upon skills she clearly lacked and become an unprecedented success. Perhaps she trusted in a fortuitous fate, but Juul feared the girl was simply oblivious to her own limitations. The odds were against her, for according to what he had heard, every freelance diver sought the golden score, but very, very few found one.

Oh, Juul was grateful that he was not going to be the one to deal with her emotional collapse when Peri's failure crushed her innocent and well-intentioned spirit. He had great sympathy for Taz Bailey, for he suspected the girl's depression was going to tax the financier's emotional stamina. Juul had been there (with his third wife), and he wished that downward spiral on no man.

He really liked Taz. The man had shown him compassion when he brought Juul to the Petrie platform, helping the defecting patrol officer establish himself as a new member of the community of freelance divers. Initially, the spacer's physiological alterations had taken some getting used to. Juul had only been in space for less than a year, so he was still uneasy in the presence of altered individuals. Such physical changes were not as popular among planetary populations, being primarily designed for zero-G environments. There had been only a few altered workers at the Natt base, with whom Juul had rare contact in the pursuit of his security duties. Among the Petrie colonists, though, the ratio of physiological alteration was in the majority. Such things still disturbed the ex-cop, but Taz's likability had helped Juul adjust to these grotesque new companions. He hoped to become friends with Taz, for trust was a valuable commodity in space.

He really respected Taz. The man had taken a lucky score and turned the profits into a self-generating money engine by investing his wealth in businesses aboard the platform. Asking around, Juul had learned that many freelancers envied Taz Bailey his fabulous luck, but many more appreciated the good he had done for the platform. Juul hoped to convince Taz to bankroll his desire to become a smuggler pilot, for a swift spacecraft was an expensive proposition for a relocated and penniless ex-cop.

He suspected that he could like Dezi Annucci too. Juul was honored to actually meet the man who ran Red Sky Radio. Plagued with worries about getting his pirate radio station back on the air, the old man was understandably not at his best right now. But Juul could see past Annucci's short temper and irritable mood, discerning how dedicated the man was to bringing music to the lives of his fellow freelancers.

Good music, that is, he qualified to himself. Harvest broadcast music too, but there was no way anyone could call what they played "good." He shuddered to recall the oppressive melodies that dominated the Corp's own transmissions. Juul suddenly felt a pang of pity for all the workers he had left behind when he had fled Harvest's contract to go freelance at the Petrie colony. To think those employees lived their lives subjected to HeeVee's dreadful marching tunes, while decent music surrounded them everyday, unseen in the form of Red Sky's pirate signal, unauthorized and unheard.

By deserting the corporate ranks, Juul had discovered the cheerful and thought-provoking music offered by the pirate station. While working at Harvest's Natt base, he had only heard *about* the pirate broadcasts. Security Domo Sloane had ranted at great length, zealously denigrating Red Sky and their insidious illegal broadcasts. Sloane had made the pirate transmission sound as if they were an affront to human decency, more than a violation of corporate policy—a crime against nature. If anything, though, the reality of Red Sky's playlists were the antithesis of the Domo's rabid claims.

So much of Sloane's policies had turned out to be mired in stale feces.

The bloodthirsty pirates of Sloane's rants had turned out to be a congenial and nonviolent bunch. The freelancers were here to pursue independent careers, not to plot to destroy Harvest and murder all their employees. The Petrie Administrators might think of Harvest as their mortal enemy, but the colony's actual populace rarely wasted much thought on the Corp. Baltuss was a huge world, it was easy to dive every day and never encounter one of the arrest squads dispatched by Sloane on a regular basis. The freelancers enjoyed the freedom and the responsibilities that came with being self-employed.

In Juul's opinion, some of that freedom could be turned to abolish some the stress and worries that nagged the Petrie colony—and a profit could be made in doing so.

There were many things that Juul Ragle had learned as result of his time spent in Harvest's employment, but the most important of them had been the realization that his dedication to justice was utterly wasted in a commercial police force. The *real* injustices were practiced on a corporate level, far beyond the reach of any sociological laws. A lone man could not fight the Corp, but the "pirates" could always use help against Harvest's arrogant oppression. Now that he was one of those pirates, he saw that they were not engaged in any battle to overthrow the Corp; they were too busy just trying to survive.

The cause of justice would be best served by improving the lifestyles of the freelancers, for the ones who were supposed to benefit from justice were the *people*. To serve and protect, to help and enrich.

Breaking contract and leaving Harvest had been the smartest thing Juul had ever done. He had longed to get out long ago, but his sense of ethics had repeatedly kept him in line, serving the charter he had adopted when he signed on with the Corp's security force. With every day, though, his security duties grew more and more like dictatorial harassment of the Corp's helpless employees. Harvest's policies were unreasonable enough without the additional hatemongering practiced by Security Domo Sloane. The brutality of the madman's assault on the freelancers who had trespassed too near to one of HeeVee's gatherer depots had been the breaking point for Juul's stoic commitment to his job.

So he had fled the scene of the attack, taking refuge in Baltuss' gaseous infinity. Considering the vastness of the gas giant's atmosphere, Juul considered himself blessed to have encountered another person so soon in the confusing clouds. He had not questioned fate, however, for finding a pirate was what he had wanted. There was no other way to join the freelancers, for the location of their base, the Petrie platform (or as crazy Sloane called it, "the Vipers Nest"), was unknown to anyone under HeeVee contract. Fortune had smiled on Juul that day, spurring him to finally abandon the cruel Corp, guiding him safely through Baltuss' dense clouds, bringing him into contact with Peri Fairchild. The girl had become his doorway into the Petrie colony, and her lover, Taz Bailey, had become his sponsor.

This was where he was supposed to be, among the freelancers who laughed at Harvest's pompous rules and dove for their own fortunes. Here, full of hopes and schemes of becoming a shuttle pilot so that he could smuggle much-needed cargoes from Greye to the Petrie platform. Here, where he had taken quite a fancy to a particular girl.

Thinking of Denise Coleman brought a smile to his lips. The tension drained from his shoulders as he recalled her voluptuous curves. Juul knew that getting Red Sky back on the air was a laudable cause, but there was nothing *he* could do to help the silenced pirate station. There was no overtone of guilt in his mind for turning his attention to another endeavor.

A happy Juul, he reminded himself, *is a productive Juul.* Maybe a productive Juul could think of some viable means of raising the creds needed to repair Dezi's transmitter network.

Even though he had just eaten, Juul decided to stop by the colony's medical offices and see if he could interest the lovely Miz Coleman in accompanying him out to dinner. Restricted by his pathetic finances, he knew he could not promise her extravagant cuisine, but he was hopeful that his charm might compensate for the platform's culinary deficiencies.

He stopped at a public washroom to freshen up.

As it turned out, Denise Coleman was pleasantly surprised by Juul's unexpected appearance. His invitation made her blush, but she accepted, informing him that she got off-duty in half-an-hour.

"I can wait," he happily announced, unable to restrain himself from giving her a sly wink. He settled into a corner, casually eyeing the empty waiting room.

The chamber was set up like most zero-G public facilities: seats were replaced by rows of back-pads situated above a bar to which the occupants secured themselves. Since the primary function here was to "wait", Juul found it odd that Admin had provided no gaming consoles or any apparatus to amuse people during their waiting. The room was shaped like a squat cylinder, and the circumference walls were lined with the seating racks. Of the remaining walls, the blunt capsule's opposite caps, one was the facility's entrance, and the other, a portal leading to the examination rooms deeper in the medical offices. Empty as it was now, the chamber seemed desolate and depressing, which Juul thought was unfortunate, for the momentary absence of any sick or suffering was actually a positive condition for the overall colony.

The door had failed to close when Denise had returned to the examination rooms. Through this ajar hatch, Juul could hear voices raised in argument. His curiosity got the better of him, and he nudged himself nearer the cracked doorway.

"—and I meant it." This voice was obviously Denise's. From her tone, Juul gathered that she was more than triflingly angry.

"Would you prefer it if I told Admin how *uncooperative* you were being?" This voice was masculine and demanding. Juul did not recognize it.

"I've done nothing wrong."

"That's for *me* to determine, not you, Nursie."

"I doubt that Admin is very concerned with whether you bed your new nurse, Doctor Petroff." Aha, so Denise was arguing with her boss.

"You must be mad if you think Admin won't do anything I demand," declared the arrogant doctor.

"You have a much higher opinion of yourself than Admin does, Doctor."

"How dare you repudiate my professional capabilities!"

"Get your hands off of me, you—"

That was when Juul chose to intervene. Up to that point, it had been obvious that the woman was holding her own, at least intellectually, against the lecherous medical officer. But Juul had spent too many hours breaking up domestic disturbances to ignore the telltale sounds of a confrontation gone physical. Doc Petroff had crossed a line, and Juul was there in an instant to slap him back. Which he did with considerable force once he saw what part of the nurse's anatomy the man had in hand.

The doctor flew across the examination room to crash into a wall of plastic lockers. A few cabinets lurched open under his impact. Bottles and vials toppled forth to immerse the man in an aerial sargasso of medical debris.

"That'll be enough of *that*," Juul declared loudly, using his cop-voice. "Are you okay, Miz?"

"I'll live," she told him. "Luckily, he didn't bite me, so I won't need an asshole inoculation."

"What the hell do you think you're doing?" cried Petroff. "You don't belong here!" Brushing aside the drifting bottles, the man angrily launched himself at Juul.

The ex-cop deflected his headlong charge with ease, sending the violent doctor crashing into another wall. More medicine spilled from freshly disturbed cabinets.

"Idiot," Juul muttered.

"I'll report this!" wailed Petroff. "You can't attack me without *severe* repercussions!"

"From what I saw," Juul remarked, "*you* were not the victim in this. I'm sure the platform's police will be interested in an objective account of what transpired here."

"Show's you what you know," growled Petroff as he regained his composure next to the dented lockers. "There are no police here. Admin's the only voice of any authority—and you can bet your last breath of air that *they're* going to side with *me*! I'm *important* on this station. You—you're just a dom cap rental to them. Look who's the 'idiot' now!"

Whirling his denunciations to bear on Denise, Petroff continued to scream, "And you—you frigid tease—you're out of a job. I'll have you deported from this platform! What do you think of that, you bitch?"

"I still think you're an asshole," Denise informed him.

"No police?" grunted Juul. "We'll just have to settle for vigilante justice then." With a serious grimace, he advanced on the doctor.

I think you broke his nose," Denise chuckled as she glided along next to Juul. They were moving through a crowded concourse, headed for the cafeteria on the far side.

"I hope so," Juul replied tersely. "This place is all screwed up, if that's the best they can for a doctor."

"He's supposed to have friends in Admin. They've been covering for him for years. At least, that's what I've heard. I'm actually pretty new here. I've only been on the platform for a few weeks."

"Really? I'm a newcomer too."

After a moment, Denise sighed, "I suppose he'll make trouble too. If what I've heard about him is true, he can get me fired, and probably bring assault charges against you."

"And who's going to arrest me? Remember? There's no police force here." He paused in thoughtful silence for a second. "If there were, he'd be the one going behind bars."

Halfway across the concourse, Juul noticed that the crowd was not in motion. These pedestrians were gathered and concentrating on something. Peering past the people hanging in the air, he saw that a man was addressing the throng. He could not hear the speaker's words, so he weaved through the milling people, drawing closer to the orator. Attracted by her own curiosity, Denise followed Juul.

"—has gone on long enough," the speaker was snarling.

An assenting growl swept the audience.

"Obviously," the speaker resumed his tirade, "they think this is going to incapacitate us. They believe we cannot survive without music. They expect us to shrivel up and go away. Are they right?"

The audience bellowed their angry dissension.

Juul realized suddenly that the man was talking about Red Sky Radio. The speaker was blaming the pirate station's silence on Harvest. More than that, he seemed to be whipping the crowd into an anti-Corp frenzy.

"What else can they think?" the speaker yelled. "They took away our music, but we aren't doing anything to get it back. That makes us all look like cowards!"

Amid the crowd's growing animosity, a lone voice shouted, "What can we do about it, Furrell?"

A frown creased Juul's high forehead. *Furrell…where have I heard that name?*

"We can fight back!" the speaker loudly proclaimed. "We can attack Harvest—and take back our music!"

The crowd's anger was getting out of control. Or was it? Clearly, this Furrell person was fueling the crowd's fury, getting them all worked up. Perhaps this was exactly what the speaker intended. First he had convinced the people that HeeVee was to blame (an erroneous assumption, but there was no way the man—or any of Petrie's divers—could know that, not as long as Annucci refused to reveal the truth behind the abrupt absence of the pirate broadcasts), and now Furrell was inciting the freelancers to challenge the Corp. This was no accident—the rabblerouser was intentionally goading the freelancers to turn their anger into violence.

That's where I know his name. With a jolt, Juul recognized the man as someone he had arrested several months ago—on the Natt base! For doing the very same thing! Only then, Harrison Furrell's anti-Corp rant had been a sham. Juul had arrested the man and another troublemaker (whose name had been something like Barker), but when he had taken them back to the Security Offices, Furrell and the seedy "Barker" had mysteriously never been booked, charged, or arraigned. Later, careful inquiries had revealed that the culprits had been released at the insistence of Exec Uwu. Juul had learned that both rabblerousers had been working for the Exec, going undercover to ferret out pirate sympathizers by pretending to share their anti-Corp sentiments. Juul had never seen Furrell or Barker again—and now he knew why!

Gradually, Juul worked his way closer to the speaker. From a distance of five meters, Juul was certain this was the same man. Despite Furrell's state of vehement passion, his distinctively narrow face was readily identifiable.

HeeVee had sent Furrell to penetrate the Petrie colony. Why hadn't the spy already reported the location of the rogue platform to his Executive master? What more could HeeVee want? Once the Corp knew the platform's location, they could send Sloane and his officers to apprehend the entire colony of freelance divers. Why was Furrell still here? What deeper, far more insidious instructions was he following?

If the divers responded to Furrell's suggestions, they were going to attack Harvest's Natt base. They would, of course, be slaughtered by the Corp's malevolent and indiscriminate defenses. Was that it? Did Uwu desire to turn public sentiment against the Petrie freelancers, justifying Harvest's "unfortunate but necessary" extermination of "invading forces"? It was a twisted stratagem, but one that Juul could imagine springing from the warped mental processes of the HeeVee Execs.

How could this Corp scheme be thwarted? The ex-cop knew he could not simply denounce Furrell as a HeeVee spy, for Juul was also a newcomer, recently defected from the Corp. In the suspicious eyes of the freelancers, Juul Ragle could just as easily be a HeeVee spy as could the rabblerouser. Publicly accusing the speaker would do no good. He had to find a more covert manner to derail this Corp-engineered massacre-in-the-making.

He pulled Denise close to hiss in her ear. "You must do something for me," he urgently whispered. "Go to the edge of the concourse, then shout that—" What? What diversion would steal Furrell's mob from his rabblerousing? "Shout that Red Sky is holding a speech of their own in another concourse."

She frowned at him, suspicion evident in her delicate features.

"Trust me, Denise," Juul whispered. "This is important. I'm trying to avert a catastrophe here. I'll explain later."

She regarded him for a solemn moment, then nodded curtly. Turning, she threaded her way to the outskirts of the angry crowd. As she departed, Juul worked himself closer to the roaring spy.

"There's only one way we're going to get Harvest to give us back our music," Furrell was shouting. "By force! We have to—"

"Hey!" a demure voice raised to call in the distance. "Red Sky's holding their own speech in Courtyard 4!"

Juul made a mental note: they were called "courtyards," not "concourses." Learning the platform's vernacular was important if he was going to become part of the Petrie community. Furrell had obviously ignored such subtleties as he implanted himself here; the spy had not picked up that the freelancers referred to Harvest as "HeeVee." This imprecise vocabulary was one of the things that had flagged Juul's suspicions.

"Red Sky!" someone near Juul cried.

"They're back!" yelled another.

The crowd surged like a unified school of fish, swarming for the exits.

"Wait!" Furrell roared. "We have to attack while—"

As the crowd abandoned the rabblerouser, Juul closed in on the man. Utilizing a nerve-pinch, he silenced the spy without a struggle. He carefully supported Furrell's limp body until the courtyard had emptied itself, then he dragged the man into the concealment of a peripheral alcove. Another pinch roused the spy from his unconsciousness while leaving him numb and incapable of movement below the neck.

"What—how did I—who the—" the man gasped as his disorientation swamped over him. "Hey—I *know* you—"

"Indeed, this is not the first time I've arrested you, Furrell," Juul grinned. "Officer Ragle."

"You're one of Harvest's Security officers! What're you doing here?"

"*I've* defected. How about you?"

"Yeah, me too."

"I don't think so," Juul shook his head with regret. "I think you're still working for HeeVee. Where's your partner?"

"Don't be absurd," Furrell disputed angrily. "Where'd everybody go? Why can't I move?"

"I think you're here to stir up trouble, get the freelancers to storm Hee-Vee's Natt base. Then the Corp can claim justifiable cause when they wipe them out defending the base from a pirate attack."

"What? That—that's absurd…"

"It's not going to happen, though. I'm on to your little scheme."

"Let me go," demanded the spy. "You can't do this. You're going to ruin everything."

"Oh, but I already have, Furrell."

"You've got no authority to restrain me. What do you think you are? A pirate cop now? They don't have police here, you fool."

"You're the second criminal to point that out to me today," Juul remarked wistfully. "Somehow, I don't think Admin will mind who it is that turns a spy like you over to them."

"You're a fool, Ragle." His eyes grew rounder. "Do you think I'm alone here? You won't get away with killing me."

Juul was going to laugh at the man's pathetic ploys when something hard and carrying a degree of momentum struck the back of his head.

As his perceptions faded down a tapering black tunnel, Juul took the image of Furrell's triumphant grin with him into abrupt unconsciousness.

Heroics were often beset with unexpected twists.

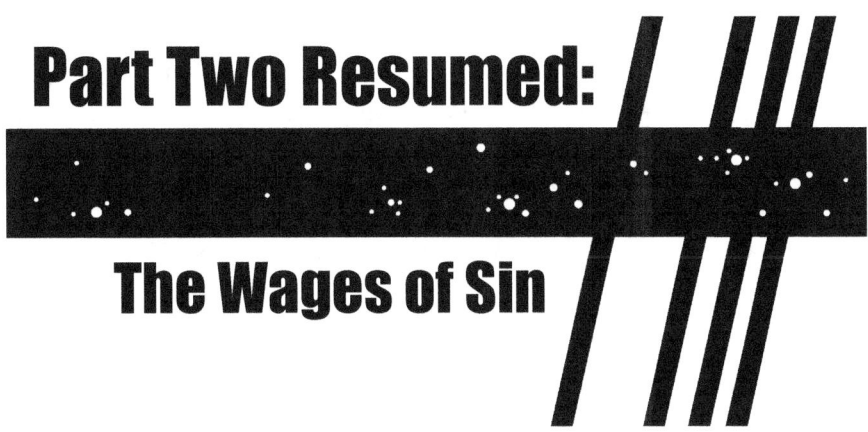

Part Two Resumed:

The Wages of Sin

There were no lulls in Security Domo Theo Sloane's life.

It took time to confirm the silencing of Red Sky Radio. Extensive investigation was required to validate that the pirate broadcasts were really gone from the regional airwaves.

More of his time was wasted managing his defense for the charges levied against him by Evelyn Hannigan. That whore—he had thought they were lovers, and she had stabbed him in the back. But Sloane knew the real culprit behind those charges was Teid Hein, the felonious nephew of Executive Bester. The nasty little nuisance was taking another crack at getting Sloane fired, payback for all of Hein's schemes the Security Domo had foiled in the past. And Sloane had evaded the trap once again. Hein was probably furious right now, devastated by his latest failure. But Sloane's vengeance wasn't about to stop there.

He imagined a picturesque and painful reward for Hein. The schemer's destiny warranted some careful planning, for this time Sloane wanted to rid himself of Hein's annoying presence once and for all.

There was time enough for such things later. All these distractions had kept him from rendezvousing with Algol Caffino. Sloane felt guilty. He had given the technician two days to follow his instructions, and here three days had gone by without the Domo calling on the spineless tech.

He's liable to think he's off the hook, Sloane mused. *And that's a completely erroneous assumption.*

To Caffino's great anxiety, a meeting was scheduled.

That afternoon, the Security Domo followed Caffino home from the research lab. He took acute notice when the tech failed to stop for a meal and headed directly for his quarters. This confirmed Sloane's suspicions that the man had obtained what had been demanded of him. Unwilling to sit through a public meal with such flagrantly illegal materials in his possession, Caffino was scurrying back to his rooms in order to hide the packet until the clandestine rendezvous that was scheduled for later that night.

Sloane had decided to doublecross his informant/spy/thief. He wasn't going to wait until evening; he planned to surprise Mr. No-Names-Please, gaining the psychological upper hand once again with his unannounced appearance.

After checking for surveillance outside the tech's quarters, he waited only half-an-hour before slipping inside. For a second time, he was puzzled to find the living room dark. The tech had obviously retreated to the privacy of his bedroom. Sloane boldly threw open the inner door and scowled at the miserable man as he cringed on his bed.

"Again, I find you listening to forbidden music," the Security Domo growled.

Slobbering with terror, Caffino's denials were undermined by the squeal of noise that escaped from the headphones as they were torn from his head. The savage motion dislodged the gauze dressing that covered his missing ear. His frantic attempt to hide the evidence was pathetic.

"That's a recording of an old broadcast, isn't it?" Sloane accused. "It has to be, because Red Sky's off the air now. You're not only stupid enough to violate Corp regs by listening to that filth, you're guilty of recording it for your own private use! You're an unspeakable deviant."

Snarling with revulsion, Sloane snatched the headphones from the miscreant and crumpled the criminal hardware in his meaty hands. He flung their ruins to the floor. Then he held out his hand and sharply snapped his fingers a fraction away from the tech's quivering nose. "The sample," he demanded. "Now!" He twitched his hand, palm up, at the recoiling spy.

Caffino scrambled, reaching under the sleeping mattress to produce a flat plastic packet slightly bigger than his hand. He offered it to the Security Domo, then retreated again to cower against the wall.

Examining the packet only casually, Sloane placed it in a sterile carry-case at his belt. As he turned to leave, the intimidated technician regained a trace of spine and objected aloud.

"What about my money?"

Sloane laughed without turning back to face the man. "Consider yourself lucky that I don't arrest you for listening to prohibited music. I am currently looking for more dangerous criminals, however, so I will overlook your trivial violation. If you run into anyone stealing materials from classified research labs—you'll tell me, hmm? *They're* the ones in really big trouble. I'm about to institute a deep investigation of all lab workers, for I sincerely believe that someone has breached the security of a particular secret project. I pity the guilty bastard, because I'm certain Harvest will skin him alive for betraying their corporate secrets."

All Caffino could do was jerk his head in a curt nod. The flush of anger drained from the man's cheeks, leaving his face pallid with desperate fear.

Sloane left the man to contemplate his fate.

Fear was the Domo's parting gift to Algol Caffino.

Panic would become his new obsession now. In Sloane's opinion, it was a justifiable reward for the man's traitorous actions against the Corp. It did not matter that those "traitorous actions" had been forced on the technician in the first place. If the man was weak enough to be turned, he deserved to be punished.

Upon reaching the privacy of his own quarters, the Security Domo settled down to examine his prize. He barely had the opportunity to pull the my-lar packet from his carry-case when his comm-link buzzed, informing him that his presence was immediately required at the Security Office.

Sloane ground his teeth with frustration over this unwelcome distraction. To finally be so close to achieving the means of vanquishing the pirates—only to be called away by some trivial Departmental matter. It was infuriating. In the end, though, he swallowed his fury and stashed the packet safely in his personal security vault. Then he departed to attend to the emergency summons.

There were no lulls in Security Domo Theo Sloane's life.

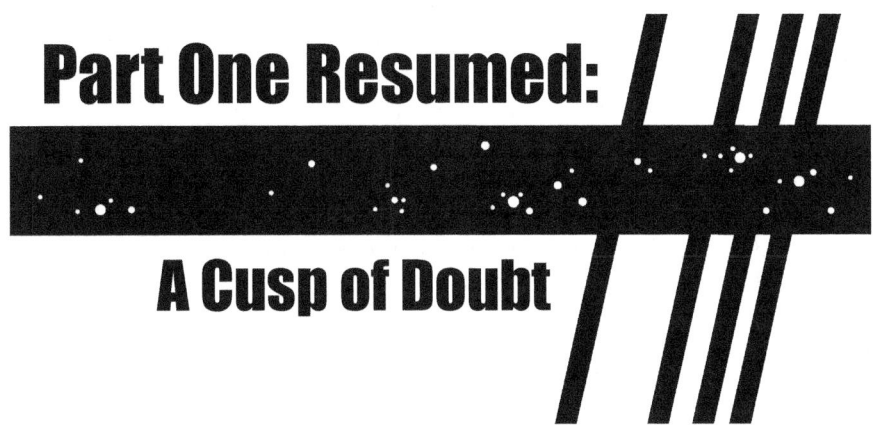

Part One Resumed:

A Cusp of Doubt

Deception was in the air.

An eager mob of freelancers coursed by her. They paid Denise Coleman no heed, never realizing it had been her voice which had announced the impromptu and nonexistent Red Sky speech in Courtyard 4. She did not understand the attraction, for she was too new to the platform to appreciate the connection which the divers of Petrie felt for the pirate radio broadcasts. Nor did she comprehend Juul's reasons for asking her to create a distraction that would clear this courtyard so rapidly. She could only assume that he knew what he was doing. After the heroic efficiency the man had displayed in dealing with Doc Petroff's lecherous advances on her, Denise felt she owed her rescuer something.

From the archway that led to the corridor outside, she peered across the vacant courtyard, watching Juul approach the man who had been speaking to the crowd. She gasped when she saw her hero attack the orator. Trepidation and confusion paralyzed Denise as Ragle moved the man to the privacy of one of the concourse's side alcoves.

What was going on? One minute Juul was escorting her to dinner, the next he was driving off this orator's audience so that he could assault the man.

What kind of madman have I gotten mixed up with this time? she wondered. After all the overt advances she had endured back on Earth, Denise had vowed that she would not be taken in so readily out here by smooth-talking deviants—like Petroff. But her trust for Ragle had come too easily, she should have been more cautious.

Had the man really been defending her honor by attacking Doc Petroff? Or was Juul the type who overreacted with violence to every "situation"? Had he been eliminating the competition, staking his macho claim on her by beating up the unprofessional doctor?

She didn't know what to do. Her initial response was to flee from the scene, but Denise rejected that impulse when she realized that she was partially responsible for the speaker's predicament. She could not leave the man to whatever deviltry Juul had in store for him. But—what could she do?

If she went for help, there was no guarantee that the two men would still be here when she brought the authorities. And what "authorities" were there for her to summon? Petrie possessed no police force, the only leaders here were the platform's owners. Could she call upon a stranger to assist her? What would she tell this passer-by in order to convince them that help was needed?

Time could be running out too. She had no idea what Juul was doing to his captive. Clumsily, she set off across the courtyard in the direction the men had vanished.

Coming to an awkward halt outside the alcove, Denise clutched the wall. She could hear voices.

One of them was Juul's: "Oh, but I already have, Furrell."

Another voice, undoubtedly the other man, replied, "You've got no authority to restrain me. What do you think you are? A pirate cop now? They don't have police here, you fool."

She was certain that Juul was planning something awful. The hard tone of his voice frightened her. Meanwhile, the other man, this Furrell, was pleading like a terrified victim. Denise was desperate to help the man. Glancing around, she spotted a fire extinguisher set into a wall niche not two meters away from her. It was roughly the size of a person's forearm, a metal tank filled with pressurized flame-retardant foam. Snatching it up, she returned to the alcove, coming up behind Juul. His back was to her as he menacingly faced his captive. Furrell seemed paralyzed by fear, but his eyes flashed large as he saw her appear over his captor's shoulder.

"You're a fool, Ragle," Furrell bristled with wide-eyed defiance. "Do you think I'm alone here? You won't get away with killing me."

I was right, Denise told herself. Juul *was* planning something awful.

Swinging the fire extinguisher with all her might, she struck Juul across the back of his head. The blow made a disgusting sound, and globules of blood spurted to lazily twist in the air. She had forgotten to brace herself before striking him; administered in zero-G, the impact sent her flying from the alcove.

She hit someone who had approached her from behind just as quietly as she had crept upon Juul and his captive. With his foot hooked around a nearby support bar, her rescuer caught her and put an end to her reckless momentum. The man's grip on her upper arm tightened, and she twisted to gawk into the leering face of Ivar Petroff!

"I warned you about severe repercussions, my dear," growled the doctor. Pulling her close, he coarsely manhandled her. Brazen and abusive, his hand crept across her breasts to toy with her neck; then he looped his burly arm around her throat, his rude hand closing over her mouth.

Petroff carried her back into the alcove, where he surveyed the unconscious Juul and the prone Furrell.

"Petroff!" called the frozen man. "You're just in time—"

"You're such a screw-up, Furrell," the doctor snarled.

"He jumped me! It wasn't my fault!"

"This fool has an annoying habit of interfering in things that do not concern him. But—with the unwitting help of our little Nursie here," he shook Denise at him like a rag doll, her fear-deadened limbs swinging with loose abandon, "it appears that we will be able to rid ourselves of this nuisance."

"He got me with a nerve-pinch," Furrell moaned. "Undo it, huh? I'll help you finish him off."

"Our instructions are to ferment discomfort, not incite riots," Petroff growled. His handsome features were contorted in a mask of abject disapproval for the paralyzed man. "If our employer wanted to destroy the platform outright, he'd send troopers to do the job. You've always failed to appreciate the Executive Mentality, Furrell. This is not a deficiency I share, for I have aspirations that will one day see me seated on the Board. It's quite obvious that this facility has commercial potential as an annex to the Corp's lunar base. If we succeed in making life intolerable for the freelancers, they have nowhere else to turn for salvation except Harvest. I can comprehend the cruel subtlety of Uwu's scheme…while you remain blind to anything but barbaric tactics."

Petroff sighed a condescending breath.

"Your incompetence makes you a liability," he told the man. Then he shot him in the face with a small palm-gun he had quietly produced. "You will serve the cause better as one of the victims of Ragle's insane killing spree."

As Furrell's blood and brain tissue fogged a portion of the alcove's air, Denise screamed with panic. She fought frantically to escape the doctor's clutches, but he was stronger than her. His arm squeezed around her neck, momentarily cutting off the bloodflow to her brain. Her surroundings grew hazy.

Terrible surprises were relentlessly pummeling Denise, giving her scarce time to understand the changing picture of reality.

Juul was a villain—then he wasn't.

Petroff had appeared out of nowhere, like the stereotypical villain in a holovid.

Furrell was not a victim, he was revealed as a villainous associate of the evil doctor, then he was dead.

Petroff had murdered his own crony!

The phrase "…one of the victims of Ragle's insane killing spree…" echoed in her dazed head. It was not difficult to figure out that the doctor was going to kill her too, blaming all the murders on poor unconscious Juul.

Whatever crime Juul had discovered, it was going to cost him—and her!—their lives. The criminals were going to win, and pin everyone's murder on the hero!

Deception was in the air.

Part Two Resumed:

A Near Save

Sometimes, there are worse things than fear.

Fear does strange things to the human consciousness.

Caffino's terror saturated the wreck that was left of his analytical mind. The traumatic flood plunged his perspective back through the years of his life.

Fresh off the shuttle from Greye, Algol Caffino was the newest technician assigned to Project Godbreath.

His job was to help refine a means of canceling a particular subatomic catalyst. The challenge was considerable, for the catalyst in question was an especially audacious one, refusing to be stopped by any material substance. It was almost as if the process was a force of nature, resilient beyond all logic. Caffino found the work intensely intriguing. He studied the target process with a passion that soon turned into an uneasy dread. The more he codified the catalyst, the more he grew to understand what it did…or what it seemed to do.

Molecules, he knew, were bound together into matter by subatomic forces. The catalyst was a form of matter that, when charmed in a special manner, was able to infect other matter and cancel this binding force. The target matter would then dissolve into loose particles. The catalyst released the bonds that held subatomic particles together, effectively disintegrating matter. While fusion achieved an accretion of matter, producing more complex elements, Project Godbreath had found a way to reverse that process, taking even fission beyond its end result—to an absolute negation of mass.

Caffino could certainly see the need for discovering a means to stifle this catalyst, but he could not fathom the need for such a catalyst in the first place. As he dug deeper through the project's database, he learned of the unholy objective pursued by the project's researchers. That purpose was neither neutral nor benevolent. The catalyst (or "matter virus" as the files referred to it) had been intentionally designed as a weapon of mass destruction. The matter virus had turned out far more volatile than anyone had imagined. As a result, current research was devoted to finding a way of controlling the deadly contagion, at least learning a way to halt the spread of the catalyst. A weapon was no good unless it could be turned off. The faction using the weapon had to be safe from its lethal effects. Otherwise it became a suicidal doomsday device, resulting in genocide for everyone.

He recalled how, during in the early days of nuclear research, scientists on Old Earth had feared this very disaster. They had mistakenly feared that a simple atomic reaction would continue to grow, consuming the entire universe. The notion was ridiculous outside of fiction—until now. Flint's matter virus was exactly that universal doom…unless a means could be found to halt the contagious attributes of the debonding process.

Because of the unstable nature of the matter virus, no actual tests had been conducted with any samples of the contagion. All experiments were digital simulations—and gratefully so too, for each mathematical model over the last thirty years had ended with the simulated virus breaking its theoretical suppression and infecting everything in a chain reaction that reduced the universe to a vast nothingness. Each proposed limiter or off-switch proved incapable of containing or deactivating the vicious contagion. For some unclear reason, the scientists had recently dared to fabricate an actual sample of the destructive catalyst.

By this point, Caffino was thoroughly scared by the work he was doing. His job was to further this insanity. In all good conscience, he now knew that he could not do that.

He discovered that he was not the first one working on this project who had been repulsed by the matter virus' implications. The catalyst's inventor had even attempted to eradicate all evidence of the process. Professor Flint's data purge had been unsuccessful, although it had set work back several decades as the new researchers struggled to duplicate Flint's original model of the matter virus. Other ethical rebels had surfaced over the years in the ranks of the project's personnel, but each of them had failed to halt or expose the research. Caffino vowed that he would not join them in defeat. He would be the one to expose the monstrous research being conducted by Harvest Corp under the disguise of a base managing a cloud-mining operation.

In his naivetÈ, Caffino approached the base's Security Domo with tales of hazardous research. In the end, that had been a terrible mistake. He had expected Sloane to expose the terrible matter virus—not steal it for his own personal use.

Caffino did not like that memory. He retreated from that failure, driving his consciousness deeper into his past.

When he was eighteen, Caffino lived in an off-campus dormitory. He liked to wander far from his rooms, exploring the weirdling avenues of Amsterdam.

Over the years, the city had grown, its skyscrapers merging and shutting out the sun from the lower levels. What had once been the grand ground-floors of every building were now mired in mud and forgotten by the decent citizens of the great arcology that stood on the Danish coastline. Those shadowed regions had become an underground labyrinth, the domain of furtive and reclusive people. The despair and isolationism drew Caffino like a cultural magnet. The architectural claustrophobia fascinated him, for he could easily picture the immense bulk of the entire arcology looming above him, threatening to crush this chthonic underbelly at any moment.

A late-bloomer, Algol was susceptible to suggestion. The loneliness of his youth made him a prime candidate for the angst of post-pubescence, especially when prompted by the teen hordes that surrounded him at college. Already possessing enough of an intimate familiarity with despair, Algol chose to involve himself in the distress of others. He befriended every loser he encountered. When he discovered the abject desolation of the city's neglected sublevels, he felt as if it existed solely for his own edification. He derived no amusement from the suffering he witnessed down there, instead the oppressive misfortune inevitably helped him to cast off his inferiority complex and face his peers as an equal. But that came later; now, he was there to gawk and be horrified.

During his repeated sojourns to the forgotten district, Algol came to frequent an Italian restaurant that was little more than a glorified pizza parlor. There, he fell in love with a girl behind the counter. Although he never expressed his feelings to this girl, he furiously fantasized about her back in the light of his days aboveground. She became the ideal, the all, the perfection that he imagined he deserved. She was moody and withdrawn and slight-figured and so obviously in need of salvation from her life in darkness. He imagined that he would save her, bringing her to bathe in the fresh sunlight and clean air. And her gratitude would border on worship. Unfortunately, the only time he had spoken to her, beyond the scope of ordering a slice of wretched pizza, had been a disaster. He had stuttered and made awful verbal gaffs, marking himself as a fool and a failure. The next time he showed up, she was gone; he never saw her again. He was too embarrassed to inquire after her, and so remained ignorant of her ultimate destiny.

The agony of this blundered opportunity was another recollection that Caffino was not fond of. He recoiled from the emotional loss, falling farther into his past.

Little Algee was the neighborhood punching-bag. Brats and bullies would come from distant streets to beat on him. His popularity as the optimum victim drove the young boy indoors, where he took refuge in literature and science.

These were formative years for little Algee, but they contained too many negative elements for Caffino to remember fondly.

While his body remained paralyzed by intense anxiety, his thoughts whizzed and whirled. Facts blurred with doubts, producing assumptions that motivated the frightened technician to think farther than his own health and safety.

It was obvious—now—that Security Domo Sloane had acted outside his proper authority, in threatening Caffino and in intimidating him to breach the security of the project. The villain was operating on his own, without the backing of the corporation that owned the Natt base. The madman had hurt him, costing him an ear. Terror had kept Caffino cowed, but now the Domo's threats seemed quite immaterial compared to the prospect of what Sloane might do with the packet stolen from the laboratory. Alone, the madman was dangerous; armed with the matter virus, the danger offered by Sloane was incalculable.

He knew he had to do something.

He had to tell someone about what he had done. To insure that Sloane would be stopped, he must confess his sin and accept whatever punishment was appropriate. Caffino was certain that the Corp would take his confession into consideration, inspiring a leniency for the one who had helped avert disaster.

"That's all that come of this," he muttered to himself as he crawled from the sanctuary of his bedcovers. "Disaster and mayhem. Sloane has no idea how dangerous that packet is. He's crazy…he'll use the cursed thing!"

He stumbled out into his living room and activated the comm-link on his console.

"Connect me with—" He paused, suddenly realizing that he had no idea who to report the outlaw Domo to. Sloane was the head of Security. Were there any officials between him and the Executives themselves? Would an Exec even accept a communiquÈ from a lowly technician? *They'll have to,* he thought, *or we're all dead…* Caffino's warning was too vital, it needed to go all the way to the top of the power structure. Pa'dash Uwu, he decided, was the one to talk to. Uwu was rumored to be the dominant Executive on the Board.

He turned to address the waiting console—and the door to his quarters opened suddenly.

His panic returned with a vengeance, for he feared that the maniacal Domo had come back to do him further harm. Frozen with blinding fear, he expected death to come at that instant. When he did not recognize the statuesque man who stepped through the doorway, he relaxed slightly, images of his murder fading from his overactive imagination.

He did not feel the pulse blast impact that vaporized his head. Only the assassin was witness to the indignity of the technician's demise.

Sometimes, there are worse things than fear.

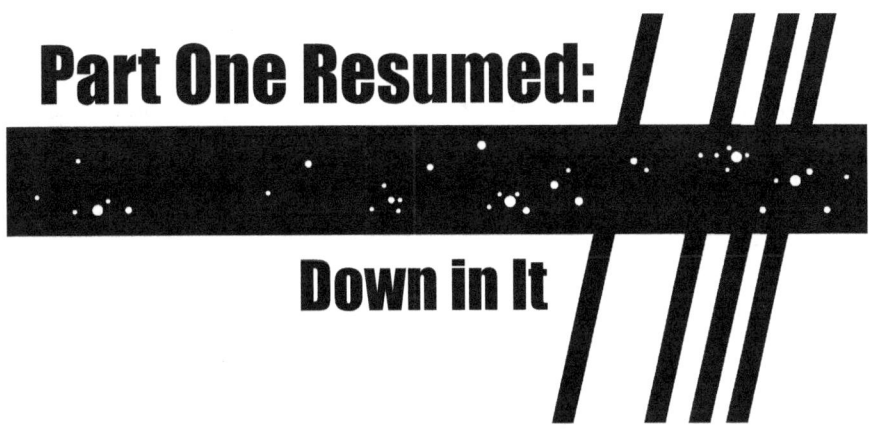

Part One Resumed:

Down in It

She had a purpose now.

Peri knew she could raise the required money. She didn't care if anyone believed her. She was determined to save the day by bagging a golden score. The payoff would more than cover the cost of the parts Dezi needed to restore Red Sky Radio. The payoff would earn her enough creds to pay off her informal debt to Taz, returning her to a position of financial independence.

As result of her endless joyrides through Baltuss' atmosphere, Peri was intimately familiar with the whereabouts of several choice clouds of absolutely ridiculous rarity. She could take her pick: precious lithium, oxygen, or perhaps a wildly profitable bag of some isotopic fermium. She could picture each particular deposit, pinpointed by longitude, latitude, and altitude in the mental image of the gas giant's vast mists that lived in her head.

Just because she didn't have a reputation as a profitable diver, that didn't mean she couldn't surprise everyone. She resented Dezi and Ragle for their lack of faith in her secret capabilities.

I'll show them, she swore as she sped along the corridors. *I'll show everybody!*

When she stopped in at their rec cap, Peri was glad to find Taz absent. A confrontation with him was the last thing she wanted right now. His concern for her health would only delay her reaching Baltuss' atmosphere. He would object to her going Down, they would argue, and she really didn't want to hurt him by openly defying his advice. She could not reveal why she had to dive right away—for several reasons. She could tell him nothing about the damaged transmitter without exposing the pirate station. Also, she wanted to avoid the chance that he would offer her the creds without asking what they were for. This time, she was determined not to accept his generosity. She knew his overprotective nature was a product of his intense affection for her, but right now she needed the freedom to prove her own skill. She could not allow her lover to distract her from saving the day. It was something she needed to do herself.

Grabbing up her decrepit bagger rod, she darted out of the living capsule and made her way along the tow lines, heading for the linear accelerator.

It never occurred to Peri that she might not have sufficient funds left in her account to purchase the launch necessary to put her in a position to bag a golden score and save the day.

Approaching the edge of the platform, she saw that many stassed figures were crowded around the entrance tube that led to the linear accelerator. As she grew closer, it became apparent that all these people were waiting to avail themselves of the facility. Everyone wanted to go Down.

Her wait in line seemed uncommonly brief; it was as if the accelerator techs were shooting off divers at a reckless rate. It wasn't until she reached the ticket booth that she discovered the reason for the volume of outbound traffic. While waiting her turn, the most cynical explanations had scampered through her mind, spurred on by her agitated imagination. Widespread panic had set in on the Petrie platform—she had witnessed enough evidence of that en route from the hydroponics garden. Were the divers deserting their home? Had the fear of further HeeVee oppression driven these brave individuals to evacuate? Where did they think they were going to hide? How long could the average diver last down in Baltuss' clouds? These people were extravagantly overreacting to the sudden silencing of Red Sky's pirate radio signal.

The truth proved to be far more surprising.

Peri finally reached the ticket booth. She drew her Ident card and started it on a vector to intersect with the account slot, but the attendant shook his head and waved her to move along.

"But—" she started to object, unclear what the man meant by this brusque dismissal.

"Free service today," the attendance flashed on the booth's external word screen.

She pantomimed utter bewilderment, but was rewarded by no clearer elucidation than the same mesage flashed at her on the booth's word screen. Ignoring her, the attendant settled back inside the booth and returned his bawdy attention to a palm holo player. Jostling from those behind her in line forced Peri to move along, entering the crowded elevator. When a few more people had followed her aboard, the open-grid metal cage jerkily conveyed the group out to the accelerator's launch tube.

The comm bands were alive with puzzled speculation, for no one actually knew why the accelerator was free today. Word of the tempting rate was spreading, though, attracting more and more freelancers to the facility. As a result, the techs were launching divers in groups in order to keep up with the increased traffic.

Peri shuddered to think how many people were strung out in the vacuum between the Petrie platform and Baltuss. She had never made the commute in the physical company of other divers.

Once the elevator disgorged the group into the accelerator, people instinctively spread out along the tunnel of rings, avoiding proximity with anyone else. Wisely done, for in a second each one of them would abruptly be moving at a hundred kilometers a minute. Accidentally bumping into another person at such high velocity could alter the trajectories of both parties, sending everyone flying off in completely inappropriate directions. *Not to mention the bruises,* Peri reminded herself ruefully. She took a position equidistant from her fellow travelers and awaited the signal that launch was imminent.

The red launch light flashed, and before she could tense—Peri was zooming through empty space. A flock of stassed figures surrounded her. They were all moving at relatively the same velocity, so the divers appeared immobile to each other. But her sensors assured her that she was racing through the void. It was a very creepy experience for Peri.

Made all the stranger by the wild rumors that were being passed around the public comm frequencies.

Red Sky had been bought out by HeeVee. (She laughed aloud at that one, knowing how rabidly Red Sky's secret owner reviled everything about the stupid Corp.)

HeeVee's killer robots had destroyed the pirate station's transmitters. (There was a surreal irony in that particular piece of gossip, for it showed Peri that *somebody* had remembered her lunatic doomsaying.)

Cacio Trumpis had gone nova, blotting out Red Sky's broadcasts. (If so, then where was the scorching blast of this stellar explosion?)

An alien invasion had shut down Red Sky's signal.

The rumors grew increasingly ridiculous as time went on.

The long voyage to the gas giant's atmosphere continued, seemingly taking forever. Without Red Sky's music to offer distraction, the passage became agonizingly monotonous. Peri felt acutely fatigued by the relentless inactivity. Although surrounded by other people, she experienced a curious detachment, withdrawing to contemplate this drastic isolation forced upon her by the oppressive hush. This deafening silence was like a psychic acid bath, dissolving away all pretense of civilized behavior, leaving her mind stripped bare and exposing the private core of her being. The raw tranquillity was a cerebral violation that she could not disregard.

The only escape was to tune into the public comm bands, where at least people's voices destroyed the dreadful absence of sound. Despite the extreme stress she was undergoing during this musicless voyage, Peri could not bring herself to contribute to the flashing conversations. She was embarrassed, but content to eavesdrop on the dialogs of strangers in order to restore her sanity. The airwaves held a plethora of irrational responses to the current Crisis. She could literally hear the capital letter in the diver's worried voices as they traded spurious interpretations of what had happened.

Again, no one seemed to know anything for certain. Everyone was mired in rash speculation, for only a handful of individuals knew the secret facts behind the silencing of Red Sky Radio.

Determined this time to honor her vow to Dezi, Peri bit her lip and refrained from extinguishing everyone's fears. The truth would set them all free, but they must never learn it. Not being able to tell them made her feel guilty.

Listening to their impractical gossip bothered her. In the end, she deactivated her comm unit, sparing herself further aggravation.

She made the rest of the journey to Baltuss in painful silence.

As Peri conducted her final approach to Baltuss' stratosphere, she beheld the grand multitude of divers whose silvered figures were spread across the face of the gas giant. There were hundreds of them! The freelancers descended on the crimson clouds like an invading army. They were coming to bag those clouds.

Down she came, penetrating cloudbanks of seething density. Down she went, passing by rich deposits of ammonia and methane. Down she dove, leaving choice clouds of fermium and oxygen for the other divers. She sought a more fabulous prize, a golden treasure to outshine all other scores.

Her wild ambition was not unrealistic. Peri knew of several prizes among Baltuss' clouds, any one of which would fulfill her present requirements, producing a score of unbridled wealth. She had only to call up the coordinates in her artificial memory and head for the designated location.

After a while, though, her gas-bag was still empty. Each premium deposit she sought was gone, swallowed by the hordes of divers that had preceded her. Even the autochthonous drifters, ordinarily unbothered by the presence of human intruders among the clouds, had abandoned the regions for quieter expanses.

She began to wonder whether she was ever going to find a profitable score with the clouds full of so much competition. This mass dive on the part of every freelancer who felt stressed by the absence of Red Sky Radio was decisively working against her. Never before had Baltuss' atmosphere entertained such a legion of voracious gas-miners.

So infrequently did Peri dive for profit, that the frustration of not being able to find a worthy target was infuriating to the normally indifferent girl. It began to seem to her that events—indeed, even the unwitting presence of all these rival divers—*everything* was conspiring against her, opposing her desire to bag and be gone.

Her only recourse was to go deeper than the others, seeking out strata that was known only to someone who had spent days aimlessly wandering the depths of this widespread environment.

Farther down she dove, leaving the plundered mists to the less discriminating miners. Farther down she went, hunting for the promise of undiscovered treasures below. With a renewed determination, she sought unpillaged gas strata, for she knew that far enough down there lay vaporous vistas unseen and untouched by human greed. In these virgin depths, she would find an abundance of precious clouds, more than she wanted or needed.

To her uneasy surprise, Peri discovered that she was being followed. Scarcely five hundred meters above her, another diver was matching her descending velocity and course. When she halted her dive or dipped left, her mystery stalker followed suit with eerie conjunction.

"Why are you following me?" she called on the public comm band.

"I know what *you're* after, sweety," came the gruff reply.

"Who are you?" she growled, for she did not recognize the voice or broadcast Ident code. "What do you want?"

"We both want the same thing," came the snide response. There was a distinctly unpleasant tone in the man's diction.

"Go find your own cloud to bag," she reprimanded him.

"Is that what you want to call it?" The stalker laughed with overtly cruel overtones.

"Leave me alone!"

His cackling persisted, and, according to Peri's sensors, the diver was swooping down to catch her. At the last second, she twisted aside, narrowly evading the man's outstretched silver clutches. His stassed body plunged by her, and the airwaves were full of his angry dissent.

A mugger in the clouds? She had never heard of such a thing before.

She dove away in another direction, but her escape was thwarted. A coarse hand closed on her ankle, tightening into a painful grip. She kicked and yelled, but the attacker drew her close with his superior strength. When she caught a glimpse of the unsightly bulge in the man's crotch, Peri abruptly understood his motives.

A rapist in the clouds!

This she had heard of.

Although her stass-skin would protect Peri from any external force or harm, the field was designed to merge with other stass fields, creating an unbroken protection for both individuals. This process allowed the freelancers to pass through the stass-hatches that served as airlocks aboard the Petrie platform, and enabled divers to physically interact out in the vacuum. She and Taz had experimented with stassed-up sex, only to find the experience awkward and ultimately unrewarding. Without a surface to provide resistance, all her lover's thrusts had failed to stimulate her.

Obviously, though, this attacker was unbothered by such unilateral passion. As with all "rapists", he was concerned only with his own gratification. There were tales of such depraved divers, but until now they had seemed no different from any of the urban myths recited by Dezi Annucci. Peri had never met anyone who could (or *would*) confirm the practice of stassed rape. And she had no intention of learning about such violations firsthand.

She kicked and pummeled and thrashed, but her struggles had no effect against her assailant's bulky muscles. He maintained his firm grip on her ankle, while his other hand searched for more intimate regions of her anatomy. She screamed for help, but knew that they were too deep in Baltuss' clouds for her signal to reach sympathetic ears. Her verbal outcries seemed to amuse her attacker, driving him to more brutal advances.

Resorting to desperate measures, Peri triggered her thigh jets. The manifolds popped from her flesh and fired twin streams of ionized gas. And away she flew. Unfortunately, her flight did not dislodge her attacker's grasp, and he was carried along with her for a harrowing blind race through the dense clouds.

The airwaves were thick with his lewd gloating. He taunted her to struggle more, for such protests only heightened his own appreciation of the interlude.

Panic clogged Peri's desperate thoughts. She deactivated her jets and strained to keep the brute's hands from achieving any vulgar improprieties. Twist and kick and squirm and gouge and yell and kick and squirm. She was losing the fight, and her stamina was draining like gas from a punctured bag. It was clear that she was never going to overpower her attacker by sheer force. Guile was needed—and fast!

If he likes my struggling so much, let's see what he makes of this…

Her aggressions abated and she relaxed, letting herself be drawn in close to the man. Their stass-fields blended into a single protective shell, allowing their skin to touch. She felt the man's rough abdomen press into her soft belly. And below that, his vile member rubbed against her leg. Swallowing her revulsions, she rubbed seductively against him.

"Hey!" he objected. "What are you doing? Cut that out!" He cuffed her across the cheek, snarling, "It's no good unless you don't want it."

Moving her hips against his, she angled her outer thigh against his revolting crotch…and activated her thigh jets with extreme prejudice. With fluid motion, her thruster unfolded from its implanted position and ignited.

The nozzle of the jet released an incandescent exhaust right into the man's privates. Pressed together as the two were, the blast occurred within the confines of their unified stass field. With a monstrous bellow, the rapist released Peri—in fact, flinging her from his scalded body with impulsive rejection.

Freed, Peri rode her jets into the depths, losing herself in the thick clouds. Although her attacker faded in her external scans, his screams remained painfully loud over the airwaves.

"You whore! Look at what you did to me! You'll regret the day you crossed my path! You bitch!"

She didn't remember switching off her comm link, silencing the brute's threats. The pounding of blood in her head drowned out everything.

She wasn't certain how long she had been diving through the clouds. Her position far exceded the maximum depth perception of her equipment. Only lunatic odders came this deep into Baltuss' mass. The pressure readings were astronomical. Her sensors detected raging forces of unprecedented caliber, compressing the clouds into quasi-liquid states. All around her flowed rivers of vibrant density and ominous composition. Down here, the environment was too crowded to demonstrate any luminosity. Her "dive" had become a laborious "crawl".

She could not recall ever going this deep before.

Obviously, Peri had blanked out after her traumatic attack in the higher clouds, leaving her unaware of the profound extent of her downward escape.

She was unfamiliar with this realm. Unfamiliar and uncomfortable.

At this depth, the pressure was incredible enough to render fumes into a viscous state. The temperature outside her stass-skin was frightening. Matter existed in a wholly different manner here than what Peri was used to. Oxygen should be a rarefied gas, not a gummy lump. The density of the flows around her pressed upon her with unpleasantly sturdy weight.

A particularly strident stream captured her, making her an unwilling piece of organic flotsam in a river of what appeared to be liquid iron, if she could believe the findings of her sensors. The ride left her bruised and disoriented. She fought her way from the strong current of iron, finding brief refuge in a less turgid pocket of runny tin.

I need to figure out which way is up *and get out of here,* she resolved.

The density of the environment muffled the range and clarity of her sensors. She could codify only her immediate proximity, leaving everything else in a peripheral haze. As to determining which way was *up*, that proved exceptionally problematic as long as the streams persisted in conveying her along in a mad tumble. With each new tumble, her vantage point changed, and the *up* marker swung wildly in a new direction. While the artificial view of the sensor graphs remained fixed and stable in her vision, the readouts flickered and flashed in a frenetic jumble, faster than she could read or fathom. Closing her eyes did no good, for the readouts were internally superimposed on her view. Only by deactivating her review of all sensory input could she banish this deranged lightshow from her mind's-eye.

For a while, she rode these rivers of glutinous metal in blindness. Dazed just as much by recent events as she was by her rollercoaster hurtle, Peri experienced another time-out.

When she surfaced mentally this time, the girl found she was no longer a prisoner of a tumultuous stream of any liquid metal. Tentatively, she peeked at her sensory arrays. Gratefully, the readouts were stable.

Peri drifted in a lethargic whirlpool of chunky ammonia. Around her seethed the edges of rivers of molten metal. Their contours pulsating with the savage currents contained within. The ammonia sludge was like an island in the fierce environment, a sweet haven in an ocean of hostile salts. She had no idea how she had managed to strand herself in this dormant pocket, but she did not question her fortune.

Minus the disorienting tumble, she was able to use her scanners to successfully determine *up* and a variety of secondary conditions. Somehow, her unconscious voyage had brought her nearer to Baltuss' stratosphere. She was still dangerously deep, well below the boundary where things grew hazardously molten. But now her long-range sensors were able to pierce the super-pressurized clouds and tell her of safe departure routes. Truly—luck had finally stepped in to rescue poor lost Peri.

Or had it? A skeptical ghost in the back of her mind whispered that the odds were simply too outrageous. No amount of random tips and turns could possibly have deposited her in this safe refuge. It was more than impossible— it was suspicious.

She became aware of a drifter hanging across the ammonia pocket from her. It hovered amid a cloud of feathery tendrils, its body concealed by those writhing limbs. The creature resembled no lifeform she knew, but that was no surprise. She had no familiarity with the beasts that dwelled this deep in Baltuss' furious soup. Suddenly the creature bolted, vanishing into a nearby escarpment of molten metal as if it possessed no physical form that might be scorched. Peri was alone now in her haven of chunky ammonia.

Questioning her survival was foolish. She was safe and once again in control of her own destiny. It was time for her to make use of this respite from environmental distress. Time to flee these dreadful depths and return to the cloud strata she knew. Before something else unforeseen and obnoxious appeared to threaten her survival.

She rode on jets of incandescent exhaust for a full minute before she paused.

She had forgotten her original reason for coming Down. The future of Red Sky Radio depended on her bagging a profitable cloud. The events of the last few minutes (hours?) had suppressed all other concerns except her own immediate survival. But now…

She turned and dove again into the molten atmosphere.

Peri refused to abandon these exotic depths empty-bagged. Down this far, each stream and eddy offered a profitable target. In this perilous abyss, everything was a golden score. An assortment of fabulous choices surrounded her…but still she swam deeper.

Drawn by an indefinable instinct more than any fleeting facts or conscious suspicion, Peri dove to unprecedented depths. Her resolve was tantamount, blinding the girl to her hazardous behavior as she searched for the ultimate prize, a score so incredible that it would become legendary, standing as the unchallenged pinnacle of golden scores for a thousand years. The impracticality of this quest escaped her, as did any thought of personal safety.

Peri was diving to save Red Sky.

Only the *best* would satisfy her unrealistic criteria now.

She found Dezi Annucci in his dom cap.

The old man's capsule was cluttered with a motley assortment of brick-a-brack accumulated over decades. There were ancient printouts taped to the walls, depicting planetary horizons of panoramic exotic splendor. There was a nylon mesh bag of loose data chips, the bag itself was blazoned with the logo of an astrophysics journal of some repute. There were clothes that spanned several decades of styles, all crammed clumsily into a cheap plastiform box. There were several carry-cases that were secured locked, which Peri now suspected were filled with the music disks necessary to run the pirate radio station. There was a profusion of innocuous objects too, simple things seen but never attributed any importance: a toothbrush, scraps of folded paper, a screwdriver, a cup. All these possessions drifted freely in the old man's living quarters.

Dezi was wrapped in the safety netting of his zero-G bed. He had not come forth to answer her buzz, admitting her by voice control of his capsule's stass-hatch. Tension and despair still tightened all of the man's elderly muscles, drawing his body into a hunched posture. He frowned, suspicious of her enthusiasm.

"I've got it," she told him.

"What?"

"The creds for the repairs."

"Huh?"

She waved her work pad. "See for yourself."

Dezi came out of his withdrawal to pluck the pad and peer at it with his squinty eyes. Those eyes widened as if tickled by an electrical charge when he beheld the seven-figure number displayed on the tiny screen. "Where did you get a fortune? I thought you claimed to be poor."

Peri smiled slyly. "I have my ways, old man."

"Is it legal?"

"What?"

"Whatever you did to earn all *this* so fast."

She nodded.

He scowled at her, but she kept on nodding.

Finally she released an exasperated sigh and confessed, "I made it bagging gas. I just came from the Gas Exchange. They were pretty impressed. It's not everyday that someones shows up with forty pouds of isotopic copper." Her grin was so wide it made her look retarded.

"Where the void did you find *isotopic copper*?" Dezi gasped.

"I'm a better diver than anybody suspects."

"You swear this is all straight?" he grunted. "I can't afford to involve Red Sky in a semi-legal transaction."

She assured the old man that everything was straight and problem-free.

The only real problem was not directly applicable to the golden score. She told herself she would deal with *that* later. Although there were no policemen to report her rape to, Peri was certain that Admin would not approve of such antisocial behavior. Such individuals were openly undesirable according the colony's bogus charter; Admin would exile the rapist the instant he was identified—if they didn't space him outright. The burns Peri had inflicted on the man would mark him as the guilty party.

Right now, she was enjoying her role as the savior of the pirate radio station. It was only an audience of one, but the old man's gratitude was more than enough to slake Peri of her guilt for being the one responsible for Red Sky's dead air in the first place. Besides that, it made her feel good. Her actions were going to benefit thousands of people, and there was no chance that any of them would ever know her name. Somehow, that anonymity made the whole thing more savory, more rewarding on an emotional level. This sentiment puzzled her, for up until now Peri Fairchild's subjective worldview had been defined by an isolationist philosophy, not any degree of compassionate empathy.

"This is far more than I need," Dezi told her.

"Use what you need, or use it all. Having money isn't really important to me." With a hidden smile, Peri realized the truth in her statement. Her own evaluation of success or contentment had never involved the accumulation of financial wealth. Her real joy was diving in Baltuss' clouds, while her next favorite pastime—she was surprised to realize—was being with Taz! Once she factored her atmospheric calisthenics out of her daily routine, Peri found that spending time with Taz was what she considered most advantageous. Obsessing on the importance of her secret vice, she had failed to recognize the other things that brought her joy. Eating, sleeping, daydreaming, copulating. With a jolt, she realized how integral Taz was to so many of these secondary pleasures.

Compared to her previous lovers, Taz was more handsome and far richer, but he exhibited one trait that had been sorely lacking in the other men in Peri's life: he was willing to allow her some emotional privacy. He did not demand her 24/7 attention. He was psychologically secure enough to remain unthreatened by her periodic need for solitude. The quality time they shared together was adequate to him…and, it dawned on her, thoroughly satisfying to her too.

Was this love?

Assessing her life through the lens generated by this new outlook, Peri found that she honestly had no grounds for complaint. Quite the opposite, in fact.

The clouds were free of killer bots.

She had a man who loved her, a man who deserved her own affections.

She had money now, more than enough to bring her financial independence.

That money could fund the repairs Dezi needed so desperately.

Red Sky Radio was coming back.

She had a purpose now.

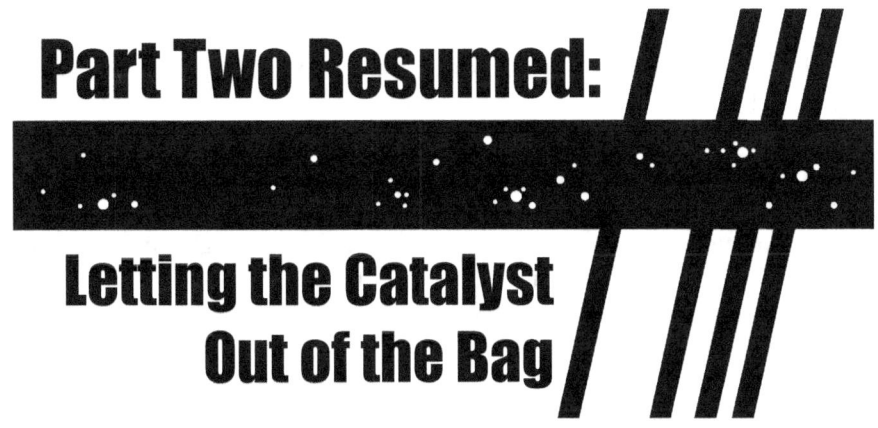

Part Two Resumed:

Letting the Catalyst Out of the Bag

How could fate have chosen to scowl so righteously on the life of Teid Hein?

A patina of ruby fury clouded Hein's vision as he witnessed his mortal enemy's victory over the carefully exaggerated charges brought against the man by the Executive Board's Inquiry Review.

After all of Hein's meticulous and devious schemes—bribing several of Sloane's "trusted" officers to "leak" the Domo's "improper" actions; conspiring with the Hannigan woman so that she would carry the accusations through official channels; indenturing himself to Uwu to guarantee that the Security Domo's downfall would be brutal and painful—and the bastard had found a way to evade his punishment. Worse than that—Sloane had received an Executive Commendation for his initiative! The trial that was supposed to have stripped the Domo of all power, prestige and dignity had gone very awry indeed.

For nearly an hour after the announcement of the shocking verdict, Hein's inner self dominated his consciousness. Freed of any cognizant restraints, Hein's dark soul sent his muscular body on a violent spree. Had this happened in public, he might have murdered a score of innocent people. His rage vented itself in the confines of his personal quarters, though, and only his mistress and four servants were mutilated and killed. When he came out of his tumultuous fugue, Hein was annoyed to find that he had wasted another perfectly functional concubine. He resented that the servants were dead too, leaving him with the unpleasant task of cleaning the bloody mess from his costly decor. Disposing of the corpses occupied the rest of his day.

Afterward, while scrubbing his victims' biological viscera from under his expensively manicured fingernails, Hein set his calculating mind to the task of achieving a penultimate vengeance against the wretched Sloane. Hein would no longer tolerate the man's slippery evasion of every disaster that was thrown at him.

All previous strikes at the Security Domo had been made through other individuals—*that*, Hein realized, had been his fatal mistake. Sloane had been able to outmaneuver the other players. The man would not be able to out-think Hein, though. It would be enjoyable—and satisfying!—to actually go against his nemesis without puppets and fall guys muffling his deadly intentions. There would be no escape this time, for Sloane could never hope to equal Hein's abilities and cunning.

Hein was enjoying a sumptuous dinner of imported roast cattle (prepared and cooked as always by himself to foil any attempts to poison his own meals), when his dining pleasure was disturbed by a private call from Pa'dash Uwu. Despite his resentment for the interruption, Hein promptly took the call, speaking with courtesy and respect to the nefarious Exec's video image.

As usual, Uwu's call was brief. In succinct terms (for calls from this Executive were more secure than any other connection on the lunar base), the Exec commanded Teid Hein to see to the immediate assassination of a group of individuals. A list flashed on the screen, and the names on it actually broke Hein's dispassionate mask. The final name on Uwu's newest hit list was: Security Domo Theo Sloane!

The others were unfamiliar to him. Lester San Germo, Alice Poindexter, Rhyss Davies, Algol Caffino, Paul Wahnfried...

No, wait—where had he heard the name Caffino? That was the technician who had covertly met with Sloane at a gaming center over a week ago. In fact, now that he scoured his mind for the other names, he recognized each of them. These were all people who worked with or had friendships with Sloane.

The Exec was ordering a purge of everyone connected with the base's Security Domo!

And he's asking me to conduct the extermination!

Because of his debt to Uwu for the Exec's cooperation in Sloane's failed Inquiry Review, Hein was bound to do the Exec's bidding without question for the next four months. It did not matter that the Domo had eluded punishment, one *never* crossed Pa'dash Uwu unless one wanted a swift death. Hein had never expected that one of those indentured duties would fulfill all his personal needs and desires.

With this Executive Order to kill Sloane, Hein was absolved of all blame for the death of his nemesis. With Sloane gone, Hein could take his rightful place as Domo of the Natt base's Security Department.

And I get to kill him myself! he reminded himself.

Hein solemnly agreed to do the Executive's bidding.

Once the face of his superior had taken leave of the comm-link's vid-screen, Hein left his meal unfinished. He collected the tools of his miscreant trade and departed his quarters in search of a more gratifying desert.

Not all of his victims were eager to accommodate Hein's murderous intent.

San Germo, Davies, and Caffino all accepted their fate without the chance to complain. The lack of any challenge soured Hein's mood of accomplishment. When Poindexter put up a fight, the assassin toyed with her, giving her every chance to defend herself; but the officer disappointed Hein, falling early to his weakest attack.

Before moving on to Wahnfried, Hein paused to send a false message to the Security Domo. The apparently official communiquÈ informed Sloane of a nonexistent disturbance in a shopping district. This false report would occupy Sloane's attention, keeping the man too busy to learn of his impending doom. Although he could see no way for the Domo to discover his fate, Hein knew to employ every caution now that he was nearing the cataclysmic strike against his hated enemy. Hein could not afford to have an unexpected accident cheat him of his final vengeance.

Wahnfried died too quickly to satisfy Hein's growing bloodlust.

Sloane, however—*he* would be the prize that would appease Hein's frustration.

After all the years of hateful rivalry, this was the first time Teid Hein had broken into Theo Sloane's personal quarters.

The Security Domo's locks were inadequate to keep out a pro like Hein.

Prowling his enemy's rooms, Hein regarded Sloane's possessions and furnishings with disdain. The Domo's tastes were clearly brutish, preferring a decor devoid of style and limiting those choices to a single color: muted off-white (commonly called "eggshell" in the catalogs). There was a single chair at the man's comm console. A solitary table occupied the center of the living room. The only evidence of character was found on the shelves that lined the chamber. There, an assortment of archaic weaponry was on display in cases and mounted on plastiform stands. Axes, handguns, blowguns, flamethrowers, an impressive collection of knives and bayonets, all carefully dust-free and sparkling (where appropriate) with polish. The Domo's kitchen niche was spartan and meticulously spotless, as if it had never seen use. The bedroom was even more sterile, featuring only a slab of foam with a hand-held reader resting on the floor beside the mattress. There were no sheets, covers, or pillows. All the man's clothing hung mutely in his closet.

No wonder Sloane was such a deadly adversary, Hein ruminated. The Domo indulged in no recreational distractions, leaving Sloane with ample time to devote to tormenting Hein's clandestine schemes.

Before killing the man, Hein was curious to discover his nemesis' secrets. He did not expect to find any incriminating evidence openly laying around the man's quarters. If there was anything, it would be locked away in Sloane's personal vault…safe from anything less than a supernova explosion.

Ha!

No locks were secure enough to keep Hein out.

Withdrawing the packets and disks from the opened vault, he spread them on a nearby counter for a detailed examination.

One by one, he popped the disks into the reader he had brought from Sloane's bedside, quickly evaluating that they contained boring personal files. An unlabeled disk offered a selection of curious folders, but he was unable to readily open them. He pocketed that disk; he would review its locked documents later when he could devote the time to crack their security codes.

Among the packets he found a thick plastiform envelope contained an assortment of archaic postage stamps, each resting in separate clear plastic bags. It took Hein a few seconds to identify the Domo's innocuous hobby, recalling the phrenological digests that came to the man in the digital mail from Earth. According to a summary pamphlet, Sloane's collection was quite valuable. Hein proceeded to tear each stamp into confetti, carefully returning the shards to their protective plastic sleeves.

Two other packets contained hardcopy documents that appeared to chronicle Sloane's enlisted years. There were no secrets there, for Hein had attained his own copies of the man's heroic Space Navy service record.

A particular, unlabeled packet attracted his attention. It was made of the type of silver mylar used in the research labs on the Natt base. *This* was something the man should not have had in his possession. Had Sloane gotten the illicit packet from Caffino? Unfortunately, in his present, lifeless condition, the traitorous technician would be providing no corroboration of Hein's suspicions.

What had Sloane been up to? What was the Security Domo doing poking around one of the base's classified research projects? His reasons could only be unprofessional, otherwise Sloane would not have been skulking around and meeting with project technicians in game centers on their lunchbreaks. Such furtive conditions implied that illegal activity had transpired between the two men. Could Sloane actually be reckless enough to think he could sell industrial secrets to one of Harvest's competitors?

It was the ultimate irony: the base's Security Domo unmasked as an industrial spy, stealing classified secrets from the Corp's research labs. It was almost too good to be true. This damning evidence would destroy Sloane's career in nuclear flames. But then, the fool was already marked for death by Exec Uwu's orders, so this evidence would only serve to tarnish Sloane's posthumous reputation…which was an additional bonus in Hein's opinion.

Curious to know what the man had planned to smuggle into the hands of corporate competitors, Hein unsealed the packet and shook its contents out onto the counter. He frowned at the tan powder that drifted from the opened packet. Another mylar envelope fell out onto the counter.

Dust? Hein wrinkled his nose with revulsion. *Sloane was going to sell* dust *to the enemy?*

Picking up the second packet, he pinched it between two fingers. He could feel what seemed to be more powder inside. Tearing off a corner of the crinkly envelope, Hein poured its gray contents onto the counter.

More dust? What profit was there in dust?

Then he noticed how the powders glittered with an electrical chattering. The tan and gray particles were mixing to become a dark brown smudge. His frown deepened when the tiny pile began to vanish. It almost seemed as if the substance was being absorbed by the countertop.

He peered close—but not too close—at the spot where the powder had disappeared, but there was no trace of the smudge left on the counter. Only a slight discoloration marked the counter's "eggshell" surface. The stain pulsed with a gentle radiance. Despite his curiosity, Hein intended to keep a safe distance from whatever the packets had contained.

What had the powders been? More importantly: where had they gone?

This is bad, he ruminated. *I finally get something on Sloane, and now I've* lost the evidence!

Taking the emptied packet, Hein held it up to look closely into its narrow depths. He needed more direct lighting to discern whether the packet held any residue of the mystery powder. He took the silver envelope across the room to examine it under the glare of a bright wall fixture. Fate never allowed him a better glimpse of the interior of the valuable packet.

Behind him, Hein heard the door to the Domo's quarters slide open, followed by a curt gasp—the sharp hiss of air being sucked in through clenched teeth. Barely a second later, something hit him from behind, pressing Hein viciously against the wall. The open packet went flying as Hein balled both hands into fists to defend himself. His fists did him no good, but his flailing feet managed to connect painfully with his assailant.

As he whirled, Hein knew who it was. Only one person would enter these quarters so casually. Only one man could catch Hein unprepared. Confronting his dazed adversary, Hein kicked Sloane in the face.

There was no point, Hein knew, of activating his stass-suit to protect him from his enemy's blows. Sloane could just as easily hide behind his own stass-suit, rendering each defense useless. The inviolate nature of a body-suit force field was impervious to everything—except another stass field. When different stass fields made contact, they flowed to become a single field. With each delivered blow, the combatants' stass-suits would unite, giving clear passage for punches, kicks, and chops.

Anyway, Hein wanted to see the pain and defeat on his enemy's face as he vanquished the wretched Security Domo. He wanted Sloane to know who was beating the life out of him.

The time for skulking and scheming was past. After all the intricate plots and slanderous innuendoes, Hein would get the chance to dispatch his nemesis with his own hands. Now, it was time to destroy Sloane.

The Security Domo had obvious problems with this goal. The man fought Hein like a rabid tiger.

"You!" growled Sloane.

"Time for our showdown," Hein advised his hated enemy.

The two men danced around the room, their limbs flying to strike each other when the opportunities presented themselves. Impacts were noticeably infrequent in this struggle, for each combatant was nimble and fast, blocking assaults and dodging thrusts with energetic ease. They moved like liquid lightning, their arms and legs in a constant blurred state. This confrontation moved back and forth in the room. Furniture was smashed underfoot, and the walls cracked under the force of the men's deflected blows.

From the extent of the lavish damage, it was quite apparent that both men possessed combat implants. Hein's stress-augmented fists crushed plastiform panels as he struck them. Sloane's movements were too swift to be attributable to womb-born muscles. Unperturbed by this, Hein was fully confident that his underworld implants far outclassed the ex-soldier's military leftovers. He adjusted his metabolism to pump extra endorphins into his bloodstream, priming him for an escalation of battle prowess.

In this flurry of destruction, neither warrior noticed as the side counter collapsed in upon itself.

Hein kept himself light on his toes, bouncing rather than standing. His left leg shot out to cave in his adversary's stomach, but the kick missed as Sloane jerked his torso out of harm's way. Hein's heel fractured a shelf unit, spilling an assortment of antique weapons. He retracted the foot instantly, and Sloane's driven elbow failed to catch his leg. Expecting the man to be off-balance, Hein brought his leg swooping back to strike Sloane in the exposed ribs—but the Domo evaded his blow with a savage twist. Part of that twist drove his fist at Hein's face, but a speedy arm came up to block the punch, sending Sloane's fist bouncing away in the air.

Both warriors paused, glancing at the knives that had fallen about their feet. Hein was the first to lunge to grasp one of the bayonets. A sharp kick from Sloane's foot sent the blade whirling from Hein's clutches. Another kick swiped the other knives aside, while Sloane drove his fist into Hein's face, crushing his nose with a gross noise.

Staggering back a step, Hein snorted mightily, expelling blood and cartilage from his tortured nasal passages.

"Taking unnecessary risks," Sloane remarked through grinding teeth.

"No risks this time," Hein told him. "I'm acting on Executive Orders."

"Always the minion," sneered the Domo.

With abrupt speed, Hein's own fist struck toward his enemy's head, catching him across the chin. As the fist struck, talons extruded to pierce the Domo's cheek, ripping flesh as the victim recoiled. Sloane shook off the wound, however, and Hein had to retreat to avoid the Domo's descending fist. Titanium caps were already glittering through the Domo's bloodied knuckles. As he danced away, Hein stumbled over the ruins of the simplistic table. His loss of balance was brief, but long enough to allow Sloane to regroup and come at him with wild screams. Hooking a piece of debris with a flailing foot, Hein flopped one of the table's detached legs up at the advancing man. Sloane dodged the flying bludgeon. And Hein regained his feet.

"At least this time, you've got the guts to come after me in person," the Domo snarled.

The battle resumed. He felt a foot catch Sloane in the knee, then grunted as one of the Domo's hands landed a painful chop to his neck. Urgent to press his meager advantage, Hein lashed out viciously, attempting to pepper Sloane's wounded knee with repeated blows. It took considerable effort to damage the man, a testament to his upbringing on the heavy-gravity world of Crunch. As Sloane's knee finally shattered, Hein took a severe blow to his own arm. The Domo staggered back and collapsed, his broken leg bending forward like that of a bird. Hein grunted with satisfaction, and moved in for the kill.

Engrossed in their mayhem, the men remained unaware as the floor began to sag near the dissolved counter.

To his surprise, Hein discovered that only one of his arms were raised against his foe. The humerus of his right arm had snapped just above the elbow and his arm was flapping like a sock full of dead meat. He tried to clench that fist, but the limb no longer answered his guidance. So Hein beat away at the Domo with his loose arm, awkwardly and imprecisely, unconcerned by the damage he was inflicting on himself.

Meanwhile, Sloane was ignoring his own injury and returning Hein's mad blows with equal fervor. From his vantage on the floor, the Domo concentrated his attack on Hein's abdomen and pelvis. A crippling blow to the crotch made Hein pause as his brain filled with a wave of searing agony. Sloane used the respite to catch his opponent's leg and snap the reinforced femur like a stout but rotten board. Hein crumpled to the floor. The Domo's advantage was fleeting as Hein came crashing down on Sloane's shattered knee. Both men wailed in pain, but they did not hesitate to instantly grapple with each other, propelling their consciousnesses through astounding agony to focus on the battle. Sprawled in a clutter of archaic weaponry, they ignored the bayonets and mace and flamerthrower. The two men restricted their battle to madly beating at each other, tearing, clawing, pounding, kicking. Growling in hate and arrogant pride, each combatant was determined to deliver the killing blow with their bare hands.

The room echoed with the smacks of meat hitting meat, the snaps of bones fracturing, the grunts of agony endured in order to inflict further pain on their opponent.

Gradually, the melee of limbs desisted, reducing the flurry to a maze of spasms and disconnected flopping.

When Hein's mind swam clear of the incapacitating flood of pain, he realized that he lay beneath Sloane's dormant form. He had won! Gasping through a bruised throat, Hein relaxed and rejoiced. *I beat the bastard! I win!* From the severe angle of the man's back, it would appear that he had broken Sloane's spine. To his frustration, he was unable to push Sloane's substantial body from on top of him. Its inert mass weighed him down.

Hein paused to take stock of his own physical resources. Both his arms were unresponsive, and he could only feel one leg. One of his useless arms was trapped beneath him, pressing into his back—into his *numb* back. He jerked and thrashed and flailed...and his body refused to respond to his mind's agitated directions.

Sloane's was not the only broken spine in the pile of men.

"But—I *won!*" Hein groaned.

"Lot of good it'll do you," came the grating reply. Sloane was *not dead!* He was not even unconscious.

"You bastard..."

"Eat me, Hein," Sloane growled. "You're the one trespassing in my quarters."

"You've been stealing corporate research secrets!" Hein spat back at the man.

That was when the two men noticed that the floor was vanishing. A section of it was already gone, and the dissolving edge was growing closer to them by the second.

"You *opened* it!" the Domo screamed.

"What's going on—?"

"You opened the sample!"

"Huh? What the hell did you steal—"

The hole in the floor was growing bigger, as if something was eating it away. A similar gap was rising up the wall where the side counter had once stood. The edge of the hole in the floor was near enough now for Hein to witness the hellish chemical reaction. Something was literally dissolving the concrete and steel.

The hole was headed right for him! Frantically, Hein struggled to pitch Sloane's immobile body from atop him. The Domo may not have been dead, but his weight was. Hein could not budge the man. His nemesis was pinning him down directly in the path of the growing hole.

"Get off me!" he shouted.

"Move yourself," Sloane snarled back. "Looks as if it's going to get us both…"

"What the hell is it? What did you steal?"

"Don't you mean: what did *you* unleash?" The Domo laughed with madcap abandon.

"What the hell is it?"

"You…you don't know, do you?" Sloane's laughter paused, to be replaced by an ironic chuckle. "It's going to kill us both, and you don't know what it is."

"It's something you stole from one of the classified research labs…"

"You're going to die, and you don't know why!" The Domo's mirth increased again, and he released mighty guffaws that would have rocked his entire body if he hadn't been paralyzed.

"Tell me!" bellowed Hein.

"Not a chance, Hein. We both die, but I do it with the knowledge of how and why. You—you just die aching to know."

Exerting himself to his limit, Hein failed to get his body to move. His head and one leg were all that he could feel, but that limb refused to stir. He could speak and move his head, but that was not enough to dig him out from under Sloane's bulk, nor were the gyrations of his neck sufficient to edge him away from the approaching hole. Trapped! He had beaten his nemesis, but could not escape whatever monstrous phenomena the bastard had stolen!

"It hasn't been programmed yet," Sloane was muttering.

The hole was barely centimeters from Hein now. An acrid ozone odor filled his frenzied nostrils. Delicate traceries of tiny electrical discharges illuminated the dissolving edge that advanced across the floor. The phenomena had an unreal quality about it, as if it were some visual effect digitally imposed on the reality of the brutalized chamber.

Again, marshaling his entire rage and desperation, he strained and failed to move himself away from the deadly precipice. *What's underneath Sloane's quarters?* he wondered. More rooms, probably. Soon, he would plummet through the incredible hole and discover what lay below.

Sloane announced, "It'll infect anything it comes in contact with."

Suddenly Hein remembered his stass-suit. It had been useless in battle against his enemy, but its force field would protect him from whatever malignant catalyst was approaching across the floor. His stass-suit could be activated by a conscious act of will in times of hazardous risk. Hein did so now, feeling the cool veneer of the stass field coating his body.

"Ha!" he wheezed. Now he was safe from whatever dangerous reaction was threatening him.

"And 'ha!' right back at you," came Sloane's snide retort.

Dammit! fumed Hein. He had forgotten that, pressed together as they were, the Security Domo would share the protection of his stass field as it flowed into a skin-tight force field containing both men.

Personal security came first, Hein reminded himself. He would address the destruction of his nemesis later, once he had survived the immediate and mysterious menace.

With an unpleasant shock, his shoulder started to burn. Hein could not move his arm, but he could feel the pain. He knew that it was impossible for *anything* to penetrate a stass-skin…but whatever was dissolving the floor had not been blocked by his stass-suit's force field! It was now eating into his flesh!

"Didn't work, did it?" Sloane gloated. "They really perfected the thing, huh? It'll eat through *anything*!"

"What the hell *is* this thing?!" Hein wailed hoarsely. Panic was starting to constrict his throat.

"That's classified," cackled Sloane. "You're on the bottom. It'll get you first."

The heat of the infection swept across Hein's back, into his chest. His flesh melted away, followed by muscle and bone, then his internal organs. There was no gushing of spilled blood, for even that seemed to evaporate in the face of the advancing contagion. He gasped as his lungs vanished. He yelled without breath as his heart dissolved. Gawking with fear-maddened eyes, Hein watched as his barrel chest caved in and the emptiness crawled up his neck to consume his face.

"I get to watch you die," his nemesis cheered.

As the infection scampered up his brain-stem to transform his wailing cerebellum into air, Hein whimpered, "Why *me*?"

How could fate have chosen to scowl so righteously on the life of Teid Hein?

Part One Resumed:
The Quest to Unsilence Red Sky

There were a lot of changes in the air today.

Of all the hardware supply shops that rented space aboard the Petrie platform's commercial districts, Dezi had no preference over any particular vendor. In fact, he chose to spread his purchases among several shops in order to conceal the scope of his buying. This left a more confused trail for anyone endeavoring to compile data that might implicate him in anything, illegal or otherwise. To protect his pirate ass and to satisfy his gut instinct, Dezi disliked commercial profiling.

This was his usual *modus operandi*, but today's crisis dictated a more direct route. Haste was motivating the old man more than caution, for he was eager to get Red Sky Radio back on the air.

He explained this to Peri as they made their way through the corridors of the Petrie station's commercial pod. She seemed to understand his motives, exhibiting a surprisingly instinctive grasp of the covert lifestyle.

Dezi could not help but notice the maturity and confidence that had blossomed in the girl. This transformation had something to do with the fortune she had miraculously found. He would have liked to believe that her growth was the result of her altruistic donation of this fortune to the cause of restoring Red Sky Radio, but he suspected that there were more levels to it that just that. Emotional epiphanies lurked in the girl's strange mind, secrets that the old man might never comprehend.

Until recently, Peri had always seemed harmless and more than a bit naive…an acquaintance who treated him like a normal human being, not an odder outcast among the freelancers. She had shown an interest in him that went beyond curiosity. It was as if she honestly cared. In response, he had returned that friendship, grateful to finally have some social contact that wasn't confined to the solicitous tolerance shown him by the other divers.

Then her personality had gotten tainted by spurious rumors and warped by anxiety. Her obsessive belief in killer robots prowling the clouds of Baltuss had twisted her likable self into an obtrusive nuisance. Dezi had mourned this emotional transformation, for he had grown to like Peri. The girl had undergone a disturbing reversal of temperament, changing from someone who was congenial and considerate into an obstinate pest. Not only had she harassed strangers with her fanatical fears, she had accused Dezi of collusion with her imaginary enemy. For a while, Dezi had dreaded that she was going to inadvertently expose his secret with her wild allegations.

When he had learned about Peri's brazen scheme to trap one of the "killer bots", he had followed her into Baltuss' clouds to prevent the girl from interfering with his network of secret transmitters. She had, he knew, already *accidentally* found two of his transmitters. He had harbored no desire to discover how successful Peri might be if she were *intentionally* trying to locate one of them.

But Peri had gotten to a transmitter first. She and her questionable companion had actually managed to injure the unit before he could arrive to warn them off.

Dezi knew he should have told the girl the truth about the "killer robots", but decades of absolute secrecy were difficult to put aside. Had he confided in the girl, none of this would have happened. Red Sky would still be broadcasting…and Peri would probably still be an annoying nuisance. It had been through her desire to undo the damage of her obsessive actions that the girl had worked through her emotional disturbances, reverting to a kind and gentle friend. The momentary silencing of Dezi's pirate radio station had been necessary for the girl to cast off her delusions. With a degree of resignation, the old man decided that it was an affordable price. Red Sky could be restored, but the salvation of a human psyche always took precedence.

He was happy to have the old Peri back. He had missed her company. Restored to her rational self, the girl was displaying an earnest concern for the fate of Red Sky Radio. It was apparent that she not only felt responsible to fix the damage done by her earlier mistake, Peri was showing signs of long-term interest in the pirate station.

Under normal circumstances, this would have worried Dezi, but he was growing aware of his own mortality. There would come a time when he was unable to maintain the pirate station's 24/7 broadcasts, when the existence of a protÈgÈ would become invaluable. Once Dezi was gone, only a trusted associate could continue his work and keep Red Sky alive.

Was Peri Fairchild that potential apprentice? Was the girl who had accidentally silenced Red Sky Radio destined to inherit the pirate station?

Armed now with Peri's sudden wealth, Red Sky's radio silence would soon come to an end. The parts required to repair the damaged unit were not many, but they were expensive. Dezi decided that they would only need to hit two supply shops to find themselves in possession of the necessary parts. Then, the old man could hastily dive Down to fix the faulty transmitter he had left in a high orbit around the gas giant.

He guided his new financial backer to take the next portal on the right. In this manner they could reach the first supply shop by cutting through a courtyard.

The last thing Dezi expected to encounter was a drama of life and death proportions.

Clouded by considerable chaos, it took a while to sort out what had happened in Courtyard 3.

Apparently, a newcomer to the platform had identified Harrison Furrell as an subversive agent in the employ of Harvest Corp. With the help of the colony's new nurse, Denise Coleman, who had distracted Furrell's audience to another courtyard, this newcomer, one Juul Ragle, had apprehended the scoundrel. While questioning the HeeVee spy about his latest agitation scheme, the hero and heroine had been surprised and subdued by the real villain.

The general population of the Petrie platform was quite startled to learn that the colony's resident doctor was that villain. Everyone thought that Ivar Petroff was a wretched medical officer, but no one had imagined that there were traitorous aims motivating his ineptitude. There was a fair amount of head-shaking and tongue-clucking, but the freelancers exhibited no trace of sympathy for the treacherous doctor. Petroff had endangered them all with his intentionally incorrect diagnoses, he had callously killed his Furrell henchman, and he had been about to cowardly murder Ragle and Coleman when he had been discovered red-handed.

Coleman had emptied the crowded concourse by announcing that Red Sky Radio was holding their own demonstration in an adjacent courtyard. When the audience had found no such lecture, they had returned to stumble upon the iniquitous Petroff and foil his craven massacre. Responding to Coleman's desolate screams, the mob had descended on the wicked villain, literally tearing him limb from limb.

Explaining all this to an ever-increasing crowd in the courtyard, Juul Ragle repeatedly made reference to the platform's need for a police force to prevent this type of sedition from reoccurring. The people did not respond well to this suggestion.

"We already got Admin watching over us," one diver called out.

"They sure did a good job hiring Doc Petroff," another observed sarcastically.

"Anyway," a woman pointed out, "what's to keep Admin from buying out a police force? Then they could sic these new cops on us for late dom cap rental payments."

Intending to quickly pass through the courtyard en route to a supply shop, Dezi and Peri had paused to listen to what seemed to be a heated public debate. The old man nodded, for he knew the woman's supposition was not far from the truth. In the past, the Petrie Administrators had maintained a bully squad to enforce their frequent rental increases. This practice had been abandoned when Admin had realized how more cost effective it was to simply turn off a dom cap's stass-hatch, ejecting the delinquent tenants into the unforgiving void.

"You need police protection," Ragle urged. "From unreasonable Administrators and subversive HeeVee spies."

"You're talking about vigilantes," someone accused him.

"Not if these police were supported by local businesses," a voice declared. Taz Bailey swam through the crowd to hang beside Ragle. The two of them faced the freelancers, frowning for their respective reasons. "I think a commercially sanctioned police force would be a good idea, and I'd be willing to finance such a program."

Ragle's scowl melted away from his pale face.

"It's about time," Bailey proclaimed, "that the citizens of Petrie platform had someone to guard them from the greedy Administrators."

"Ain't no citizens here, Bailey," someone laughed from the crowd.

"Yeah. We're all independents," someone else professed with egocentric pride.

"Oh, get real," muttered Denise Coleman from the side. Suddenly everyone was staring at her. She blushed, trying to evade their mass scrutiny. Unable to escape their glaring regard, she spoke up, "You're a community here, not the band of ragtag pirates that HeeVee calls you."

"You're the new nurse," some accused her. "What do you know? You haven't been here for more than a couple of weeks…"

"That's enough time to recognize a colony when I see one," she responded. "You people depend on each other more than you realize. It's human nature to establish social relationships with other people. You all think you're frontier individuals, but none of you are self-sufficient."

A growl rose from many throats.

"She's right," declared Bailey. He pointed at a person at the edge of the crowd, "You, Din. How long's it been since you slept alone?"

Dezi chuckled, for Din Gacy's womanizing was legendary aboard the platform.

"That's one form of social interaction," Bailey pointed out. "Commercial trade is another. How long would any of us last if we were deprived of basic necessities or entertainment? We even have our own radio station."

Why's he looking at me? the old man fidgeted nervously. He finally convinced himself that Bailey's fixed stare had been coincidence, nothing more.

"The only ones who don't want us to become unified are the Administrators, because it would cut into the financial stranglehold they have on each one of us. As individuals, we're slaves to their price control. As a group, we're a customer base that can challenge their business practices. As a community, we could reject their oppression."

What's he doing? Dezi frowned. *Is he suggesting we oust Admin?*

"You're talking about revolution," someone gasped.

"Not at all," Bailey attested. "I'm talking about fair trade practices. Communities do not tolerate commercial monopolies or price gouging."

"You're advocating the violent overthrow of Admin…"

"There'll be no violence going on while I'm on duty," growled Ragle. He puffed up, looking quite authoritative.

"Who put you in charge?" called out a hidden member of the crowd.

"He's not in charge," Bailey announced. "He works for me—if he wants a job heading up the Petrie police force." He glanced at the ex-cop, who nodded grimly in return. "It's his job to protect the community."

"Admin's not going to like any of this," another person hidden in the crowd grumbled loudly.

"I'll deal with Admin," Bailey declared. His voice conveyed a stern finality. With that, he left the impromptu stage—basically the tallest slab in the concourse—and disappeared into the crowd.

He's crazier than I thought, ruminated Dezi. *Admin will never cave in to his demands. They'll starve us all out of our dom caps before they relinquish control of the platform.*

"Nothing more to see here," Ragle was instructing the crowd. "Let's clear the courtyard, okay?"

With a sigh of resignation, Dezi signaled Peri to follow him. Whatever the fate of Bailey's revolt, the old man and the girl had their own mission to complete. The crowd was dispersing as they swam for the chamber's far exit.

As they exited the concourse, Taz Bailey swooped from the shadows to join them. He followed them down the empty corridor.

"Peri!" he called. As he drew near, Bailey whispered, "So, you two are talking again, hmm? Good. I was hoping to have a few words with you…"

"I'm busy right now, Taz," Peri told him nervously. "Can I catch up to you later? In our rec cap?"

"Actually," the financier smiled, "it was Annucci I wanted to talk with."

"Huh? Me?" the old man scowled. *What's he got to say to me?*

"Privacy would be advised. Follow me." Bailey kicked off into a side passage. He paused a few meters down the new hallway, glancing back. "Please?"

Dezi followed the man. After a momentary confusion, Peri came too.

Bailey took them directly to an elite restaurant nearby. At first, Dezi thought the man was mad, expecting to get a table at Real Food Central without a reservation, but Bailey and his companions were immediately escorted to a private dining room.

The old man had never before been inside RFC, he had never had the creds to spare for such a lavish experience. Dezi marveled at the exquisite decor.

The restaurant's antechamber was walled with paneling that looked like— no, it actually was!—organic wood tiles. Strips of golden chrome framed the timbered walls, arranged in craftsman designs that implied opulence-with-taste. The material muffled the echoes of their words, bestowing a strange calm to the room's acoustics. A matre di podium was located at the rear of the cubicle, flanked by a pair of—again, surprise, they were genuine!—potted ferns. The doorway that led deeper into RFC was curtained with a film of beaded satin threads that comfortably parted as they slipped through the barrier. The corridor beyond was paneled with a noticeably different grain of authentic wood. In contrast to the bland functionality of the rest of the platform's interior design, the restaurant's extravagance seemed all the more resplendent.

"What's all this about?" Peri inquired once the trio was alone in a private dining room. "Dezi and I have things to do."

"I can imagine," replied Bailey. He gave the old man a cold look, "She knows then?"

"Knows what?" Dezi commented as innocently as he could.

"I do not have time for games, Annucci," Bailey told him sternly. "If Peri doesn't know that you're behind Red Sky Radio, then she's about to find out."

"That's absurd," Dezi laughed.

"I've got money invested all over this platform. Your purchases and incoming shipments leave a damning paper trail, old man. You'd have been unmasked long ago if I hadn't erased your telltale receipts."

"Umm…"

"I have no interest in exposing you, Annucci. Nor do I have any interest in taking you over or becoming a silent partner. Okay? You do a damned fine job, you are to be commended. You have your own reasons for doing it in secret, and I don't care what they are. I need to ask a favor."

Dezi stared at him with his best expression of disbelief, but it was doing no good. He could see that the financier had uncovered his secret in a manner that no bluff could effectively explain away. There was no point in maintaining his denial.

"What kind of favor?"

"I saw you back there in the courtyard. How much did you hear?"

"You're inciting a revolt to overthrow Admin," the old man muttered. "And I want no part of it."

"That's not exactly what's going to happen, but the end result will be getting rid of the Administrators."

"How long have you been planning this?"

"Trust me, I've had this in mind for a long time, but I never thought I'd have the guts to put it into action. Things seem to have pushed the situation upon me—and on everyone."

"You're going to get a lot of people hurt doing this, Bailey. I really think you should forget about the whole thing."

"It's too late for that now. It's time this platform grew up and became a community. We can't do that as long as Admin treats us all like guests in a hotel."

"But that's what this place really is—a hotel for pirates."

"No, that's what it used to be. You've been here longer than anybody—surely you've noticed that things have changed. People interact now, they socialize and interbreed. There are *families* living here now, families with children. This isn't just some spacelanes stop-over for freelance divers. It's their *home*. We've got to stop thinking of ourselves as the Petrie pirates and act like the colony we are."

"All righteous opinions," Dezi admitted. "But Admin will never relinquish control to anyone without a fight."

"Trust me, nobody's going to get hurt."

Their conversation was interrupted by the arrival of a waiter and an assortment of entrees. As the waiter distributed the bowls to magnetic plates set into the central table, he chattered about the astounding rumor that was sweeping the platform. "Did you hear, Mr. Bailey? They're saying Doc Petroff was a HeeVee spy, and he was to blame for silencing Red Sky Radio. There's talk of armed retaliation."

"You know better to listen to rumors, Roget," Bailey chuckled in response. He jerked a thumb at Dezi and remarked, "This is Dezi Annucci. If anybody knows about rumors, it's him."

Dezi blinked with surprise. "Yes…umm…no. There's no revolt brewing."

"That is reasurring to hear," the waiter commented calmly as he stepped back from the table. But—the man wasn't a waiter—he was Roget Thibuit himself, the master chef. Suddenly, Dezi realized that Bailey must have holdings in this restaurant, that explained his royal treatment.

The old man eyed the bowl of food before him.

"Enjoy," Thibuit grunted before he disappeared.

Alone again, Bailey resumed his pitch for independence from the owners of the platform. Dezi heard very little of it as he tasted, then gobbled his delicious gourmet meal. The spices were not the only unfamiliar part of the food, he detected exotic vegetables and meats that were utterly foreign to a spacer's diet.

"...these people deserve to decide their own destiny," Bailey was saying. "I've got the backing of a lot of the local merchants, even some whose businesses I don't have money in. We were hoping to deal with things quietly, but the scheme's out of the bag now. So I have to act fast, before Admin can react to a threat that doesn't really exist. I need your help."

"I remain unconvinced," Dezi grumbled, "but you have me at a disadvantage. If I don't do this favor for me, you'll expose Red Sky, right?"

"Hmm," Bailey paused and stroked his chin with one of his four hands. The luminous tattoos across his dark face lent the gesture ominous overtones. "I hadn't thought of that. That's tempting...but I think I'll rely on your civic spirit instead."

Dezi snorted, expressing that he still opposed the man's scheme.

"I need Red Sky back up and broadcasting," the financier-turned-revolutionist explained.

"It is not down by choice," muttered the old pirate.

"We're trying to get it back on the air," Peri spoke up.

"What's the problem?" Bailey asked. "Do you need money?"

"We've already got the creds we need," Peri retorted possessively.

Bailey cocked an eyebrow at Dezi; the old man nodded his head the slightest fraction.

The other tactfully skirted the matter, returning to his casual inquiry, "How long before you can get it back up?"

"Four hours," admitted Dezi. "Once I get the necessary parts."

"I want you to support this revolt on the radio. In fact, I need you to advocate the violent overthrow of Admin."

Peri gasped.

"No way," Dezi declared. "No way in hell."

"You've got to trust me. This will help insure that there is no violence."

"That's absurd!"

"Do as I ask, Annucci, and I promise you: there will be no bloodshed or violence."

"I trust him, Dezi," Peri remarked. "I think you should too. Taz is not a violent man. He's a businessman, not a rebel."

"I know it sounds crazy, but it'll give me the leverage I need to pull off this coup in a bloodless manner."

"Red Sky's never had a disc jockey speak on the air before," Dezi grunted.

"There're a lot of changes in the air today, old man."

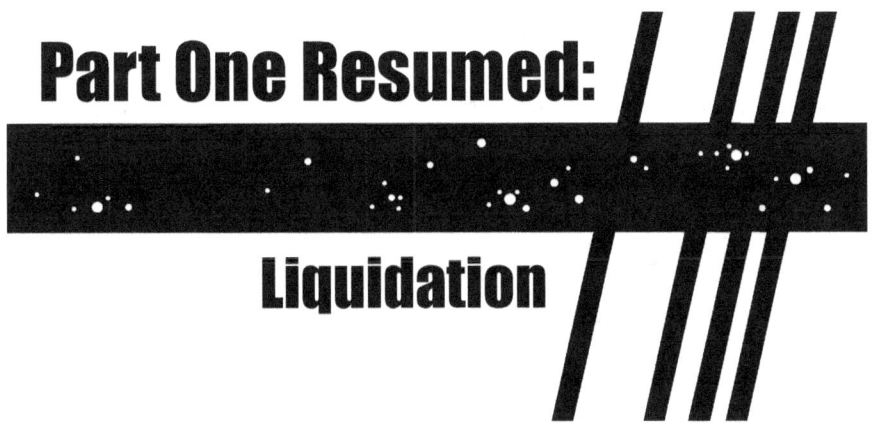

Part One Resumed:

Liquidation

Calls for help began to flood in.

Cataclysm was gnawing away at Harvest Corp's Natt base.

Every comm-link on his console was screaming for Nigel Bester's Executive attention in his private sanctorum. Each message brought word of a dire disaster that was sweeping through the Natt base. The calmer of these reports were vague, but the majority were panicky and illogical.

"—the walls are dissolving—"

"—people are disappearing—*literally*—"

"—can't find the Security Domo—"

"—need help down here—"

The base was undergoing some kind of attack, and from all accounts: it seemed as if the enemy had struck from *within*. Calling up an on-screen schematic, Bester plugged in red dots to correspond to the horde of incoming warnings. The dots were clustered internally in the base's geometry, they defined a ragged sphere of disturbance that was swelling from the core of the cubic citadel. Call lights ceased to blink on his console as this unresponsive area swallowed more of the schematic.

Such widespread destruction could not be the doing of the gas thieves. They simply did not possess the means to inflict this kind of damage.

It had to be one of the classified research projects. Bester had opposed these operations, advocating that, if they *had* to exist, at least the labs should be located a safe distance from the base's personnel. But no, Exec Uwu's influence had swayed that decision, and the research projects were kept on-base, where their unethical secrets could be better guarded from outside curiosity.

This was the price of such sloppy management. Something had gone wrong, and the base was disappearing under their very feet.

There would be time enough for recriminations later, if he survived. Now, however, Bester needed to order a complete evacuation of the facility. Was there time to divert crews to salvage the collected gas stocks? A glance at the inflation rate of the affected area told him the sad answer. The precious cargo tanks were doomed. The lives of the workers were far more valuable in Bester's opinion.

This attitude was not shared by the rest of the Board. When Bester went to sound the evacuation siren, he discovered that circuit was solidly blocked by Evelyn Hannigan. Tuning into the command link, Bester found that in Uwu's control. The nasty Exec was ordering work crews into the contaminated area, commanding them to retrieve the threatened cargo tanks.

"No!" wailed Bester. "Are you insane?"

Uwu's swarthy face popped up on a peripheral screen to sneer at Bester's agitated outcry. Too aloof to bother to argue with Bester's pathetic dissent, Pa'dash Uwu wasted no words on the man.

"It's a lost cause," insisted Bester. "You're ordering those workers to their deaths!"

"We have to salvage something," Hannigan informed him. "Do you expect the three of *us* to go down and unhook the tanks?"

Bester pleaded with the cold-hearted woman, "They're human beings—not disposable tools!"

"They're employees. They're paid to do what we say."

"You're insane!"

"The base is under attack," Uwu announced tersely. "Those damned pirates are behind this."

Blame was unimportant. Only survival counted now.

Playing a trump card that had taken years and thousands of creds to insert into the base's system, Bester initiated a usurp-virus into the base's computer network. The disruptive code knocked Uwu and Hannigan out of the command loop, leaving control of all lines in the hands of Bester. He instantly ordered the immediate and unconditional evacuation of all personnel from the base.

Leaping from his hover chair, he dashed over to the decorative base of one of the faux columns that lined his sanctorum. Hidden here was his escape pod; each of the Execs had one. As he pulled open the secret doorway, Bester paused, a dark thought crossing his desperate mind.

His usurp-virus had effectively locked the other Execs out of all command lines—including those used in their own quarters. Wherever Hannigan and Uwu were, they could not escape—all doors were secured against them, all systems refused to answer their orders.

There was no question that Hannigan and Uwu deserved to die. The financial ruin of millions stained their greedy hands, not to mention the actual blood of not a few individuals. Just now, the pair had been willing—no, *eager*—to throw away the lives of their loyal employees in a futile attempt to salvage a commodity. The only human lives that mattered to the two wicked Execs were their own. Oh yes, they deserved to die. But Bester refused to lower himself to their vile level and be responsible for *any* deaths, even theirs.

Flinging himself back across the ragged cobblestones of his facsimile castle, Bester scrambled to modify his usurp-virus, returning a degree of control to the trapped villains. He would not condemn them, but neither would he take the time to rescue them. They could achieve their own escapes now. He had his own to worry about. A glance at the on-screen schematic told him the affected area was getting close. Turning away from his console, he caught a glimpse of something sparkling in the shadows across the mock-stone chamber.

The phenomena froze him. With eyes widened with fear, he poised in mid-turn over his desk and gawked at the strangeness that was creeping into his sanctorum. A twinkling edge seeped up the wall, transforming the faux stone into nothingness. Whatever the cataclysm was, it was relentless and incredible. Crackling like a living current, the glowing edge caressed fresh wall, and the material simply vanished. It was some horrific chain reaction transmuting all matter into vacuum. A similar dissolution line was traveling across the floor, eating away the rotund cobbles. As the gap in the wall grew, Bester stared with shock through the hole, gazing upon a vast depth that had once contained the bulk of the base. Floors, halls, quarters, everything was gone! In the distance, he could see the opposite side of the expanding sphere gnawing away at the lower corridors.

It's the matter virus, he gasped. The force destroying Harvest's base was the matter virus! Designed and cultured in the Corp's illicit labs, this artificial annihilator was consuming its place of birth like some insane evil offspring. There was nothing that could withstand the unnatural contagion. According to the latest reports from Project Godbreath, though, a limiter had been found. Bester wrestled with his memory to recall what the researchers had devised. *Vacuum,* he remembered. The virus stopped when it ran out of matter to consume. *A lot of good knowing that will do the base.*

The cracking edge of dissolution was barely six meters away and coming strong, advancing across his doomed sanctorum. In seconds, it would sweep upon Bester and end his miserable life. It was Flint's revenge.

Without another thought, the terrified Exec threw himself away from his console. He staggered and almost fell en route to the yawning hatch of his escape pod. By sheer stubborn defiance, he managed to keep his footing, finally stumbling across the threshold and falling on his face inside the pod.

Behind him, the hatchway slammed shut. Activated by his entrance, the pod's preordained emergency systems kicked in without hesitation. Thrusters exploded into action, driving the pod up the escape chimney. Acceleration increased, pushing his injured features painfully into the metal floor. By the time the pod ejected from the base's rooftop, it was traveling with enough speed to achieve escape velocity from the frozen moon. The crushing pressure of several Gs drove the shards of Bester's shattered teeth ripping through his tattered lips. The cartilage in his nose was reduced to a chunky paste. He screamed, his breath sputtering blood through his ruined mouth, and he gratefully passed out.

But only for a few moments.

Through a cloud of agony, the Exec's mind struggled back to consciousness. Desperation wrenched him from the warm and welcome embrace of dark relief. He knew he had escaped the terrible disaster, but his job was not done. As ranking Exec, Bester needed to coordinate the evacuating workers, gathering them together in the void beyond Natt.

Protected by their stass-suits, they would be safe in the vacuum. But this escape was impermanent, incomplete without some place for them to regroup. The air contained in their body tanks would not last indefinitely.

Dragging his gangly and bruised form into his pod's launch couch, he fumbled with the controls until a monitor screen sprang to life. Hanging over his head, this screen showed him the view below: the ice moon his pod had just left. A flick of finger zoomed the view in on the dwindling base.

Perched precariously at the lip of an enormous chasm, the base's cubish black shape was starkly visible against the frozen methane. As he stared at it, the structure began to collapse into itself. Unsupported by any internal mass, the huge walls and ceiling buckled. The pieces—small on his screen although he knew them to be hundreds of meters in size—fell into the depths, vanishing from view in a crackling glow.

Bester gasped.

As he watched, the vicious contagion spread from the crumpling exterior of the Corp's base to sweep across the lunar plains. The awful matter virus had eaten its way to freedom, consuming labs, technicians, hallways, floors, the entire base—and its hunger was not sated. Spastic tongues of molecular fission danced on the ice, leaving a void in their wake.

Within minutes, the moon was gone.

The matter virus had effectively eradicated Harvest Corp's holdings in the region of Baltuss. Had it been Project Godbreath losing control of the contagion? Or had Exec Uwu been right—had it been part of a pirate attack on the Natt base?

There was only one person outside Harvest who knew about the matter virus, and Bester knew that was the virus' inventor, Professor Donald Flint... who had fled Natt over thirty years ago after attempting to erase all trace of the project from the base's databanks. The Corp had searched long and hard to find the renegade scientist, fearing the classified data he held in his brain. No trace of the man had ever been discovered.

Had Flint taken refuge with the pirates?

Was the defector behind this attack?

No, Bester decided. Flint had been so ethical that he rebelled against the research because of its hazardous nature. The scientist would never condone the use of the matter virus as a weapon against anyone—even the corporation he so loathed.

Would anyone ever learn who had been responsible for Harvest's defeat?

Eighty percent of the divers under contract to Harvest Corp escaped the destruction of the Natt facility. It turned out that most of these individuals had completely ignored Uwu's lunatic orders to salvage the threatened cargo tanks. They had fled the base at the first hint of disaster.

Only twelve of the three hundred technical employees survived. It was presumed that most of these techs perished in the early stages of the contagion's outbreak. Going about their business in the central labs, the odds were good that they died before they knew anything was wrong.

No signs were ever found of Executives Evelyn Hannigan or Pa'dash Uwu. The catastrophe left Exec Bester in absolute command.

Command of nothing, he ruminated. The base was gone, so was the entire moon that had harbored it. He was left with thousands of bewildered and terrified divers. A few small Security pursuit ships had escaped the base's dissolution, but none of them were capable of reaching distant Greye.

The only other human habitation in the immediate region of the gas giant was the pirate's secret base.

Calls for help began to flood out.

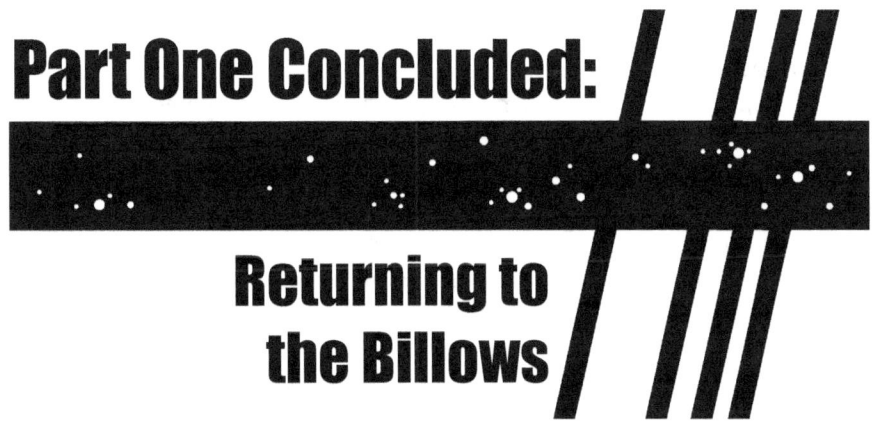

Part One Concluded:

Returning to the Billows

There was no turning back now.

Taz accompanied Dezi Annucci and Peri as they visited a hardware supply shop. There, the pirates (it was amusing to think that, after years of unprofitable diving, his lover had become a *pirate* by association with the illegal radio station) purchased a motley collection of equipment. At first, the merchant refused to accept money, using Taz's presence as an excuse to be generous. Peri's outrage at this had predicated the shop owner backing down and taking payment.

Aha, noted Taz Bailey. *She's discovered her new fortune.*

He understood Peri's need to be financially self-sufficient, and recognized that she was determined to help out Red Sky Radio without any financial assistance from him. Taz could respect that, her spunk was one of her most attractive emotional features.

Glancing quite innocently at the balance code on Peri's Ident card as she used it to pay the merchant, Taz's expression of casual curiosity widened with astonishment. The seven-figure number he saw bore little resemblence to the 3,042 creds which he had secretly slipped into Peri Fairchild's account earlier.

Where the fusion did she get all that money...?

When he looked up, Taz found that everyone (Peri, Dezi, even the apologetic merchant) was staring at his slack face, each with their own brand of bewilderment. The merchant seemed uncertain about the entire transaction, perceiving Taz's shocked look as evidence that something was amiss. The old man's dubious scowl slowly melted into a knowing smirk as he drew some private conclusion about the whole thing. Peri laughed aloud and drove a playful elbow into his brown ribcage.

"See?" she whispered. "I can bag like a pro...when I want to."

"What...?"

"I scored some radioactive copper," she told him with unembarrassed self-satisfaction.

"Okay..." He smiled at her, and his confusion dissipated in a puff of dazed approval. He wondered whether she had noticed his ghost deposit before the Exchange Office had paid the girl for her miraculous score. It didn't matter now.

Peri was suddenly extravagantly flush with funds. Her unexpected wealth was of her own doing. With this monetary declaration of self-preservation, she had apparently shed her "killer bot" mania, returning to her old, chipper, unbearably sexy self. Taz longed to smother her with welcome-back kisses, but the moment was not neccesarily appropriate for such an impulsive display of affection. There were things to do—*serious* things.

Peri and Annucci had a pirate radio station to mend.

And Taz had a revolution to lead.

Carrying their purchases in a pair of lumpy satchels, the old man and the girl hurriedly departed to catch the linear accelerator out to Baltuss. There, repairs would commence, and, according to Annucci's confidential estimate, four hours from now, Red Sky Radio would return to the airwaves.

Taz desperately hoped he had convinced Annucci to do as requested.

Among the apparatus the old man had gotten had been a voice synthesizer. Taz assumed that Dezi would use this device to debut a disc jockey in conjunction with Red Sky's triumphant return. Whether that DJ announced or denounced the imminent violent attack on Admin...this remained to be heard.

In four hours...

Four hours...not a lot of time to prepare, he mused. There were a lot of details that needed to be confirmed before he could go before the Head Administrators.

And, now that he thought of it, *I'd like to have Officer Ragle with me when I confront the enemy. Just in case...*

He faced the four Head Administrators and told them bluntly, "You're facing a revolt, you know."

They scoffed at him, but Taz could tell that they were aware of the unrest that was sweeping through the platform. It was no secret that Admin monitored activity throughout the Petrie platform via hidden cameras.

Taz had spoken with the colony's merchants. They had all agreed to establish rebel training camps, signing up earnest freelancers who desired to become citizens. The actual purpose of these camps was to avert any violent attack on Admin, distracting possible militants with the arduous preparations for an armed revolt that wasn't supposed to happen. If all went according to Taz's plan, by the time these rowdies were ready, there would no longer be any Admin to overthrow.

Word of these rebel camps had undoubtedly reached Admin, though. *That* was what mattered.

Beside him, Juul Ragle hung in a uniform manufactured in the last two hours. In it, he looked every bit the part of a military leader. (Later, a few alterations would transform the costume into an innocuous but functional police outfit.) Officer Ragle scowled and remained silent—as Taz had instructed.

The Administrators were wearing intolerant scowls as they faced Taz. His gut response to their bravado was contempt. In fact, he was finding it difficult to handle the situation without feeling abject repulsion for the greedy bastards. For years and years, he had watched Admin gouge the freelancers, milking them financially dry and then treating them with scorn when there were no more creds to squeeze from this captive market. Even with his own wealth, Taz had felt the sting of Admin's avarice. It was no wonder that he personally loathed the greedy bastards. The wonder was that he had managed to contain his outrage for so long.

Annucci had perceptively identified that the overthrow of Admin was not a new scheme in Taz's mind. The financier had been working on the notion for nearly five years now, quietly broaching the topic with merchants throughout the colony. Together, they had devised a plan that might oust the greedy bastards.

When he had discovered the incident in Courtyard 3, Taz had recognized the volatile mood of the crowd. They were already emotionally charged by the loss of Red Sky, primed to blame HeeVee for silencing the pirate radio station. With the discovery that Doc Petroff had been a HeeVee spy, the freelancers were ready to attack the Corp's lunar base—and get themselves killed. That last part would not have been part of the mob's plan, but it would certainly have been the outcome of any stupid assault on the Corp's defenses. Against his better judgment, Taz had stepped up and turned the crowd's animosity against the Administrators. Ahead of schedule, his own private scheme had been forced into play.

"Your days—your *hours* are numbered on this platform," Taz informed the nervous Administrators.

One Administrator warned that all external hatches would be turned off, exposing the entire station to the vacuum.

Taz reminded them that everyone aboard the Petrie platform had a stass-suit that would protect them. "They'll just come after you in the vacuum."

Another Administrator wanted to know why Taz Bailey was here.

"I'm here for many reasons," Taz declared. "One of them is to make sure that you understand the forces about to take you out."

"We are fully capable of defending our ownership of this platform against a mob of lunatics."

"They're not lunatics," Taz pointed out. "They're patriots. They're fighting for their freedom. There's a lot of historical precedent implying that in such a conflict, they can expect outside assistance, while *you* can expect to be crucified by the press. That's not the kind of battle I think you want to fight."

"What press?"

"How about Red Sky Radio?" he smiled.

"What? Everyone knows that HeeVee knocked the pirate radio station off the air half-a-day ago."

"That's entirely a vicious rumor. You'll find that Red Sky is back now, and they're calling for your heads."

An Administrator fumbled with a nearby console. After a minute, the dry hiss of static echoed from the controls.

Sneering, an Administrator remarked that some "vicious rumors" appeared to be true.

Dammit, Taz fretted. *Come on, old man...give me a signal...*

The Administrators were regaining their composure. Three of them grinned with malicious victory. Wearing an arrogant scowl, the fourth decreed that Taz's audience was over.

"Okay," Taz shrugged. "I'll tell the freedom fighters you rejected my offer, and they'll come after your heads."

"What offer?" asked one of the Administrators cagily.

"I've got a proposal that might just save your collective butt." He paused, toying with their anxiety. They were playing a cool front, but Taz knew that the prospect of armed insurrection had them scared. It certainly frightened the wits out of *him.*"This platform is a business to you. You pull in what—two mil a year on the rentals and concessions, right?"

"Three point seven mil a year," an Administrator grunted pompously.

"I've seen the figures in your off-line books," Taz revealed. "It's two point zero one mil. And I'm willing to offer you twenty."

"Twenty mil..."

"Twenty mil, that's right."

"For what?"

Beside him, Taz could sense Ragle's disorientation. The man had expected to hear an ultimatum presented to Admin, not a buy-out offer.

"For the platform," Taz declared.

"You're offering to buy us out?"

"I'll guarantee your safe departure from here too, as long as you leave within twenty hours. Call it my 20/20 deal."

"What makes you think we're looking to *sell* in the first place?" the arrogant Administrator growled.

"Surviving the upcoming revolt and showing a profit sounds like a pretty good deal to me."

"We are not—" started one Administrator. His declaration jammed in his mouth as the radio static transformed into a clear signal.

The strains of an archaic classic filled the conference room. The lyrics crooned: "You say you want a revolution…"

The Administrators stared with hollow eyes at Taz. He returned their regard, as if facing a group of teenage thugs caught red-handed at some embarrassing illegality.

"Twenty-four mil," one of them demanded.

"Twenty," Taz responded clearly.

"Twenty-three point five."

"Nineteen."

"We'll take the twenty."

"My offer is now nineteen," Taz announced. "In five seconds, it'll be fifteen."

"All right! All right, we accept—nineteen mil," the arrogant owner bellowed.

Red Sky's broadcast of pop music provided an eclectic backdrop as they drew up the terms of sale. Once signatures were recorded, Taz authorized a transfer of funds into an account in a bank on Greye.

"I'll cut you a break," Taz told them once the deal was a done thing. "You can still have twenty hours to vacate the platform."

Accompanied by Officer Ragle, the new owner of Petrie platform left the ex-Administrators to their hasty packing.

"You call that an ultimatum?" Ragle grumbled as they swam away from the Admin district.

Taz chuckled. "I call that a bloodless coup."

"You knew Red Sky was coming back. You expected the pirate station to support the revolt…"

Taz shrugged. "A lucky coincidence."

Ragle shook his head, unconvinced but unwilling to challenge the man's statement.

Taz felt drained and exhausted. It had been a high risk, but it had paid off. Armed with a collection of rumors and threats—and a corpulent cred account assembled from his own fortune and donations from sympathetic Petrie merchants, he had faced the enemy. He had won, but the illusion of a violent revolt had been his actual weapon.

"Come on, Juul," Taz remarked. "Let's go tell everybody the good news." Especially before any hothead rebel wannabes ruined everything by giving reality to the grand illusion.

There was no turning back now.

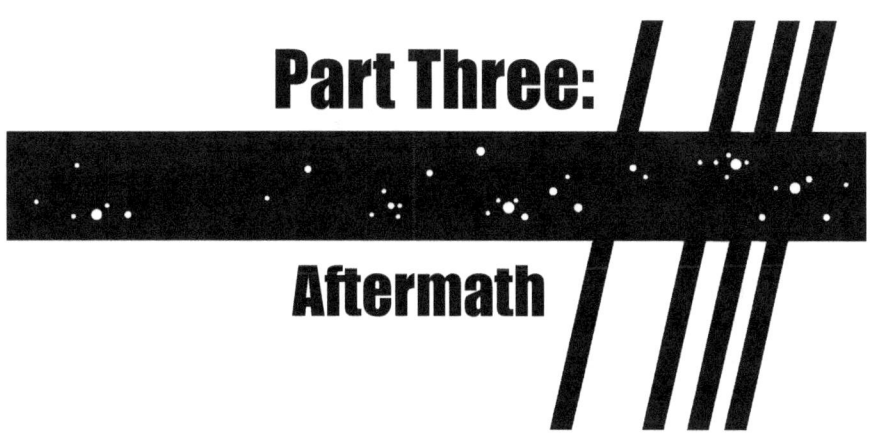

Part Three: Aftermath

Much to his surprise, Taz Bailey enjoyed his new social standing.

There was considerable controversy and severe skepticism in response to Taz's claims that Admin had bloodlessly relinquished ownership of the Petrie platform. Even when he produced the legal documents, the freelancers were leery to believe that the revolution had been averted. It was not that they distrusted the financier, but his story was simply too *simple* to be credible. They were finally convinced when the Administrators and their retinues booked passage with outbound supply ships and departed from the platform. *Then* a cheer rang through the station, celebrating everyone's freedom from the oppressive owners.

Behind closed doors, though, the future of the Petrie colony was arranged by the station's merchants. With Taz's assistance, a charter was drafted bestowing equal representation on each freelance diver. The methodology for free elections was mapped out, along with fair taxation to fund the station's existence, and plans to expand civil services such as socialized medical facilities—staffed with *trustworthy* physicians. The model produced by these businessmen was surprisingly unmerchantile.

When they were done, Taz signed over the platform's complete rights to the new nation of Petrie. Announcements were made, and elections were scheduled. Until an inaugural government could be voted into power, the station would undergo a period of readjustment under the temporary guidance of a privately hired police force headed by Juul Ragle. The pirate base was a colony now.

Like any colony, their long-term survival would depend on competent trade agreements. If the Greye Authorities recognized Petrie's sovereignty, the new colony might be spared any further harassment from Harvest Corp. The ability to openly conduct business with the pirate station would profit Greye as much as the platform. If Harvest's protests grew too boisterous, Greye would hopefully defend the Petrie colony's right to exist—if only to maintain their elevated dividends.

Once Taz had transferred the deed for the platform over the colony, he felt drained and exhausted, emotionally and financially.

The buy-out figure of nineteen million creds had taken the combined wealth of every merchant aboard the Petrie platform. All of these individuals were now penniless, except for the value of their services or the wares currently on hand in their shops. Taz Bailey had no merchandise or trade. He politely refusing all attempts to nominate him for the colony's first President. He had no time for politics. If he was going to rebuild his cred account, he was going to have go diving for clouds. It would take a lot of premium bagged gas to replace even a fraction of the fortune he had recently lost, unless he stumbled onto another golden score. He knew the odds of *that* happening again were too flimsy to be a sensible expectation.

His poverty was an acceptable burden, though, for it was a battle-scar from winning the platform its freedom. His dream of the pirate base becoming a community had become a reality.

He would not starve, nor go unclothed or unhoused. His lover was quite rich now. No matter how much Peri spent on Red Sky Radio, she would still have funds left over to cover their expenses in a more-than-lavish fashion. Taz might even borrow creds from her; he knew how amused she would be by that irony.

But her response to his impoverished status ran deeper than simple amusement. She accepted the reversal of their roles, easily adapting to responsibility. Their relationship changed as passion replaced her former emotional distance. Some part of Peri's recent adventure had stimulated her feelings for him. He could sense it, she wanted to be with him now as vibrantly as he longed to share her days and nights.

Whatever had happened, it had won him the heart of the woman he loved.

It was no surprise that Taz Bailey enjoyed his new social standing.

There were surprises for everyone.

The Petrie platform was shocked to receive Bester's distress call, almost as startled as the Exec was to discover that he was pleading help from a newly formed sovereign state. The freelancers had recently evicted their pirate leaders, declaring themselves a colony.

Careful to reveal as little as possible about the nature of Natt's destruction, Exec Nigel Bester explained the plight of his surviving employees, negotiating amnesty and refuge from the hostile vacuum. Unexpectedly, the "colonists" responded to his pleas with compassion and not trace of aloof resentment. Bester almost suspected that they were only luring him into a trap—but no, the pirate base conducted itself with utmost professionalism as it offered sanctuary to the desperate Harvest personnel. No reprisals or punishment awaited Bester's people when they docked with the platform.

He doubted that this civility would be practiced by the Home Office when they learned about the destruction of the Baltuss operation. The disintegration of the Natt base left Harvest without the equipment necessary to mine the gas giant's atmosphere. It would take countless billions to rebuild a presence here. Would the Corp bother with such an expenditure? Or would they finally come to grips with the competition and enter into a business relationship with the pirates? They were dealing with *colonists* now. The legal ramifications of a Petrie "colony" were myriad.

Whatever happened, Bester was certain that *he* would not be involved in any of it. The Home Office would need someone to punish for losing the Natt base, and he was the only surviving Executive to be a scapegoat. It was in his own best interests to befriend the Petrie colony's new leaders, he might indeed require political asylum from the Corp's savage vengeance.

The problem was: those leaders did not yet exist. Elections were still pending. Candidates were still in the process of declaring themselves and launching their campaigns. In fact, despite the fervor in the air over the colony's new independence, the platform was in a state of social chaos. The oddest part was that the freelancers seemed comfortable having no existing power structure. They continued with their own lives, diving and eating, losing no sleep over the political vacuum that watched over them in the colony's weeks of infancy. This lack of any governing body left Bester with no one to discuss the transportation of his displaced employees. He needed to arrange temporary lodgings for over two thousand personnel, then passage had to be booked to distant Greye for them. He was unsure whether Harvest would approve the funds to pay the merchants who donated food and offered dormitory quarters, for the Home Office could be expected to still perceive the Petrie colony as trespassers in Baltuss space.

It took nearly twelve hours, but Bester finally managed to get his people settled into their interim accommodations spread throughout the platform's commercial districts. Courtyards were partitioned off and converted into impromptu dormitories, and cred chits were circulated among the Harvest employees so they could feed themselves at Petrie's cafeterias. A list of survivors was assembled; when matched against the Home Office's records of the Natt base's personnel files, families of the newly deceased could be contacted.

There was an endless succession of details that required someone's Executive attention, and the tasks all fell to Bester.

Early on, he had received medical treatment for the injuries he had incurred during his speedy escape of the lunar base, fleeing with the matter virus gnawing at his heels. He wore his bandages through all his negotiations, suspecting that his gruesome injuries only reinforced the impression of how needy the Harvest refugees were.

Whatever trick or quirk of fate had convinced the pirates to offer succor to their downfallen enemies, Bester was grateful for the outcome.

He was pleased to learn that Red Sky Radio was back on the air. He had worried that the pirate station might have been another casualty of the recent disaster that had claimed so many innocent lives. Bester was confident that the station's entertaining transmissions would help bolster the spirits of all the survivors, freelancers and displaced workers alike.

The ex-Exec was taking a meal in one of the cafeterias when he recognized someone.

It is possible? Bester wondered. *It's been decades since I last saw the man…*

He was more wrinkled than Bester's recollection of the man, but age did that. The man's overlarge head was memorable, with its protruding ears and hatchet-nose. His beady eyes sparkled with considerable intelligence. The man's chestplate was the telltale, though. Few spacers wore such archaic tech these days.

No, it was him.

Professor Donald Flint had hidden himself superbly from the Corp's trackers. The defector had chosen the one place guaranteed to remain "unseen" to Harvest—the Petrie pirate platform! All these years, while corporate agents combed far-flung colony worlds for the renegade scientist, he had been hiding at the edge of Harvest territory.

Bester approached the man. When Flint finally noticed him, he did not seem to recognize the Exec. With half his face concealed by bandages, Bester wasn't surprised. He settled across from the man.

"Can I do something for you?" the hiding scientist asked innocently.

"You're Professor Flint, aren't you?"

"You've got the wrong spacer, pal."

"We never met, but I know who you are."

"I'm nobody."

"You used to work for me," Bester chuckled mildly.

Flint started to leave, but the Exec called him back. "You've nothing to fear from me, Professor. Situations have changed, and my days with Harvest are numbered. I wish you no trouble."

Pausing, Flint muttered, "You've got me confused with somebody else…"

"Indulge me," the Exec smiled. "I'm an old man."

"I'm older than you."

"I feel so old right now." Bester closed his eyes and massaged his forehead. "Running the base was becoming so difficult, what with all of Uwu's schemes and Hannigan's antics. The catastrophe proved how trivial it all was. All the plotting and rivalry vanished along with the lunar base. Eaten by your matter virus."

"What?" An expression of panic flashed across Flint's loose face. "What did you say?"

Surveying the scientist's confusion, Bester remarked gravely, "So…it wasn't you who set it on us. I wonder who it was then…"

"Who the void are you?"

Bester smiled. "My name is Nigel Bester. I used to be on Harvest's Executive Board."

"You're on the level," Flint gasped, drawing near. "You weren't joking—somebody released the Godbreath contagion?"

Bester nodded. "Wiped out the entire base, moon and all—gone now."

"What happened?"

"I haven't a clue. All the evidence got eaten. It all happened too quickly."

"Was research still being done?"

"That's the most probable explanation, yes. Some experiment got out of control and the virus broke out of the lab and spread through the whole base. We'll probably never know for certain."

"The reaction stopped, though?" Flint's critical tone was insistent.

"Yes. The Project had determined that vacuum would limit the virus' infectious capacity. I read that in a recent report. Apparently, it works that way. Once it had consumed the moon, the process stopped."

"It took your researchers this long to figure that out?"

"I cannot speak for the competency of the research Department, my expertise involved the financial aspects of Harvest's interests. I should point out—I was always opposed to those classified labs being on the base."

"You should have abandoned the Project when I…left. The damned thing is too dangerous to use for any reason. Believe me…I know…

"Is that why you took off? You were *afraid* of the research?" Bester was shocked. All these years, he had imagined that Flint had fled from the unethical nature of the project, not scared off by personal risk.

"You've seen what the contagion can do," Flint hissed angrily. "So have I. The thing is an abomination. It has no commercial application—it can *only* be used for destruction. It scares me the same way a supernova scares me. Theoretically, they're both interesting quantum incidents, but morally it's an unspeakable atrocity if you get in the way of an exploding star or the Godbreath contagion. I want no part of either."

So, it *had* been the scientist's ethics all along. This pleased Bester on some vague level of respect for the man.

"And you can forget you ever saw me, if you're looking to start up the Project again. I'll never cooperate."

"Will you chill out?" Bester sighed. "The Home Office is going to professionally castrate me for losing the Natt base. I'm history as far as the Corp will soon be concerned. Anyway—I would never support continuing any of the secret research that was being done at Uwu's direction. I objected to it then, I reject it still."

"Then…what *do* you want…?" Flint inquired slowly, as if dreading whatever hidden agenda he had asked to be revealed would be even more terrible than the subject of their conversation so far.

"Nothing, really. I suppose I wanted to confirm that it wasn't you who sicced the virus on Harvest." He shook his angular head wearily. "The prospect that you had given the pirates such a monstrous weapon was unsettling."

"No one here knows who I am," Flint confided.

"A new life," Bester nodded with a wistful expression. "One of those would be nice."

There were surprises for everyone.

Some of those surprises were best forgotten.

Dezi did not know what to make of his unexpected meeting with the former Harvest Exec. The man's lackadaisical attitude was quite unlike what Dezi would have expected from a member of the Corp's Executive Board…at least, under normal circumstances. But then, these last few days had hardly culminated in "normal" circumstances.

The HeeVee base was gone, destroyed by an outbreak of the contagion Dezi had helped invent decades ago. HeeVee's cloud-mining operation was history here at Baltuss. Thousands of Corp workers were suddenly unemployed and stranded far from their homes. Exec Bester had intimated that he was uncertain whether Harvest was going to foot the bill to ship the refugees back to Greye. The only thing the tired old Exec had seemed sure of was his own dark destiny at the mercy of Harvest's inevitable vengeance.

Dezi felt a vague culpability for the disaster that had ruined the workers' lives. If he had never invented the contagion, or if he had been successful in eradicating all the project's files from the base's databanks decades ago, or if everyone had simply backed away from the cursed research…if someone had forcibly used some sanity, then none of this would have happened. Dezi knew his sense of guilt was implausibly motivated, but that didn't spare him the ache of the emotion.

He had never really gotten over the horror of releasing the contagion so many years ago, using Godbreath to rescue the platform from HeeVee's vicious attack. Despite that situation's desperate nature, no crisis warranted unleashing Godbreath.

The terrible abomination served no benevolent purpose, it was only capable of ruining people's lives. Even as a weapon of war, its destructive aptitude was too awesome. Perhaps now, with the Natt base gone, all trace of the dreadful contagion had been extinguished from existence, swallowed by its own insatiable hunger to reduce matter to an absolute vacuum. Perhaps now, the universe was safe.

The formula still survived in Professor Flint's stifled memory, but Dezi would never reveal this secret to anyone. Nothing could force him to recreate the monstrous catalyst.

His displaced guilt cheated the old man of his joy over the many miracles that had befallen the freelancers of Petrie platform. No, it was Petrie colony now. That was one of the surprises—the pirate base had finally become an actual free colony.

Taz Bailey had lived up to his word, achieving a bloodless coup and freeing the platform from the tyrannical ownership of the Administrators. Dezi endlessly pondered on how the financier had pulled off this maneuver. There were many mysteries surrounding Bailey. How long had he known Red Sky Radio's secret? Years? And yet, never once had he revealed what he knew—to Dezi or to anyone. The man's honor was admirable, and not the sort of ethics that the old man expected from a wealthy, powerful individual.

That boy was just full of surprises.

Her lover was just full of surprises.

Denise Coleman was suitably impressed by how much Juul Ragle had changed since the man had appeared on the Petrie platform.

Juul had arrived as a HeeVee defector, penniless and brimming with colorful misinformation regarding the nature of the "pirate colony." Somehow, he had managed to enlist the financial backing of the platform's most renowned entrepreneur, securing himself lodging and pocket-creds until he was able to commence his new existence as freelance diver. Juul had quickly adjusted to this new life, learning the nuances of the platform's mores and routines.

For a brief moment, she had suspected him of nefarious activities, but he had swiftly been exonerated of that suspicion. Indeed, he had been identified as a potential hero for his attempt to apprehend the HeeVee spy in their midst. He had promptly been appointed the platform's Chief of Police. It was even rumored that Juul had accompanied Bailey when he had confronted Admin, but Juul declined to discuss that meeting. Why he might even have been instrumental in helping the entrepreneur wrestle control of the platform from the tyrannical clutches of the corrupt Administrators. He was a hero.

And he fit ever so nicely beside Denise in bed. He was helping her grow accustomed to sleeping in zero-G.

Not to mention: introducing her to fascinating new amenities, like the music of Red Sky Radio. Ever since his promotion from freelancer to police commander, Juul had become a devout listener to the so-called "pirate" broadcasts. He played the music boldly in his new offices, and set up speakers in Denise's walk-up apartment so that she could enjoy constant tunes. She found the change exciting, surprised at how much more colorful each day seemed with a soundtrack.

He had so many surprises to show her.

He enjoyed life because it was so rich with surprises.

In one capacity or another, the grizzled old man had spent his entire lifespan in the void. Never once had Dirk Masterfield descended into the gravity well of Greye or any other planet. Born on Victoria Terminal, Dirk had been raised as a spacer brat. His choice of trade had been obvious, for there were few non-tech-maintenance jobs aboard the space port. Through a series of menial services, Dirk had mastered enough know-how to score himself a position on a spaceline freighter running cargo from the Harvest Corp's cloud-mining base on Baltuss' twelfth moon.

During his duty as a drive system grunt aboard the *Erbe*, Dirk profited professionally, financially, and personally.

Working on the *Erbe's* drive system gave him the opportunity to learn more intimate details of keeping such equipment operational. He became expert at numerous tech jobs, making himself invaluable on every deck of the freighter. While enjoying this popularity, he took private pride in the ever-increasing scope of his technical expertise.

Saving every cred he earned, he was able to afford a downpayment on his own spacecraft. Time and subsequent profit allowed him to supplement the crude vessel with upgrade portions, bought piecemeal and grafted onto the ship where needed or possible. Most of the actual expenditure went into maintaining the ship's temperamental ramscoops. The wisest expense, though, had been incurred acquiring a durable and oversize cargo hangar, for the more he could haul, the more his profit-margin became. With a ship of his own, Dirk resigned from the spaceline and went into business for himself.

Many friendships had been forged aboard the old freighter, among crew members and with the infrequent passenger traveling to Harvest's Natt base. Sometimes there were even individuals looking to secretly escape the Corp's lunar facility. One such deserter was to become his closest friend over the years. In Dirk's confidential opinion, his friend had also become one of the most influential people in this region of the void. Greatness was often born of humbling defeats.

Relaxing his spindly limbs in the refreshing caress of zero-G, Dirk allowed the memory of their first meeting to replay in his frontal lobe.

Although Dirk Masterfield was dedicated to keeping the freighter's machinery in optimum condition, he was not adverse to conducting a little semi- or blatantly-illegal smuggling if it managed to sweeten the financial nest-egg he was building. The other crew members indulged in similar activities, sneaking smokes and porn past the Corp's staunch customs and into the greedy hands of addicts and perverts stationed on the lunar base. According to ship's lore, Smilin' Eddie had scored a fortune last trip by supplying one of the station's Execs with something unspeakably loathsome. There were considerable opportunities to supplement one's income by catering to the deviant needs of the corporate personnel.

Dirk was somewhat unprepared when his chance came. Expecting to find himself approached by someone in the market for illicit disks or designer hallucinogenics, he was caught off-guard by the man's desperate plea.

"I have to get away from here! Can you help me?"

How could he ignore such an emotional imploration? The man looked so pathetic with his oversized head and flap-like ears and wide-eyed, begging stare. Dirk was compelled to give the wretch refuge from whatever corporate demons he was fleeing. The downside was that the man had no fabulous ransom to purchase his escape…so Dirk helped him without payment.

The deserter had a clever escape plan all worked out. He would leave the base through the facility's waste dump pipes, then rendezvous with someone who would transport him to the orbiting freighter. Haste was vital, the deserter assured Dirk, for the Corp would go ballistic once they realized that he was gone.

Borrowing a tug from the Erbe's *cargo fleet, Dirk secretly ferried the man from the frozen surface of the methane moon to the freighter. He hid him in unused quarters on the lower levels, sneaking the man food from the cafeteria. Their tension eased away as they began to imagine that they had pulled it off.*

Then an alarm swept the ship. Loudspeakers announced that Corp Security Officers were boarding the freighter in order to search for a possible stowaway. Leaving his post at the drive core, Dirk hurried to the cabin where the deserter was hiding. At the time, he had no idea what to do. There was no place to hide a person from a complete search of a space vessel. Harvest's cops would uncover their prey, and Dirk would be arrested for complacency in the crime.

Panic set in when he found the cabin empty. Of the refugee, there was no trace.

Where did he go? Dirk fretted. *Where* could *he go? Any hiding place was as ineffectual as the next aboard the finite corridors and chambers contained within the space freighter's hull. The only possible way to escape might be to jump ship—but again:* where *could he go? There was nothing outside but empty vacuum.*

Was the fugitive that *desperate to evade capture?*

He must have been, for the Corp cops never found their stowaway. They were forced to allow the Erbe *to resume its flight for the commercial docking station in orbit around distant Greye. The deserter never reappeared—at least, not aboard the freighter.*

Languidly drifting in his personal quarters aboard his patchwork ship, Dirk relaxed to the soothing orchestral music provided at this time by Red Sky Radio. Such tuneage always made him wax nostalgic. He recalled how surprised he had been when he had run into the refugee years later.

By then, Dirk had retired from the *Erbe* and was flying his own vessel. He was not happy to discover that Harvest refused to hire freelance freighters, restricting all their cargo business to the official spacelines. This left Dirk with a worthy ship but nothing to haul with it. After a few jobs ferrying junk around Greye's stratosphere, Dirk opted to become a smuggler. It was no secret that there existed a pirate platform out near Baltuss which harbored freelance divers who fed off the Corp's licensed clouds. These reckless independents needed supplies. The pirate base was a prime market for anyone courageous and foolhardy enough to brave the Corp's blockades.

Guarding the location of the pirate base was an unspoken rule among the smugglers; the wisdom in this was obvious: if Harvest ever destroyed the freelancer's platform, the smugglers would lose all their customers. Perpetuating the secrecy was simply good business practice. The smugglers policed themselves, meting out terrible punishment to anyone brazen enough to betray this secret to the Corp. Over the years, there had been several ambitious traitors, some of them unscrupulous divers who imagined they could elude the smuggler's code of bloodthirsty ethics. Every traitor had met a grisly retribution for their crime… while the secret they had sold was useless by the time Harvest dispatched a squadron, for the pirates were constantly moving their platform, roving the void on the outskirts of Baltuss' lunar collection. It was more than a simple matter of honor-among-thieves, it was justice- and punishment-among-thieves.

Regardless of the economic basis for this relationship, Dirk deeply respected the smugglers for protecting the freelancer colony. He was proud to be able to help the divers. The pirate base represented a bastion of free trade, a valiant island in the shadow of the arrogant corporation.

It was aboard the Petrie platform that Dirk encountered the fugitive again.

Flint wore a new name but the same top-heavy head and protruding features. Apparently, he had indeed jumped ship all those years ago, leaving the *Erbe* to flee into open space in order to evade capture by the Corp Security Officers. Giving himself to the void, he had accidentally discovered the pirate platform and taken refuge there. Over time, his hiding place had become home. Now, his name was Annucci, and he bagged gas for a living.

Pleased to see each other again, they retired to a tavern to swap their tales. By the end of the evening, a strong friendship was cemented. Both men had been forced by circumstance to reject their previous lives, finding solace and even prosperity in livelihoods outside the realm of legality. Annucci acknowledged a debt to Dirk for being instrumental in delivering him from the Corp's lunar base, while the spacer felt simpatico with the deserter for they had both tasted—and suffered from—the aloof disdain of the pompous corporation.

As the years passed, their friendship deepened. Although Dezi never discussed the reasons why he had fled Harvest's Natt base, there were other secrets that passed between the comrades. Some of them were intentionally shared, others were obvious and needed no disclosure. Some secrets were unearthed by accident.

Not unlike other residents of the Petrie platform, Dezi placed orders with Dirk for certain purchases. While others requested luxuries and delicacies, the HeeVee deserter asked for hardware and copious amounts of musical disks. Dirk did not have to be a genius to realize that he was providing equipment and software to Red Sky Radio.

He never did confront Dezi with his suspicions, for Dirk had grown accustomed to his old friend's distrustful nature. A man who harbored dreadful secrets needed to practice extreme caution. Dezi was on the lam from HeeVee, he had reason enough to be paranoid. Any fame derived from his pirate broadcasts would only endanger his safety. Not only was he a wanted deserter, but the Corp had attached a bounty to the head of the subversive mastermind behind Red Sky. To reveal his identity was the same as a death sentence for Dirk's closest friend. (Would things change now that Harvest was gone from the region?)

Over the years, Dirk developed a protective attitude toward his friend's secret endeavors. He had helped the pirate station expand by releasing transmitters into orbit around Greye, bringing Red Sky's music to the landbound colonists. And when he had heard that girl ranting about "killer robots down in Baltuss' clouds", Dirk had instantly realized what the attractive fanatic had actually found. As soon as she had left with that Ragle fellow, the smuggler had contacted his friend and warned him about the girl's "dangerous delusions." He could only hope that Dezi would figure out the potential threat to Red Sky's transmitters hidden in the gas giant's stratospheric clouds.

That warning apparently came too late, for as he launched his ship from the platform that afternoon, the pirate signal had vanished. Silenced, no doubt, by accident…but silenced all the same. Dirk mourned the loss.

Days later, while cruising the void halfway between Baltuss and Greye, Red Sky resumed transmission. And Dirk had celebrated its return. Trusting in Dezi's resourcefulness and dedication, he had known his friend would emerge victorious from whatever difficulty had stifled the pirate radio station's voice.

Arriving at Victoria Terminal, Masterfield learned about the startling revolution that had taken place, in which the freelance divers had liberated the Petrie platform from their Admin leaders. The pirate base had declared its independence, announcing the formation of the Petrie colony.

Soon after this came the astounding news that the Natt moon had disappeared, taking with it Harvest's lunar base and a percentage of the Corp's personnel. The survivors had been offered refuge by the ex-pirate colony!

What further surprises would Dirk find when he returned to the Petrie platform?

Every day seemed to offer new and exciting surprises.

As she descended into the scarlet clouds, Peri decided that she had achieved a satisfying fulfillment.

No longer was she impoverished. A golden score had turned her into the wealthiest person aboard the Petrie platform. (No, it was the Petrie *colony* now. The liberation of the platform had drained the accounts of the richest freelance divers, leaving her newfound fortune as the greatest local wealth.) Her father had been right: "Money could solve all problems." But—only if she used it unselfishly.

No longer was she beholden to Taz to pay her bills—in fact, circumstance had done a turn-around, and now the man was financially indebted to her. Peri had finally achieved her independence, and through that attainment had come happiness

No longer was she an aimless failure. She had found purpose and redemption through saving Red Sky Radio. Her actions had rescued the pirate station from silence.

No longer did she fear or distrust the attention of other people. She had learned the value of cooperation. Peri had also realized that her satisfaction was greatest when she was helping others.

The soundtrack that filled her head expanded with a symphonic flurry. Percussives drove the melody into an epic frenzy, the emphatic rhythms resounding like the collapse of heaven. As the crescendo ebbed, flutes emerged to escort the coda to its imminent conclusion.

Listening now to Red Sky's music filled her with a benevolent connection to every person listening to the same broadcast. If not for her, all their lives would have been condemned to dreadful silence. Their joy and enjoyment of the music was a direct consequence of her actions. The public would never know the debt they owed Peri Fairchild, and in her own opinion, that made it all the more rewarding.

She liked having a new secret.

But *this* was the part she liked the best: descending toward the scarlet clouds, all billowy and inviting like a forever wall of baby's-bottoms.

Bonus Feature

How "Diver" Became Red Sky Radio...

In 2001 Gregory Benford put me in contact with a digital SF magazine called *Oceans of the Mind*. Looking for experimental science fiction, the mag took an interest in my graphic stories and asked me to a few short comic strips for them. In 2002 I did three strips for the mag: two Keif Llama pieces, and a strip entitled "Diver."

I've always been keen on gas giant planets (as evidenced by my novels *Itself* and *Imaginary Numbers*, and my comic book series "Star Crossed" for *Helix*), and "Diver" allowed me to explore the clouds once again, this time as the backdrop for a tale about freelance gas miners and the pirate radio station that helped keep them sane during their long excursions into the dense atmosphere.

While working on the "Diver" strip, my mind persisted in developing tangents for the tale, tangents too elaborate to include in the short graphic story. I enjoy drawing gas giants, but I was daunted by the prospect of doing so for a longer version of the tale. It seemed easier to tackle the tale as a prose novel, which would allow me the freedom to delve into even more aspects which continued to spring forth in my mind. So...I wrote *Red Sky Radio*.

In 2004, Trantor Publishing (*Oceans'* publisher) produced a digital book of the novel.

When Merry Blacksmith Press expressed an interest in doing a print edition of the novel in 2011, I thought it might be nice to include the original comic strip as a bonus feature.

Enjoy...

– Matt Howarth
July, 2011

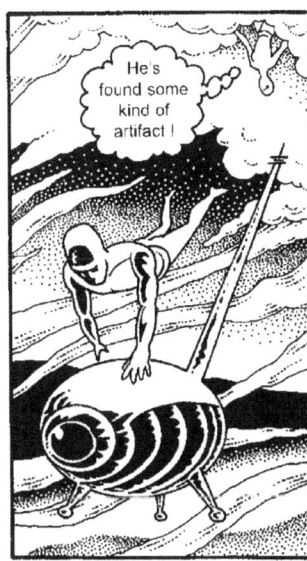

You're the *radio pirate* !
You're the one flaunting the corp's no-unauthorized-music edict with your illegal broadcasts !
Yes.
I could just *kiss* you ! In fact—**I will** !
I simply **adore** your broadcasts ! Diving without them would be so *boring* !
Umm... That's nice to—uh— know....
So...you won't tell anyone, will you ?
Silly boy. Come dance with me !
Umm...
Peri's secret passion has evolved. With a partner, her diving has become a duet.
There are happy endings, even in the jovian billows.
5

COMING SOON BY MATT HOWARTH FROM MERRY BLAKSMITH PRESS

SCIENCE FICTION COLLIDES WITH ARCANE HORROR as Matt Howarth pays homage to H. P. Lovecraft's Cthulhu Mythos in this lavish science fiction novel. Hundreds of years in the future, mankind has colonized the galaxy. Meanwhile, Cthulhu has risen and conquered forgotten Earth. Answering a distress call, a team of mercenaries find themselves facing unspeakable horrors as they struggle to rescue Princess Eden from the Old One's hideous minions.